Trevor Stubbs was born in Northampton, England in 1948 and studied theology in London, Canterbury and Exeter. He has lived and worked in West Yorkshire and Dorset in the United Kingdom, and Australia, Papua New Guinea and South Sudan. He currently lives in Keynsham, nr. Bristol.

Trevor Stubbs is married with three adult children and two grandchildren.

For more information about Trevor Stubbs
or to contact him visit:
www.whitegatesadventures.com
and follow him at
www.whitegatesadventures.wordpress.com
or on Twitter
@TrevorNStubbs

BY THE SAME AUTHOR

Fiction

In the *White Gates* series:

The Kicking Tree
Ultimate Justice
Winds and Wonders
The Spark

Non-fiction
*WYSIWYG Christianity: Young People and
Faith in the Twenty-First Century*

THE
KICKING
TREE

TREVOR STUBBS

Matador
9 Priory Business Park
Kibworth Beauchamp
Leicestershire LE8 0RX, UK
Tel: (+44) 116 279 2299
Fax: (+44) 116 279 2277
Email: books@troubador.co.uk
Web: www.troubador.co.uk/matador

ISBN 978 1783063 871

British Library Cataloguing in Publication Data.
A catalogue record for this book is available from the British Library.

Printed and bound by CPI Group (UK) Ltd, Croydon, CR0 4YY
Typeset in Aldine401 BT Roman by Troubador Publishing Ltd

Matador is an imprint of Troubador Publishing Ltd

*This book is dedicated to all those
who, for whatever reason, have never been
able to have an adventure.*

Reviews for The Kicking Tree

"Wonderful Story. Its a great adventure that made me cry. I love the two main characters who meet across the Universe..."

Miss S (Amazon ☆☆☆☆☆)

"An Interesting Read. Was encouraged to read this book by a friend at church. Was not disappointed. An excellent way of putting Christianity in a modern perspective. Very thought provoking too."

Aidie (Amazon ☆☆☆☆)

"... a perfect book for the adult-literacy teacher trying to encourage teens to read, with its strong narrative structure, simple vocabulary, and positive, active role-models. There are all too few authors who write well for this market, and Stubbs is one of them."

Church Times

"Trevor Stubbs has an interesting philosophy of life: 'I hate injustice and oppression, especially against the weak and the vulnerable and want to speak out.' Trevor uses his undoubted skills as a master storyteller and a magical weaver of tales to bring about such justice."

That's Books and Entertainment

"Five Stars. Very good. Suitable for young people. I am a bit old for it but enjoyed it nevertheless."

Glenys Brown (Amazon ☆☆☆☆☆)

"This book is one of the most special books I've ever read. In a good way. It's a love story. But it's not really a love story - it's about two people falling in love. It's an SF-book. But it's not really an SF-book: there is some time- (or perhaps wormhole?) travelling going on, and there are space ships. It's also a fantasy story. But it's not really a fantasy story…"

Linn (Good Reads)

"I think this book is amazing. I like the fact that almost nothing bad happens, but that you still want to read more. It is hard to put away, and there is not a sentence in the book that is boring."

Ebba (Good Reads)

1

The bus rounded the last bend on the descent onto the Zongan coastal plain. The driver heaved a sigh, slapped the side of his dashboard and drew to a halt behind a queue of traffic. It extended as far as he could see into the stand of trees two yukets ahead. They were now less than ten yukets from the village of Zonga where all of his passengers were headed. He knew they were impatient to get to the village and had been longing to get home or to see their relatives who lived there, since the earthquake two days ago.

A few anxious passengers stood up, craning their necks to ascertain the cause of the hold up. Little Jalli stood up on her seat to see too but her grandmother quickly pulled her down. If the bus made a sudden movement the three year old might have fallen and Momori was not going to deliver her granddaughter back to her parents with bruises after all they must have been through. Although the earthquake had been felt all along the coast, including Wanulka City, the capital some sixty yukets away, the village of Zonga had suffered the most.

Remarkably, there had only been one dead and two seriously injured reported so far, but there were still half a dozen missing in a single collapsed building near the centre of the village. Mercifully the phone connections had not stopped working, except for an hour or so due to overloading. The authorities had kept people away from the village for two days, fearing further shocks. They were also wanting to keep the road clear for emergency traffic. But now the way was clear, and Momori, Jalli and hundreds of others in cars and buses were on their way back, not knowing quite what to expect.

As the bus had set off along the coast road some two hours before, the passengers were all chatting excitedly to their relatives in Zonga on their phones. Not long into the journey they had gone out of range of the final mast and they had calmed into a murmur of anticipation. But now they were getting frustrated.

The traffic queue was not moving at all and the bus began to heat up. The passengers threw down the windows and the scent of ripening ibon, the staple crop of that part of Raika (the second smallest of the planets in the Jallaxa solar system) filled their nostrils. It had been a good growing season this year and, in under a Raikan month if the weather held, the farmers would have a rich harvest.

All three suns were now high in the sky and the glare on the yellow sand that lined the road caused the occupants on the nearside of the bus to avert their eyes. If the passengers on the offside had been attentive, they would have noticed that nothing had passed them in the opposite direction for some time.

The bus driver turned off the engine. He might as well conserve his fuel, and besides, the people in the car behind would be grateful not to have to breathe his fumes. Gradually the other vehicles in the queue that now extended up the hill and around the bend behind began to do the same. The silence was almost deafening.

Suddenly, from behind them the scream of sirens could be heard coming round the bend. Two police vehicles hurried by on the wrong side of the road. They were followed a moment later by a fire engine. Two minutes after that there was a spate of emergency vehicles and soon it seemed that the whole of the uniformed services from Wanulka City was on the move.

One of the last police cars drew up about a yuket ahead and two policemen approached a lorry driver. They spoke to him and he manoeuvred his lorry to form a kind of road block and then a police car turned round and started back. As they passed, the officer shouted through a megaphone:

"The road's flooded. No-one can get through. Go back and clear the road."

Flooding? But it hadn't rained for several days!

The bus driver started his engine, but several passengers stood up and stated their intention to walk. Others called on them to sit down because it would take them far too long at the hottest time of the day of the hottest time of year. People were flushed with heat and frustrated, and soon became angry. Jalli put her hands over her ears.

Then from somewhere at the back of the bus, a man with a big voice shouted loudly and authoritatively for everyone to "shut up!" A slight woman beside him was listening to a portable radio which she held against her ear.

"The dam's burst," she declared. "All communication has been lost with Zonga. The government fears the worst."

The passengers stood, sat or perched where they were in stunned silence. The woman sobbed, "They think that a giant body of water has smashed into the village. The sea is full of debris."

The news had clearly reached others in the traffic queue. People were streaming from the vehicles and running down the road. Two police cars pulled up from alongside the truck. One of the policemen addressed the crowd with a megaphone.

"The way is blocked. No-one can get through, even on foot. Please go back to your vehicles and get them away from the road to allow the emergency vehicles to pass."

The bus driver did not hesitate, he pulled across the road while it was clear, did a three point turn and headed back up the hill.

Three hours later they were back in Wanulka City bus-station. Momori took Jalli and looked for somewhere they could stay for the night. All she could do for the present was to ensure the child was safe. She dare not think about anything else.

2

Fourteen years later. Jack: Age: 18. Home address: 68, Renson Park Road, Persham, England, Planet Earth.

Jack kicked out at the bush by his front gate as he had done every day since he was eight. It was a habit he had indulged in for the last nine years. He had no idea what variety of bush or tree it was – he simply called it his "kicking tree". It no longer resembled a tree now but a stunted shrub. But that battered bit of creation simply refused to die, no matter how many times it was kicked. He called it a "tree" because once it had actually been a tree – a young sapling with bright green shoots in the spring. It had grown more quickly than he had, and, when he was aged eight, it had suddenly appeared to be bigger than him. It was then it came in for its first ill-treatment. Jack had taken hold of the pliant young trunk and had swung on it until it splintered. He left it broken and torn, just hanging on to life through its sheer toughness. When Jack's efforts were spent, he had taunted it. "That will teach you to be bigger than me!" he had hissed.

But the tree persisted in producing new growth each year, and Jack never ceased assaulting it. Now, at the age of eighteen he did it more out of habit than anything else – the tree still got on his nerves.

In truth, lots of things annoyed Jack. He had little concern for anything outside of himself. The fact was that Jack and contentment simply did not go together. It wasn't that he hadn't got a brain, or average sporting ability, but he resented the rest of the world and what he had decided it had thrown at him. Here he was, sharing a house with his mother who made him do jobs and live an existence he hated. Other young men his age lived in much nicer places he told himself. And they had fathers at home, and brothers and sisters too. They didn't have to help with this, clean that, and do the other. Their mothers tended their gardens, but the garden in front of his small house was a heap of junk and weeds that his mother rarely got round to doing anything about. It didn't occur to him that he might clean it up and tend it himself – it wasn't *his* junk. Those other eighteen year olds had fathers who brought home wages that bought clothes and luxuries that he had never known. For Jack, life sucked, or so he decided. It owed him plenty, and he owed it nothing.

He had had a father of course, but Matilda, his mother, told him that his father had gone off with another woman while Jack was still a baby. Jack hated him for not being there – he hadn't bothered with either his wife or his son since. He had never contacted them – not even on Jack's birthday or at Christmas. Christmas. That was the worst season of the whole year for Jack because it brought to the surface all that Jack didn't have.

Jack spent a lot more time thinking about his father than he would care to admit. Some of the time he speculated about the kind of man he might be. Most of the time, though, he wanted to meet him so he could kick out at him and beat him, and tell him what a sod he was, and get him to plead forgiveness, and then send him away and tell him not to come back again. If his father had ever sought to come by that is precisely what Jack most likely would have done. But, of course, he didn't come by. Had he done so and received the rejection he deserved, it might have been better for Jack. Could his father have just been there to take it, to let the hatred pour out of his son's heart, it might have set him free. But, as it was, the absent parent left a gap in the centre of Jack's heart which fostered the smouldering resentment that affected so much of the rest of his life.

Jack's mother was a survivor too. Life hadn't been easy for her bringing up a wilful son all on her own. She had been bitter because of the poor choice of husband she had made, and had always seen some of this ungrateful man in Jack. Yet she knew Jack was not him and that this must be resisted. Still his anger and self-centredness made it increasingly difficult to get close to him. Everyday life, making ends meet, did not allow much time to dwell on what might have been. The last of her own parents had died five years ago disappointed in the mess their daughter had made of her life. She hadn't heard from her brother since then. He had his own life and he didn't bother with her and she wasn't going to bother with him.

But her son worried her. He could have turned out worse though, she thought. He had never got into trouble with the police like some of the boys at his school, and somehow he had avoided getting caught up with the drug-taking layabouts she saw on the street corners in the town. She had been outspoken about this – but she felt that it wouldn't have made any difference what she had said. Jack lived in his own world, and didn't do anything he didn't want to do.

In fact Jack had not shown much interest in having friends. His naturally introvert nature had probably been his saving grace in this regard. And his innate intelligence had meant that he had got on at school, despite his preoccupations. He had stayed on simply because there had been nothing else he wanted to do. He needed to get out of the house, away from his mother, and occupy his bright brain with something. He might have been the kind who spent his time surfing the 'net or playing computer games but he did not have a computer at home, there was no way they could afford one. He did most of his homework on the computer at school after hours. (In the senior class people without their own computers could make special arrangements.)

That morning Jack was going to the school but it was to be no ordinary day. This was the last time he would go there. He was going, not because he wanted to meet his friends, or participate in any leaving ceremony, but because this day was the one in which he would receive his results. What he was going to do from now on he did not know. If his results were good he might consider going to do further study somewhere. Not a local place though. He wanted somewhere far enough away so that he would have to find digs or a college hall. He could have applied earlier in the year but he had not decided which subjects he wanted to pursue. Some of the other students had done the research, paid visits on open days, and got excited about this or that course. Jack had not known where to begin, or what he was capable of, and when it came to these things his mother might as well have been on another planet. So he decided to have a "gap year" and apply for the following year. But he hadn't done much about that either. He resolved to call in at the library on the way home and see if there were some ideas there. He had already asked other students what they were doing and how you found a gap year opportunity, but they all seemed to have had "connections". One had an uncle in the diplomatic service and was going out to do something in some remote corner of the world, another had decided to pursue a year in industry and his next door neighbour had got him a post in a local factory office. A third had gone off to the antipodes on his father's yacht. But when it came to uncles, useful neighbours and fathers, Jack, as usual, fell short.

Later that day Jack felt good. In fact he couldn't remember ever feeling quite so good before. He had got his results and had done better than anyone had expected. His teachers were pleased. Fellow students were impressed. He knew he had been lucky with some of the questions. If they had been on other parts of the curriculum which he hadn't revised he would not have done so well. But the teachers and the others didn't know that. So he had a spring in his step as he headed off for the library.

Perhaps his good fortune would continue and he would find a line to pursue. His way took him past his former middle school. This was in an older part of the town with red brick terraced houses and tiny front gardens in different styles. Some had pots of bright flowers, others a small patch of grass, one or two were unkempt like his own, and one had a large greenhouse. "I wonder how long that will last?" mused Jack, remembering what some of the pupils had been like in his former school. He found himself actually caring, actually wanting the greenhouse to survive! He *was* in a good mood!

As he passed the long brick wall that surrounded the St Paul's Middle School Jack had left five years before, he was suddenly aware of a new white gate in the wall. "What have they been doing here?" he asked himself. He could not imagine why they wanted to put such a gate in this wall. It looked so out of place. It was a low wooden gate, with a solid frame and a rounded top. Vertical bars carved into curves and swirls gave the gate an ornamental air. It shone with the lustre of new, pure white, gloss paint. Jack stopped, looked at the gate and then beyond it. The remarkable thing was that the gate seemed to lead to a short, narrow path about two metres long through a high dark-green hedge. He remembered no hedges around the middle school! But the really astounding thing was that the path didn't lead to a school yard but a garden with a green lawn overhung with trees. The corner of a country cottage was just visible. It was completely incongruous. There was nothing akin to this anywhere near Jack's part of town. Indeed Jack could not remember ever seeing anything quite like it, not even in books.

Jack deliberately closed his eyes for several seconds to make sure he wasn't seeing things. But the gate, the hedge and the lawn were still there when he re-opened them. Jack reached out and touched the gate. It felt good and solid. He had an irresistible urge to open it. Somehow, in a way he couldn't explain, the gate, he felt, was there for him. For a moment it crossed his mind that perhaps he had died and was being invited up to heaven. But his body seemed real enough, and anyway there was Persham on the other side of the road as he always remembered it. He didn't know what he believed about "life after death". He had not given it much thought, but he always imagined dying to be a painful thing, and you would feel it when you died. But here he hadn't noticed a thing. He could still feel the stony path beneath his feet, and now the shiny paint hard under his hand. The gate had a simple catch on the inside operated by a circular iron handle on the outside, although it was low enough for him to lean over and lift the catch by hand. This he did. The gate swung open readily without a sound as he leaned against it. Jack stepped gingerly onto the short path and took a pace forward.

3

Jallaxanya Rarga: Age: 17. Home address: 127, Sikilai Buildings, Wanulka City, Wanulka, Planet Raika

Jalli was not sure exactly how it had begun. She had been engrossed in her book in the local public library when this man had appeared, and the next thing she was aware of was that they were walking down the street together. She could not recall exactly what he had said to her inside the library – she had been deep into the life-cycle of parmanda colonies – but he was there, waiting for her, when she had emerged with her notes and her head full of how she was going to begin her essay for the biology teacher in the local secondary school. She had been attending the school for over six years. Now she was coming to the end of her final year and people were talking about her future. At seventeen many of the girls in Wanulka City had already left school and were actively seeking husbands. They had dreams of leaving their parents to establish new homes of their own. How proud they were when they found a respected, good looking boy – especially if he had a decent income, or at least the potential of one. But ambitions of this nature did not occupy Jalli's mind. She could never imagine leaving her grandmother, Momori, with whom she had been living for the best part of her life.

Their story, looked at from any point of view, was a tragic

one. And yet they were happy because they had each other, and because they had learned to smile, and even laugh together. Some had said that they should not do that. How could they after what had happened to them and so many others. Yet Momori had always felt she had been blessed, and was still being blessed – especially by her granddaughter of whom she was very proud.

Fourteen years had passed since the earthquake that had taken Momori's family. Her husband, her mother and father, all four of her children and their families, her brothers and sister and their children, along with nearly every one of their neighbours in the village of Zonga, had been swept away in one single catastrophe. In fact she and Jalli were the only two of their whole extended family who had survived. They had done so because they had not been at home that day. Momori had brought little Jalli the sixty-eight yukets into Wanulka City, a dusty middle-sized place, to attend the hospital and do some shopping.

The earthquake had not been a big one in terms of earthquakes, but it had fractured the dam in the hills behind the village. In the quake a building had collapsed, and all the inhabitants had gathered from their homes and fields to dig in the rubble for survivors. Nearly everyone had been there in the centre of the village beside the small stream that for centuries had flowed under the bridge beside the inn. There had been a small after-shock and the dam had given way. A huge body of water had rushed down the stream bed without any warning and had hit the village with a force that hardly left one brick standing on another. In a matter of seconds there was no bridge, no village and no people. Only half of the remains of Momori's family had ever been found. They had been buried along with other inhabitants in a mass grave.

The village had never been rebuilt. There was no-one left to populate it. Momori had been forty-four years old then. She had found a room, then later a small house (with a flat roof like all the others) in one of the suburbs about three yukets from the centre of the city. Then this grandmother had invested all her energy and devotion into bringing up her bright little girl who loved her dearly, and who, despite everything, had such a happy disposition you could not help but smile. Momori felt that she had been chosen, kept alive, to look after this child whom, she felt, was destined to be a blessing to more than herself.

But now this stranger in his late twenties had suddenly appeared and decided Jalli needed, for the first time since she was old enough to remember, to be escorted back to her home. Not that he could have known where she lived, she thought. But he had asked her, and she had told him. Why had she told him, this person she'd never met before? Just half a block from the library she couldn't believe her naïvety. She had been so delighted to find the books she was looking for on the shelf (the library didn't always come up with what she wanted so easily) and had become so wrapped up in her parmanda hives and feeling good about things, that she failed to register this young man's eccentricity.

At first, he had seemed harmless, even kind. But what did he want with her now? As they walked, he explained that he had seen her in the library a couple of times and had been intrigued by the expressions she made as she wrestled with her books and researched their contents. She had "interesting eyes", he explained. Apparently, he had asked the librarian who she was and thought he would introduce himself.

By the time they had reached the first crossroads near the bus-stop where she could take a bus home, she had decided that this man was really weird – or, at least, he was talking weird. Generally in the dry season, when the town was hot and dusty and there was no risk of rain, she would walk home from the library. She enjoyed the exercise. On other days when she didn't go to the library she would train for the sports, or go down to the beach with some of the girls she knew – not that she regarded any of them as more than school friends. She never invited them home, or joined in any of their sleepovers, but she had an open nature, and they welcomed her among them when she wanted to go to the beach or join in the sports. Sometimes they would talk about the homework they had to do – but not so very often as Jalli did not share their dislike of the work. She did not want to seem to judge them on their lack of interest. But she was always pleased to help if they got desperate the day before assignments were due and they wanted someone to explain what was needed. She had patience to help them, but it always stopped short of doing the work *for* them. Their talk about clothes, make-up and especially boys, left her cold. It was all so pointless. Why they needed to pander to the boys, who seemed to think it impressed girls if they "acted stupid", as she called it, she could not imagine.

But at that moment she would have been glad to have seen anyone she knew from school. In less than ten paces, she had made up her mind that she was not going to allow this man to walk her all the way home. Today she was going to catch the bus. Even if she had to wait fifteen minutes for it, it would be preferable to having to walk with him right up to her home. So she stopped at the bus-stop and thanked him for his attention, dismissing him as politely as she could. He didn't seem to take the hint that he had done enough. What he said next really alarmed her.

"But you do not generally catch the bus," he proclaimed, "you walk home."

"How do you know that?"

"I've seen you, swinging your bag and thinking as you go. I like that. Come, let us walk together to your home."

Jalli stopped and looked him in the eye. "Have you been to my home?"

"I know where you live."

"How?"

"I've followed you."

"You've followed me! It is wrong to follow people." Jalli was not a person who had difficulty in stating her mind. Her grandmother once observed that she felt sorry for anybody who got the sharp end of her tongue.

"I only did the once. You have such an interesting face and I wanted to know about you... speak to you." Jalli was now properly alarmed, and steadfastly refused to move beyond the bus-stop. He continued, "I know you live alone with your grandmother and have no other family. Not having connections is not easy. Many girls of your age are already destined for marriage or dating people. It is not easy for you, not having family and all that. You need a boyfriend, and I thought you would be grateful to have someone of my standing. I have a job in the Registry that pays well, and prospects of promotion to head of department in a few years. My father would need persuading, but after he has met you and seen how intelligent you are and …"

"Stop! Just stop there! Who do you think you are? I *don't* need a boyfriend. I am perfectly happy as I am. I am *not* looking for anyone and, in any case, I have a grandmother who is as good for me as some people's entire family. I *don't* know you, and I *do not want* to know you. I don't even know your name! And I haven't told you mine! So please leave me alone!" she exclaimed rapidly. His mouth remained open for about two seconds, but he quickly recovered.

"Of course, all this is rather sudden and you need the time to think about it. I do know your name. It is Jallaxanya Rarga – the librarian told me – and mine is Maik Musula. I will speak to you tomorrow."

"I do not want to speak to you tomorrow. Just *go away*!" Jalli was almost shouting now and people were staring as they passed. There were others in the bus queue. Maik Musula smiled innocently, offered his hand – to no avail – and lifting it in a wave, stepped backwards and smiled, "See you tomorrow!"

"Not if I see you first!" Jalli asserted under her breath.

She was suddenly aware, for the first time since she dressed that morning, of the clothes she was wearing. Faded blue jeans and a large floppy white T-shirt with the words, "DARE TO BE DIFFERENT" printed across it. It had appealed to her precisely because it was different, not like the figure hugging blouses or skimpy tops that some of the girls wore. Jalli was not shy, but she had a modesty about her that set her apart. Whatever it was that had intrigued Maik Musula she wished it hadn't. She had never thought about the

17

expressions she made that only others could see. For the first time in her life she felt really vulnerable, and began to wonder what was going on in the heads of men. She got on the bus, conscious of the fact that the bus-driver was a man. His mind was probably far more on his tea than on the identity of his fares, and to her relief he didn't betray any sign of weirdness. She sat beside a middle aged lady. She would normally have taken one of the empty seats but this time she thought it best to sit beside someone rather than have an unknown person sit beside her after the next stop. The man (what did he call himself?), Maik, had unsettled her. This wasn't fair. Anyway he had gone, she had dismissed him.

By the time she got home she had reflected on her performance and thought she had dealt with the situation rather well, and her normal buoyant self returned. The smiling face of her grandmother completely restored her faith in humanity.

"You're home early today," observed Momori who, despite her smile, looked rather older than her fifty-eight years.

"Yes, I decided to take the bus."

"So, Jalli Rarga, you're getting lazy in your mature years!"

"I wanted to get on with my essay," responded Jalli. It struck her that she had not told Grandma the truth. She was not in the habit of lying. But she did not want to say anything about her admirer. She wanted to forget him and did not want to talk about him. She was angry with him again – now he had made her lie! How dare he! But again she took a grip on herself and cheerily went into her bedroom – but not before Grandma had noticed the shadow on her expressive features.

The wise lady was no inquisitor, and knew that she would be told, if and when, Jalli needed to tell her anything. After all, this girl was now fast becoming a woman. Momori had not wanted it to happen, but she had always known that the time would come when she would lose her granddaughter to a home and life of her own. This, after all, was the role she, the child's only relative, had accepted. She would delight in seeing her granddaughter blossom and flourish. The thing that bothered her the most now was that clearly her bright girl was quite capable of further education, and how they were going to pay for it she didn't yet know. But she was a lady of faith who believed in some kind of divine providence. "He has provided for us so far," she told herself, "and He will see that we get what we need. All we need to do is be faithful and patient." And, indeed, it had been true ever since she had taken that sad little three year old to that small flat in the city all those years ago. Something had always turned up.

Some of the other women in the church ladies' group could not quite understand Momori's faith. Yes, they went to the church but they did it more from a social motive than a religious one. If they had had all their family wiped out like that then it would have been difficult to believe in a loving God, let alone talk about Him as a provider. Momori had explained that it was precisely because of the disaster that she believed so much in God. When you have nothing of your previous life left, she had explained, you become acutely aware of the presence of God. Somehow He is with you, alongside of you, weeping with you. Her friends couldn't understand that if He cared so much why hadn't He intervened and stopped the dam bursting, or got the people out of the way? Why did He allow earthquakes in the first place? Momori said she didn't know the answers to all of that.

Perhaps He couldn't for some reason. All she knew was that He stood beside her when her life was shattered – and had given her a little adorable three year old to care for.

Momori never wanted to be a leader of any kind in the church – but in many ways she was. Her faith gave much strength to the fellowship, and her gentle witness had a power of which she, herself, was not aware. She knew God loved her and that was sufficient not just for herself but for the other ladies too – and for her beloved granddaughter who was seen in church beside her even when no other young people were present. It did not surprise anyone that Jallaxanya chose a T-shirt which declared to the world that she was not afraid to be different! She was a real tribute to her grandma.

"Some people have whole families who do not give as much to their children as that one lady gives her granddaughter," people observed.

That night Jalli spent longer on her essay than she normally did. Her mind was upset. But by bedtime, after reading to her grandma, and saying her prayers she felt more herself. And the next morning Maik Musula was almost forgotten.

But, across the city, Maik Musula was carefully laying his plans for a second attempt. He had been too sudden, he concluded. He needed to take it more gently. He would wait a few days and then approach her again – apologetically. It had never crossed his mind to let this fascinating, innocent beauty escape him. After all, she needed him as much as he needed her. He was sure of that!

4

Three days after handing in her essay to Mr. Bandi, the biology teacher, Jalli found herself heading towards the city centre again. The books she needed were all missing from the school library, taken out by other students. She was told they were due back in two days but Jalli was not going to wait if she could find something in the city library. Had not the library produced exactly the book she wanted last time?

But Jalli never made it to the library. She had almost forgotten about Maik Musula, and was again wearing a cheerful, distinctive T-shirt – this time one with a bright yellow sunshine on a deep green background. She had not seen her persistent admirer the next day and she had decided he had reflected on his stupidity and was not going to reappear. But she was wrong. As she approached the Municipal Gardens, a small park in the centre of the city, where on fine days office workers ate their lunch under the trees, he accosted her. He had followed his own advice and felt that she would now be pleased to see him. He greeted her with a cheery, "Hi!" Before she could say anything he apologised in a humble voice for alarming her the other day. He had been too hasty.

"You certainly were," asserted Jalli, relieved that he seemed to have reflected on the previous importunate approach and was sorry to have alarmed her. "Apology accepted."

"But perhaps you have missed me?" he volunteered. "Would you like to meet for lunch tomorrow? I work right over there. We eat at the place on the corner."

"Thank you, but no. I am really not interested in striking up a new friendship right now."

"They do a good lunch, and you can have anything you like on the menu."

"Look, the answer's *no*! *Please listen* to what I am saying. I don't want to hurt you, but I don't want you to make a fool of yourself, so just…"

Musula grew agitated. "I am no fool. Who said I was a fool?" he demanded. His voice was raised, his eyes flashed. He was beginning to "freak out", as Jalli later described it. She was feeling frightened by him all over again.

"May God bless you!" she heard herself saying, "Goodbye." Jalli made to walk on but he caught her arm causing her to veer towards the wall that surrounded the Municipal Gardens. It was then that she spotted a small white gate, slightly ajar. Anything to put something between herself and him – she was thinking fast. With a tug she wrenched her arm from his grip, then she swung the gate open, stepped through and shut it behind her.

What happened next was completely unexpected. Maik Musula's expression was amazing. He had stopped by the gate. He was less than two metres away from her but his eyes were focused somewhere beyond her left shoulder. She turned, following his gaze but all she saw was a high green hedge. She wondered what had caused him to look so confused. He put his hand up against the hedge and pushed. He patted the air above the gate just feet away from where she stood. He clearly couldn't see her. He stood back, stared in the direction of the gate for a further five seconds, then turned and headed down the street.

Jalli breathed a huge sigh of relief. But then she fell to wondering why he had acted so strangely. She was sure he had a problem – probably some kind of mental illness she decided. But the way he had looked through her was not consistent with anything he had signalled before. It was as if she had simply been taken from his sight. Jalli considered what to do next. He had gone in the direction of the library so she decided she would cross the park and go back to the school another way. She did not want to meet Musula again. She could tell Mr. Bandi, her favourite teacher, what had happened and ask him what she should do. She turned round and, for the first time, looked in the direction of the Municipal Gardens – or what she expected to be the Municipal Gardens. What she saw astonished her. There, before her, was a beautiful green lawn with fine grass. Flowering trees, the like of which she had never seen in her whole life, hung over it, and behind it was, what Jalli considered, an oddly shaped building with a sloping straw roof. It had low windows and a porch with another little roof. The walls were painted a pale cream and were covered in a climbing plant with pink flowers. The scent of this garden filled the air.

Jalli could no longer hear the sound of the traffic behind her, all she was aware of was bird song and a gentle buzzing that she associated with parmandas – the life-cycle of which she was now an expert (or so Mr. Bandi had said). Everything about Wanulka seemed to have vanished. She appeared to be in an entirely new world. The very quality of the air was different – it was softer and sweeter than anything she had experienced anywhere. Even the green-grassed borders beneath the trees beside Wanulka beach that the city council always watered felt very coarse compared with the carpet of lawn on which she now stood. It was a wonderful experience. She wondered if she had "passed over" somehow, as Grandma might say. This was exactly like the place she expected heaven to be – so different and so beautiful.

She couldn't see anyone else there, but she felt an overwhelming sense of welcome. Strangely she did not in the least feel like an intruder. In some miraculous way it was "hers" to enjoy. Why? She had only just stepped onto the lawn and now she was feeling like she had belonged here forever. Had she experienced something like this as a child perhaps? Was she in some kind of dream? Yet she had her bag in her hands, and was still dressed in her deep green floppy T-shirt with the large smiling sun on the front. She looked down and saw that her trainers were making little dints in the lawn and she instinctively took them off like someone stepping on "holy" ground. The cool, gentle grass caressed her toes and instep. She felt herself being drawn further into the garden and tiptoed to a rustic wooden bench beneath a tree laden with pink blossom, sat down on it and looked about her. This was, beyond doubt, the most beautiful place she had ever been in, she thought.

For the next ten minutes, she deliberately pushed the question of how she had arrived in such a place to the back of her mind, and just absorbed its wonders. Jalli was the kind of person who would make the most of anything that came her way, and she was not going to waste this miraculous moment. She revelled in the delightful scents of the blossom and the chirping of the birds that she caught sight of every now and then as they crossed from one bush to another. She wondered who lived in the house with the grass roof. All the houses she knew in Wanulka had flat roofs – you only put grass over grain stores. In fact, come to think if it, this house looked like a very big grain store. The straw roof was crossed with ornate binding. It wasn't really grass, she observed, or even straw. (Much later she learned that it was reed from the marshes, called thatch – but that was some time in the future). Jalli crossed over to the house and peered in through one of the windows. Inside there was furniture and furnishings, so clearly someone lived here. Then she pulled herself together – however she felt about the sense of welcome, she was being far too curious, she told herself.

Then it occurred to her. If she had "passed over" then she had left Wanulka behind forever. She had never imagined going before Grandma, and the thought of leaving her all alone in the world after all that had happened to her was almost unbearable. But the white gate was still there in the hedge. She hurried across to it, and over the top, to her relief, she could still see the street in Wanulka. Jalli picked up her trainers and stepped through. The gate now seemed to be on the inside of the two metre thick hedge. Pushing her way along the little path she felt stones beneath her feet and then the hot pavement of Wanulka City Centre. The sun beat down and the traffic was deafening after the silence of the garden. She turned, and the white gate was now on the outside of the Municipal Gardens' wall. When she looked over it, however, the lawn and trees and the straw roofed house were still there. She turned and bent down to put her shoes back on. Not fifteen metres further on people were going in and out of the usual iron gates of the Gardens, but no-one gave a glance towards the white gate.

Jalli took several paces to the iron gates and entered the Gardens. She turned up the path that ran around the edge of the Gardens and looked at the other side of the wall where the white gate should have been – not a sign of anything but a herbaceous border and a solid wall. Then she walked back outside the Gardens. The white gate was still there, bright and newly painted. She measured the steps and went back along the pavement and counted the same number of steps along the edge of the border. The white gate simply did not exist on the inside. A gardener was weeding the border and Jalli asked, "Excuse me. Is there a white gate anywhere in that wall?"

"No love," he replied, "no white gates anywhere in these gardens. And I should know, I've been working here for the past thirty years."

"Thank you. The gardens are always lovely. It's just that I thought I saw a gate on the street side of the wall."

"No. Never been any gate in that wall except the big iron gates you came through. They are always locked at night."

"Thanks," said Jalli, "it's just that I thought I had seen one on the other side."

"No, not here, love."

"Thanks."

The gardener smiled to himself. "Young people get stranger all the time. White gate? Still, she seemed a nice sort of person." He went back to work happy that someone had noticed him – especially a cheery sort of person like Jalli. He smiled as he hoed. Without knowing it, Jalli had spread another little blessing!

Jalli reverted to her original plan and crossed the Municipal Gardens, but not before popping outside once more to check on the gate. It was still there, bright and new looking with the lawn beyond it. She decided she was not going to tell Mr. Bandi about Musula, well not today anyway. Her mind was too full of the garden with the straw roofed house.

From the school she took the bus home. For the second time in four days Jalli kept something from her grandmother. This time she had decided not to lie, and had worked out what to tell Grandma that simply left out the man and the white gate and the garden.

Going to sleep that night she wondered whether just not telling someone constituted a lie. But she couldn't possibly tell her grandmother everything forever. Some things you needed to keep to yourself, she concluded. After all, that's exactly what Grandma had said when she had asked some years ago what it was like making love to Grandpa.

"Some things you just don't talk about!" she had said. Could this be one of those things? Well, for the moment, yes. But somehow she didn't feel in the least like keeping it a secret from God. It was something she and God already shared because, of course, He knew everything – He already knew about the events of that day.

Jack's good mood had filled him with a sense of curiosity. He stepped through the hedge and emerged onto the lawn. Wow!

He was in a different universe! This wasn't a conversion of the school yard he had played in as a boy at St Paul's. It was so different, but he didn't feel at all like a trespasser. Amazing! He was in a country garden with a thatched cottage in it. But somehow he didn't expect anyone to yell out of one of the bedroom windows, "Get off my lawn! Before I send for the police!" as had happened the last time he inadvertently strayed onto someone's private property whilst trying to take a short cut home. "OK, mate. Keep your hair on!" he had barked as he scampered back the way he had come. What amused him on that occasion, after he got over the shock of being shouted at like that – like being hit in the back by one of the school bullies when you weren't expecting it – was that the man was completely bald. "Unfortunate expression," he had said to himself.

But, here, now, he felt entirely different. He had never visited a place like this before. It was not like anywhere he had ever been, and yet he felt he, somehow, "belonged". Odd that. Jack could honestly say that "belonging" anywhere was not in his experience. He lived with his mother but he felt that he was only there till he could move. Secretly, though, he had to tell himself, he would never abandon his mother as his father had. He was not going to be a sod like him. He had not even felt he belonged in Persham, and certainly not St Paul's Middle School. In fact the nearest he had come to feeling acknowledged in the world was that very morning when he had amazed everyone with his exam results. But this was not that world. It was so completely new – and yet he seemed to belong here. It was home! But how could that be?

He looked around for some sign of another person. He

shouted, "Hello!" but instinctively not too loud. His voice rang with a timbre that seemed to fit in with the place. There was no response. "Anyone there?" he called. All he sensed, in a way that he couldn't really describe, was a welcome. He surveyed the scene. There were trees with lots of blossom – some pink and some white – around the soft green grass. The garden was quite big and was surrounded by hedges, as far as he could see, on all the sides. Only one entrance was apparent, the white gate through which he had come. Behind the cottage he could just make out the corner of a greenhouse.

Consumed by curiosity, Jack crossed the lawn to the cottage door. He knocked. There was no response. He knocked again, louder. By this time he would have been surprised if someone had come – and, in truth, he did not want them to. He tried the handle – the door was unlocked. He opened it and peered in. There was a hallway with a flight of stairs leading up from it. The plaster walls were painted an off-white and the doors and stairs were in plain varnished wood. "Medium oak," thought Jack thinking of the colour charts in the DIY store he had worked in last summer holiday. To the left and right were doors that, he guessed, led into the front rooms with the windows that gave out onto the lawn. The door on the left stood open. He looked in and saw an inglenook fireplace with a country landscape painted in oils above it. There was a dresser laden with plates and earthenware against the inner wall, and a fine table in the centre of the room complete with four solid looking oak chairs. In front of the window was a window seat with a fitted embroidered cushion. The full-length curtains were pale green with a delicate flower pattern. It was like the pictures that you saw in some of the holiday brochures advertising country accommodation; but this was real. It was "lived in". It was a home.

Jack decided to touch nothing, just look. He explored the other front downstairs room which was a sitting room to match the dining room he'd already seen. There was a kitchen with modern equipment, and a sink with taps above it. Beside the long work top was what he guessed was a fridge but he didn't open it. The larder beyond smelled richly of vegetables and fruit stacked on the racks. From the kitchen window he could see the greenhouse and beyond that more grass. Next to the kitchen was a bathroom with a beautiful enamelled bathtub against the far wall, a toilet pedestal and sink that matched the bath, and a shower cubicle. Jack had never had a shower in his life. When he was a child his mother had a great struggle to get him to wash at all! Even now Jack scanned the bathroom but did not linger like his mother would have done. She would have admired the tiled walls and floor, the full-length mirror and the electric light fitting in the centre of the ceiling. But Jack was mounting the staircase two steps at a time and, gaining the tiny square landing, encountered three more wooden doors, and to the right, above the sitting room, a narrow corridor lit by two small windows. He began with the room on the left. This was above the dining room. As he entered it his heart sang. There was a strong feminine presence. To the right was a huge double bed with a plain white cover. On the wooden floor were three rugs made of coarser material. A dressing table stood beside the window through which he could see the garden seat under a tree with pink blossom, and beyond that the white gate that led back to his world. But he did not want to leave this place. He felt so welcome. There was a delicate fragrance about this room that intrigued him. He opened the wardrobe opposite the bed. It was filled with dresses, skirts and blouses in cheerful colours and pretty lace. This was a young woman's room he decided. After a while he felt that perhaps he should leave, and not pry further.

The second door opened onto a room that overlooked the greenhouse. "This would be above the kitchen," he surmised. It contained two single beds, a wardrobe, a chair and a low chest of drawers. He strode across the room and opened the wardrobe. Men's clothing. It was a mixture of smart and casual, and also some overalls that seemed a little incongruous because no-one appeared to do any work about the place. He hadn't thought about how the house kept clean, or the grass mowed, or the clothes washed, but someone must do it. From the window he surveyed the hedge at the back of the garden, the entirety of which he could see above the greenhouse. There was no back entrance visible. He decided he would walk the perimeter when he had finished surveying the house. He tested the beds. "Just right!" he said to himself. For a moment he felt guilty that he was behaving like Goldilocks invading the privacy of the "Three Bears". But the feeling was immediately dispelled. No. He belonged here. Sitting on one of the beds he reflected that he shouldn't feel that. In fact he couldn't belong, could he? But, somehow, he just could not shrug off the gentle and insistent embrace this house gave him.

Jack continued his tour. The third door was a small upstairs bathroom with just a sink and pedestal that he passed over quickly. (His mother would have declared, "A second toilet!" and rejoiced.) Jack continued down the low corridor under the pitch of the roof. On the left were two small windows that gave onto the rear of the house, and on the right two doors, exactly like all the others. He opened the first and stepped inside. Whoops! He shouldn't have done that without knocking! Why? The room was not occupied any more than the rest of the house was. The furniture was simple and differed little from any of the other bedrooms. There was one single bed. To tell the truth, at this moment he felt exactly like he would have done had he entered his mother's bedroom at home without knocking. Her room was her preserve. When she was in there she wanted to be private. When he needed her as a small child, he would knock and wait and, mostly, she would come to him. But he had never crossed the threshold. Jack quickly withdrew from this room back into the corridor and closed the door firmly behind him hoping his incursion would not be noticed.

The last room was at the end of the little corridor and he made his way towards it. This time he knocked, waited and then opened the door. After the last room he was quite nervous about going in. He quickly checked the room out. It was a twin of the other one he had just left but not quite as forbidding. Why that should be when they were so similar he didn't know, but he firmly closed the door before retracing his steps to the top of the stairs. Perhaps he should leave the house now. Regaining the little landing he saw that he had not closed the door to the first bedroom he had entered. He laid his hand on the doorknob and was again filled with a great desire to enter the room. This was definitely a lady's room.

And yet that seemed to make it even more irresistible! It just seemed to invite him and as he stepped over the threshold so his heart warmed and the room seemed to smile. He stole over to the chest of drawers and pulled open the first drawer. There were things that young women wore in their hair, bangles and other trinkets. There was no real jewellery. This is what thieves would do, he recollected, but he touched nothing. The second drawer contained underwear. He slid the drawer shut and opened the bottom drawer which contained night clothes. The nightdress on the top had a big bright yellow sun on it with a smiling face and, as he looked at it, he fancied it was smiling at him. "I would like to meet your owner one day!" he told the sunshine, and the embroidered eyes seemed to dance a reply that perhaps he might. In fact, he thought, she might be coming home right now and he blushed at the thought of being caught in her bedroom. He hastily shut the drawer and stepped out of the room making sure all the doors were shut as he had found them. He descended the stairs and out into the garden, closing the front door behind him. He stepped into the middle of the lawn and surveyed the house. It was even more attractive now he had been inside. His eyes looked up to the bedroom window on the left above the dining room and wondered if he would ever meet its occupant.

He then walked to the white gate from which he had come. He could see the street in Persham as it always had been, but he turned to his right and walked around the garden with the hedge on his left. It was quite a long way, and the whole length of the hedge was thick and dense. At no point was it possible to see through it. He confirmed the conclusion that the white gate was the only way in or out and no sounds from outside seemed to penetrate the thick hedge. In all his scrutiny of the place, however, Jack saw no evidence of anyone. There were things that belonged to people, the whole place belonged to people, but there was nothing to indicate that anyone had been here recently – except, just inside the hedge a few metres before he regained the gate, the dent of a shoe much smaller than his own. He glanced across the lawn. The whole of it was covered by similar dents, but they were all made by him. No-one would have any difficulty in realising he had been there, yet this person had left just one single dint. But then he noticed that all around it the grass had been trodden on, but very lightly, and with care.

Jack was proud of himself. Perhaps he should look into being a sleuth as a job! But whom could this footfall belong to? He examined the hedge behind the dint, but it was just as dense there as everywhere else. How could, whoever it was, manage to step here without coming through the gate or from the house? The person looked to have stepped straight out of the hedge. It belonged to someone with much smaller feet than his, a woman perhaps. Jack thought of the girl whose bedroom he had recently explored. He reflected with surprise again at just how he had gently invaded its secrets. He couldn't believe he had done that. In fact, how could he have gone into the cottage uninvited at all!? There seemed to be some force outside of himself inviting him in. With the exception of the one upstairs bedroom, had it not just opened itself up before him, and told him to feel "at home"?

Jack checked his watch. It was now too late to go to the library, it would be closing in ten minutes. He decided to make his way straight home. It just occurred to him that now the white gate appeared to be on the inside of the hedge and open outwards, away from him on the inside. He was sure it was on the roadside before or he would not have seen it. Strange again. He lifted the latch, stepped the two metres through the hedge and was back in Persham. An old car was mounting the street making a huge racket and children were shouting from the school yard. The sounds, smells and atmosphere of the town flooded back into his senses. He turned. The gate was now on the outside as he remembered it, shiny and new and looking oddly "out of place". He spotted the school caretaker leaving his house next to the school and hailed him.

"Hi!" he yelled. Running up to him he asked, "Someone told me that a white gate has been put into the school yard and, as I was passing, I thought I would check it out. As a former pupil, like."

"White gate? New white gate, you say?" Jack nodded. The man was looking straight at it behind him. "No new white gates here, no new gates at all!"

"What about a cottage?"

"Cottage! What cottage? You've got the wrong place mate."

"OK," said Jack. "Sorry to bother you."

It hadn't surprised him at all. The whole thing was so strange. "Perhaps it's the entrance to a 'worm hole'," smiled Jack to himself, "like on the *Startrek* TV series where they travelled around in space from one 'quadrant' to another with ease. The cottage is in the 'Delta Sector'!"

He decided he would go to the library the next morning, and then check out the cottage again!

"Had a good day?" called his mum as he stomped into the house.

"Cool," he replied. "Got better results than expected." And before his mum could respond and get on to what he was going to do with his life (which would not be long in coming beyond the expressions of delight), "I'm going to the library first thing tomorrow to see about a gap year and research career options. Now I know what I have got, the options should be easier to research."

Matilda was genuinely pleased. And it pleased her even more to see her son in such a good mood. "Perhaps things will get better," she hoped to herself. "I do wish he would stir more enthusiasm to sort out his future though." But, somehow, his present demeanour urged her to be patient – at least till he had been to the library.

5

The following morning Jack was "up with the birds", as his mother would have said. He ate a good breakfast and shoved an apple and a bottle of water into his shoulder sack, and was out of the house before his mother could shout, "Mind how you go!" in her usual way. She'd never seen him so positive! It was even lifting her own mood as she set about the washing. She noted that Jack had not put on his scruffy jeans either.

Jack passed the kicking tree and realised he didn't feel like kicking it. It occurred to him that it was trying to live – just like him. Before, it had been some annoying thing that needed kicking. So Jack strode off towards the library. He arrived almost as soon as it opened. He was directed to several pamphlets about different options for a volunteer gap year. Only one did not require him to pay them a lot of money before he got there. Then, they all expected him to find air-fares which were quite high in some cases. After that he glanced at the university prospectuses. There were quite a shelf-full of these and he didn't quite know where to begin. He thought about the Internet, but the computer stations had been quickly commandeered by some young lads engaged in what looked like a bloody on-screen battle but must have had something to do with school research or it would not have been allowed in the library. This was going to take a long time, at least a day, and he was impatient to see if the white gate was still there. There was no urgency, he concluded as he put some free leaflets into his bag.

He stepped outside the library, took a drink from his water bottle and made his way up the hill to St Paul's school. He reflected that he must get a job and earn some money, whatever he was going to do in the end, so he found himself getting a bit impatient again.

But not for long. When he got to the top of the hill he looked towards where the white gate had been. It was still there! He glanced around him, decided no one was in sight, pushed the gate open, and slipped through the hedge.

★★★

In Wanulka, Jalli was eager to get to the city centre and check out the white gate again. "Her white gate" she was calling it because no-one else seemed to see it.

On the way she contemplated how likely it was that it would still be there that day and was deciding how disappointed she would be. To be honest, "very" was the answer. So, as she approached the place and looked across the road to see her bright little gate clearly visible in the Municipal Gardens wall exactly where it had been the day before, she was elated. The street was quite busy. She was conscious that someone might see her go in and try and follow her. So rather than crossing the road and walking straight up to the gate, she decided to cross further up and slide in the way she had done the first time.

The gate opened under her hand and she stepped into the

channel through the hedge. Bending to remove her shoes she looked across the lawn. "Someone else has been here," she thought. She immediately noticed the dents of large shoes across the lawn leading up to the front door. She thought of retreating – she must be intruding. She felt both welcomed and uncomfortable at the same time. While she stood barefoot on the edge of the lawn, she heard someone call from her left, "Hi! You live here?" It was Jack who had just arrived himself.

"N…No," she stammered, "I…I'm sorry I just found this place yesterday and thought I would come back and see if anyone was here today."

Jalli was standing on the spot where Jack had found the footstep the day before.

"How did you get in?"

"Through that white gate here," she explained.

"It wasn't there yesterday," stated Jack, noticing a new white gate behind her for the first time. "I came through one too. Over there." Jack pointed to the gate leading to Persham.

"You've come through a white gate too! I didn't see yours yesterday either. I just liked this place so much that I wanted to come back today. I hope that is alright."

"It's alright by me," replied Jack, "but it's only my second time here myself. It isn't my place. Have you met anyone else here?"

"No-one," stated Jalli. "Have you?"

"Not a soul. No-one in the garden and no-one anywhere in the house."

"You've been inside?"

"I just thought I would try and find someone. There was no-one in the cottage, but its seems lived in."

"What did you call the house? Cot…" asked Jalli.

"What? 'Cottage'? It's a country cottage."

"I don't know that word," explained Jalli. "…and I've never seen a house like this before."

"True, you don't get them like this in Persham. You have to go out into the country a bit…usually," he added, looking at the very real cottage.

"Where did you say?" marvelled Jalli.

"Where? Persham? The town out there."

"It's not out there!" stressed Jalli, pointing to the gate from which she had come. "Out there it's Wanulka. The Municipal Gardens to be exact. Come and look." Jack walked across to Jalli's gate and looked over. There, beyond, was the busy street in Wanulka.

"Astounding!" exclaimed Jack.

Then they went together to Jack's gate and beyond it they observed the road outside St Paul's school in Persham.

"Mind-blowing!" announced Jalli.

Somehow they had both found a white gate that no-one else appeared to see in their own lands. Those gates had taken them both through to an isolated garden and cottage that appeared to be lived in, yet deserted apart from themselves. Just what were they to make of all this?

"Look let's sit over there under the tree on that bench and compare notes," suggested Jalli. She tip-toed across the lawn to the bench.

"Why do you take your shoes off?" Jack inquired.

"Because this lawn is so perfect. You dent it with every step."

"Like I've done?"

"Well. Yes…"

"Perhaps I should…"

"No. It's me," interjected Jalli. "I was afraid of making any impression on this place. It wasn't mine."

"But you're not so afraid of doing it now?"

"No. No, I'm not. I feel this place has welcomed me."

"So do I!" exclaimed Jack. "It's as if, well, somebody wants me here."

"Exactly!"

"Somehow I feel I 'belong' here in some strange kind of way. But I didn't discover it till yesterday. And to tell the truth I could not wait to come again. It's a very beautiful place, but it's more than that."

"I know just what you mean. I felt really drawn to come back. I was so worried the gate wouldn't be there today."

"Just the way I felt. And I was so glad it was. I opened it, stepped in, and then you appeared."

"Perfect timing! Perhaps we were meant to meet."

"Do you think, all this is some kind of 'plan'?" queried Jack.

"Well. I do believe that God looks after you and has a 'plan' for each one of us. But I never thought it would be in a strange new garden with strange white gates. It's like in a new world. There's nothing like this anywhere near where I live. The air is different, the trees, the birds. It is as much about how it feels as how it looks and sounds. And yet, at the same time I like…kind of…know…" Jalli weighed her words, "It's as if I'm at home."

"I'm not sure what I think about God…" said Jack, "I've never given him much thought. Mum always reckons He exists but she never calls on him or anything. But I agree about your 'another world' thing. Yet I just cannot understand how it works. I mean, it is not in St Paul's school yard and not in your…what did you call your park?"

"Municipal Gardens. But where is it then? Where are we?"

"I really don't know. This cottage could be England but the plants and trees are not quite right. It's definitely not Persham. It could be some virtual reality but it is extremely advanced if it is. One possibility is that we are on board some kind of alien spacecraft with technology so advanced we can't detect it beyond the sensory experiences the aliens give us to experience.

"Aliens. You mean people who are strangers?"

"Yes. People from other planets. There could be more advanced civilisations than ours who could travel without being seen and land on Earth and take us over without us knowing it. At school we learned about Plato talking about the world we know being mere shadows projected on the wall inside a cave. The people in the cave can't see reality, only a shadow of it. But they could not know what it was truly like outside the cave in the real world. They weren't even aware that there was a world beyond what they could see. Coming here might be like stepping outside Plato's cave and seeing the real world for the first time…

"Then I was wondering about wormholes, but I think that is only fiction."

"Wormholes?" quizzed Jalli.

"Yes. Passages through space and time that lead from one universe to another. But that would mean we would have had to have travelled millions of light years."

"Do we have to work it out? I mean, must we know how it happens? Perhaps we should just enjoy it and explore it as it presents itself. All I know is that, in one way it is all very different, but in another way I do feel so at home."

"I feel like that too. That's a good way of putting it." Jack studied, a thoughtful expression on his face. "At home"! Jack pondered the words. This belonging thing was probably the strangest thing about the whole experience.

"At one time I thought I could have died and gone to heaven!" stated Jalli. "But quite clearly I haven't, because my grandma seemed to think I was normal enough and people in Wanulka all treated me normally."

"Tell me about your place," asked Jack. He was beginning to like this girl. She was different from any of the girls that went to his school. She wasn't like anybody he knew. All at once it came to him. She belonged in that bedroom he had been so ungentlemanly in inspecting yesterday. Those were her things. She did belong! Wasn't she wearing a green T-shirt with the same sun face on it?

Jalli started to tell him about Wanulka. She told him how it was hot and dry at the moment, how the suns were at their brightest and the rains were not due for another month. She told him about the Municipal Gardens and how the white gate was not visible to anyone else, even to the gardener who had worked there for years.

Privately, Jalli thought of Maik Musula and how he had made her feel about men. Perhaps she was being naïve all over again? But Jack seemed great – she had only just met him, but everything he did, and everything he said, seemed to dispel any doubts she should have had.

Then Jack explained about St Paul's school yard and the hill on which it stood with roads leading down into the centre of Persham. He told her about how he had just finished high school forever, and about his exam results yesterday. Then he explained how he had discovered the gate on his way to the library. He was also convinced that no-one else could see his white gate.

"Except me," remarked Jalli.

"Except you! So, hi! I'm Jack."

"Jalli, Jalli Rarga."

"Jack Smith."

"Jack Smitt?"

"Jack Smith."

"Smitt," she tried.

"No. Smith. Put your tongue between your teeth. You must be able to say it because you're saying all the other 'ths' perfectly."

"I have never said a strange word like that, Jack Smitt… Sm-i-ss." She laughed.

"Oh. Jack will do! Jalli Raa-ga?"

"Perfect!"

"But look. Your Wanooka…"

"Wa-nul-ka."

"Wa-nul-ka. You said 'suns' – more than one?"

"Yes, of course, there are three."

"Wow! You're kidding! We only have one sun. I mean on Earth we only have one. That must put us in a different part of the sky. No, I don't get that. How could we have travelled across millions of miles by just walking through a hedge? You're having me on!"

"Having you 'on'? What does that mean?"

"It means you're teasing me. You can't have more than one sun in your Wanulka!"

"But we do," retorted Jalli, concerned that he thought she was not telling the truth. "Why should I tease you?"

"I don't know. I mean…I'm sorry. It's just too fantastic."

"It's a mystery. God's mystery. But like lots of things He makes, it's…"

"But that makes it all too easy. I mean the universe just doesn't work that way."

"Maybe not the universe you know about. But the universe is very, very big. Many things could happen that we don't understand yet… And I don't think this place, and you, are just in my imagination, a sort of dream… It's not like anything I've ever imagined before. It's far too real and different to be a dream."

"No. I agree. I think it's real alright."

"Then, perhaps it is one of your 'wormholes'."

Jack did not know what to say next. They both had to try and get their heads around this. The only thing that made sense was that they had somehow transported through space-time. This was indeed mind-blowing as Jalli had said.

They sat in silence for a bit. Everything was surreal and fantastic, yet everything about it was so cool. After a few minutes Jack said:

"Three suns. I like that idea. What do you call them?"

"Jallaxa, Suuf and Skhlaia."

"Jallaxa, Soof and Claya?"

"Suuf and Skhlaia."

"Whatever. You only have one sun on your T-shirt."

"That's Jallaxa. The biggest and brightest."

"Jallaxa! I can say that one!" They laughed.

"That's good. I'm named after it, Jallaxanya. It means 'little Jallaxa'. They call me Jalli for short."

"That's a nice name. I like it."

"Thank you kind sir!" They laughed again.

"But," continued Jack, "if you live in a different world you must speak an entirely different language to me. So how come you're speaking English? Where did you learn to speak it so well?"

"English? What's that language? I speak Wanulkan."

"So, you're not speaking English…now?"

"No! I am speaking Wanulkan."

"Am I speaking Wanulkan?"

"Yes. But some of the things you say are a bit strange. And sometimes you use odd words like…What did you call the house?"

"Cottage."

"Cot-tage. Things that I don't know the name of. And there's a slightly different sort of accent to your voice from what I am used to."

"Your English sounds like that to me. I like the nice way you pronounce it though…"

"Do you know what I think? I think we are talking, each of us in our own language, and 'He' or 'She' or 'It' – whatever it is that has brought us to this place – is doing some kind of dubbing. You say it in English and I hear it in Wanulkan, and vice-versa."

"That would have to be so, because I have never heard of Wanulkan, and it would be strange coming from different planets if we spoke the same. If you're from a different planet that makes you an alien!"

"Me, an alien?"

"Yes, from outer-space. But when people in Britain draw

pictures of 'aliens' they usually have odd shaped bodies and funny faces. They're often thought of as 'little green men'."

"Green? Are you saying I look green?" Jalli was almost horrified.

"No. That's the point you look…human. Like you come from Planet Earth… Look, I wonder whether what is true for our language is also true of our appearances as well? What I mean is, if our speech is being translated, is the same thing happening to what we see? I mean, you may not have three arms and two blue heads like me!" Jack found himself enjoying talking about appearance to this girl whom he thought was quite attractive. He also liked the way she laughed.

"You do not have three arms and two blue heads!" giggled Jalli.

"That could be quite offensive if I had!" exclaimed Jack. "But you're right I don't. I have two arms and one head and it is not blue! Let's test this further! Describe yourself to me, and I will say if what I see is what you think you are."

"OK. Good idea." Jalli was beginning to feel really happy with this boy from another planet. "I'll start at the top," she said. Why should she feel entirely comfortable describing her body to this alien boy she had met less than an hour before? Perhaps it was because he was from a different planet – but he was also someone she was beginning to like.

It felt just the opposite to the way she had felt about that Musula guy. Imagine if she had met him here! But, somehow, she knew she never would.

"My hair is long," she began, "down to the middle of my back. It is brown – nothing special. I have greyish blue eyes –

two of them – and a large bulgy nose, beneath which is a small mouth and a chin that sticks out too much…"

"Enough!" chuckled Jack. "Let me try! Your hair is a delicate shade of chestnut brown. Your eyes are a pale blue, and your nose is the nicest nose I have ever seen and… I think you're altogether quite good looking!"

"OK! Stop! Praise will get you everywhere!" They were both laughing out loud.

"This is fun!" said Jack. "OK, we've established that our appearance is probably not being translated."

"But, if you think I'm as good looking as you say then there must be a 'Translator' who is doing something remarkable!"

Jack wanted to say that if that was the case he didn't care. He did think she was quite special looking. Better than anyone in his school, he thought. But he felt that he hadn't known her long enough to tell her all that, so he decided to continue with, "And 'He' or 'She' has done a really good job on your wings if they are just as I see them!"

"Wings?" she began then realised it was like the three arms and blue heads. "Yes. Exactly! So I can take off at a moment's notice."

"Go on then!"

"OK. But there's one problem. I have to confess the wings are only in your imagination!" and they laughed some more.

"Seriously…" said Jack. But somehow "being serious" was not easy. Some of it was the nervousness of meeting somebody of the opposite sex for the first time that seemed really nice, and some of it was that being in this place was so far beyond reality. Perhaps it would all vanish as quickly as it appeared. Eventually, Jalli managed to ask, "Do you want to go inside? Inside the cot-tage?"

"Haven't you been inside?" asked Jack, a little surprised.

"It wasn't my house when I came yesterday, and I felt I shouldn't. But I did look through the windows."

"I wondered at myself feeling so welcome inside. I looked everywhere!" said Jack. "That's your room up there!"

"My room!?"

"Well, I went in. The cottage didn't mind – and it's full of your things."

"My things?"

"Yes. Dresses and…things. Girl's things."

"How do you know they are mine?"

"They just are! You belong here. They are the sort of thing a girl like you would wear. They kind of…fit."

"You mean you even checked their size?" Jalli giggled.

"No. I meant that they suit you. They're your style. As I was talking to you I knew that you and they belonged together."

"I've hardly worn a dress in my life!" exclaimed Jalli. "I wouldn't even know what was my style myself."

"But 'He' or 'She' does. The One who brought us here. There was a nightdress with a sun face on it exactly like the one you are wearing."

"So you've been into all 'my' things!" teased Jalli. "Opened all 'my' drawers?"

"Well. I didn't know you then, did I? And, somehow you, or 'He', or 'She', or the cottage, or whoever, was telling me you wouldn't mind."

Jalli was now looking forward to exploring everything herself.

"Do *you* have a room?"

"Kind of. But it's got two beds in it. There are some nice things in the wardrobe though."

"Then I shall poke around in 'your' stuff too!" Jalli had never found anyone quite so good to be with as this boy from a different planet. Weird, but nice.

They crossed the grass to the cottage. "Should we knock?" asked Jalli.

"No need. I don't think anyone is here." But Jalli knocked lightly in any case. Then Jack opened the door. They stepped inside.

"Are you sure this is OK?" Jalli hesitated.

"The cottage tells you what it wants you to do. Yesterday it drew me into it. Honestly. I was worried like you at first, but as I went I kind of felt I should be here, and should be looking around. I didn't touch a thing. Just opened doors and cupboards and looked. Come on, I'll show you around. I started with this wonderful dining room."

They went round the downstairs rooms in the same way that Jack had done the day before. They kept telling each other what an absolutely beautiful house it was.

"But who looks after it?" queried Jalli. "Someone must clean it and dust it. Everything is so neat and tidy too."

"Yes. I keep wondering that. It's so 'homely'."

"Exactly. This has people attending to everything and loving it."

Going upstairs, Jack motioned to the first door on the left. "This is your room!"

"Don't keep saying that! I've never been here before. It can't be mine."

They stepped inside and were enveloped in a huge sense of happiness. Jalli was not prepared for it, and it even surprised Jack, despite his being so impressed the day before.

"Wow!" he uttered.

Jalli just stood open mouthed for a full ten seconds. "Do you feel what I feel!?"

"It's exactly like I said. Only today it's even more powerful."

"This is a room that would make you feel happy no matter how sad you are. It is a place where hurts can be made better," contemplated Jalli out loud.

For at least a minute they surveyed the room from just inside the threshold, standing together in some kind of trance.

Jack broke the silence and took Jalli's hand, "Come over here. Open the wardrobe and look at the things."

Jalli, still stunned by the power of this room over her, crossed softly with him to the long wooden wardrobe that stood opposite the bed. She opened it. It contained a rail of dresses that all seemed so beautiful. There were bright colours, and subtler ones with dainty lace. The more practical things were at one end. There were shoes too. Jack had not touched anything, but Jalli was suddenly free of all her inhibitions and was in among them. Delighting at one, and then another. Taking them off the rail and holding them up, admiring their line and the cut and the stitching.

"These are all so beautiful," she cried. "I've never seen so many things I like together in one place!" It was a veritable treasure-trove.

"You see," explained Jack as Jalli began to examine the drawers, "I told you. This room, and the things in it, all match you. You fit. I knew you would like the stuff. And you…you know what… you are the most perfect girl I have ever met!" What was he saying? Fancy saying that! It was true but he had had no intention of saying so! Whatever would she think of him? So he quickly continued, "This is the most perfect place I have even been in…If you want to try anything on I'll wait downstairs."

Then he wished he had said "outside the room" instead of downstairs so she could have opened the door and let him see her wearing those pretty dresses! He was just working out how he might still manage that, when Jalli blurted out a resounding, "No!" She had suddenly become self conscious. All this was happening far too fast. The fact that she didn't want any of it to stop was probably what frightened her the most. What was she doing? If somebody this morning had told her that she would be exploring a bedroom with a boy possibly from a different planet with one sun and a strange language, she would never have believed them! And here she was inside a strange house with…

"Look, these are not my things. They are not mine, even to touch let alone try on! How could I have even come in here? Come on, we really ought to leave!"

For a second this took Jack by surprise, but he quickly recovered.

"Hold on! You're… you're probably right," he stuttered searching for the words, "your parents would probably be horrified if they knew their well-brought-up daughter was with a perfect stranger in a bedroom in an empty house. But… but I do think we were invited in in some way. We both felt it, didn't we? It came from outside of us. Just like all these amazing things. And – this might sound silly – but to rush out seems almost as rude as being too curious."

Jalli relaxed. "You're right," she said. "I think we should… should say, 'Thank you' or something. I mean to the house, or Whoever, before we leave."

Jack had not been the kind of person who had said many "Thank yous" and this speech made him feel a bit awkward. They stood still together in the doorway, looking into the room. Neither spoke.

"Are you going to do it, or shall I?" asked Jalli after the silence became profound. But before Jack could answer, Jalli spoke up. "Thank you, house, 'cot-tage', for being so kind to us. We are very sorry if we have done things we shouldn't have. You've been so welcoming to us and made us feel so 'at home'. Everything is so lovely here, and you've made us very, very happy. Thank you!"

And the odd thing was that the room, the cottage, and everything seemed to smile on them in acknowledgement. Especially the face on the appliqué sun – Jallaxa? – on the nightdress, that Jalli had laid on the bed and had not put away!

They shut the bedroom door behind them and descended the stairs. Outside they stood on the grass looking back at the cottage.

"It doesn't look too unhappy with us," remarked Jack. "You really said a lovely thank you."

"It was a bit like praying," explained Jalli.

"I can't remember ever praying. I guess I would feel a bit silly talking to someone out there who might or might not exist… and if anyone caught me, I'd feel a right idiot."

"Oh, He exists alright," said Jalli emphatically, "Grandma would never have come through without Him. And you needn't feel a 'right' anything if you wanted to pray when I'm around. I do it all the time."

"Does He answer your prayers?"

"Well I don't just ask Him things, or talk to Him when I want something. It's more like talking to Him because He's there. Sometimes He is a She – He/She keeps changing, but at the same time is always the same. Do you want to say anything to God about anything now?"

Jack was about to say, "Perhaps another time," when Jalli began saying, "Thank you, Lord God, for this place and, whoever owns it and tends it. Sorry if we have trespassed. And… please, can we come back again one day? Oh, and thank you for Jack and bless him. Amen."

"That was lovely, Jalli. I want to ask you so many things. You must tell me about your grandma and what happened to her."

"One day, perhaps. But I think it's time for me to leave now."

"Yes. I suppose so. But you will come back here won't you?"

"If you want me too. When?"

"Tomorrow?"

"No. I have an essay to write. I am already too late to go to school today."

"You go to school?"

"Only for another fourteen days and then I finish for good. This is my last essay. If I get good marks in it I will have enough to go on studying."

"How long will it take?"

"Give me four days. I will come back on Saturday. The same time as today."

Jack took Jalli's hand. "I hope the white gates will still be there!"

"So do I! But if not, it's been a wonderful time." She scanned the scene. "Thank you garden, thank you cot-tage," and meeting Jack's eyes added, "and thank *you* Jack Smitt!" and she squeezed his hand, tiptoed towards her white gate, picked up her shoes, waved a smile and was gone!

"Wow!" cried Jack. "Unreal!"

During the next three days Jack worked hard. He researched his options thoroughly and decided he could be a teacher of children with disabilities. He felt he wanted to make a difference to kids with a rotten start – like himself, only worse. He was a model son for the first time in his life. (His mother wondered if he was "sickening for something"). And, in passing, he even thought about apologising to his "kicking tree". Amazing... and how stupid! What had got into him? Here he was thinking about talking to a bush! Yes, he had been with a girl who had spoken to a cottage. But that was different. Life had suddenly become really good, and he liked being Jack Smith, or even Jack Smitt!

As for Jalli the last biology essay on "The role of the worm and soil production and maintenance" was the hardest to write because she simply couldn't concentrate. Mr. Bandi spotted her in the library. He was amazed she had not already handed anything in. Jalli gave excuses like the books were out, which was not entirely untrue, but she said nothing of her adventures. Her wise biology teacher was not fooled though. Jalli's expressive features betrayed something different.

"Holiday can't come soon enough?" he asked.

"Yes... I mean no!"

"Don't let yourself down on this last effort, Jalli."

"No Mr. Bandi, of course not! I'm doing it right now." And, to herself, "That is when I'm not being interrupted!" She smiled a Jalli smile, and the teacher replied.

"Fine. I'll leave you to it. I won't bother you any more."

"I swear," mused Jalli as the teacher breezed out of the door, "he knows everything I'm thinking. He's guessed I'm up to something."

She could almost hear him say, "Now, Miss Rarga, tell me about this boy you met yesterday. What's so special about him?" As she studied a response it took her into another round of contemplation on what exactly it was about Jack that had done this to her.

Five minutes later she realised she had not read or written a single word since Mr. Bandi had "left her to it".

"Pull yourself together, Jalli Rarga," she ordered herself. "This just will not do!" She thought of her teacher and his disappointment if this essay didn't turn out right, not to mention that of her grandma. Jack had said that he had just left his school and done well. So she had no choice. For everyone's sake the worms had to be tackled! And actually, they were quite interesting. She caught herself thinking, "I wonder what a worm feels when it meets another worm for the first time?... Jalli Rarga! Stop it!"

Somehow the essay got written, and she handed it in on

Friday afternoon. "Great," said Mr. Bandi. "Looks as if I shall be working over the weekend," he teased.

"Thanks, Mr. Bandi." She would miss this teacher. Lessons were done with. Just the results and the organising of what happens after the long holiday. The local university would confirm that she had a place on their biology course – so long as her "worms" did not fall below forty percent!

6

Saturday came. In two households in two galaxies separated by untold dimensions of space-time, two young people eagerly made for the bathroom! And a mother and a grandmother were both thinking the same thing. Their young people had met someone special. This could be the only explanation for them acting so strangely.

"I'll be out all day, Mum," sputtered Jack over his toast. "Can I take something to eat? A banana or something."

"I'll make you some sandwiches. Where are you off to?" Of course she was going to ask him, and he had his answer ready.

"I'm off to St Paul's Middle School. There's a garden project that I want to join in with. I'm meeting up with someone. I might not be back early."

"Well, ring me and tell me where you are if you're going to be late. You have got some credit on that phone of yours?" Jack checked his rather sad looking mobile. The truth was he hardly ever used it because, for the most part, no-one ever rang him and he didn't ring them. To his relief it had some charge in it, and he knew he must have plenty of credit. "I promise I will phone you Mum. I said I'd be at the school at a quarter to ten." He did not want to be late. He had worked it out. He would go in his normal things, but he would put his new T-shirt and clean trousers in his bag and change when he got there. If he were early he would have a minute to do that before Jalli arrived. As he left Jack did not even notice the kicking tree. The little green shoots had now started reaching for the sky, and the deeper green leaves were opening out.

Jalli took the bus. She had her newest jeans on and a long, floaty, deep red and brown top. It was the most feminine thing she had, apart from the dress that she had worn to a friend's sister's wedding the previous year and never had occasion to wear since. "I should like to wear pretty things sometimes," she thought. But if no-one else wore them how could she? Anyway she felt good in the things she had chosen today, and glowed.

She had told Grandma she was meeting a friend and they were exploring a garden. Biology stuff. Grandma gave her a packed lunch that included little rolls of bread, fruits and a home-baked Wanulka pie she would definitely hide at the bottom of her canvas shoulder bag. It would not fit into the atmosphere of the house, or "cot-tage" she must say.

The bus seemed to take a long time that day. It only just got going before it was in another traffic queue. Jalli checked her phone. Nevertheless, she still had plenty of time and she didn't want to be early. She had thought about it, and decided that the right time was about one minute after ten. At last she stepped lightly from the bus a block away from the Municipal Park. She had fifteen minutes to consume, so she decided to walk slowly around the block and look into a few shop windows.

Ten minutes later she was nearing the street in which she would, she hoped, spot the little white gate. She was so intent on looking to the corner from which she would be able to see it, that she failed to notice Maik Musula standing in her path. She walked straight into him!

"Hi!" he was holding her shoulders. "Great to see you! I was just going into this coffee shop. Fancy a coffee?"

"Maik Musula! What are you doing here?"

"I'm in town doing a bit of shopping. Nothing special. Hey, I like your top."

"I have an appointment," announced Jalli. "At ten o'clock. I must go!" But Maik had not changed. Now he had met her he was not going to go away very easily.

"What happened last week? You kind of just vanished. I mean, literally. You walked through a wall. I checked on the other side and you weren't there. One time you were there and the next, 'pop' you had gone!"

"Really! Are you sure it wasn't something to do with you freaking out on me?"

"What do you mean 'freaking out'?"

"Look. Every time I have seen you, I have told you, as politely as possible, that you are not the guy for me. Are you stalking me?"

"Stalking you? What do you mean?"

"I mean following me. Laying in wait for me. Or whatever it is that you do. Now, I am late for an appointment, and you are going to make yourself scarce." Jalli was quite cross, and really fed up with him. Politeness was not working so, she judged, an aggressive dismissal was the only option. She tried to push past him, but he again barred her way. Jalli was an accomplished ball player. Without warning she suddenly put her weight on her other foot and sidestepped him, passing him on the inside. If it hadn't been for her bag, she would have been away and through the crowd and he would never have caught her. But Maik instinctively grabbed at her as she passed and just managed to grab the strap of the canvas bag. Caught off balance, she twisted round and pitched into a hairdresser's salon window. She was lucky it didn't break she hit it so hard.

The people in the hairdresser's all looked up alarmed. What were these people playing at? But an elderly couple who had been passing as it happened saw everything. Jalli was shouting. "Let go! Just let… go!" She was tugging at her bag as he held tenaciously onto the strap.

What happened next took only a few seconds. The elderly gentleman spoke up, "The lady says to let her go!" Maik Musula was too intently set on holding on to Jalli to hear anything. "Let her go young man!" the man ordered. And then he brought his walking stick smartly down on Masula's wrist causing him to release the bag and Jalli to step backwards away from him. Musula yelped, clutched his wrist and turned towards his assailant.

Whether or not he would have gone for the elderly gentleman no-one would ever know because, standing behind him, the elderly lady had hooked her stick handle around Musula's ankle and pulled. He was still off balance and fell his full length on the pavement. She stood over him, stick at the ready. "If the lady says let go, you let go!" she barked.

The hairdresser had got onto the police within seconds of the crash against her window. A crowd gathered, and Maik was dragged to his feet. He struggled to get away but was held tightly with his arms pinned to his side by a big strong fellow who had also joined in. Maik was shouting and really "freaking out".

Two police officers arrived.

"OK. Someone tell me what's happening here!" one commanded. The elderly couple explained what they had seen.

"Are you hurt?" a woman police officer asked Jalli.

"N… no. I'm… I'm OK," she stammered.

Two police cars arrived and Maik Musula was bundled into one and driven away. The police woman shepherded Jalli into the front passenger seat of the other and noticed the wince as she sat.

"Are you sure you're OK?"

"Yes. I hit the window rather hard and my hip's sore that's all."

"OK. Tell me what happened."

Jalli told her the whole story. She told her this was the third time Maik Musula had accosted her, that she suspected him of stalking her. He had never actually hurt her, but he could not take no for an answer. He had freaked out last time when she had remarked that he was making a fool of himself. This time he had grabbed at her as she tried to leave.

"Fine. I need you to make a statement. I think we have had trouble with him before. My colleague and I will drive you to the station."

"But I had an appointment!" responded Jalli. "At ten o'clock."

"Well you've missed it now. It's twenty past already. Just hop into the back. We won't keep you long." What could Jalli do? She couldn't really ignore the police. Would Jack still be there when she had finished? In fact he might already have gone. He might have concluded that she didn't really want to see him again. "Oh God," she prayed, "give him patience, please!"

"What did you say?" asked the policewoman getting out of the car.

"Oh. Nothing. Just praying." The policeman shrugged and indicated the back seat. Jalli opened the car door and stepped out. As she put her weight onto her left leg a pain shot up it. It didn't take an expert to read Jalli's features this time.

"We'll get you to the hospital and get that X-rayed!" declared the policewoman. By now Jalli had decided the best thing was to go with the flow. She probably ought to get it checked out. That Maik Musula was an absolute liability. His stupidity had denied her the opportunity of meeting again someone really special. And it had landed him in a big mess, and if the police thought charges were appropriate she was going to have to put up with him for some time to come. She would probably have to go to court.

As she lowered herself into the back seat, the elderly couple came up to her. "Are you alright?" asked the lady.

"Yes. Thank you. I shall be alright. Thank you both for coming to my aid."

"Always ready to help a maiden in distress," smiled the gentleman.

Of course, the statement took much longer than the police officer had said, and the wait in the hospital had been quite long. It was half past one before Jalli emerged from the examination room. "Just bruised," the doctor had pronounced. She would find walking painful for a few days. Not to worry if it felt worse when she got up the next morning but the trick was to keep it moving. She wouldn't do it any harm. Nothing was broken.

Jalli assessed her options. Should she go home or on to

the garden? It was probably too late to meet Jack now. He would have given up on her a long time ago. She limped off to the bus-stop.

Jack had arrived in the garden, as he had planned, at a quarter to ten. He knew the gate would be there, he would have been shocked if it hadn't been. He glanced around. Jalli hadn't arrived yet so he quickly slipped off his jeans and T-shirt and put on his new ones. He hoped he looked smart. He sat on the bench and waited, drinking in the clear air. Somehow the garden and the smiling house were not enough in themselves though.

The lustre had paled without Jalli. The bird-song and the blossom were just as sweet, but without Jalli there was a shadow. He missed her sunny laughter. Ten o'clock came and went. No Jalli. 10.30 and still no Jalli. Jack resolved to explore the greenhouse to pass the time. "I wonder if she is locked out of the garden?" he considered. The greenhouse was empty apart from a few tools. He returned to the front of the house. Jalli's gate was not there. Perhaps whoever it was did not want her in the garden and house anymore. But he had been far more impertinent than she had. He had been the one to pry whilst she had initially taken her shoes off and tiptoed across the lawn. If anyone should be excluded it should have been him. He contemplated what to do. Should he leave and come back later? Or should he stay a little bit longer? He loved this place but it was not the same without Jalli. She belonged here, he was convinced of that. "God, or whoever you are in charge of this place," he heard himself saying out loud, "tell me what's happening. What should I do?"

All of a sudden he felt a peace come upon him. "It's OK. Just wait. Be patient," it seemed to say. "Wow! Was this a kind of 'answer?'" He turned to the house. "You're talking to me, aren't you?" And somehow, in a way he couldn't explain, he felt it was. Jalli was late. If she was this late something must have happened, because he was sure, he was really sure now, that she was on her way. "I hope she's OK," he thought, and then he added out loud, "You will make sure she's OK." He knew then she was loved and so was he. "Thanks," he muttered.

Half past twelve and Jalli still hadn't come. He had spent the time wandering about or stretched out on the lawn reflecting on his new found capacity to talk to gardens and houses and whoever it was who provided them, but whoever it was he never showed himself. He felt hungry and hunted for his packed lunch. He had thought he wouldn't reveal this in front of Jalli because it was not "cool", but since she was not here he was grateful for more than a banana and a can of coke. He put them on his lap and thought, "I bet Jalli turns up right now and catches me eating Mum's tuna paste sandwiches!" So he ate the most embarrassing things first leaving the banana and biscuits till last. He was careful to put every single bit of litter back into his bag. Normally he wouldn't have bothered. He had a habit of drop-kicking the empty can to see how high and far he could get it! That behaviour here was quite inappropriate! He thought even Persham could be nice if people looked after their gardens like this one. He wondered if the greenhouse was still there in the front garden down the road.

Jack resolved to stay till half-past-two. After that time he would leave a note on the bench. He had seen a pad and pencil on a table just behind the front door of the cottage. "Funny," he thought. He just did not feel the faintest urge to go inside without Jalli. It would feel empty without her. He glanced at his watch. Half past one. Just one hour to go and then he would leave that note.

He was just wondering what he would say in the note when Jalli emerged from the hedge.

"Jalli!" He was across the lawn in two bounds. "Jalli! I had almost given up on you!"

Immediately he knew something was wrong. There was pain in her face, and a tiny tear in the corner of one of her eyes. "What's wrong?"

The next thing he knew she was in his arms and her tears were flowing freely. He could feel the wetness through his shirt as she sobbed and clung to him. He just held onto her as long as it took for the pain to flow from her and she became calm.

"I… I almost didn't come," she stammered. "I thought you would have gone by now. The bus home from the hospital passed the Municipal Gardens and I saw the white gate in the wall and got off at the next stop and came back. You waited!"

"I wasn't going to, but somehow the place just told me to be patient and keep waiting. I guessed something had happened to you."

"See!" exclaimed Jalli, "Praying does work! I was praying for you to be patient and… and you were."

"OK. Come over to the bench and tell me all about it." She began to move and winced.

"It's OK," she said, "I've just bruised my hip. The hospital checked it out. It's not broken."

She winced again on the second step. Then Jack just put one strong arm behind her knees, another around her back, and carried her over to the bench and gently sat her down.

"Thank you, kind sir! My, you are strong!"

"Now. Tell me what happened."

She began to tell the tale beginning with Maik Musula who would now definitely not be bothering her any more unless he was really stupid. Well, he might even be in prison after today. She got to the bit when she had realised that whatever she did she had probably missed Jack and prayed that he might be patient.

"I talked to the cottage too. It kind of told me that you were loved."

"Thank you, cot-tage," smiled Jalli. "I'm hungry. Really hungry now. You and this place have made me feel so much better. I've got some lunch in my bag," she explained, "if it isn't too shaken up." She then remembered how it was packed in its special box, a box that shouted, "Lovingly prepared by Grandma!" Oh well. Nothing for it. She was now feeling ravenous!

"It's my grandma's special," she revealed. "I wasn't going to eat it if you were looking." Jalli's sparkle was returning. "But needs must!" She set about eating and got almost three quarters through it. "But what about you? I forgot about you." Jack smiled and pulled out the wrappings of his lunch stuffed into its bag. "My mum does the same! I had mine an hour ago when I got bored waiting." They were laughing now.

"I tell you what," said Jalli, "next time we'll swap."

"But you haven't seen what my mum produces!... I do like the look of yours though!"

Jalli then popped the last piece of Grandma's Wanulka pie into Jack's mouth.

"Grandma's cooking!"

"Wow!" he exclaimed. "I like your grandma!"

The next few hours were spent on the bench or hobbling round the garden together.

Jalli needed to keep moving. This time it didn't occur to them to go into the house. They told each other all about themselves. What they were doing, their interests, their whole story. Much time was spent in listening to Jalli talk about the earthquake that took her family, and Jack spoke freely about his father for the first time ever.

"I've never told anyone about him before. I even vowed to pretend he did not exist. But he's out there, somewhere. You are a great listener."

"And you too. I want to tell you everything. If I'm not boring you."

"Boring me! Jalli Rarga, you could never bore me!"

"I like it when you call me that. That's what I call myself sometimes, when I'm telling myself off!"

"Then I shan't say it because I don't want to tell you off!"

"Oh. But it's different when you say it, Jack Smitt!"

They made a date for the following Friday because the next day, Sunday, Jalli was expected at the worship centre, and the following week was the final week of the school year – Jalli's last – and it would be packed with all the things she needed to attend.

"Let's make it earlier. Say nine o'clock and it will be less busy getting here. And we'll have more time."

"That's fine by me," declared Jack. "And I'll bring my tent and camp here until you arrive!"

"Don't you tease me!" she cuffed him playfully. And then kissed his cheek. "Your turn to leave first this time!" Her hip was stiffening up and she didn't want to hobble off stage, so to speak. Jack stood up.

"OK. You sit there demurely, looking all lovely, and I will just slip through the hedge," he whispered. He kissed her cheek too, and carefully tiptoed in an exaggerated fashion across to his white gate. "Bye!" he waved and leaped through the gate! Whoops! He nearly knocked a boy off his bike charging down the pavement into Persham. The boy didn't look up. "Where's your helmet?" he yelled after him. He was getting a bit like those annoying grown-ups he decided!

Jalli put her hand on her mouth remembering how automatically she had kissed his cheek. What a day it had been. She hobbled across to her gate. The bus-stop was a good hundred metres from the white gate! Still, she would get there. Got to keep it moving. Whatever would Grandma say!

Jalli did not make it to the worship centre the next day. The hip was very sore and the bruise was "coming out" as Jack's mum would have put it. In the afternoon one of the congregation came round with a huge bunch of flowers. It was a combination of contributions from different people's gardens. "Jalli Rarga," she told herself, "you are loved aren't you!" And her mind drifted to Maik Musula. What must he be feeling? In trying to make things happen when he shouldn't, he had lost everything. His impatience was the very opposite of the way her Jack had waited. "My Jack? Why not? *My* Jack!" she whispered to herself.

7

The next week seemed the longest in Jack's life. He had begun it researching all the possibilities of helping children with disabilities. The prospectuses suggested some relevant experience would be useful before starting an education degree or something, so it seemed to be a good idea to have a year before going on. He had asked one of the special schools in the area and they were interested in volunteers in the autumn. But he would have to get a job to earn money. He had been to the DIY place again but it was too late for the summer. They told him to come back in September after the school term had started. OK. That would be fine. He could do voluntary work in the mornings and work the late shift there. He would also be available for Saturdays and Sundays.

The thought of work brought him down to earth. He started to wonder how he was ever going to have time to visit Jalli and the garden. He had found the most wonderful thing – beyond his dreams – and then life seemed to be telling him he couldn't have it. After three days he was almost more cynical and cross than he had been before the exam results, the white gate and Jalli. If there was a God why was he being taunted like this? It was a classic trick of the bully to wave a lolly in front of a kid, pretend to give it to him and then snatch it back with a mocking laugh.

The days dragged. He couldn't go to the library every day.

Only sad people did that. His mother wasn't happy about him not getting a job straight away. It wasn't about the money, she said, but that without something to do Jack was going to become unbearable. So she nagged him – and that made it worse. But Jack didn't want a job – well not straight away. After the weekend Jalli would be on holiday and then he could see her every day.

He and his mother never went away on holiday. Fed up with being got at, Jack stormed out the front door. "OK, OK! I'm going. I'll try to find something!" He slammed the door on his mother's reply. He didn't want to hear any more. Instinctively, he went straight to the tree – and then stopped. If Jalli could see him now she wouldn't like him any more. She would not like a boy who took out his anger on a bush. He didn't like what he saw. In that kicking tree was reflected the bitterness of his life – and he did not want Jalli, sweet pure Jalli, to see that. So now he could not take it out on the tree, on life, without feeling guilt and shame. Things had got complicated! And, perhaps for the first time, he began to see himself as his mother saw him – and he didn't like it. OK, so his mother was horrible at times but, he had to admit, life sucked for her too – really sucked. If he felt trapped, how might she feel?

Jack swung his leg out toward the tree, but deliberately missed it, and stomped off down the road. He headed in the direction of St Paul's School. Now he had stopped feeling good he half expected the gate to be gone – stolen away from him like the lolly in the bully's hand. His behaviour might be judged as unworthy by a perfect Creator. If Jack himself had been "the owner", would he have let in someone who kicked trees into his lovely garden? If Jack could but know this new found sense of guilt was one of the first steps on to a road of joy, and his confusion was caused by being confronted by goodness, he would have been less unhappy.

To her huge delight, Jalli's last essay was a good pass. Mr. Bandi had commented that Jalli was not so keen on worms as she had been on parmandas. That was not surprising she told him.

"Oh, But we all need worms so very much. They are vital."

"Because they produce really nice muck out of their back-ends!" she retaliated.

"Among other things. Whatever have you been doing?" He noticed her limp.

"Had a row with a shop window. It won!"

She had confirmed her place at the uni too. Some of the others were really excited because they were going abroad to study. One or two others hadn't done so well as they had hoped. They only had themselves to blame, thought Jalli. It would have been better for them if there had been less beach and boys, and more books. She spent some time with a couple who had not succeeded but who had really tried. They chatted about other options, and then a teacher came along and did the same, which seemed to cheer them up. "Uni is not everything," he told them. They could do with a white gate, thought Jalli, or somewhere to open up when the door they were looking at stayed firmly closed. She silently sent up a request for a way to open for them that would excite them.

The other bit of good news was that the Maik Musula

thing had been dealt with, and there was no need for Jalli to attend any hearings. It turned out that he suffered from some sort of mental condition that could be treated successfully. If he took the medication he could lead a fairly normal life but, for one reason or another, he had ceased taking the stuff which had resulted in his unreasonable behaviour. Because of his condition, when he was younger, expressions like "freak out" and "fool" made him feel bad and Jalli's use of them hadn't helped the situation. She was very sorry. However, she was quickly reassured that, first she wasn't to know, and secondly, whatever the cause, his behaviour had indeed been unreasonable, and thirdly, it was his own responsibility to take the medicine. Anyway, he was in hospital being stabilised and the only real harm done was to Jalli's hip – which didn't feel very much better, it would take several weeks before the bruising cleared up.

Friday came. Both Jack and Jalli arrived early at the garden. Jalli was there only a couple of minutes before Jack. Each was really pleased to see the other. They met with a bit more reserve than they had had when they last parted. A week is a long time. Jack felt a completely different person in Jalli's presence. She seemed to bring out something good in him – and he felt all the frustration and guilt evaporate. "How's the hip?" he inquired.

"Much better. Still sore though. You ought to see it! It is a terrible colour."

"I'll wait till it's better then I'll take a good look."

"You cheeky young man!"

But he was to see it sooner than either of them imagined!

They were just thinking about how they might spend the day, when Jack suddenly spotted a third white gate.

"Do you see what I see?"

"Another gate!"

"I was just about to invite you to look through mine," remarked Jalli, "but it seems we are meant to explore in this direction instead." They approached the gate and looked over it. They could clearly see a world beyond, but it was like neither of their worlds. It was a bright green, blue and white world with strong sunlight!

"Look! Beside the gate." A small garden tool-shed had suddenly appeared. Opening the door that released a strong smell of creosote, there were two small suitcases on each of which were neatly stacked a large towel and a small pile of clothes and two sun hats. A pretty straw one and a handsome white cotton one.

"Do you think these are there for us?" asked Jalli. Jack began to explore one of the piles.

"Well this one is not for me!" he exclaimed producing the top part of a two piece swimsuit. "But it must be for you. Look the colour and design matches your outfit perfectly." Indeed it did. The deep red and brown swirls were an exact match for Jalli's floaty top. It must be meant for her. "I think we are meant to wear these things when we go into this new world," deduced Jack.

"Looks like it," agreed Jalli. "But I haven't worn anything quite like this before. It's quite revealing."

"All the better for it!" thought Jack, but he didn't think it appropriate to say so out loud because he guessed wearing a revealing thing like this for the first time might be a little alarming for a girl. He examined the other pile. There was a pair of long legged swimming shorts, that came almost to the knee, and a loose T-shirt with long sleeves. It was pure white with brown side panels – the same brown as Jalli's stuff.

"We belong," he declared, offering up the brown bit against Jalli. "I wonder what is in the suitcases." They were clearly overnight bags that included nightclothes and washing stuff – soap, shampoo and razor etc.

"Wow! This is posh stuff!" exclaimed Jack sniffing at one of the bottles. "And look your nightdress has got a Jallaxa sun on it. Can only be yours. That's rather pretty." It was, thought Jalli.

"Well if we are to head off for this place overnight we'd better let our parents know," concluded Jack. Jalli was quite unsure about doing this, yet it felt right to.

"What should I do?" she asked. But Jack knew she was not talking to him. She studied, looking at Jack. He did not interrupt her. After about a quarter of a minute a smile spread across her face. "OK let's do it! – If Grandma will let me. I am going back through the gate to ring her up. I won't be long." Jalli disappeared through her gate and Jack waited patiently. It seemed to take a very long time, but eventually Jalli returned beaming a smile that indicated her grandmother's consent. She had given it reluctantly, but was happy to know that Jalli was not going anywhere alone and had promised to avoid spending too long in Wanulka town centre. Jalli had explained that they would be outside the town.

Then Jack went through his gate and told (rather than asked!) his mum. He listened patiently to her directions about making sure he didn't get into bad company and asking the name of the person he was going with. "You don't know them Mum," he truthfully stated, "'s called Jalli." He deliberately slurred the pronoun. He didn't want to give any indication of gender because he knew that would result in yet more questions and exhortations to behave himself. "I'll see you tomorrow. Must go now." And he hung up.

"I have received lengthy instructions about how to behave," said Jack after he reappeared through the gate.

"I hope you promised to be good."

"Of course! Would I do otherwise? So come on, let's visit our new land." Jack rolled his beach clothes in the large colourful towel and tried the gate. It wouldn't open. "It's stuck!"

"Perhaps we're meant to change before we go. We don't know if there will be anywhere when we get there." Jalli was checking through the contents of a beach bag, that also had a smiling sun on it, and came out with a purse with what looked like bank notes in it. "Money!" she declared. "Whoever has decided we should visit this place has thought of everything. Why should we be given a free holiday? I wonder what the catch is?"

"If we can get in we'll find out that's for sure. Who's changing first then? Ladies first. That is if the lady wants to."

Jalli got inside the shed and shut the door. It was poky and dark! She opened the door a little and peered round but Jack had his back turned and was re-examining his new things. She opened the door a little and began getting into the swimsuit. It was all bows that took some adjusting. Her bruised hip was going to be exposed for all to see, but fortunately there was a pair of shorts too, which she donned. Obviously her own top was part of the outfit. She folded her underwear inside her towel and stepped out of the shed. Jack was modestly looking in the other direction.

"Ur-hum," Jalli coughed. Jack turned.

"Wow I like the legs!"

"Thanks. I'm looking forward to seeing your knees too!"

"Not my most beautiful asset."

"That will be for me to decide!"

Jack entered the shed and changed in fast order. Nothing too complicated for him.

"Knees not bad," smiled Jalli.

"Thanks. What shall we do with our own things? I don't think we're going to need them. Let's leave them in the shed."

"OK." Jack dropped them inside the door. "It would be better if there was some attempt to fold them."

"You sound just like my mother!"

"She's clearly a good woman."

Jack hadn't thought about his mother as being good or bad before. He had been so caught up in himself and his own problems. But all she did in trying to make sure he turned out OK was not just for her but for him. He was beginning to see that now. He took his clothes and folded them obediently.

"You're right," he said thoughtfully, "My mum is a good woman." Jalli took note of that, and was aware of the fact this good woman had a good son too.

"Right. Let's try the gate again," said Jalli, and put her hand to the latch. It opened. She waited until Jack was right behind her and, tentatively, they advanced into yet another unknown place. The first thing they noticed was the noise. The place was full of music and animated conversation on the left, and delighted children's voices from the right. The next thing they remarked upon was the smell of the sea! It was clearly a beach resort. They were standing on some coarse grass under the shade of palm trees. Their white gate stood in a short hedge between two blue gates. People dressed in swim suits with towels over shoulders were entering and leaving the blue gates – women to the right, men to the left. A toilet block!

"Always useful to know," said Jack, indicating the signs.

The children's voices were coming from a white strand in front of a blue sea with a big white surf. The children were grouped into what was clearly a patrolled zone. Nobody paid Jack and Jalli any attention. They were just holiday makers like everyone else, and dressed as they were, they blended in perfectly.

"Where to?" pondered Jack. "Let's go on the sand, lay our towels out and take a swim."

"You can't wait to see me in my swimming costume!" said Jalli.

"Got it in one," he teased. Although he did think that he would quite like to see Jalli so dressed (or undressed!). "And I am going to witness the bruise after all."

"I'm afraid you are. This costume covers hardly anything!" But glancing around, it was pretty clear that all the girls her age were wearing the same sort of thing, so it didn't feel quite so bad. They laid out their towels on a patch of sand in among others but not too close to them.

"The sun's hot," remarked Jack. "How many are there?"

"I can only see one, but it's a hot one." It was about the size Jack was used to, but he quickly decided that they had better have their swim and then get into the shade. Jalli slipped off the shorts and then the top.

"Wow it *is* a big bruise! I can't believe you did that hitting a shop window. However didn't it break?"

"No idea. But if you think that's bad you should have seen it last week." The black bruise that covered a large area of Jalli's upper thigh was now giving way to grey-blue with a sort of yellowing around the edges.

"No wonder you had a job to walk."

"Did you think I was putting it on then? Just to get you to carry me to the bench?"

"Actually no. But I am ready to carry you down to the surf if you like!" He had laid his T-shirt on top of her things and made as if to pick her up.

"Thought you were a gentleman!" she shouted. "Race you!" Despite the bruise Jalli's head start left Jack well behind. Splashing in the surf behind her he spluttered, "You're fast!"

"I train," she explained. "Fastest in the year and can outrun all but two of the boys." She splashed salt water over his chest. It was remarkably warm. Jack had only experienced the sea around the British coast, and then only once. Weston-super-Mare he remembered they called the place. He was told the "super-Mare" bit meant "on-sea" only he remembered that the sea itself had small waves and was a long way from the sand across a very muddy beach. This place was cool! They splashed and ducked into the waves. For Jalli this was a common experience as Wanulka had a beach not too unlike this one. Jack was impressed with Jalli's swimming ability and felt overawed by her for the first time. She was so much more confident in many ways than he was. Sure he had been less diffident about going into the house but that was probably more ignorance than confidence. He went on instinct, but Jalli went on the knowledge of her own ability. She was much more self assured than he was, he felt.

If he had been able to see it from Jalli's side he would have realised that a lot of her confidence was actually down to him. She would not have even gone swimming in this way with the school friends in Wanulka. She would not have worn such a swimsuit for a start. He gave her strength to express herself and access those qualities and abilities that had not previously emerged in her. Jalli had not met anyone like him. Whatever his sporting or intellectual abilities, here was a boy who was different. He had depth and a sensitivity to her that she had not come across before. With him she felt entirely safe and very comfortable. He was not changeable like some of the other young people she knew. He appeared dependable, and quite clearly felt the same about her as she did about him. If he had known how many of Jalli's contemporaries regarded her as dull, a swot or odd he would never have believed it.

"You are much cleverer than I am," he observed as they made their way back up the beach. "I hope you don't get tired of me. I am only average at sport, two left feet when it comes to ball games – and my looks are nothing special. In this outfit you can see I'm quite a weedy person really."

"Dear Jack! All this because you were outrun by a girl! Sensible girls look for sensitiveness, kindness, dependability, respect – and you have all those qualities. And, in any case, you're quite good looking! Come on let me put some sunscreen on your back and we'll move our things into the shade. That was fun. I really enjoyed that surf."

"I've never seen a sea like this before. To tell you the truth I haven't been away from Persham much, and never outside England. I can see why all these folk want to come on holiday here… I wonder where we are to stay? We have our stuff." As Jack was speaking a young woman approached them.

"Hi," she greeted them. "Have you just arrived here?"

"Yes, about an hour ago," replied Jalli.

"I thought so. Can I introduce myself? I'm Kakko."

"I'm Jalli, and this is Jack."

"Pleased to meet you. Are you two on your own?"

"Yes. We were just thinking about somewhere to stay."

"You are better in a group," explain Kakko. "You see it's not entirely safe here."

"But it seems such a nice place."

"Well, it is, but we have people who come here and steal and make trouble. I thought you were not aware of this when you left your stuff on the beach and went swimming. You really need to have someone look after it because it might just disappear. The thing is we have people here who are on drugs and who spend their time in the bars and quickly run out of money." Kakko indicated a bar with some fairly noisy people sitting around it. "They're half drunk now, and it's really not safe to wander about after dark unless you are with a group. You would be very welcome to join us. Our parents only allow us to come if we agree to stay together." Kakko gestured to a group of about a dozen young people further up the beach playing with a ball.

Jack looked at Jalli and weighed up the options. They

looked normal enough. "Why not," he said, at last. These people seemed OK. Kakko escorted them over to the group.

"Hi guys. This is Zhalli and Zhak who have just arrived from a foreign place. Can they join us?"

"You're very welcome," spoke up one of the lads. "My name is Tod."

"Hi Tod," said Jack, and offered his hand which Tod took. Not quite the custom it seemed but good enough. Jalli bent into a Wanulkan curtsy. They were then introduced to all the people. It is hard to remember names when they are not ones that you have heard before, thought Jack. Quite clearly the "j" sound was difficult for them, so "Zhak" and "Zhalli" became their names as long as they were there. It was not easy describing where they came from either, but a place called "White Gates" seemed to be acceptable.

"This is indeed a great place," they agreed when Jack expressed his delight in the sand and the surf. "But you do need to be in groups of more than four to be really safe," Tod explained. "We spotted you when you came onto the beach, and have been keeping an eye on you and your things."

"Shame that this place is being abused by people who are 'out-of-control' (a Grandma expression)." Jalli saw too much of the same sort of thing on the beach at Wanulka.

"Well, they don't bother us when we are together. And we have fun in our group. We all belong to various spiritual fellowships and our parents let us come if we are together."

"What do you do here?" asked Jack.

"Same as everybody else. The sea and surf, but we sometimes have beach sports – and in the evening we sing songs together." Singing, thought Jack. Well at least he would have the excuse here of not knowing the words. Spiritual fellowships seemed to do a lot of singing, and since that was one thing he never did it was one of the reasons he had always steered clear of them. Jalli would be alright though. Sports, singing – she would be in her element. But that day proved them both to be in their element. Jack turned out to be good with the bat. He'd never rated cricket at school but so long as he didn't have to kick the ball he could do well. He also enjoyed the surf boards. Jalli spent more time chatting than in the games. She was finding out what you had to do in school in this country. It seemed to be much better in Wanulka she thought. These people seemed to have to put in very long hours.

Later in the afternoon the group took them round to their hostel which was just behind the beach in a beautiful tree lined road with attractive gardens. The flowers were big and colourful. "One or two beds?" asked Kakko.

"Two please," replied Jack and Jalli in concert. They looked at one another and smiled. As far as anyone else was concerned they were well and truly an "item". It seemed odd that they had only known each other a couple of weeks. It felt much longer.

They were escorted upstairs by Kakko and Tod (who were also clearly together). "Your room is just across from us," they announced, and before Jack and Jalli could say any more they found themselves in a pleasant room overlooking the garden.

"Two beds but one room," observed Jack.

"Well I trust you not to take advantage of a vulnerable maiden," teased Jalli.

"As long as I can trust you not to take advantage of me," laughed Jack. "Which bed do you want?"

"The one you're not sleeping in! Seriously though, we'd better not let on to Grandma that I have been sharing a room with a boy."

"No. You will not have shared with a 'boy', but a 'gentleman' offering you protection in a strange land."

"In fact," said Jalli, "I am glad I'm not in a room on my own. This place doesn't seem to be the safest place in the universe."

"Sad that."

They unpacked and used the bathroom and then went downstairs where the group was deciding what to do that evening. A beach barbecue was quickly agreed upon. They left to buy meat at the local market. Jalli produced her money and the group helped her buy what seemed as plain a piece of meat as any on offer.

That evening proved to be unforgettable for both of them because they had not been in the company of so many kind and welcoming people before. Neither of them had really fitted into the "youth society" in their respective home towns that well. These people turned out to be an absolute delight. By the end of a couple of hours, it was amazing how many of their names they had already learned.

They soon ascertained that the group took it upon themselves to look after people like them who were vulnerable in the beach resort. "Why do you do that?" asked Jack. "Many people would come with their group and take no interest in others."

"It's part of what we do," Tod explained. "If we want to be looked after ourselves, we also need to be aware of the needs of others." That was so simple, thought Jack. Why don't more people do it? He even found himself joining in with some of the choruses of the songs. "There," Jalli had declared, "you *can* sing." Jack was discovering so much about himself first from Jalli, and then this group. He seemed to be far more "likeable" to others than he ever imagined himself to be. He decided he had never been so happy as he was at that moment. He was partnering a lovely girl, on a tropical beach, with a group of great people. It was straight out of Hollywood! He half expected them all to get up and sing and dance as if they were in some incredible musical!

But what happened next remained in the minds of all those young people for many years.

8

Without warning, as the fellowship group were sitting together on the edge of the sand, a half empty can landed in their circle. It narrowly missed Tod's head spraying beer as it went. The can was followed by jeering and cat-calling.

"Better to ignore it," advised Tod. "Everybody OK?"

"I smell like a brewery," sighed Kakko, trying to wipe beer off her front, "but the can landed safely."

Then things got worse. The group of drunken young people had started disturbing a street front restaurant. One of them upturned one of the tables tipping all the food, plates and cutlery over the people around it. A second got onto one of the other tables, tottered and fell off dragging everything behind her and breaking one of the chairs as she fell.

The owner came out of his restaurant remonstrating. But you cannot argue with someone who is drunk, let alone a group of ten. He was pushed and manhandled. Horrified diners quickly deserted the place and left. The unhappy man was incensed. "I am sending for the police," he shouted. But before he could re-enter his restaurant, one of the group had hurled a large stone at the plate glass window that divided the inside from the outside from floor to ceiling. It shattered. Two of the drunks, screaming delight, rushed through the space and kicked over more tables. Others set about scooping bottles from the shelves and snatching pictures from the walls. Decorative paper flowers flew as a drunken girl, looking to join in but incapable of reaching anything else, hurled the vase into the air. In all the mayhem it was amazing no-one was hurt.

The police did not take long to arrive. The "fellowship", now huddled together further down the beach for safety, could hear the sirens approach before the revellers. But as soon as they did some were off down the street, while others were quite incapable of flight. Fleeing or not, however, all were soon rounded up and bundled into the back of police vans as they tried to argue and protest their innocence. The scene was an ugly one.

After they had all gone the police looked for witnesses, but it was amazing at just how quickly the crowded street had cleared! "People are scared to come forward," explained Kakko. But that did not stop her approaching the police herself to tell them that she had seen the whole incident. Tod took Jalli and Jack to one side.

"When something like this happens," he said, "most people don't want to know because they are afraid of reprisals from the families of the drunks. But we think that if no-one is willing to help and people get away with things that doesn't help anyone. It's OK most times because the families don't usually do anything."

"Kakko's brave," remarked Jack.

"Sometimes you have to be brave to do the right thing. But," he added quickly, "whatever you do, think twice before actually tackling someone who is drunk or on drugs. You can get seriously hurt, and you may even be arrested along with them. Leave the fighting to the police."

A police-officer came across to the fellowship group to confirm Kakko's story. He urged them to look after themselves and warned them about being about after dark. "Stay together!" he ordered.

Eventually the police-officers finished talking to the restaurant owner, a Mr. Pero, put their notebooks in their shirt pockets, and indicated the direction of the police station. It was clear they would sort out the rest tomorrow. No sooner had they stood up to leave when another officer from beside one of the cars shouted across to his colleagues. They quickly got back into their cars and left. Another incident.

The restaurant owner picked up one of the chairs and sat down with his head in his hands. He was in shock. The staff, who had been hiding in the kitchen, emerged and looked around them in disbelief. They starting righting the tables and chairs. "Put them all inside," murmured the owner. "The police are sending somebody to board up the front early tomorrow morning. Then that's it. No insurance – couldn't afford it. Come back tomorrow and I'll pay you what I owe you, then we're all out of a job." The staff picked up the worst of the mess. The fellowship group came over and helped. Soon the poor owner was left sitting on the pavement at an empty table all by himself, still dazed.

Jalli instinctively approached him. "Are you hurt, sir?" she inquired.

"No. Just ruined," he sobbed. And soon he was pouring it all out to them. He had come there three years previously and gradually built up the business. He had re-invested all he earned into it.

He had decided to upgrade the place and soon he had established a reputation, but he still owed the bank a lot of money and had taken a risk with the insurance. "The premiums were so high," he mumbled. This was the incident he dreaded, and no-one would want to come near his place after that night, would they? He took one look into what was, just an hour before, a bright, cheerful, well-ordered and inviting restaurant. Tomorrow it would be all boarded up. Even new plate glass would be beyond him.

"But you still have to pay your bank loan!" This was Tod who had come over and was listening.

"Don't tell me about it!" despaired the owner. "If I'm lucky, I might sell the place for what I owe."

"But you live here! Where would you go? OK, here's the deal," said Tod. "You promise to open up tomorrow at ten o'clock in the morning and we'll guarantee the place will be ready."

"How can that be! We don't open until twelve noon anyway, and there will be no staff."

"No problem. We'll do coffee and jam sandwiches until they arrive. There are twelve of us. Ros" (Tod indicated a large lad with broad shoulders) "and I will stay here overnight and guard the place while you rest. Everyone will be here at sunrise and we'll put the place to rights."

"But what about the window?"

"We'll order a new one first thing."

"But I told you I haven't any money for a new window."

"You will have by tomorrow evening when you close at eleven o'clock," said Tod. "We'll insist that the glass is installed by three o'clock at the latest." Tod had a father who talked like this, and he knew that if all else failed he could turn to him.

The parents of this group were proud of the way their children looked after everyone else.

"But what about your holiday weekend?"

"We'll still have time for a swim in the afternoon, but this'll be better fun than anything else because it will make people happy," explained Kakko.

Tod and Ros went back to the hostel to get a blanket each, and the girls went into the kitchen and made a cup of tea for Mr. Pero. "The kitchen's full of scrumptious food, with no-one to eat it!" exclaimed one. "Mr. Pero. There is a lot of good food getting cold in the kitchen. Can we eat it? We'll pay." They had brought the owner into the kitchen and sat him down with his tea.

"Why not? It'll only go to waste."

Beginning with the pavement, the whole group swept the glass into a heap. Two of them went into the bar from where the drunks had been drinking and asked for brooms. The people from the neighbouring flats appeared and helped too. When that was done all the tables were set out once more and the remaining food distributed. The group insisted that everyone pay for it by putting a large cardboard box by the door. One of the group had written in large letters – FOR THE RESTORATION OF THE CAFÉ! on the side of the box. Mr. Pero would never have called it a "café" but these young people were incredible. He really believed they meant what they said!

"Why are you doing all this for me? I will never be able to pay you back."

"We would not be doing it, if you could," said Kakko. "The unions wouldn't wear it!" and they all laughed. "We are doing this because you need someone to help you, and we like helping people. Besides this is fun!"

"Helping people is what this group seems to do," interposed Jalli. "They've looked after us since we arrived this morning."

"My, this food is good!" declared a cheerful girl with rosy cheeks.

"Best in the resort," mumbled Mr. Pero.

"In that case, we'll be doing everybody a favour," stated Kakko.

"Far too good to allow this place to close," declared the girl, tucking into a delicious looking pie.

"Don't eat the stuff that will keep till tomorrow," warned Kakko.

Jack and Jalli tried different dishes they had not tasted before. Not only was this a quality place, the ingredients were different from what either of them were used to.

"Out of this world!" declared Jack. Jalli laughed.

"No. Out of our worlds you mean."

"Right. But it's amazing how quickly you can get caught up in a new world. We have only been here just over twelve hours and we're involved in everything."

"That's because of this fellowship," reflected Jalli. There needs to be more groups like this. We could do with one in Wanulka."

"And Persham," added Jack. "I think I can see why the Owner wants us here now."

They had taken to calling the invisible owner of the white gates the Owner for want of any other name. "He wants us to learn from these people."

"And help. If we can."

"You certainly can," declared Kakko just coming over to them. "You don't mind, do you?"

"Not at all," replied Jalli.

After everyone had eaten and done the washing up, and Kakko and a couple of the others had taken Mr. Pero upstairs to his flat, Tod and Ros made a couple of beds from cushions and laid out their blankets.

"We'd better get back to the hostel to sleep now," said one. "We've got an early start." They waited while Kakko and Tod took their leave of each other.

"It started last summer," the group explained. "They hate being apart."

Back in their room, Jack waited, while Jalli went into the bathroom, undid her bows, took a shower and put on her nightdress. He washed too. He didn't tell Jalli until later that that was the first shower he had ever taken in his life! And it was also the first time, for either of them, being without siblings, to share a bedroom with someone else. They didn't think about it for very long though, because they were soon asleep. And, before the sun rose again someone was knocking on their door saying they were leaving for the café in half an hour.

Dawn saw Jack and Jalli, along with the rest, setting about the clearing up of the mess with a will. It was amazing just how rewarding the task was. One of the lads immersed himself in a sink washing the stained tablecloths, while a second rinsed (exercising some quality control and rejecting any that were still marked), a third wrung them out whilst two others straightened them and ironed them dry. The shelves were washed down, and the bottles and ornaments that survived were washed and put back on the shelves under the direction of an artistic looking girl who also restored the paper flowers, putting them into far more ambitious arrangements than they had been. All the pictures were replaced on the walls with the exception of two with broken frames that Tod took with him when he went into the town to order the new plate glass.

The police turned up and were amazed at what was going on! They had ordered a skip and some men to come with boarding. They left the skip but cancelled the boarding up. Jack found himself using the woodwork skills he had picked up in school to re-glue some of the joints on the tables that had come loose. A couple of the chairs, however, were damaged beyond use and they put them into the skip, together with the broken glass and the rest of the rubbish.

The girl with the lettering skills had made big posters for both sides of an A-board belonging to the bar (which they had willingly lent – persuaded by a couple of the lads). It read "OWING TO VANDALISM 'RESTAURANT PERO' WILL OPEN CONTINUOUSLY FROM 10 am TO 11 pm." She wrote three other notices declaring "Restaurant Pero OPEN" and arranged them on the pavement. True, the lettering was not quite in the style that Mr. Pero would have chosen, but as he looked at them his heart filled with delight. Despite his worries he was enjoying being looked after. Their energy and openness was amazing and the fuss they made around him as he was preparing food in the kitchen restored his belief in young people.

A newspaper reporter and a radio broadcaster came down to report on the vandalism and write the usual things about "youth violence" with headlines like "Drunken Teenagers Wreak Havoc In Local Restaurant!" but when they arrived all that Mr. Pero could talk about concerned the fantastic young people who had rescued him. He proudly showed them the clean linen and restored decorations and the cardboard box for the collection towards the new window. "I'm having to stay open all day today because these young people want to make sure we have enough customers to pay for it," he explained. "They have promised to work for me for nothing!" So the word about what was happening went out very quickly, and people started to come down just to watch and put contributions into the box.

The girl with the rosy cheeks had purchased a small bunch of fresh flowers, and she and Jalli were busy making them into table arrangements, when a dishevelled teenager approached them. His appearance and posture betrayed a heavy weight somewhere deep inside him. It was in stark contrast, Jalli remarked, to the fellowship group of which she had so quickly become a part. "I've come as soon as they let me go," he stammered.

"I… I have come to apologise. I kind of got caught up in the crowd yesterday and was drinking too much. The next thing I knew I… I was inside this place when the police arrived. I don't know what I was doing. I just wanted to say sorry to Mr. Pero – if he'll let me?"

"You'd better sit down here and I will go and find Mr. Pero and see if he wants to speak to you," said the rosy cheeked girl. The boy took a chair opposite Jalli. She looked at him. He hung his head, he looked in pain and his heart was full. He looked ill and broken and his hand shook. "Why did you do it?" she asked.

"I don't know. I was drunk I suppose."

"No. I mean, why did you get drunk?"

"Well, nobody really cares where I am, or what I do, and then I just do what other people are doing. They buy me drinks and I drink them. But I've just slept it off on the beach before. This time it got stupid."

"But couldn't you find friends that don't drink?"

"Well, not really. Nobody really wants to be my friend. I haven't got a rich daddy like you people."

"I don't have a father," stated Jalli. "And I'm not rich." Jack, who had seen Jalli talking to this stranger and feeling a pang of a mixture of protectiveness and jealousy, had come and sat in the empty chair.

"I don't have a father, either. We've next to nothing in our house, my mum and I. But I don't need friends that drink."

"But I bet your mum loves you. My mum turns me out so she can have her boyfriends in."

"Rough," said Jack. He was learning all the time what a good woman his mother really was.

Kakko appeared with Mr. Pero. "This is Mr. Pero, the owner," she said to the young man.

He immediately got to his feet, but unsteadily. "I… I want to say sorry." The word seemed very lame when he considered what had been done in those short minutes last night. "I was here and I… I want to say that I really regret being part of it."

"So they let you go?" inquired Mr. Pero.

"Not all of us. They have let some of us go. But we all have to go to court next week. To tell you the truth I was too drunk to remember much about it." He still looked very much the worse for wear.

"Head hurt?" asked Mr. Pero. The boy nodded once,

gently. Mr. Pero indicated a bottle of water from the shelf and one of the fellowship brought to it him. They were all gathering round now. "Sit down and drink this!" ordered the restaurateur. The young man drank carefully, gratefully. "Thanks," he muttered.

"OK. Apology accepted," said Mr. Pero, "So long as you promise to be in court, take your punishment and to learn from this."

"Thanks. I am going to plead guilty. I promise. Can I do anything to help?" He spotted the cardboard box and dropped a note in it. "All I have left," he said.

When he had finished drinking the water, Kakko looked into his eyes. "Stand up," she barked. He stood. "You'll do. Washing up!" she ordered.

After he had staggered in the direction of the kitchen, Jack exclaimed, "Wow! He's a bit brave isn't he coming back here after last night."

"He is," said Jalli, "but I don't think he's bad inside, just unloved."

"If you've got someone to love you," declared the rosy cheeked girl, "then life is a different slice of pie!"

"… or kettle of fish," murmured Jack

"What?" laughed Jalli.

"Kettle of fish. We say 'kettle of fish'. Life is a different kettle of fish. Things are different."

"And we say 'planted in a different field'. Life that is different. If you've got someone to love you then it's like planting seeds in good soil. I can't imagine putting fish into a kettle! How does that work?"

"I don't know. I've never thought about it. It's just a saying.

I expect they used to have fish kettles somewhere in the past. It's not as silly as like when we say 'it's raining cats and dogs'."

"What? I'm not coming to visit you on a rainy day! It sounds positively dangerous."

"So you two don't come from the same country then?" asked the girl.

"No, different universes," replied Jalli, "but he's good for me."

"Life with him is a good kettle of fish then?"

"The best!" she giggled, giving Jack a kiss on the cheek.

At nine-thirty the staff started arriving. They weren't due till eleven but they had heard on the radio that Pero's was opening at ten. At a quarter to ten customers began to roll in and by half past ten Mr. Pero was down at the market with some of the young people buying food. It looked as if they were going to have a good number of people all through the morning. In fact, this was the first of three visits he had to make to the market that day!

"I don't usually buy on a Saturday," he explained.

There was soon a queue of people who had come out especially to patronise Pero's. They wanted to applaud his courage. "It's a good job you have such a big family," observed one customer seeing all the industrious young people. "All yours?"

"All of them! They are my very special friends," smiled Mr. Pero, as Tod walked in with the repaired frames and began hanging them on the wall.

"The plate glass will be here before three," he stated.

That morning all the young people stayed around to help, but soon only a few of them were needed. Tod led most of them off to the beach where Jalli and Jack had an awesome time in the surf followed by some form of beach cricket. Jalli was really good at it and had to keep running. But after a long stint, Jack detected a fleeting wince of pain in Jalli's face.

"Time to declare," he shouted.

"Declare? Declare what?" asked Tod.

"It means that you give someone else a go because no-one can beat you."

"Great idea," said the rosy cheeked girl stepping forward and taking the bat from Jalli.

"I was just getting into that," breathed Jalli.

"You were playing with an injury. It's hurting you."

"How do you know that?"

"It was in your face – just a little bit."

"Can't hide anything from you!"

"Don't try. Got to let people love you."

Jack reflected. Love. It can mean so many different things in English. When he said that just then he didn't mean it in the same way as he had said he loved her top yesterday. Or in the same way that Tod and Kakko had said they were all called to love one another. He wondered how it would be translated for Jalli. But she must have understood what was in his heart because she looked at him and smiled and squeezed his hand. He held onto it.

"It's arrived!" One of the fellowship was charging down the beach. "The window. It's arrived."

They quickly gathered their things and went back to the restaurant. They helped to take tables and chairs across the street onto the grass under the trees where people could continue eating their food while the glass was put in. Tod counted the money out of the box to pay the men.

"We're doing this at cost," they explained. "We heard what happened and we want to help." Tod found there was just enough to cover everything. But the box remained all day and throughout the evening and at the end of the day Mr. Pero had enough to have painted on the glass "Pero's Family Restaurant". It used to read "The Restaurant Pero" but he said that now he had a super new family of young people, he had decided to rename it. "You are all my family," he declared. "And whenever you come here, you eat for nothing because you are family." After the window had been finished, and the tables and chairs returned to their rightful places, a photographer from the newspaper came to take a picture. "I want all of my family in the photo," Mr. Pero pronounced, and so everyone was arranged around him.

"Wait!" called the restaurateur, "where is the young man doing the washing up? He must be in the photo too. He is part of the family. He has been washing up all day." So the young man whose life had presented him with a "different slice of pie" was pulled into the group bearing a sheepish smile that turned into a laugh when "Rosie" gently dug her fingers into his waist.

The rest of that afternoon was just as busy. Mr. Pero had to set off for the market again and a different shift of young people took over. The repentant lad was taken from the sink to play the beach games and was accepted into the fellowship just as easily as Jack and Jalli had been. After a couple of hours as a waitress Jalli was tired. Jack came over to her and said that they really ought to be going and Jalli agreed. They sought out Kakko and thanked her for a wonderful two days. "We think there should be fellowship groups everywhere," they affirmed.

"Then start one up," replied Kakko. "What you have to do from the beginning is agree that the purpose of the group is to help other people and have fun at the same time… and it helps if you can pray about it."

"Jalli's good at that," responded Jack. "Thank you!" They waved a goodbye to everyone and promised that they would definitely look everyone up if they could come that way again.

"And don't forget. You eat here free any time," promised Mr. Pero.

"Thanks. Your food is the best," said Jack.

"I know!" he agreed.

The tired couple returned to their room and paid the bill. The money they had just covered it. "The Owner has given just enough," remarked Jalli.

"And that makes us rich!" rejoiced Jack.

Jack carried both bags as Jalli was beginning to limp. They walked up to the toilet block, turned to take a last view of the beach resort, and stepped through the white gate.

Inside the garden the air was soft and quiet. There was a gentle breeze that wafted the scent of flowers into their nostrils. Jalli put her arms around Jack's neck and held onto him. She was really tired and in some pain. "Too much fun!" she declared. Jack lifted her off her feet and carried her to the bench.

"You need to rest a bit," he suggested as she snuggled up to him.

"Look I've been thinking."

"You've had time to think?"

"I'll have to tell Grandma… everything."

"Yes, I suppose you must. And I'll have to tell Mum. Not that I feel like it."

"Everything," murmured Jalli. "White gates. This garden. Beach resorts. And, especially, you! My grandma will want to meet you of course."

"But I may not be permitted through your gate."

"Then that would be a disaster!" shuddered Jalli. "Grandma just wouldn't countenance me sloping off into a different universe to meet a boy she can never meet." Jack then became aware that Jalli was talking quietly to her God. "Please let Jack into Wanulka. Please!"

Silently, as lovers do, they held onto to each other for a full ten minutes. Then Jack returned to the practical. "We're both rather salty," he observed. "It did occur to me to shower before we left. But then, I thought, I was too tired to bother."

When they looked back across the lawn the white gate through which they had just come had disappeared. So had the little shed, and their clothes were in the neat pile in which they had left them. "I'd better put the jeans on," muttered Jalli. But when she stood to move, her leg had seized up again. "Ow!" she yelped. She stood but no way could she bend forward to her feet. Jack fetched her jeans and trainers while she undid the shorts and let them fall.

"Exciting!" declared Jack.

"And I was going to tell Grandma what a gentleman you were!"

"So, an excited gentleman." He knelt down and held the trousers for her to put her feet in and then tugged them up into her reach. Then she sat down as he put both her socks and shoes on.

"Whatever would I do without you?" she smiled.

"You won't have to, ever, if your white gate allows me through." He sat beside her and she put both her arms round him and kissed his face. Their lips met and it was as if the whole universe, all the universes in creation belonged to them at that moment. They enveloped one another and felt the power of the Owner of the cottage as He or She too revelled in their joy.

"Everything," whispered Jalli, "I have to tell her everything!"

"OK! I do not want to be a hidden secret. But, now, however are you going to make it home?"

"I have to catch a bus. It stops nearly outside my house."

"I know what we will do," pronounced Jack, "if I can get through your gate I will come with you to your bus-stop and see you onto the bus. I can help you get there. And then we will know for sure whether or not I am allowed through your gate."

"That is a brilliant idea!" They hobbled to the gate. But before they opened it, Jalli lent up and kissed Jack again. After all she may not get another chance! She then opened the gate and she pushed Jack through in front of her. It worked! They stood together in Wanulka beside the Municipal Gardens.

"Wow! This place is really different from Persham. I like it!"

"A different kettle of fish?"

"Well not exactly. But there is a really strange smell here."

"It smells like home."

"I suppose it does to you. It's not a gentle smell though is it? Like in the garden."

"Some of it's the soil, I suppose, and some of it's the sea – and some of it's the mess people don't look after properly," she sighed. "The bus-stop is this way." She gave the towel with her underclothes wrapped in it to Jack as she thrust her hand into her jeans pocket and pulled out a small purse with the fair. She was still wearing the swimsuit.

"Looks as if we're allowed to keep these things," said Jalli, as she took back the bright towel.

"Souvenir of the trip!"

Fortunately for Jalli they did not have to wait long for a bus. As it approached they remembered they had almost forgotten to make arrangements for their next meeting.

"Tuesday," suggested Jalli, "early – nine o'clock. I'll meet you in the garden and I'll take you home to meet Grandma!"

"Fine." He kissed her on the cheek and helped her up on to the step and into the bus. The bus pulled away and Jack stood staring after it, his arm raised, suddenly alone in a strange land. The strangeness of the land, now, had far more to do with the fact that Jalli wasn't with him, than that he was probably standing in a different universe light years away from his own.

As he re-entered the garden and collected his things, Jack spun around and around, and shouted, "THANK YOU" as loud as his lungs would permit!

9

Later that evening, Jalli limped in from the bus-stop. She was exhausted but radiant.

"What on Planet Raika have you been up to?" Grandma stared in amazement as she beheld her granddaughter. Jalli had suddenly exploded into colour – in pain from the hip, in ecstasy with her first kiss, and filled with wonder at the whole weekend with such super people.

"Grandma I just have so much to tell you!" she blurted out. "I've had an absolutely super time. I met this boy called Jack and…"

"Doesn't surprise me, Jalli, I've known for weeks that there's been something going on. Are you going to tell me all about it now? Can Grandma be let into the secrets?"

"OK, Grandma. I am going to tell you everything – but you won't believe me. I've been to two different planets!"

"You've been to the beach that's for sure. But not round here. You're covered in sand, but it's not from Wanulka beach. And what's this you are wearing underneath your top with this bow round your neck? Where did you get that? The first or second planet?"

"The first… to wear in the second. You see…"

"OK. I have no doubt you will tell me everything, but before you spread any more sand around why don't you go and take off those beach things and have a bath. Then come back and have a cup of tea and tell me all about it." Gratefully, Jalli made her way to the bathroom scattering sand and bikini as she went. "And Jalli, I am delighted to see you so happy," called her grandmother after her.

"Thanks, Grandma!"

A universe away, Jack emerged from his white gate into a drab and wet Persham. There was a rough wind driving the rain into his face as he made his way down the damp pavement that led to Renson Park. By the time he arrived home he was as soaked as if he had taken a shower fully dressed. The leaves on the trees in the park offered no shelter. In fact it was probably wetter under them, and the short cut across the park, he decided, was a mistake because the paths were really muddy. It must have been raining here a long time. As he turned into Renson Park Road he spied the kicking tree and he felt deeply guilty. What he had done to that tree over the years was no better than the way those drunken revellers had behaved in the beach resort. OK, he may not have done that to a person – no he was not a vandal like that, he had never been part of a gang of youths wreaking terror – but what he had done to the tree was a kind of vandalism all the same. The only thing it had done wrong was to be there – and it couldn't run away! Jack almost apologised to it but he didn't. He told himself that talking to a tree (or a bush as it now was) was rather silly – but he was also conscious that he was too ashamed to face it. After all, had he not spoken to the cottage and the garden?

He let himself in, dripping wet. Unlike Jalli scattering sand, all that Jack's mum was aware of was Persham mud in her hallway! "Where on Planet Earth have you been?" she cried, "You'll catch pneumonia! Why ever didn't you take a coat?"

"The sun was shining when I left," explained Jack.

"Quite! It's been raining here for twenty-four hours. You've been a long time. I was getting worried."

"I said we might be gone overnight," said Jack getting annoyed – and getting annoyed with himself for getting annoyed. He felt himself sinking back into the moaning Persham mood. Some of it was probably due to the weather – raining, grey, and mud-soaked for twenty-four hours without a break. He thought of his impending visit to Wanulka. There they had three suns in the sky…

"We?" Matilda was asking. "Who have you been with?" Jack remembered Jalli saying, "Everything. We have to tell them everything."

"Jalli. A girl called Jalli. I'll tell you everything, from the beginning." Matilda was about to wade in and demand a full explanation but stopped herself just in time, as the import of Jack's words entered her brain, "You'd b… everything? Did you say you'd tell me everything?"

"Yes, Mum. Everything. We decided we would tell our mums everything – well, Grandma in Jalli's case." Jack sneezed. He was still standing inside the front door with a large puddle forming around his feet.

"Goodness. Look, you'd better take a bath. There'll be just enough hot water, I expect. Then come and eat something. You are hungry?"

"Ravenous!" Jack breathed a sigh of relief and hurried upstairs to a welcome bath. That had gone better than he had anticipated, he reflected, as he lay in the warm water. Jalli was really wise. Following her advice he had used the right words, and it had stemmed the tirade that he was used to. Perhaps in the past he may have been as responsible for the way his mother talked to him as she was. Up till now he had, instinctively, blamed her for being cross with him. Jalli was teaching him how he could say things in a way that reduced, rather than inflamed anger – she was just so good! Telling his mother what he had been doing was not easy. He felt exposed. He risked being misunderstood. In fact he knew he would be, because there was no way his mum in her limited world was going to get her mind round all he had been doing. But he had to try… for Jalli. As he talked he kept thinking about Jalli telling her grandma everything. He mustn't keep secrets about Jalli – even if his mum didn't always understand.

Jalli's hot soak did wonders for the hip and she felt really relaxed and fresh despite the excitement of the last forty-eight hours. Sat beside Momori with a hot mug, she began at the beginning – the white gate, the cottage, and Jack. But long before she had finished, Jalli had gone to sleep, trailing off in mid sentence about Kakko, Tod, Rosie and the others.

It took two whole days to tell the whole story as she kept remembering bits that she hadn't told. Momori had known something was afoot, but all of this was far more complicated and phenomenal than she had ever imagined – or, she told herself afterwards, she ever could imagine. In fact that applied to many things in life, she reflected. She had always been astonished at what life brought – both for the bad things, and also for the blessings.

Creation, she decided, was all about healing and all about putting right that which had fallen apart as well as destruction and disorder. She had experienced a cataclysmic event, but nature had immediately began to heal. If you go to the site of her old village now, you come to some of the most beautiful and productive countryside in the district.

And out of the same sadness had grown this lovely girl with a capacity for enjoying herself and in doing so, bringing good things to other people. She had been part of the process of restoring Mr. Pero's belief in young people and Momori was proud of her. She was also grateful for the way she could trust her granddaughter absolutely. More than once she had been on the point of demanding what was going on, but she had been patient enough to wait and was now rewarded with an openness that made her feel really good. Her trust had been vindicated.

Momori found it hard to believe in the story of the different planets. This was too far fetched to swallow, but she knew Jalli believed it and was not making anything up. And now, quite rightly, she wanted to bring this young man, Jack, home. She hoped that Jalli wasn't deceived by this boy. She was usually a pretty good judge of character, but Momori knew how teenage hearts could be taken in by charm and appearances.

Matilda thought Jack had "lost his marbles" as she put it when he first began to talk about the garden behind the white gate. The other white gates that led to a planet with three suns and a beach resort were very difficult to come to terms with. But Jack had definitely been somewhere hot because he had a real tan, and the beach shorts were proof of something. He couldn't have taken a plane to the Mediterranean because he had no passport – nor any money as far as Matilda knew, and he didn't appear to be making any of this up. What delighted her was that Jack seemed really keen on bringing his Jalli to see her, and you can't actually make up a real girl. Once he had started he couldn't stop talking about her. She seemed to be bright and good at sports, great looking, kind and sensitive and not stuck up – everything you could wish for in a Jane Austen heroine (the BBC had just scheduled a repeat of *Sense and Sensibility* – but Jack hadn't seen it. It was not the sort of thing he would dream of watching).

"Well then, you'd better bring her," declared Matilda. As soon as she had said it, however, she was conscious of her surroundings. If this girl was all that Jack had said she was, she would no doubt be coming from a well-appointed house – definitely middle class! Whatever would she think of 68 Renson Park Road? "What kind of a house does she live in?" she asked.

"I don't know, I haven't been. It won't be too grand though," assured Jack who guessed what his mum was thinking, "because her grandma isn't well off at all. I believe she's had to work hard since all the family died in the flood. Jalli has no-one but her grandma." Jack explained about the earthquake and the dam.

"How will she take to this house, do you think?"

"I don't know. I've not thought about that. She's the sort that takes people as she finds them. I'll tidy my room though."

"Goodness, we are talking miracles here! She must be something! Then you and I must have a go at the front garden." Jack promised he would help. Then he wished he could undo the damage to the kicking tree as easy as he could clear the front garden and tidy his room. He hoped Jalli wouldn't notice it and ask questions about it.

On Tuesday morning Jalli was walking much better and she hurried off to the Municipal Park to find Jack. She was so excited about introducing him to Grandma. It never crossed her mind that they wouldn't take to each other. It seemed entirely natural that each would find equal pleasure in the other. They were wholly compatible, assumed Jalli, just as they were both compatible with her.

The bus journey to the town centre seemed to take even longer than usual but Jalli knew it was because she couldn't wait to meet up with Jack again. As soon as she descended from the bus she hurried the one hundred metres to the white gate and simply walked straight in – just as she would the front gate of her own house. She had given up thinking about people seeing her "disappear" unless they were right in front of her or behind her. Most people seemed to walk down the street without taking much notice of other people. It would have amazed Jack to think that the most fantastic girl he had ever met, after a survey that had involved more than one planet, should not be noticed by so many other people!

Jalli was early, but so was Jack. As soon as she came through her gate he was there on the other side. The air in the garden was just as sweet as always, but Jalli had no time to think about it before Jack's arm was around her.

"Hi!" squeezed Jack. Still breathing hard from her walk, Jalli stood on tiptoe and kissed his cheek. Their eyes met and, moving Jalli's hair from her face, Jack bent down and he kissed her lips. They remained in their embrace several minutes.

"Come!" urged Jalli, "come and meet my grandma. She's dying to see you."

I bet she is, thought Jack. Then out loud, "I hope she likes me."

"Of course she will!"

"You sound so sure. Loving adults are very protective. She's going to be quite critical. I'm not exactly the boy with the most to commend him compared with you, am I? But *you're* clever, good at sports and the best looking girl I have ever met. I know *my* mum would be absolutely delighted in *you*. But your grandma will see the deficiencies in me you don't seem to notice."

"Now, Jack Smitt. I tell you, you will be just the sort of person Grandma would approve of. I have told her what a gentleman you are! All you have to do is be polite and… and not be scared! You weren't nervous at the beach resort were you?"

"That was different. If people didn't like me, it didn't matter. But I don't want your grandmother disapproving of me, do I?"

"And she won't. Come on." She took him by the hand and led him for the second time into Wanulka. This time they both got on the bus, Jalli paying his fare along with her own. Jack absorbed the atmosphere of the bustling city and felt the heat of the dry season about to give way to the rains. In fact over the sea he could see great black clouds with the occasional flash of lightning illuminating them. However up ahead, as the bus proceeded west to Jalli's house, were three suns almost in line but not quite, the largest being the highest in the sky.

"Jallaxa?" he pointed.

"Right. And the others are… ?"

"Sklier and… I've forgotten the other one."

"Not bad, Skhlaia is the smallest. The middle one is Suuf."

"They're beautiful! They make this place quite hot."

"Yes. It gets much cooler when the rains come though. That will be any time now."

"I like the buildings. And the people look much like they do in England – only brighter!"

"The young people have started to dress differently from the older generations. Women in trousers is fairly new for example."

"Same as in Britain. Funny that."

"I think our two planets are at the same stage of development. If we weren't about the same we would find it much more difficult to interact. The Owner of the garden knows what he is doing."

"You really believe it is all meant to be don't you?" Jack was not as certain as Jalli. She was more confident about most things. It hadn't been long before this that Jack thought life sucked – for the most part anyway.

"Certain of it. We were meant to meet."

"Then, does this mean we only think we have freedom to decide what we do?"

"Oh, no. We are perfectly free to do what we want to do. We don't have to go through our white gates. But we want to."

"Yeah. I was just curious at first."

"Exactly, God invites you – but you can kick your white gate just as much as go through it if you chose."

"But I didn't! I do… but… I suppose I have kicked things that annoy me."

"Like gates and walls… but not people?"

"No. Not people, let's not talk about it." He grew alarmed that Jalli would extend her inquiries and be shocked that he had attacked a living thing. How could he have done that all those years? "I feel bad about the things I did in the past. I was angry most of the time."

"Why?"

"Well, life didn't give me things like other people. My dad disappeared when I was two, my mum was bossy and school was boring most of the time. I only stayed on there for something to do… Jalli, until I met you I really couldn't see the point of life most of the time… Look let's not talk about this. I'm here in your wonderful planet on a bus with people all different, the suns – all three – are shining and I'm with the most fantastic girl in the universe!"

"Are you certain of that? You haven't seen them all!"

"Absolutely certain. You can't beat perfection!"

"You just keep thinking like that, Mr. Smitt!"

"I will. At least as long as you want me to… and as long as your grandma approves of me. If she does, you must come and visit Persham and my mum."

"Of course I will! And don't be worried, Grandma will like you."

Jalli and Momori's house was just as Jack had expected. It was smaller than his own, being all on the same level. It was furnished with cushions and throws all embroidered by Momori, Jalli or one of their friends. The walls were festooned with pictures and hangings and the low tables had crocheted doilies and little ornaments on them They clearly relied on candlelight more often than in Britain because there were several candlesticks with half-consumed candles scattered about.

Momori was wonderful. Jack was very polite, and his initial diffidence only helped to recommend him as someone who cared much for her approval. Jack was really impressed with her. He was expecting to be questioned about his past and his prospects and so on, but it wasn't like that. Momori simply wanted to be friendly. Of course, as Jack and Momori shared, so they talked about themselves and Jack was soon saying all sorts of things about himself. The day came to a climax when Momori brought out the food. The Wanulka cuisine – well at least as cooked by Momori – was superb, and Jack could not do anything but praise every mouthful! "Wow, Mrs. Rarga. This is really good!" he kept saying.

The meeting was a great success. Jalli was just the same in front of her grandma as she was anywhere else. Jack felt at home in a way he could not believe but which, nevertheless, he found amazing. "Can I call you Grandma, too?" he asked.

"Why of course, so long as my Jalli is not jealous!"

"I like it," proclaimed Jalli. "But if he does he will have to behave, and be good all the time, like I am!"

"Of course," joked Jack, "that won't be difficult. I am naturally perfect."

"You two are as bad as each other! So that's alright… 'Perfect!' That'll be the day! But you're good enough. And I dare say you're perfect for one another – at least for the moment. Now, why don't you show Jack around the garden, and then he may look into your room and see just what a perfectly tidy girl you are, Jallaxanya Rarga!" But of course Jalli had tidied it up – a bit.

"It's lovely. Just full of you," smiled Jack. "I wish I had known you when you were little."

He patted one of her dolls sitting on the side of her bookshelves.

"But I didn't like little boys, then."

"You certainly wouldn't have liked me. I was horrible. But, then I thought all little girls were a pain. Come to think of it I still do. You're the huge exception."

"I'm glad. You're only supposed to like one." Jalli took his hand and turned him away from looking at the room to her and kissed him. There was something special about kissing Jack, here, in her house, in her room. Jack felt that that embrace was not only Jalli's but that of her whole surroundings too. He had never felt as privileged as he felt at that moment.

The following day it was Jalli's turn to visit Persham. To Jack's great relief it had stopped raining. He hadn't had much time to tidy his room but he had collected the soiled clothes and put out about eight dirty tea mugs – some of them dating back three weeks.

Matilda had wondered why they had been so short of mugs. Perhaps the most disturbing find was the remains of his sandwiches from the last time he had been to the school. The banana skin had virtually melted into a brown mass and the bread was so thick in blue mould it was hardly recognisable.

"Jack Smith!" exclaimed his mother. "Put that straight into

the bin! I think I will have to offer this girl an anti-germ mask – especially if she's coming from a different universe!"

Jack was not proud of his town. He had never thought of Persham as anything special. No-one, except perhaps the mayor and corporation, seemed to think of the place as anything special. The general view was that there were worse places, and here at least you knew people and you belonged. Many young people left though, especially those that stayed on to do A-levels. They were excited by the idea of the city and its special culture, and for the most part, they never came back. They didn't even have a decent football club to follow – unless you counted lowly Persham Wanderers. But, as he prepared to usher Jalli through into his world, he felt special.

As soon as Jalli looked across Persham from the hill on which St Paul's school stood, she exclaimed, "Can't you see a long way from here!"

"I suppose you can," he hadn't thought about it before but Jalli lived on the flat, near the sea and the hills were behind the city. Here, the town was built up the hillside, away from the river. He stopped and explained. "The town centre lies that way and the river comes through that gap, see."

"Where do you live, Jack?"

"Down there." He pointed to his right. "You can't see it from here… It's beside Renson Park – part of an old estate. Some of the park is still there. I learned to ride a bike in the park – although there are big notices saying 'No cycling!'" he laughed.

"Bike? What is a bike?"

"You ride it. It has two wheels." Now he thought about it, he hadn't seen bicycles as such in Wanulka. "Look, I'll point one out when we see one. Come on, we go this way."

They descended the street of terraced houses with small front gardens. The greenhouse was still there, and tomatoes were to be seen growing in it. Jack marvelled every time he saw it. Soon the park came into sight and they crossed it avoiding the muddiest bits. The park was covered in cycle tracks. Then they saw one, zooming across the football pitches. Jalli thought the contraption looked funny – especially as the rider had a muddy streak up his back.

"It is the rainy season," observed Jalli.

"Every season is the rainy season in England," grumbled Jack, "especially in the school holidays! You're lucky it's not raining now!"

They entered Renson Park Road and Jack indicated the doors as they numbered up.

"Sixty-eight," he explained. He was consciously trying to get Jalli to look at the houses rather than the street and the trees. If only she could avoid noticing the kicking tree. He was so conscious of it now, every time he went out and came home! But the plan almost backfired. Jalli was counting off the houses and looking at their numbers and actually stumbled into the edge of the kicking tree. "Sorry bush!" she exclaimed. Jalli had just touched the tree with the outside of her foot, accidentally, and had apologised to it! Jack turned red. Thinking that Jack was embarrassed at introducing her to his mother, Jalli assured him, "Don't be worried, Jack, I will be good. I promise!"

"Of course, you will. You couldn't be otherwise. Mum will think you're fantastic."

Then the door opened. "You coming in?" asked Matilda.

"Hi, Mum, this is Jalli."

"Pleased to meet you," said Jalli, giving her a little Wanulkan curtsy. Matilda was taken aback. This girl was indeed straight out of *Pride and Prejudice*!

"Enchanted," said Matilda – for indeed she was. "Come in, come in!" And she took Jalli's hand and drew her into the hallway and into the living room. "Will you take a cup of tea?"

"Yes, please," responded Jalli.

"Jalli won't have tasted our type of tea, Mum," advised Jack, "better not make it too strong!"

"Do sit down," beckoned Matilda and bustled out into the kitchen to put the kettle on.

"Mum's a bit scared of you, I think," whispered Jack.

"Why? Am I frightening?"

"No. It's just that she doesn't get many visitors. I don't bring friends round. I have not brought friends in – not for years! You're the first."

"I see," smiled Jalli. She stood up and looked around her. "You have a big house!" exclaimed Jalli as Jack's mum returned with the tea. "I like it. Your world is very different."

"How is our world different from yours?" Matilda was intrigued by this girl's accent.

"Ours is hot and dusty. Yours is cool and soft and green. The gardens have lots of flowers. It is much quieter inside your house. The walls are thick."

"So where is it you come from?" Jalli told Matilda all about Wanulka and her grandmother, her school and her interests. Jack didn't have to say anything. It was clear that they were going to get along because his mum was growing easier. She was definitely impressed with Jalli.

"You see, she does come from another planet!" cried Jack.

Jalli talked about the white gates just as Jack had done and described it from her angle.

"Well, I must confess I found that bit the hardest to believe but I shall believe it now, even if it's because I want to. Now let's eat." It was Jack's favourite, "toad in the hole" and greens and potatoes followed by ice-cream.

Plain, thought Jack after Wanulkan fare, but Jalli seemed to really enjoy it. For her it was quite as different as Wanulkan food to him.

The visit ended with a tour of the house, a kiss in Jack's bedroom(!), and a promise by Jalli to call again. It was clear that Jack had his mum's blessing in pursuing this relationship. Later, after Jack had seen Jalli back to the garden, his mother privately wondered how he had found such a superior being.

"Must be something about me you hadn't noticed before," expressed Jack.

"Oh, you've got 'it' – what it takes to attract a girl. Just you look after her! You behave yourself and make sure you deserve her!" she entreated.

"I will, Mum. I promise. I know she is good."

"So you be good too!"

"Yes, Mum. Don't nag!"

Matilda suddenly felt the way the conversation was going and caught herself from saying anything more. "I just think," she said, "you have made an excellent choice."

"Thanks, Mum."

10

A couple of days after the visit to Persham, Jack and Jalli met as they had arranged, with the object of doing "nothing special". They had had so much excitement and much to talk about. "Let's just bring a picnic and 'chill'," suggested Jack. So they had brought their favourite foods to share with each other. When they had laid it all out on a cloth on the lawn it was an impressive spread.

"I hope you're feeling hungry!" exclaimed Jack. "There's enough here for ten people."

"I reckon that if we start now we'll make quite a dent. We needn't eat tomorrow!"

"Life is great! I am pleased I met you!" laughed Jack.

"Do you mean you are glad you met *me*, or my grandma's pie?"

"Both. Definitely both. And at the moment I reckon it is touch and go which I love the most!"

Jalli chased him round the garden and shouted that she wouldn't let him near the food again until he had paid proper attention to her! After several minutes of strenuous activity spent in this game in which Jalli's sporting skills denied Jack even one opportunity to get back to the food, he eventually grabbed her and swung her off her feet and they fell in a giggling heap. He admitted defeat and kissed her tenderly. She allowed him to crawl back to the food so long as he agreed only to eat things as she gave him permission. They had much fun exploring the various names for things. They had a wonderful picnic which included pies and tarts, meats, fish, cheese and fruits of all kinds.

After they had finished, they used the cottage toilet. Jack emerged from the house and there he saw, across the grass, a new white gate – and a small shed beside it, exactly like before. He waited for Jalli to join him. She caught the direction of his gaze. "I wonder where that one leads?" he asked.

They had had such a pleasant morning eating their picnic and just enjoying each other's company that the new white gate came as a bit of an unwelcome intrusion. It sort of said, "OK, you've had a good time 'doing nothing' now it's time to do some work!" The Owner had a new place for them to visit.

They looked over the gate. It was quite a different looking land with dark green pine trees in view and meadows with what looked like snow in places. The shed contained piles of thick clothing, fur hats and two large rucksacks – the hiking sort.

"This looks like energetic work!" exclaimed Jack as he checked out a pair of heavy duty hiking boots.

"Doesn't look like just stuff for two days either," commented Jalli as she pulled out several sets of thermal underclothes and five pairs of socks! Jack put on a fur hat, to Jalli's great amusement. She readjusted it for him, making sure his ears were properly covered.

"If we're going on this," said Jalli, "then I'm going to have to phone Grandma."

"And I'll contact Mum. Jalli, I don't think we have much choice in this, do we?"

"You know, Jack. I've been thinking about all this business of choice. Yes, we do have choice here. I don't think the Owner will force us if we decide just to ignore this gate. He or She didn't make me get out of bed and come here this morning. I am sure I came because I chose to, I didn't have to. I was invited to play a ball-game over near Parmanda Park. But I really wanted to come to be with you. That's the thing, I want to do what He or She seems to want me to do."

Jack was more doubtful about going through the gate. He found trusting the Owner more difficult than Jalli did. How could they be so sure of all this. It was a strange situation, all of it. He was reminded of the line in the film *Notting Hill* when the heroine says of her unexpected new encounter in the house with the blue door, "Surreal, but nice!" But what evidence was there to say it would stay like that? What if the Owner were putting conditions on their access to the garden. "If we decided not to go through this gate," ventured Jack, "we may not be allowed to come back here again."

"But that would be awful! How dreadful if we couldn't get through to see each other!"

"This is the point about the choice thing. We can choose to be part of all this, or not. But are we permitted to pick and choose the bits we like from the bits we don't?"

"I suppose we can. If we did pick and choose though, it might not come out as well as it should… I mean, if we only did what we thought was going to be good, in advance, we might not even be here. We have gone along with it up to now, and it's been great. And, looking back, I wouldn't have changed any of it."

"No, exactly. But there will be times, perhaps, like this

one, when we're having a great time and suddenly we are asked to do a job. When we're started we'll probably be glad we did it. But, right now, in this lovely garden that backpack doesn't look terribly inviting."

"But the prospect of having a couple of weeks with you on an adventure holiday is a great idea though!" exclaimed Jalli.

Jack smiled. To have this great girl by his side without having to go home and check in with Mum each day would be cool. But, then, he was not entirely convinced. Jack hadn't forgotten that until the day he went through his white gate, he had decided that life sucked.

"Bet it's not a holiday!" he said in a negative tone.

"I bet it'll be fun though. Like last time at the beach resort… OK. So we may be able to turn down this new white gate. But I think we could be silly if we do," affirmed Jalli.

"And I know what my mum will say. She'd reckon we'd be stupid to let ourselves in for something without thoroughly checking it out first. She'd basically be telling me to think very carefully about this."

"And my grandma would certainly be worried."

"So, what are we going to do?" queried Jack.

"This is what I think," said Jalli decisively, "the Owner here wouldn't ask us to do this if it wasn't important. And I think we might regret turning anything down that He or She has asked us to do, because it's all been great so far. Actually, I think Grandma would agree with me. If she were here she would go."

"My mum wouldn't. But some of that is because too many people she has trusted have done things to her that turned out wrong. OK. So are we agreed we're going?" Jalli nodded. "I'm going because you are too good to resist, and because I'm getting really curious about what's beyond that gate! I'll pop out to Persham to ring Mum." And Jalli did the same in Wanulka. Soon they had the older peoples' permission – provided they were sensible and looked after themselves and each other. In fact Grandma was quite positive Jack would look after Jalli, and Matilda was so impressed with her son's choice of Jalli she was quite ready to accept his logic about "having to go". "Mind you look after that girl," she had pressed upon him. Jack had assured her that he certainly would, and, to his amazement, she seemed to believe him. He was so used to his mum not trusting him to do what he said he was going to do, even when he meant it. What he had not reckoned with this time was that Matilda had seen so much change in him since he had met Jalli and, so long as Jalli was with him, she was ready to trust him.

They ate some more food and then packed up the rest of it to put in the top of their backpacks. They laid out everything neatly on the grass, took note of the contents, and then re-packed them carefully, item by item, making sure they had lined the packs with the waterproof plastic provided. They then took off their jeans and T-shirts and put on the cold weather clothing, beginning with the layers of thermals. They trusted the Owner on this. If they were given this stuff, they would need it. Jack was more used to winter things than Jalli because Wanulka never really became cold. Snow was something Jalli had only seen in pictures. This adventure was clearly going to be more of a challenge to a warm weather girl than a resident of Britain!

They surveyed each other in their new outfits and decided that, apart from their faces, they were in total disguise! They helped each other on with the backpacks, adjusting the straps. Like the rest of the gear the fit was perfect, and they quickly became confident as they walked around a bit.

"OK! Let's go!" said Jack unlatching the white gate.

The cold fresh air hit their faces like a blast from a freezer. They stood beside a path at the edge of a pine forest with cones and dried needles beneath their feet. On the other side of the rough path there were tufts of grass, dead and brown but with tiny green shoots around the base. In front of them was an open area covered in low scrub beyond which was a shallow valley with more evergreen forests on the low hill beyond them. They could identify a lighter green area at the lowest point which hinted of water. Splotches of white snow could be seen in the hollows of the land that rose again beyond it. Nearer to them further down the path, there were more patches in the places where the trees gave deeper shade. From a distance their white gate could easily have seemed like one of these.

"We need to take special note of this place," stated Jack thoughtfully. "Let's take great care we do not lose our way back to the gate."

"Can we mark this tree?" asked Jalli.

"I can't see it will do any harm to draw a mark on the trunk but I think a rock would be better." Jack took a whitish coloured stone and quickly discovered it was like chalk. Handy, he thought. He drew a circle on a darker coloured outcrop just up the path, and on another just below the gate. "There, now we need to make marks as we go. They need not be obvious but they should be where we will look for them."

"And here are three big trees closer together than the others," observed Jalli getting excited by this awesome place. So far she was delighted they had come. They looked out across the valley and lined up various land marks.

"Which way?" asked Jalli.

"Downwards? To the left?" suggested Jack. The path wound slightly downhill around the edge of the forest.

"Fine. Is that snow?"

"Yeah."

"I've only seen it in pictures before."

"Well, it isn't very good snow. It's not fresh. It looks like it's melting now for the spring. Look," he said, putting his foot into a medium sized patch, "it's wet and coarse." But for Jalli it was a big deal. Real snow for the first time in her life. She picked up a handful and felt the cold seep into her finger tips. What is it about snow and the young? It is a mystery, but wherever they are in the universe it seems, they have to make snowballs and throw it at their friends! It took Jalli just three minutes to make and throw her first snowball! Jack retaliated. They might be seventeen or eighteen, thought Jack, but it was good to be children. (They were just emerging from that period of teenage life when being sophisticated mattered. At seventeen it's generally cool to be childlike again.) And, anyway, here, there was no-one else from among their acquaintances to notice. In fact, they didn't care if anyone thought they were being childish! After half an hour they resumed the path – hands, numb with cold, now stuffed inside their furry mittens!

The walking was enjoyable along the well trodden path and they quickly began to appreciate that exercise is the key to keeping warm in cold lands. Eventually they emerged, rosy cheeked, from the path onto a wider track. Jack marked a small rock by the junction. They continued on down the gentle slope. A hundred yards further on, they came across a fork. They pondered whether to bear left or right. Eventually deciding to go right, Jack stepped off the road to mark another rock. Then a man came running up the left fork shouting at them. "What do you think you're doing?" he yelled. But before they could make any response he demanded Jack come back onto the road at once.

"Don't you know anything? You cannot leave the road for any reason. You risk instant death. Don't you know there are mines all over the place here?"

Jack froze. A short middle-aged man dressed in rough farmer's clothes – a woollen jumper tucked into a pair of thick trousers held up by a broad leather belt – was shouting and gesticulating wildly.

"Sorry, I didn't know. Mines? Why?" asked Jack hesitantly – terrified.

"Where are you from? What kind of accent is that? Whose side are you on?"

"We're new here," interjected Jalli. "We've only just arrived."

"Arrived! Arrived from where? Nobody just arrives in this part of Tolfanland… You don't appear to be armed," he said more softly.

"Armed!" declared Jalli, "What with guns and everything? Of course not!"

"You *have* just arrived haven't you? I can't imagine how you've got this far without knowing what you've got yourself into. You'd better come this way."

Jack returned to the road in one bound, and breathed a sigh of relief. He and Jalli then followed the countryman. He led them down the road along which he had come.

"Looks as if we've stepped into the middle of a war!" remarked Jack when he judged the man was out of hearing.

"This is scary. Do you thing he's OK. He's not going to do anything to us, is he?"

"I don't know what he plans to do, but if he was going to do us in he probably wouldn't be so concerned about me stepping on a mine."

"That's true."

After about three hundred metres they caught sight of a low croft that stood some way off the road at the end of a narrow footpath to the left. Proceeding down this path with some determination, the man turned and checked the couple were following. They hurried after him. As he got to the croft the man shouted something. He bade the couple stop and wait. A moment later a woman appeared at the door dressed in what appeared to be the female equivalent of the man's country clothes, a brown woollen long-sleeved dress and a beige shawl about her shoulders. A sturdy, practical looking sort of person, thought Jalli.

"They look innocent enough," the woman declared. "Foreign that's for sure. They haven't wintered here either. Just look at their skin." And, addressing Jalli and Jack directly she spoke in a gruff but not unpleasant tone, "You'd better come in. Take off those packs. My, they look hardly used. Very fresh all round!" she assessed.

When Jack and Jalli had removed their boots, hats and outer fleeces and were seated together on a wooden settle in front of a fire that served both as a kitchen range and source of heat for the whole croft, the questioning began. They explained how they had come down the track that led beside the wood after arriving from a different land.

"We don't doubt you've got here from somewhere quite foreign," declared the crofter.

"Do you know what is happening here? The rebels are a few kilometres down the road you were about to take, and in that direction" – he indicated the way they had come – "the government soldiers are re-grouping. Where they'll meet this time we just don't know."

"What's the fighting all about?" asked Jack.

The crofter looked at his wife. Were these two spies? He decided they were not, they were very convincing if they were. So he began to explain, "That way, in the west, they speak a different language from those in the east. Always have. There are some among those from the east that are fed up with being ruled by westerners and they have rebelled."

"And some of us that just want to get on with our lives and don't care who rules!" asserted the woman. "The rebellion has made things so bad for us."

Her husband continued, "One lot of soldiers after another come making demands – east and west. They mostly demand food. Last winter we barely had enough to survive on ourselves. I've just managed to save them" – he gestured to a sack of tubers – "to plant for the new season, if they will let us alone long enough to plant them."

"But the worst thing," said the woman with tears welling up in her eyes, "is that the rebels have taken two of our sons barely old enough to look after themselves to fight in their army. No more than thirteen the younger one," she sighed.

"Thirteen!" exclaimed Jalli, "but that's criminal. How can they ask a child to go out to fight?"

"Ask! There was no asking about it. He had no choice. Either they went and were taught to use a gun, or a gun would have been used on them." Just then a teenage girl, perhaps about the same age as Jalli, came in.

"Our eldest," explained the man. "These here are foreigners that are just 'passing through'. Sorry don't know their names," he explained to her.

"Jallaxanya – Jalli for short."

"And I'm Jack."

"Told you they were foreigners. Strange names you have for our ears. This 'ere is Tillithy."

"Hi," said Tillithy, "I get Tilly most of the time."

"Family name's Somaf," added the crofter.

"And these are our youngest," said the wife as three younger ones arrived. A girl of about ten called Bonny, and two boys with names sounding like Mod and Gan. They showed a lot of interest, the youngest touching and stroking Jalli's long hair.

"They've not seen hair that dark in colour before," said their father. "Come on now you two, give her a little peace."

Jack and Jalli tried to tell the family a bit about themselves. About how they were both only children and how they had met. And about the white gates. "Well I wouldn't have believed it," said the woman. "But that you are here and could hardly have got here any ways else that I know of."

"We think that the Owner has something for us to do and

we want to do the right thing. But we don't know what it is until, well until just before we're doing it."

"So, do you think your Owner wants you to stay here?"

"We don't know where else we might go," replied Jalli, "it… well it sounds rather dangerous to go in any direction. We had better not travel in the dark."

"If I might say," ventured Mrs. Somaf, "a good looking girl like you should not be out and about on the roads at all. And a young man such as you," she said to Jack, "cannot say you don't know what side you're on. If you're not with them, then you're against them, and that means being shot." The prospects of moving anywhere seemed disastrous. Maybe this time Mum's caution might have made sense after all.

"I could say I'm a journalist from an international agency," declared Jack bringing out a note book and pencil from the front pocket of his backpack.

"May work," declared the crofter, "but journalists don't usually have girlfriends in tow! In any case you'd be safest here keeping your heads down. If the weather's right, and they leave us be, we could start the planting tomorrow – and since you're eating here you might as well do some work." Despite having stuffed themselves full of picnic earlier in the day the mention of food sounded welcome to Jack.

"But we can't eat your food when you've barely enough for yourselves," protested Jalli.

"Can't see that you've got much choice – unless you can live on fresh air!" surmised Mrs. Somaf.

This was the second time the question of choice had

arisen – and Jack noted that, in both cases, it was in the expression "no choice". He looked at Jalli, and they both silently reflected on the discussion they had had earlier in the day. Yet the truth was that they still did have a choice. They could leave right now and go back to the white gate not very far away, and leave this war-torn land – or they could stay. These people hadn't the same privilege. They were stuck here inbetween warring parties. Even if they took to the road as refugees they couldn't have got far with two young children. Things would have to be very bad for that to happen. No words were spoken but they knew they had made the decision.

"Thank you," said Jalli. "Your cooking does sound good. We have got some food. It's not much, but you're welcome to it," and she unwrapped the remains of the picnic that she and Jack had brought with them.

The effect was dramatic! The family had not seen anything like the cold treats that Matilda and Momori had packed up for their children. Jack and Jalli carefully shared all they had and it was a delight to see their faces as they tasted the strange delicacies.

"Well, your Owner has sent you to us to give us the treat of our lives!" declared the woman. "How does your grandmother make this pie?"

"You need to be near the sea and collect a special kind of seaweed for a start. And then the meat has got parmanda honey in it. Jack's country hasn't got any parmandas so his mother can't make it. It really is a rare treat though. And my grandma knows that Jack likes her pies so much she couldn't resist making one specially for him."

"But your food is special to us too," broke in Jack, "because it is just as different."

"There's nothing special about what we grow in our gardens, or what our cattle give us," commented the wife.

"But it's very special to us," said Jalli. "It's special being here altogether, and, if we're not going to be in the way, we'd be delighted to stay…"

"… and work," added Jack.

"Let's pray that the weather will hold and the soldiers keep away then," said Mr. Somaf.

Jalli and Jack spent the night on two beds covered with furs laid on top of what seemed like a kind of bracken. They slept in the end of the croft that the two oldest boys had once used before being taken away. It was divided from the rest with a curtain. Tilly and the children all slept at the other end whilst the crofter and his wife stayed in the main room by the front door. There was a back door that led out of the same room that they used to go to the small shed in which the "earth closet" was situated. Jack had not seen one like this before but he knew they were common in other parts of his planet. "In Australia," he had explained to Jalli, when they were settling down to sleep, "they call them dunnies I think. In the army they call them latrines. In fact we have more names for the toilet than any other place, I reckon. Mum likes to call it 'the loo' because she thinks it's more middle class. In the United States I'm told they call it 'the john' and that's the same name that Jack comes from…"

After a moment, Jalli inquired, "Why do they call it that? Why call it a 'john'?" But she got no answer. Jack had drifted off to sleep as if he had been sleeping on furs and bracken all his life. Great, thought Jalli, I hope I don't need to go to the "what-do-you-call-it" in the night. It's so dark outside, and I didn't ask if there was a candle. But she needn't have worried because she, too, was soon soundly asleep and did not open her eyes till it was getting light.

11

Jalli woke just as it was getting light to the sound of vehicles and men's voices. It sounded like several large trucks were manoeuvring around the fork where they had met Mr. Somaf, but something was up because men were barking instructions to each other.

She got up to glance out of the window.

"Keep your head down! Don't be seen," ordered Mrs. Somaf. "It's the rebel army. I hope they go right by, at least the fighting won't be on our doorstep."

"From what's being said it sounds like one of their trucks has broken down and they're trying to get by it," said the crofter. "Just go back to bed dear until they've gone. It looks like a big drive." Jalli obediently returned to her bed. Jack took her hand as she passed.

She had just sat on the edge of the bed when there was a huge flash. The morning light increased in intensity several times. A fraction of a second later there was a deafening crunch. They both heard the explosion, and then felt it. The whole croft rocked. A bottle fell off the shelf and smashed on the floor. The crashing lasted several seconds, and then for one uncanny moment there was silence. Jalli wondered if her ears had stopped working. But then the dogs started barking, the birds were up all screeching their own calls and one of the boys in the croft started crying. The soldiers' voices were now raised with some panicking while others were beseeching order and calm.

"They must've hit a mine," declared Mr. Somaf. "I didn't hear a shell coming in. Girls! You'd better go to the bunker. They'll come down here for certain. Jalli you should go with them. Put all your things – everything that you're not wearing – in your pack and push it well under the bed. Quickly. Girls, you do the same – you know the drill."

"Yes Dad," replied Tilly, almost already completing the task. "Bonny, come on!" She grabbed a bottle of water and a blanket from the corner, which lay in readiness for such an exercise. Within two minutes Tilly, Bonny and Jalli were being ushered out the back door by Mrs. Somaf. "The bunker's through the toilet," explained Tilly to Jalli who was quite confused. "Follow me!"

Meanwhile Jack had got up and put on his things. "Why do the girls have to leave?" he asked.

"Soldiers in wartime take liberties," explained Mrs. Somaf. "They not only steal food and make your sons become fighters, they can also take your daughters to satisfy their carnal appetites. We have built a bolt-hole out the back of the toilet for the girls to hide in if any soldiers come round. That is why we have a back door. Crofts like this don't usually have back doors."

Tilly led Jalli into the toilet. It was just a hole in the floor with a wooden cover. She stepped over the hole and, bending down, removed a panel from the bottom half of the back of the shed. Behind it was an opening about a metre wide into the bank that passed along the rear of the toilet shed. The entrance opened into a small room lined with wood. Tilly ushered Bonny inside, then Jalli, and finally squeezed herself in, pulling the panel back into place behind her. The bunker was no more than three metres deep, one and a half metres wide and a metre and a bit high. Not even Bonny could stand up in it. In the roof was a pipe through which faint dappled light shone onto Jalli's legs as she sat hunched between the girls.

"How often do you have to do this?" asked Jalli.

"This is the third time," replied Tilly. "Now we have to remain very, very quiet because our voices will travel easily up the air-vent and be amplified."

They listened to what was going on. The noise of men's voices was definitely coming their way. The parents had been right. The soldiers were in trouble and were looking for some place to get themselves sorted out. They heard a loud banging on the front door of the croft and a gruff voice demanding a bed for an injured comrade.

Inside the croft the rest of the family had quickly put away anything tempting to steal. Jack was stuffing the seed corms under his bed when the officer banged on the door. He stepped away from the bed to the centre of the room as the crofter swung open the door and three men staggered in with a bleeding soldier. "Over there!" barked the officer and the soldier was lowered fairly roughly, thought Jack, onto the bed Jalli had been using. It was pretty obvious the man was in a bad way. He was bleeding heavily. One leg was clearly broken and blood was pouring from the man's upper arm.

Before he was sixteen Jack had intended leaving school as soon as he could. One of the things he contemplated doing was going into the fire service or becoming a paramedic, and he had taken a first aid course to improve his chances. For some reason, that he could not quite explain, instinct took over and he shouted, "You've got to stop that bleeding and quickly. Somebody give me a long sock!" Whether it was the tone of voice or some other reason, the officer backed him up yelling to the rest of them, "You heard the boy. A sock!" The crofter's wife was there with one of her husband's socks before the others had quite taken in what was happening. Jack was examining the arm and the leg.

"Both socks, and a towel!" he ordered, as he began tying the first around the man's thigh above the break. He suspected that there was little hope of repairing the leg that was smashed in several places. He tightened the tourniquet and the blood stopped gushing.

The arm was more difficult. It would have to be direct pressure decided Jack and he folded the towel into a large pad and bound it to the wound. Then he began to examine the rest of the man's body. He was quite unconscious. His side was also damaged, and then Jack spotted the blood on the man's head. Jack said in a calm voice, "I think he's bleeding inside as well, and his skull is probably broken. The only chance this man has is to get him to a hospital straight away."

"The only hospital is three hours that way and the government troops are fleeing up that road right now," returned the officer. "Are you a doctor?"

"No," said Jack, "I'm a writer. I'm doing a piece for the magazine I work for on what it's like living in a war-zone."

"Where did you say you were from?"

"I didn't," said Jack. "It's a country a long way from here. I live in a town called Persham."

"Never heard of it."

"No. Very few of my people from there have ever been here. That's why I have come."

"Don't you have wars in your own country?" asked the officer.

"None recently," replied Jack. "There was a big war that finished more than sixty years ago, but it was before I was born. The only civil war we've had was more than three and a half centuries ago."

"So you have come here to find out what it's like?"

"A bit like that," said Jack.

"So, where did you learn how to treat patients?"

"A first-aid course. I wanted to be an ambulance man once – before I became a writer."

Jack checked the injured soldier's pulse. It was very weak, and Jack didn't like the look of his eyes. He was deeply unconscious. Jack asked what had happened.

"A bloody mine," stated the officer. "Didn't you hear it? He was trying to get his truck round our lead truck that broke down in the middle of the road."

"Anyone else hurt?" inquired the crofter.

"Three dead! Too many pieces… So you'll have plenty to write about today. How do I know you're not a spy?"

"I'm afraid it's four dead now," sighed Jack. "He lost too much blood." He stood back and allowed the officer and the other soldiers to examine the body. "Sorry I couldn't save him."

"Well you did what you could. Which was more than this riff-raff (indicating the men in rebel uniform). When we leave here you're coming with us."

"But, I… I have a story to write."

"You'll get a much better story if you ride with us. We can do with your medical knowledge, and there are two ways of dealing with spies, take them with you so they can't report, or shoot them."

"But I'm not a spy," protested Jack.

"Perhaps not. That's why you're not being shot."

Mrs. Somaf spoke up, "This young man is our guest!" She could not just let him be taken, like her sons were. Hadn't the officer got a heart?

"I've got a heart," he replied. "That's why I'm going to look after this boy." He turned to the other soldiers, "OK, get this body out of here. We'll bury him. 'Grandpa' you tell them where. I don't want any more mines going off.

"Who else have you got here?" he demanded of the crofter's wife. "These your only children? You're old enough to have bigger ones."

"I have. Two sons that have enlisted in your army," she complained.

"Enlisted have they? Volunteers?"

"No," she bit her lip. "They're only fifteen and thirteen."

"Huh. If you want my view," said the officer candidly, "for what it's worth. I don't hold with that. They don't make good soldiers. Can kill themselves with their own weapons, and spend too much time crying to go home. What are their names?"

"Hak and Vic Somaf."

"I'll look out for them."

"Thank you," said the woman with genuine gratitude.

"OK, don't get sentimental. Doesn't do in war. Where

141

does this door lead?" The officer unlatched the back door. "Ah, the khazi," he said as he spotted the toilet shed, "I could do with a decent crap. You," he turned to Jack, "what's your name?"

"Jack Smith."

"Get outside and help with the burying, Jack Smiss. And write down the names of the dead for me. Then take note of what happened in your book." With that he left through the back door. Jack looked at Mrs. Somaf with some panic.

"Just do as he says," she urged. "It's your only chance. The girls will be safe, they'll be sensible," she whispered. Jack went out the front door and saw a large truck on its side in the ditch. The bodies had been lined up on the road. Some of them not complete. Jack felt sick. Mr. Somaf was directing operations on the other side of the road from the cottage.

In truth he could not be certain there were no mines there, but he was not going to let them dig beside his house in his vegetable plot, or near the girls.

Meanwhile Bonny, Jalli and Tilly held their breath as the officer tugged open the door to the toilet. "Bloody dark in here," he mused as he positioned himself over the hole not more than half a metre from where Tilly was crouched behind the panel. The girls were treated to a few "rear" noises followed by some sighs of contentment from the relieved soldier. "Bloody war!" he muttered. "My own khazi's a sight better than this one, and here I am in the middle of bloody nowhere fighting for God knows what. I wonder what food they have stored here?" he breathed as he fastened his trousers. "Strange that it's all boys. Bet she thought she was lucky until she realised that male children make good cannon fodder. Still, better than girls!" The door of the toilet slammed shut.

Bonny began to cry. Jalli put her arm around her. She could just make out Tilly signalling to remain still. They would have to remain in the hole until Mum or Dad came and told them the coast was clear. At first the bunker had been very cold. Jalli was still dressed in her pyjamas with just a coat on top. But now they were beginning to feel quite hot, and the air was bad. The officer's contribution hadn't helped, and the pipe was not very wide. They took it in turn to put their heads under it and draw in fresh cold air. After ten minutes it went all quiet again but the soldiers clearly hadn't left. Tilly passed round the bottle of water. She whispered, "I hope they don't all come!" They could still hear voices on the other side of the house and the vehicles were all stationary.

Two hours later the driver from the first vehicle announced his vehicle should be able to continue. The broken spring had been replaced. The bodies were laid in the grave and the soldiers were formed up. The officer recited a prayer, which may or may not have been appropriate. Three soldiers were ordered to fire a volley into the air. And the graves were quickly filled in. The officer barked an order and the convoy got back under way, with Jack seated in the back of the lead vehicle, his backpack between his knees.

The silence after the men and vehicles had moved off was almost deafening. Then Jalli could hear the life slowly coming back into the countryside. The insects and the birds, that had taken shelter from the cacophony of humanity, gradually came back into song. It is amazing, reflected Jalli, just how much most people miss of the life of the countryside by simply never stopping to listen.

Jalli also reflected on the terrible ability of humanity to destroy – including other humans.

She wondered just what people who made the bullets, bombs and landmines felt about their work. She could understand how people wanted to resist oppression, and seek to defend themselves and their "tribe" from ignominy. But what was it that got into the hearts of men that made it necessary for the family of her two new friends to plan and construct a hiding place like she found herself in now? She knew it was no better in Wanulka than here, and Jack had known immediately what was meant by a landmine, so Earth was no different. This same species was capable of such selfless giving as this family who were treating her as one of them, feeding them when they hadn't enough for even themselves, and risking their own security in taking them in. What a weird race we are! mused Jalli.

She wondered what had transpired in the house. Fifteen minutes after the noise of the soldiers had faded away Mrs. Somaf came into the toilet shed. "Girls," she said. "You alright?"

"We're stuffy but fine," said Tilly.

"OK." The crofter's wife bent down and removed the panel. "Stay inside for a few more minutes until we're sure no-one's coming back over the ridge." It was great to have a blast of fresh air. And the girls felt free to talk.

"I really am sorry to have to squeeze in with you and make it so much more uncomfortable," said Jalli.

"That's OK," said Bonny, "we always hold onto one another, and last time it was so cold, but having you this time warmed it up nicely." Jalli had had her arm around her much of the time.

"It must be dreadful living like this with soldiers coming by, and mines, and not being able to grow food," observed Jalli.

"Or go to school," added Bonny. "Tilly has had years more lessons than me."

"And I have had twelve uninterrupted years that I have just taken for granted," said Jalli. "Some people hate going to school where I come from because they don't like working."

"That was never the case here," said Tilly. "We can see the advantage of education so clearly. When (or if) this war finishes people could still be going to school well into their twenties."

Mod came into the shed. "You can all go back into the house now Dad says. And be quick, I want a wee, and they wouldn't let me come until you could come out!" The three girls did not need a second invitation.

When Jalli got back to the croft she immediately looked for Jack to see if he was alright and to ask him what had happened. It was a horrid shock to find he had been taken away. For a few minutes she was very quiet and lost. She was frightened for him, and she missed him. Here she was now, without him in this very strange land. It had been easy to be brave with Jack. The pain of his absence was so acute that it was hard to understand. For the first time she could begin to feel what it must have felt like for Mrs. Somaf to have been parted from her sons – only, she quickly told herself, it must have been worse because Jack was not thirteen.

"Is he their prisoner? Or do they expect him to fight for them like your sons?" she asked anxiously.

"No, it appears he's a handy first-aider, and they don't trust he's not a spy," replied the crofter.

"We're so sorry," sighed Mrs. Somaf. "You are our guests and we feel bad about it, but there was just nothing we could do."

"No," assured Jalli, "I know you have absolutely no choice here. Things happen to you beyond your control. It's just that it is something we're not really used to, Jack and I. But we didn't have to come here. Look, I don't want to be in your way. I can go home."

"How can you do that on your own? Nobody, especially not a lone girl, should go around on their own here. And besides how can you leave without your boyfriend? He clearly means the world to you!" said the mother.

"He does, and thank you… Jack was going to help with the planting today if the weather was good. I can do that."

"You could if we still had the seed tubers to plant," responded the crofter. "But they've gone. As have three-quarters of the chickens, the calf we were hoping to fatten this summer, and the last of our cheeses! And it looks as if your boots are missing too, lass."

Where Jalli's boots had been by the door there was now nothing more than a damp patch.

"They didn't get the cheese!" said his wife. "It's been in the loft for the past week with the rest of the flour. I thought it was safer there!"

"Clever girl!" exclaimed the crofter. "You're a bright woman!"

"Of course," she replied.

Jalli wanted to get dressed. She looked towards her bed.

The bed and floor were covered in large clots of blood. It was horrible. They told her the soldier had died there. Jalli stood in silence. She wondered if he had a wife or girlfriend who was waiting for him to return. She went cold at the thought that the same could happen to her Jack. "Why do people do this to each other?" she cried.

"Come on, let me clean up!" declared Tilly. Jalli moved to help her. "No. Not you, you've had too much to cope with already. Sit up the other end with the children." Jalli did as she was bid, aware of the quiet children for the first time since she had come back into the croft. They took her into their arms, and in that tragic hour, she became like a sister to them. She gave comfort to them and they comforted her. Tilly and her mother took the pelt outside. Then they went under the beds to get the stuff out before they began swilling the floor.

"Look at this! Your Jack's a marvel!" declared Mrs. Somaf. "He's stashed both your boots and our seed corms under his bed! You know, he showed such authority in taking charge of the dying man. He got us all organised. I reckon he can look after himself, *and* everybody else!" Jalli was proud of him. Tears flowed down her cheeks. He had only been her friend for a short time, but he was so good.

"Great," she said. "I know he can. And he's given me no choice but to help get the corms planted out – whatever the weather!"

"You don't have to," intervened the crofter.

"Oh yes, I do," said Jalli with determination. "I am beginning to understand about choice. If you want to be the kind of person that the Creator can rejoice in, you have to make the right kind of choices. If you want the universe to be a better place, you have to choose what the Creator has chosen for you. And He has led me to meet Jack and brought me here to this wonderful family. Now, as soon as I'm dressed, tell me what to do and I'll get digging!"

Mrs. Somaf could see immediately that activity was going to be the best thing for Jalli. And her husband and the rest would benefit from it too. "Right. That's a good idea. But we all eat breakfast first. Pancakes. Tilly, wash your hands and get up to the loft for the flour and start cooking while I finish up here." Her directions were obeyed without question.

By mid-afternoon all the tubers were planted.

Meanwhile, Jack had quickly taken stock of the situation he found himself in. Most of the men were not there out of any conviction. It wasn't that they believed they wanted to stay under the yoke of the westerners – but they clearly all thought the price was too high.

What was keeping them going now was that they appeared to be winning. There had been a coup in the rich country that had kept the oppressive government in arms and money for the war. The enemy could no longer keep their planes in the air and there were no longer any spares for the most sophisticated weapons.

Jack's company had made good progress up the road, passing evidence that the enemy had quickly withdrawn. The sound of gunfire that had been up ahead had ceased some time ago. Rounding a bend the convoy encountered a number of enemy troops with their hands aloft waving white handkerchiefs! The leading vehicle screeched to a halt.

"The war. It is over!" shouted an enemy officer. "Do not shoot! The government has been overthrown!"

"Wait here!" commanded the officer in charge of the rebel force. He took two men and approached. After a while all the enemy soldiers, clearly unarmed, sat on the road under the direction of the two men. The rebel officer returned. "It appears," he announced, "that the government army has overthrown the president and has joined us! At any rate these soldiers here are not offering any resistance."

Just at that moment a dispatch rider on a motorbike came up to the convoy from behind. He delivered a letter to the officer. "This confirms it, men," he shouted, "the war is officially over!"

This was met with cries of delight from the men. "Does this mean we can go home?" asked one.

"Not yet. We have to return to barracks immediately."

As they were turning the trucks, the officer noticed Jack still sitting in the back of the lead truck with his backpack between his knees. "You can go!" he barked.

"No!" said Jack. "You have left that crofting family without food, and without their children. You might be going home as victors, but what about them?"

"You are a feisty character aren't you? Get off with you!"

"If you want me to report on the use of child soldiers in your war, or the way you just kidnap or abandon reporters at your whim, then dump me here. But I don't think your leaders will thank you for it. I would guess that now that the military war is over they will be turning their attention to being seen as nice people! Do you want me to report that?"

"You're young for a reporter!"

"But not for a soldier, it seems! Look, if you see that the crofter and his family are compensated for their contributions of food, and…" Jack stopped the officer from butting in, "their two boys are returned to them unharmed, I will report favourably on your regime, and commend you in particular."

"You know I don't approve of children as soldiers."

"Exactly. Help me find these boys and I will see that you are favourably reported."

"So, you tell me, how am I to do that?"

"Take me with you. Tell your people that I am looking to write an article on the caring they have for children and families disturbed during the conflict, and that if they could find just these two it would give me the anecdotes I need to give the report with that human touch our readers enjoy. I could be a good propaganda tool.

"… and, in the meantime, send one of your vehicles back with the food the croft supplied you with. And take a message to Jalli that I will be back by and by."

"Jalli? Who's Jalli?"

"Oh, sorry… I mean Mr. Somaf, the crofter." Jack was glad he wasn't connected to a lie-detector! But fortunately, the officer didn't seem to react to his gaff.

"How long have you known this family?"

"Not very long. Long enough to know Mr. Somaf's family nickname."

"OK. What are you going to write about child soldiers?"

"Nothing. If the Somaf boys are returned unharmed within the next two weeks."

"And you'll report me favourably?"

"You are an efficient, caring officer with a compassion for his men, and the people. A man who helped find two missing boys. I shall tell them the truth."

"It's a good job I like you!" grinned the officer. He turned and barked over his shoulder, "Sergeant!"

"Yes, sir."

"Take the third truck with your platoon back to the fork from which we have come to return the beef and chickens the croft supplied us with – we have no need of them now, and we, the victorious force, is a compassionate one! And tell them the reporter is going to travel on with us and will be back within two weeks. And... for God's sake, keep off those bloody verges. We don't want any more mine casualties."

"Yes, sir!"

"And then join us at the barracks... Well what are you waiting for?"

"Sir!" The sergeant bustled away, organised the loading of the third truck with stuff they had taken from the croft, and directed the driver back down the way they had come. The officer ordered the enemy soldiers to get in the back of the lead truck with Jack. It was tight getting everyone in but, he announced, weren't they compassionate victors!

12

Before it was dark they were driving into a compound containing the soldiers' barracks in an eastern town of Tolfanland. Jack was put up in the officers' quarters and enjoyed a good meal and a shower. After breakfast the following morning he was taken to the commanding officer and interviewed. He had noted that they had intended to treat him well and were using him, as he had intended, to be an agent of their propaganda. He assured them that he would report their kindness, and he meant it – but exactly how and where, he hadn't a clue. Although he was clearly young, the authoritative way in which he spoke earned him the respect he needed, whilst his obvious ignorance of the whole situation made him unlikely to be any kind of spy. He amazed himself. It seemed that, given a mission, he was as adept as anyone. The fact that he was not known here seemed to give him added power. He knew that he couldn't have done what he was doing here in Persham. (Wasn't it a problem even Jesus had had? A prophet is not honoured in his own land etc.) The Owner of the white gates seemed to know more of what Jack was capable of than he himself, or anyone else for that matter.

The commanding officer had been informed that he was on the Somafs' case. He was assured that these boys would have been taken care of for their own protection as the croft had been in the front-line. (The "front-line bit" was clearly true – the mines were evidence of that. Jack was assured they were not laid by the rebels. Maybe true. Yet it would have surprised him if stuff hadn't been laid by both sides in all sorts of places. The sad thing was that if the war was truly over for the present, these mines would probably still be claiming victims for years to come.) Jack expressed his gratitude and said all the right things about the way his investigation had been facilitated by the "very caring officer" whom he had first met, and he looked forward to being acquainted with the boys.

In the meantime Jack was put into the care of a young officer, a lieutenant, who was clearly charged with saying all the right things, and Jack dutifully made notes on his pad as he was shown round the less sensitive parts of the barracks. Then it was lunchtime. The officers did not seem to lack food. In the afternoon Jack asked if he could go out into the town. He was granted permission so long as he was accompanied by the lieutenant.

Jack was shocked by what he saw. The people were clearly doing their best with worn out clothes. There were long queues at the few market stalls that still had food to sell.

"It's the war," explained the young officer, "difficult to get things. If you've got money though you can generally manage – and the army has to be fed first. We also generally get paid in the army, which is not the case for most people even if they have jobs."

"Is this going to change now the war is over?" asked Jack.

"Hope so," ventured the soldier. "There are so many of us in the army though, peace means it won't be good news for some."

"What will you do if you leave the army?"

"I hope it won't come to that. Some people want to leave, but I don't."

The officer indicated a bar and they settled into a couple of chairs outside. "What'll you drink?" asked the young officer.

"I don't know," replied Jack. "I've not been out drinking stuff at home. I've kept myself to myself really."

"Have a beer!" He went into the bar and came back with two large frothing glasses.

Jack smelled it, and had a sudden shock. He couldn't understand it, but the smell of that beer frightened him. It resonated with something in the past – a long time ago. He felt anxious, and pictures of his mother distressed and angry seemed to emanate from the back of his mind. Could these long forgotten memories have something to do with his father? Could it be that beer and his father were strongly associated? This frightened him.

"You alright?" the officer was looking at him in a puzzled way.

"Oh… fine! Just remembered something from a long time ago." Jack was contemplating what he was going to do with the beer when he became aware of a touch on his elbow. He turned and there was a child, silently begging for food. Then there was another....

"Don't give them anything!" ordered the soldier gently. And turning toward the children, "Get on! Be off with you!" They persisted with Jack, but ran off when the officer got to his feet. "These street children can be a menace!"

"Street children?"

"Yes, kids that don't have homes."

"Where are their parents then?"

"Abandoned them mostly. Too many mouths to feed. Many of them never had fathers in any case."

"Why, what happened to them, the fathers? Killed in the war?"

"Some of them. Mostly just not interested. You're rather ignorant for a reporter, aren't you? Soldiers on leave get sex wherever they can and then have no idea they have left a woman pregnant. Mostly they don't even know the girl's name. Isn't it like that where you come from?"

"We have not had a war in my country for generations. And orphaned kids are taken care of by the local authorities."

"You must have a very rich country."

"I suppose we have. I hadn't really thought about it. Mostly I, and the kids I went to school with, thought of ourselves as poor because we didn't live in the big houses on the other side of town. I didn't have a father around, but we were never hungry, and my mum always saw I had clean clothes to wear."

"Half the kids here don't go to school at all."

"Now that the war seems to be over, you will be able to put your money into schools instead of weapons?"

"Perhaps. But we don't have enough teachers anyway. It's going to take a long time."

Jack had to acknowledge to himself that he had always felt deprived, but he would always be grateful he was born in Britain after this.

"I had to leave at the end of primary school," continued the young soldier, "not enough money."

"But don't you feel deprived?"

"Mostly not. I've done alright for the past year in the army."

Just then they were joined by three rather daringly dressed young women, no older than Jack. They approached the officer and one walked straight up to him and put her arm around his neck. "Who's your handsome friend?" she asked, looking at Jack.

"A reporter from some foreign land where they all go to school rather than war," he replied.

Before he knew what was happening to him, one of the others had her arm around Jack and squeezed herself against him. "You're nice!" she declared. Jack had been full of authority in the barracks. He now felt completely overwhelmed. Girls had always thought of him as being rather dull in Persham. Here these perfect strangers were making it quite clear they were very interested in him.

Jack struggled to his feet. "I think I have to be getting back now," he said to the soldier. "I have a lot of writing to do!"

The young officer sighed. "Sorry ladies," he said, giving the first girl a kiss on the cheek. "Next time perhaps, Loops." The girls looked quite upset.

"Won't you tell us about your foreign land?" one asked. "We can have a lot of fun. Don't you have fun in your country? It must be a very dull place. The girls there must be totally bored!"

"It's just… that I have work to do!" blurted Jack, amazed at how he could lie when he didn't really need to. But somehow he just felt he didn't want to offend them. He was frightened. He just wanted to run. As they left the bar, Jack was very relieved to leave both this pack of pawing girls and his untouched beer!

"They're OK, they're clean," stated the soldier. And then, "I bet you've never had a girl, have you?"

"No, not like that."

"You should. They don't ask for much. And the money you give them makes them happy and helps them buy more clothes and eat regularly."

"But that's selling sex!"

"Yes, of course. But what's wrong with that if they want to sell, and men want to buy? Nobody's forcing them."

"But they wouldn't want to do that if they could make money otherwise," suggested Jack. He knew Jalli or his mum would rather starve than do that. He shuddered at the thought. He wouldn't want that – it had to hurt a person to sell sex.

"Maybe not. But who knows. That's the way many girls live around here. It's part of life. Many of them are grateful that they can earn good money whilst 'having fun'."

"But there's no future in it," said Jack.

"Who knows what the future holds. We all live for today here. That's what war does to you."

Jack saw acutely the stark difference between sex for its own sake, and sex in a committed loving relationship that presumed a future. These young people had never known anything like the wonder he had experienced in that first kiss with Jalli. Oh, how he missed her! He wondered how long it would take to find these boys. He hoped not very long… but he was determined to see it through.

That night he thought about those street children who

never had mothers or fathers, and the girls of his age selling themselves for a night of "fun". He had always taken Matilda for granted. She wasn't a happy woman, and there had not been much laughter in their house, but she loved him and had always been there for him. He began wondering where his father was. As a child, he had often imagined him living somewhere, but he had never thought it possible to try and find him. After all these adventures, he might have enough courage to look for him. He shivered. But this place was not as daunting as he would have thought had he been told all that he was going to do in advance. When you're actually doing it, he reflected, it is not as bad as it might seem when just thinking about something. How many things had he never done because he was too scared to start? Loads. Perhaps if God (if that was the right name to use) wanted him to look for his father it might all work out. Of course, he had grown up hating him, but mostly for not being there. And what was all that about the smell of beer? Could he have been a drunk?

That had never occurred to Jack before. He made up his mind that when he got back he would start looking. Perhaps Jalli would come with him. That would be nice. And it was with the sweet thought of Jalli that Jack drifted off to sleep.

Two days later, Jack was called to the commanding officer's office.

"We have your two boys," he declared.

"They're both in one piece?" asked Jack.

"Fine as can be."

"When can I take them back home?"

"Tomorrow morning. But I will need their father to sign

for them. My lieutenant will accompany you to the croft and supervise the handing over. The letter will declare that they volunteered to serve and lied about their age. And I want a copy of the report you will be making to your editor."

"Of course. I will bring it to your office before the end of the day." Jack had been anticipating this and felt they would be pleased with his efforts. He wrote about the helpful way he had been treated. He simply left out anything that he knew would not please them. He entitled the report, "Speedy Efforts to Bring Compassion into War-torn Land". A bit long winded, he thought, but he wasn't writing it for a magazine readership, but to facilitate the return of the boys.

The following morning he was introduced to two confused-looking young men who were not quite sure what was going to happen to them. They were not aware of anyone else being sent home from their regiment. They were simply summoned to the HQ and told that they were going home with a foreign journalist who wanted a story. They were told, under threat of arrest and other dire consequences, that they were to say nothing of their time in "the service". In particular, they were to tell the foreigner that they were volunteers who had lied about their ages, as their papers said. Of course they merely accepted that they should do all that they were ordered to. But were they really going home? Jack was not like anyone they had ever met before. But he seemed to really want to help and genuinely appeared to know about their home.

They were all to travel in an army vehicle with a driver and the young officer who had been assigned to Jack. They left the barracks and drove through the town. In the main street with the bar the lieutenant ordered the driver to stop.

Waiting for them was the young girl, Loops, who had approached the soldier in the bar three nights earlier. She was not dressed up but looked attractively ordinary, thought Jack. To his surprise she climbed into the back, her belongings lifted in after her. "I'm taking her home," declared the officer from the cab. "She would rather go back to school than have a whole week of nights of fun with me! Keep off the drink," he warned Jack, "you might promise things you later regret!"

It transpired that after he had had a few the soldier had asked her what she really wanted and promised that, if he could afford it, she should have it. He was thinking of clothes or bling. Instead she had asked for a recommendation and reference to rejoin school from the commanding officer in the garrison. With such a document she would get priority back in her village. It would also guarantee her reputation at home. She was ambitious, he explained, she had also wanted her school fees for a year, and money for a uniform! But somehow it made him feel good to give her the things she needed to get back to school. He had left her feeling happy and for some reason he now felt more fulfilled than any "night of fun" had done. He had bribed the commanding officer's secretary to produce a standard copy of the recommendation in her name. She had simply put it with the others and the CO had signed it. He was pleased to see her there waiting – it had occurred to him that she might have been too drunk to know what she was saying and, today, might have forgotten – or think better of it.

"Thought you might have changed your mind," he said as she got in.

"No chance!" she declared. "I thought you might." The

lieutenant feigned disbelief. "Got the letter?" He handed her the official letter in an imposing looking envelope. "Thanks."

Jack spent the journey listening to her story. She had been tempted by what seemed a short-cut, an easy way to combat the grind that she had witnessed among her family. In fact she still only half regretted it. Was she not better off than her sisters who had stayed at home labouring? She had told them she had been working for the army. Now she wanted education – she had seen the difference it made. So long as people didn't think ill of her, she reckoned she had done about the right thing. Jack asked whether she loved the young soldier.

"Of course not!" she exclaimed. "But he has been kind to me. He has not treated me badly like some of them!"

Jack wished her well. Education had worked for him – and Jalli, he explained, but he had always taken it for granted. (In some ways, he reflected, in Britain he hadn't been living in the real world but a kind of cocoon that shielded him from reality. The white gate into this place had helped him see that.)

"Jalli? Is she your sister?"

"My girlfriend."

"What's she like?"

"She's the nicest person you could ever hope to meet."

"Clever?"

"Yes. She's good at biology."

"Bi – what?"

"Biology. Animals and plants. She especially likes insects."

"That's weird!"

"She finds them really interesting."

"She teaches you things?"

"All the time. Not just about insects and school things either. She's got good ideas. And she can just talk to God like he's there beside her all the time."

"That sounds creepy."

"No. It isn't. It could be, I suppose, but not how she does it, kind of naturally. Like she talks to anyone. God is a sort of friend to her."

"So does God look after her?"

"She says that knowing God is with you doesn't stop things happening to you, but He helps you through. Apart from her and her grandmother, when she was only three, all her family were drowned when a dam burst."

"And she still talks to God!"

"Well, He didn't exactly make the dam burst."

"If God were God he could have stopped it."

"Jalli says that that is not the way God works. He doesn't always intervene to stop bad things happening, but He helps people when things happen to them. And Jalli believes in heaven of course."

"Heaven!"

"Yes, the place you go to when you die."

"I know what heaven is. Some of the older people have stopped believing in it here. They blame God for this war."

"What about you?"

"I don't know. I don't believe in the old priests. They're a waste of space. They go on about the war being a punishment for being bad. I don't believe that. The war is because some people want to be in charge, and some people just like fighting. Take my soldier here, he likes his job. He would hate it not being in uniform carrying a gun. But he's not a bad sort.

He hasn't got anything to do with God punishing people or anything." Jack agreed. If anything the young lieutenant was being an agent for good – restoring two lads to their parents, and this girl to her place to get back into school.

"Perhaps God is still helping people despite the war? It's just that we don't recognise Him," ventured Jack.

"You mean He might be working through my soldier?"

"Well, yes, I suppose so. He certainly works through Jalli, and her grandma, and…" (it struck him for the first time) "through my mum too – only she would not say so. I guess He can work through anyone."

"Is He working through you?" The question made Jack think.

"A month ago I would have laughed at that idea, but not now. In a way I suppose He is. Jalli would say so. But I don't think about it most of the time."

"Would He work through me?"

"He probably already is, by getting you to ask all these questions about Him, and me!"

"Sorry."

"No. I mean it. I reckon God could do all sorts of things through you."

"But, I'm not a good person."

"I don't think that matters – so long as you keep wanting to be better. He keeps showing you that there is so much more to you than you would ever guess. Since I've been here I've learned so much about myself. I never reckoned myself as good."

"But you are. You're different. My friends – well those girls you met the other night. They thought so too. They respected you for leaving. They knew you had a good heart… How do you speak to God?"

"Jalli just talks to Him, like He is here beside her. She just talks to Him like you're talking to me."

"Perhaps I'll try it one day. When it doesn't seem so weird! Where is your Jalli?"

"Can I trust you with a secret? I don't want to lie to you. She's waiting at these lads' croft for me. The soldiers don't know she's in the country."

"So I can meet her! I'd love to meet her. Can I go with you?"

"But aren't you on your way home?"

"I'm going with you. He can drop me off on the way back. Hey, soldier," she shouted into the front. "Go straight to the croft and call into my village on the way back!"

"OK. You having 'fun' with our foreign journalist?"

"Sex! That's all you can think about isn't it?"

"Only when I'm with you, darling!"

Loops just shrugged her shoulders. "Soldiers!" she sighed.

It was the middle of the afternoon before they approached the croft. The boys had grown less agitated and more excited as the day went on. At first they hadn't known whether to believe Jack or not. Now it became clear they were really going home. Jack wondered whether the family would find them much changed.

Their arrival was unheralded. The approach of an army vehicle had been watched with apprehension and when it stopped the girls were packed off out the back door. They hadn't got properly into the bunker though before Mod came running up. "It's OK. It's your Jack! And he's got your brothers!" The girls dashed back down the garden path.

"Jack! Jack!" shouted Jalli. They ran into each other's

arms. The boys were being hugged and kissed. The young lieutenant, Loops and the driver just stood and stared.

"You see why I wanted to come," proclaimed Loops with tears running down her cheeks, "I got an idea that it would be like this. These people know how to love!"

"Seems so. Bit mushy I'd say," observed the lieutenant.

"It's real though, isn't it?" breathed Loops, "I wonder whether I could ever love like that? I want to meet that girl, Jalli. She seems a marvel. I can see now why Jack wanted to escape us girls the other night. What we did was wrong."

"You never thought that before."

"I mean, what we did in trying to get him."

"What's different about him that he should get special treatment?"

"This!" she indicated the family that were now all clustering round Jack and singing his praises, "All this genuine delight these people are taking in one another."

Mr. Somaf came across to the three of them. "Do excuse us," he said. "We're not looking after you properly. Come in! Come in! Take tea!" And the two soldiers and the girl were drawn in as friends too. After an hour, Mrs. Somaf declared, "It's too late to go back to the town tonight. You must all stay the night."

"But there's hardly room for us all here," replied the officer.

"Nonsense!" This was Mrs. Somaf. "We have floor space enough for everyone. It's not as cold now and we have spare pelts in the loft." There was no argument to be made, and they accepted the invitation with gratitude. Loops had sat herself beside Jalli and spent hours talking about everything.

She was interested in finding out whether Jalli genuinely believed God was real. Jalli had to admit that she had just "grown up with Him."

And she also had to admit that in her grandma she had had a much better start in life than Loops had had. But perhaps because of that, God could do things with Loops that He could not do through herself, suggested Jalli.

Bedtime was quite interesting with the two youngest lying on the floor between the beds, Tilly, Loops and Jalli all squashed in together, with Jack in the bed next to them. Jalli was overjoyed to have Jack back near her. And she was so proud of him. "How did you manage to do all that?" she whispered.

"No idea. You must have been praying for me."

"I was."

"And I was praying for you too. In my way."

"I know. Thanks… Jack? I love you! I missed you so much," she whispered.

"Thanks. And I missed you. And I love you too." He reached out to take her hand.

They all rose with the daylight. It was amazing how much breakfast there seemed to be. "Mrs. Somaf, you're a marvel," rejoiced Jack.

"Well we've got enough food for the time being. We'll soon have to send these two out hunting."

"And it's time for the wild strawberries," added Bonny. "I'm good at collecting them."

"But you must all take a lot of care," said the driver. "There are mines about."

"Quite right," agreed the crofter. "You hear that, you youngsters?"

Soon the soldiers and Loops were ready to set off for Loops' village. "Thanks," she said earnestly to Jack, taking his hand. "You've done something for me."

"What have I done for you?" queried Jack. "I haven't done anything."

"You treated me like a respectable person... and you talked to me about things that last. And thanks for introducing me to Jalli. I'll not forget you... Will you be coming back?"

"I don't know. Maybe."

"Well, if you do, look me up." And she wrote down her address and gave it to Jalli. Then kissed her on the cheek.

"I hope you get a good teacher, Loops. I know you will work hard," encouraged her new friend.

"Talk to God for me."

"I certainly will," assured Jalli.

When the soldiers and Loops had finally left, the Somafs were all over Jack. The day they had got their food back they couldn't believe it. Especially when they had heard the story of how Jack had refused to leave the convoy. And now here he was, back with the two boys. It was clearly going to take some time for them to get over the experiences they had been through.

Jack said that the people he had met were not that bad. Clearly in wartime people just did things they would never dream of doing any other time. Jalli promised to pray that the peace would hold, and that the people of Tolfanland would be left alone to sort out their own differences without outside interference from international pressure groups.

After lunch, Jack and Jalli felt it was time to leave. They helped put things straight in the croft and, having reluctantly accepted things for the journey, they packed their backpacks and set off for the white gate. Mr. Somaf, Tilly and the youngsters went with them. They followed Jack's marks without any difficulty and had no trouble spotting the white gate in the hedge halfway up the hill. The Somaf's could see nothing of course.

"OK," said Jack finally, "this where we just disappear."

They took their leave once more. Tilly was crying, saying she would never forget Jalli. It had been really special having her with her during such a difficult time.

"Let's hope we can meet again," whispered Jalli, giving her a big hug.

Back on the lawn in front of the cottage, Jack threw off his backpack and lay full length under the sun. Jalli joined him.

"I could sleep for a week," declared Jack.

"Me too. Tell you what, though. In this garden, surrounded by the scent of the flowers, you stink! And I bet I do, too."

"No," returned Jack, "you just pong! Do you think we could use the showers in the cottage?"

"Why not?"

"I'd like to nip through to Persham and ring Mum first though."

"And I'll ring Grandma. But don't get lost! Don't be gone long. You know Jack, I really missed you!"

"And I you. There's only one Jalli in the whole wide universe – and the more we do together – the more we have shared, the more important you become… Look! The gate into Tolfanland. It has gone!"

Jalli breathed, "You know God, you did ask us to do the most amazing things. I hope we did them OK?"

"The Somaf family said some real nice things about you, Jalli."

"And they thought you were absolutely wonderful! And so do I!"

"The Owner of the challenging white gates does seem to know what He is doing. OK let's call our people and then come back and shower."

After half-an-hour, they were looking like the old Jack and Jalli again. "I've decided I'm going to look for my father," asserted Jack. "In Tolfanland I met kids without any fathers at all. At least I have one, somewhere. And I've decided I'm going to find him. Jalli, will you help me look?"

"I'll have to. Because I'm not letting you out of my sight again! When do we begin?"

"You are eager! We can meet here tomorrow, and you can come on down into Persham and we'll begin asking my mum. I think she might have some idea of where to look. But I'll need you to help me because I'm really scared of talking to Mum about my dad… and I haven't the faintest idea where to begin otherwise."

"You shouldn't go looking for him without your mum knowing."

"Exactly. But she won't like it."

"I think she may understand."

The exhausted couple kissed and, reluctantly, Jack saw Jalli into Wanulka and on to the bus. She was almost asleep before she reached home.

13

"Platform four for… the… 10.33 to… Newcastle," announced the p.a. system. Jack and Jalli pushed their way onto the crowded platform. Jalli had never travelled in England before, nor been on a train. Jack took pride in leading her onto the train and finding two seats together. He ushered Jalli into the window seat. The day was cold but fine. Coming from sunny climes Jalli had found the draughty platform especially cold, even with several layers of British clothing. They found themselves on a coach with an interesting assortment of people. Jack's attention was drawn towards a girl in a white mini-skirt and hot pink blouse with a low neck line despite the weather. She had knee high boots and large earrings beneath a shock of jet black hair that fell across one shoulder.

Jalli was glad that from where they were sitting Jack could only see the top of her head!

"Keep your eyes on me!" she laughed.

"Willingly!" said Jack. "But you can't help noticing someone like that."

"That's the idea!" stated Jalli, "Don't fall into the trap!"

"Too blatant. The skilful ones just capture your heart in more subtle ways."

"Exactly. By just being naturally impressive."

"Like you! I'm afraid I am totally captured."

"Good job. I wouldn't know what to do on this rail thing in a strange land."

"Train. We say 'railway train' in England. Well I feel great sitting with you. Let all the other guys look at me and be beside themselves with jealousy! Seriously I am so pleased you're helping find my dad. If you weren't here beside me I would be really scared. So scared I might not actually have got on this train."

"Are you very frightened of him?"

"Not so much frightened *of* him, but what he will *be like* when I find him. I don't know how I will feel when – if – I meet him. I can't even imagine what I'm going to say to him."

"Don't worry about that bit now. You can't decide that in advance. It doesn't work like that."

"How can you be so sure?"

"Well, like when I was trying to work out what I would say to you when we arranged to meet for the second time. I had it all worked out, but it did not go like I thought because you said something first, and then everything turned out quite different."

"And, in fact, what I said bore no relation to what I thought I might say."

"Right. And if you don't know what he's going to be like you have no idea what you might want to say."

"I might not want to tell him who I am."

"That's always a possibility. Anyway, what you have to do first is find him."

"And with a name like Smith that might prove quite hard."

"How come?"

"You know, you learn so fast that sometimes I forget you're

from a different world. You know so much, and then the things that everyone from England knows, you don't. Smith is probably the most common name in English. We got our names from our professions back in the Middle Ages. Then there were so many different sorts of smith – anyone who worked with any kind of metal really."

"So there might be quite a few Shaun Smiths."

"Yes. But I have the address he was last known to be at. That was ten years ago so he could have moved long since. If he has, someone might know where he went. When we get to Newcastle Central, we are to take the Metro to North Shields. We might have to stay overnight. I've never been to Newcastle before."

"This whole venture sounds expensive."

"Mum is paying. She wants to find out about him too. And with you here it kind of makes it possible, it makes it safe."

"How?"

"Well, she knows she won't lose me too because you will look after me. She thinks that you will keep me from harm. In a way she's right."

"I think I understand."

A succession of interesting people entered and left the train. Miss Hot Pink and White was replaced by a man with a white beard who spoke endlessly on his mobile so that everyone knew the names of all his family and the delicate health of his dog before they arrived at Newcastle.

"I never knew there were so many treatment options for pets," declared Jalli.

"You learn lots of things on trains," replied Jack, "most of it excruciatingly boring!"

After getting out at Newcastle Central, they were swept down the platform by people all of whom seemed to know where they were going. In this new environment it was Jalli who sussed where to go first. She spotted the large "M" sign of the metro. It was remarkably easy to follow and in no time they were rattling along in the direction of North Shields. Jack got out the address and asked someone on the train who looked as if he knew where he was going, where the place was.

"Yes, just go though the Beacon Centre to the Library and across Northumberland Square, turn left along Upper Norfolk Street and cross the Albion Road. It's not hard to find."

It wasn't. They were soon knocking on a door of a terraced house. They were pleased to find someone at home. A middle aged lady came to the door. She was simply dressed with an apron over a pair of blue jeans. She stared at this unlikely couple who were clearly not local.

"Well?" she ejaculated as Jack struggled to find the courage to ask her about his father.

"Excuse me," he stammered, "I… I am looking for a man called Shaun Smith. I believe he lived here once… recently."

"Are you, then?" the lady replied, "'e don't live here now – but a' believe 'e once did. Ma husband's away wi' the Magpies so we can't ask him. Why don't you try next door? They've lived here donkey's years."

"Thank you," said Jack, "we'll do that."

"They in't in till six o'clock. They're minding their daughter's bairns while she's shopping."

"We'll come back, thank you very much."

"I'll tell 'em you came," said the lady. They thanked her again and continued down the road.

"Well that looks hopeful," muttered Jack. "I would have been very surprised if we had found him first time."

"Magpies? Donkeys?" asked Jalli. "Didn't you call the big black and white birds in Wanulka magpies? And why donkeys?"

"Donkeys? Oh, 'donkey's years'. It means a long time! I don't know what it's got to do with donkeys… And quite right, magpies are birds. But here in Newcastle it is the local football team. They wear black and white. I hadn't thought of that. If they had been 'at home' the train would have been crowded with supporters all coming to Newcastle."

They walked back to the Beacon Centre and bought two lattes and doughnuts. Jack explained about the English football league system and how important it was for teams to be in the Premiership. As detail followed on detail he failed to notice Jalli's eyes begin to focus more and more on the shops and the people bustling in and out of the centre. He was just talking about Michael Owen and his stunning goal for England against the Argentinians in a World Cup match, and how he once played for Liverpool and…

"Michael who?" asked Jalli. "Did he know your father?"

"Very unlikely!"

"What about him then? How can he help?"

"He can't help. He's a footballer. And anyway he's not here – well, I don't think he is. Haven't you been following what I've been saying?"

"Honestly, no. Is this football stuff important?"

"Yes, of course! Well, no, not really. It's a game. But it's very popular all over the world, and we invented it here in England. We have one of the best leagues in the world.

Millions of people go to watch football matches every weekend. And even more millions watch them on the telly. Even in the middle of Africa and the Far East."

"But not that lady we met. And the people next door whose daughter had gone shopping."

"But they're women!"

"So football is a 'man' thing then?"

"Er… yes. Mostly. There are quite a few women though who…"

"I can understand that now. I couldn't imagine why people should get so passionate about the smallest details like a – what do you call it – a 'goal' in Michael."

"A goal scored by Michael Owen. But that is not a small… well, OK, it wasn't actually that important in the end I'll grant you. We still lost the match. The really big thing was in 1966 when…"

"You weren't born in 1966!"

"But we won the World Cup. The only time."

"I think I would like to do some shopping like that woman next-door. There are some interesting shops here. Can we go and look at some of them?"

"Well, if you like. There's nothing special about this place. Same as every other shopping centre."

"But I have never been to a shopping centre in your country."

"But we haven't any money to buy things with."

"No. Not *buy*! Just look."

Jack inwardly sighed. How much happier he would be watching football. He hadn't realised how much he had missed it – he didn't even know how his team were doing this season! He had been so caught up with Jalli and their adventures. It then occurred to him how much this girl had changed him, had changed everything. For her he would go round window shopping and he would not say a word of complaint. He never would have done that for anyone else. He reflected how cross he had been with his mother the last time she insisted they go shopping for clothes. Clothes he really needed. But then he knew his mum would go round looking at things she had no hope or thought of buying, and that annoyed him.

They wandered from shop to shop with Jalli asking questions, delighting in this or that display, asking about certain shops that looked especially unusual. She spent some time examining women's underwear while Jack did not know where to look or stand. If he stood too close to her, he thought, then it became excruciatingly embarrassing. (He was glad he was not anywhere where anyone was likely to recognise him!) If you stood too far away though, people might think you were on your own, and just hanging round the lingerie because of some odd fetish you might have! But Jalli was fascinated by the huge varieties of things people in England apparently wore underneath – something she had not seen on her travels before. She had lots of questions but it was quite obvious that Jack, not having a sister or anything, really had little idea. He explained that he was only interested in clothes when people were wearing them. They stayed in the centre until things began to close down and people were heading off home.

"We must go round to these neighbours just after six," said Jack, "in case they go out again or get into watching the telly

– and then we'll find somewhere to stay for the night and get some fish and chips."

They knocked on the door at about ten past six. An elderly lady, short and a bit dumpy (what Jack's mum would describe as "homely" looking) opened the door. But before Jack could utter a word she declared, "Well. I never! You're Shaun's kid, if I'm not mistaken. Next door told me to expect someone asking after him."

"I... I... I am looking for my father," responded Jack, "how do you know I am Shaun's son?"

"You're the spitting image of him! Well, don't keep standing there, come in."

Jack and Jalli followed her into the house and found themselves in a medium sized room that seemed to serve for everything except sleeping and washing. An old gentleman was sitting opposite a television with some quiz show on, but instead of watching it he was reading a newspaper.

"Tom! We've guests!" announced the woman. The man looked up from his paper and caught sight of Jalli, then Jack, and pulled himself to his feet. Quite clearly they were not used to strangers in their home, least of all imposing young people who dressed a "bit posh". (Jack was wearing smarter clothes to travel than he normally did about Persham.)

"Er... welcome," Tom spluttered. After he transferred his eyes from Jalli to Jack, he asked, "Don't I know you from somewhere?"

"Sit down, sit down!" insisted the lady of the house. She found them a settee from under a pile of newspapers and some knitting in progress. "Tom, put the kettle on. You'll have a cuppa tea, no doubt."

"Er… thank you," said Jack.

"Tom, put the kettle on. Milk and sugar?"

"Yes. thank you," said Jack again.

"Both on you?"

"Yes. Please," replied Jalli.

"Did you hear that?" the old lady shouted to her husband who was filling the kettle from a tap.

"Tea for two with milk and sugar. That right, Marge?"

"That's right!" and more quietly to Jack and Jalli, "He's a bit deaf these days, you know. Got that way in the works. Now then. You are Shaun's boy?"

"Well, yes. But I wouldn't know him if I saw him. He left home when I was two. I've been wondering about him all my life."

"What do you know about him?"

"Nothing much. Mum didn't like talking about him. There was another woman, but I think they had fallen out before that."

"So why do you want to find him now. Is everything alright at home?"

"Yes. Fine. It's just that… that I want to know what… I'm curious about him."

"Course you are! And this is your… girlfriend? You're foreign aren't you?"

"Yes," said Jack, "this is Jalli. I'm Jack. You seem to know a lot about people before they tell you anything."

"I've always been good at that. Now take your father. There was a lot of good in him underneath that many people didn't see."

"Where is he now?"

"He left here six years ago, but we got a Christmas card from him only last year so he's still in the same place, Leeds. Well he was then. So you're a bit too far north."

"So you have his address. Great."

"But you can't get there tonight. Where're you two staying?"

"I thought we might stay in the city, at a budget hotel near the Westmorland Road. We'll go there when we've finished the tea."

"Now, no need to do that if you don't have any objection to staying here? We have a spare room upstairs and if you don't mind sleeping in here," she addressed Jack, "you can make yourself comfy on the settee. The bird'll quieten down when I cover him." She indicated a bright yellow budgerigar who was competing quite successfully with the television and the conversation. "We don't see too many people. We'd enjoy having you."

Jack looked at Jalli who spoke up with assurance. "That would be very nice. But we would not want to make you work."

"No trouble, I'm sure."

"In that case we'll accept with many thanks."

"You two eaten?"

"No. We were going to look for a chip shop."

"Then we'll all have some. Chips tonight Tom?"

"'Bout time Marge. Chippy would go out'a business if it were to rely on us!"

"Let us buy for everyone," insisted Jalli. Marge made vociferous objections but soon realised she wasn't going to deflect Jalli when she had made up her mind. So Tom was dispatched to the chip shop while Marge talked about Jack's dad.

"He was a good man underneath. I can't say he didn't have his faults and I'm not surprised his Daphne left him. She had much to put up with at times. When he hadn't been drinking he was the kindest of men. But after he'd had a few he was a real tyrant. He became so argumentative. Aye, she put up with a lot at times. After she left, he used to come in here regular, and I used to feed him. He were terrible for looking after himself. I did all his washing – he 'adn't a clue. The truth was he were sick. He used to say that the drink had him. He wanted to stop, but he just didn't know how. He drank all his benefit. He finally met this women from Yorkshire. She was a funny sort who wasn't worth half of him. She kind a moved in. But it did'na last. It came out that, after Daphne left, no rent had been paid at all. Eventually landlord arrived with some official types and he had to leave. They went down to Leeds – to the woman's daughter. A place called Middleton it was called. Throstle something. Anyways we kept in touch with Christmas cards. He said ours was the only one he got, so we've kept it up these past four years. He didn't say much about his past but I gathered he had a son somewhere. He said he'd had to finish with all that – he wa'n't wanted. But a son always wants to know 'bout his father."

"I didn't know I did until recently. I just hated him for not being there."

"Well. Now you're looking. Jalli here changed your mind?"

"In a way. But it was understanding that I really wanted to know him all along. And now I feel I can begin to look. But it is frightening a bit, looking for someone that's so... so important."

"And so Jalli is 'holding your hand'."

Jack looked at Jalli who had not actually been holding his hand at that moment. "She means you're giving me the courage and standing beside me on my quest to find him."

"I am glad to do that," said Jalli looking at Jack.

Something raucous began happening on the TV. Marge lent across and turned it off.

"'Ad it on for the scores," she said, "shouln'a bothered. They lost again."

"The Magpies?" said Jalli.

"Yes. You learn quickly," replied the old lady warming to this imposing young lady more and more. "You're a real lady you are. Where do you hail from?"

"Wanulka. It isn't in England."

"No I guessed that. Bet it's a cut above this place. Are they all as good as you?"

"Thank you for the compliment. We have our problem people. Some people are selfish and mean and some people are sick" (her mind turned to Maik Musula). "But lots of people are very kind." Jalli hadn't thought of Wanulka as a particularly good place – but, now she thought about it many people were good. "But there are some very good people here in England too," she continued.

"Aye, there are. More than people give them credit for." Marge and Jalli were warming to each other more and more all the time. Tom returned with the fish and chips which they all enjoyed. These were good too. Newcastle had some good people, and good food.

The spare room was neat and tidy and kept especially for the unexpected guest. Jalli learned that they were the only unexpected guests Tom and Marge had had stay in thirty years!

It was as if the room was kept especially for her all that time. Jalli appreciated all this. Jack was amazed. He would never have thought about things like that, but he did his best to be equally attentive and volunteered to wash up the pots. He was instantly turned down and couldn't argue. He was beginning to realise that the world was full of confident women who ran the domestic affairs. Tom winked at him. "Let 'em have their way, lad. It's safer," he half joked. "I were the foreman at work – not here. Do you want to see out back?" He escorted Jack through a back door and here Tom was in his element. Next to the house was a row of dahlias all carefully staked and the garden was full of vegetables of all kinds in neat rows without a weed to be seen. At the bottom of the garden was a coop with pigeons of every hue. "A race 'em sometimes. In the summer. But mostly I just keep 'em and breed 'em," he explained. "You know your dad were interested in 'em. He said how it was great to see them wheel in the sky in a big flock and watch them all come back one at a time. He thought it was cruel to send them away many miles though just to race 'em back. But I think it is hardest on the owners, 'cause you gets anxious if one is late… Take my advice lad. You've got a good girl there. You look after her… and stay away from the beer. It don't do no-one any good. If you want company join the pigeon fanciers. We're a great crowd."

"Thanks," said Jack, "I'll do that. I've got an aversion to beer. It might be from when Dad was at home. But I can't remember."

"Well, he did you a favour lad. Good man at heart, Shaun. I hope you find him. Take him our love."

"I will," promised Jack.

14

Jack and Jalli slept better than they could have imagined in a strange house. Jack woke to a gentle knock on the sitting room door.

"You decent?" It was Tom. "Can I come in and make a pot of tea for me and the missus?"

"Of course," said Jack, "come in."

"We always wake at the same time every morning, even on a Sunday. We usually go to the chapel for ten o'clock, but don't worry, this morning we'll see you off from the station."

"No need to do that," responded Jack, driving sleep from his brain, "we'll see ourselves off. No hassle. No, you go to church – they'll miss you."

"No. Think no more about it. Would you like a cuppa tea?"

"Please."

After Tom left the room, Jack got dressed as quickly as he could and folded the sheets that Marge had given him. He washed in the sink, and then shaved – all the time keeping an ear open for the others. He was soon ready for company. He had just finished combing his hair neatly in the mirror over the fireplace, when the tousled head of Jalli appeared round the door. She was still half asleep. "How's Mr. Jack Smitt this morning?" she inquired.

"All the better for seeing you!" He pulled her into the

room and gave her a passionate kiss. As she came to, Jalli struggled free with:

"Jack! They might see us."

"But they are not here!" He made to kiss her again, but Jalli stepped back.

"No, listen Jack. They usually go to church on Sundays. I told Marge that we will go with them. Hope that's OK… The train to Leeds does not take long. Marge said about an hour and a half… OK, Jack?"

"We'll be strangers in their church. And in church they might ask lots of questions."

"So. We're in Newcastle for the weekend. You don't have to say any more than that. We'll ask Marge and Tom not to say anything about your dad. OK?"

"Well, OK if you want to… But I can't remember ever going to a church service, Jalli."

"Neither have I. Not in England. That's why I want to see what happens. You scared? The boy who can take on an army is scared to go to church?"

"No! Yes… well, no, not exactly scared. Uncomfortable. You never know what they're going to be like in a church. They judge you in a church. They might think I'm rather scruffy. You can't go to church in jeans, and I haven't got anything else."

"Of course ye can!" This was Tom coming through to start the breakfast. "All the young people in the church wear what you are wearing. Don't take any notice of us old 'ens. Chapel has changed since I was a lad. It isn't stiff and starchy like it used to be. Well, ours isn't. Ministers these days are quite different. Ours is quite 'trendy' I suppose you would call it. We like her."

"Her?" asked Jack rather surprised. He had not heard of a female minister before.

"Yes, Alice is her name. You are behind the times if you think they are all men. In fact women ministers are getting quite common these days. Unless you're Roman Catholic of course."

"Roman Catholic?" quizzed Jalli.

Jalli wanted to know about all the different churches. So over breakfast Marge gave a potted history of the Reformation.

"But we all get along together quite fine these days, at least around here. We call it 'Churches Together'. Our church is not in this area though. We still go back to where Marge and I grew up. We met in that chapel... we'll leave just after nine and catch the bus so if you're coming you'd better make sure you're ready."

"I'm all ready," replied Jack. Jalli gave him a playful scowl that turned into a smile and took off upstairs.

The chapel turned out to be quite an experience for them both. They sat with Tom and Marge and were introduced to their friends among the older members of the congregation who sat around them. There was, however, a group of about eight teenagers sitting together near the front who kept turning round to look at them. The service began with a hymn quite unlike Jack was expecting. They projected the words on a screen. It was quite a catchy tune that the young people obviously liked. "Be Not Afraid" it was called. The music came from a keyboard situated to one side and was amplified through a speaker system. There was an organ, or at least organ pipes, but it wasn't in use. Neither Jack, nor Jalli of course, knew any of the prayers either. Even the "Lord's Prayer" used contemporary words – all the "thys" and "thous" had gone.

The reading Jack did recognise. It was the one about a good Samaritan. (The one where muggers had left a man for dead. Some religious people walked by pretending not to notice but a traveller from an enemy tribe – the Good Samaritan – stopped and put him on his donkey and took him to an inn.) Jack wondered if Marge and Tom had acted like this and had looked after his dad because they found him washed up and in need.

The minister challenged the congregation to take risks to be good neighbours to strangers. Well, at least, thought Jack, this couple practise what this minister preaches. He wondered how risky it must be to be a minister in that city. As a child he was aware ministers experienced quite a bit of hostility. He knew some who despised priests and religious people because they were a "waste of space", or "always after your money", or "there to stop you having a good time" – and even because they reckoned they deemed themselves to be a cut above everyone else. But most of the ones Jack had come across as a teenager didn't seem that stuck up. Certainly, this lady didn't appear to be. In fact, he could imagine her looking after an injured man like in the parable. Some of his school mates would have said that that was stupid, but you had to hand it to people that did that. Jack asked himself if he would have stopped on the desert road with muggers about? A month ago there would have been no doubt of the answer. He would have had nothing to do with anyone who had nothing to do with him. After Tolfanland he had begun to think differently.

But what was it that made people want to take risks? He wondered if it was only about wanting to help people, and he reflected on his own idea of "working with children". Would that be taking risks? He hadn't thought about it like that.

After the service they were immediately surrounded by the young people. They were full of questions. Had they come to live in Newcastle? Were they going to join the church and come regularly? Would they like to come to the mid-week club? Were they Christians? Jalli was quite up for this. She was in her element because they were behaving exactly like the young people back home a universe away in Wanulka. No, she said, she wasn't a Christian because there were no Christians where she came from.

"What is important for a Christian?" she asked.

"Christians believe that God made the world and the whole universe and everything in it," said one.

"We believe we should love one another and look after the people in need," replied another.

"… because God gave himself for us in Jesus… because he loves us so much," chimed in a young girl with long blond hair that reminded Jack of a character in *Harry Potter*.

"Where does God live?" asked Jalli.

"In heaven," declared one of the younger ones.

"… and in us," said the minister, as she came across to join the group.

"That is exactly what our Scriptures teach," responded Jalli.

"So where is it you come from?"

"Er… Jalli doesn't come from this world," explained Jack, "she's an alien!"

They all thought that a really good joke and were still laughing when the biscuits arrived. "Save the jammy dodger for the alien!" said one. "It says in the bible that you have to look after aliens! Do you folk want tea or coffee – or do aliens like lemonade?"

"Are *you* an alien?" asked one of the boys of Jack.

"No," assured Jack.

"What's your team then?"

"That's a dangerous question!" he replied. "We don't have a local team unless you count Persham Wanderers."

"Who are they?"

"Exactly. I follow West Ham on the telly. I knew someone once who lived near Upton Park."

"So you know how to suffer too, like us, Geordies. Never quite there, and with frequent excursions into the Championship."

The conversion had now moved well and firmly into Jack's territory. The minister and some of the girls moved off.

"So are you coming again?" one of the girls asked Jalli.

"I don't think so," interjected the minister coming back across with Marge and Tom.

"They have to take a train to Leeds today. Jalli, would you and… er…"

"Jack," put in Jalli.

"… like a quick sandwich at the Manse? Then I'll run you into Newcastle Central on my way to the hospital to see a few people. Trains for Leeds are roughly every hour."

"Thank you," said Jalli. "But look, you've all been so kind already."

"But you've got to come back to Newcastle – even if

you're Hammers supporters," said one young lad who had really taken to Jack.

"Even if we're what?" asked Jalli.

"Football," replied Jack. Jalli rolled her eyes in mock horror. But she was beginning to see that football could break down barriers for boys where perhaps traditional religion could not.

An hour and a half later, Jack and Jalli shuffled down the carriage of their second train in two days. "I don't think I have found so much welcome anywhere in so short a time," said Jack.

"Churches can be like that. Churches should be like that!" observed Jalli. "God is certainly in this place. He lives in these people. You can really sense Him." Jack could almost see what she meant. But since he had not knowingly met God like Jalli seemed to have done, he still felt on the outside looking in.

"Don't think like that." Jalli was reading his thoughts. She was becoming good at it. She seemed to know everything he was feeling, but he was pleased that someone clearly so wonderful wanted to bother about him. "All you have to do is talk to Him and you'll find Him inside you too."

"Maybe. But don't hassle me. I'm still coming to terms with the culture shock of a church where they don't do what I expected them to. There is so much to learn about this God thing. I couldn't join in anything. I didn't even know if I should stand or sit most of the time.

"And I really could not understand half the 'I believe' thing they said, so how could I ever believe it. I was not brought up with it. It's a different world, more different even for me than Wanulka! It's not really my scene."

"But the thing is you don't have to learn that stuff to be part of God's people. That'll be different wherever you go. But God is the same. That's what I've just learned, whatever world you're in."

The train sped through County Durham and then the Yorkshire countryside. Jalli remarked on how it was all so green. They passed through York with it's towering Minster. Jalli stared at it with huge interest and couldn't believe it was as old as Jack said he thought it was. At least six hundred years he thought. (But in fact it is much older than that!) It had certainly lasted well.

"I'd love to go inside it!"

"One day, perhaps. But you're not getting me into two places of worship in the same day!" They laughed.

Soon after that the train was drawing into Leeds Station. People left the train to make their way up to the entrance above. A young couple with a toddler in tow were labouring up the platform with more cases than they could really manage. As the man lifted one of them, the case just burst open strewing clothes and books around him. The couple stood in shock for a moment. As they bent down to pull things together Jack instinctively approached and offered his help. He and Jalli helped hold the case together while the couple found a piece of string and a belt to tie it. Then Jack offered to help carry something to the taxi rank outside the concourse. The couple were very grateful indeed – a "Godsend" they said – and Jack felt really chuffed at being able to help. After they had gone Jack just stood in the concourse deep in thought.

"You, OK?" inquired Jalli.

"Yeah. I don't know what's come over me. A month ago it would never have occurred to me to do that. I would have walked past thinking that it was nothing to do with me. I would have thought, if I had thought about it at all, that if they had an old weak case and too much to carry, that was up to them. It was their look out. But today I just went to help without thinking. It's all to do with you, Jalli."

"And the One who brought us together," added Jalli, "the man called you a 'Godsend'."

"That's just an expression. He didn't really mean God sent me!"

"But he might have done."

"Well, if my dad wants to see me, I might begin to believe that! Now, how do we get to Middleton?"

"They asked a person who was waiting for a bus in City Square outside the station. She pointed in the direction of the Corn Exchange – down Boar Lane and Duncan Street.

"You'll need the number 3 or the number 10. I'm sure they both go to Middleton Park Circus."

Jalli and Jack went in the direction indicated. It was further than they had thought but after asking someone else to confirm they were going in the right direction, they found the Corn Exchange and a line of bus shelters. They were very soon sitting on a number 10 as it made its way south through Hunslet and Belle Isle. The driver told them when they got to Middleton Park Circus and they got off.

Jack glanced at his watch. "I think we should find somewhere to stay first," he said. "This isn't a place with lots of hotels and things." They walked back up the road to a parade of shops and checked out some of the ads in the windows. "Here's a bed and breakfast place advertised. It's in a street called Lovewell View."

"Is it far?" asked Jalli.

"I don't know." He spotted a lady coming along the pavement and called, "Excuse me. Can you direct us to Lovewell View?"

"Yes. It's there. Just there on the left."

"Thanks. So it seems we're nearly there," said Jack. "Come on let's see if we can find a room."

The house wasn't a big one but the owner didn't have anyone else staying at the time and she took Jack and Jalli in and showed them two very comfortable rooms, one with a single and one with a double bed. Jack insisted Jalli have the double bed and the bigger room. "You're so old-fashioned," smiled Jalli.

"So! I can't help it."

"Don't try. I like it." She kissed him.

After they had settled themselves the landlady offered them a cup of tea and Jack explained they were looking for someone in Middleton and showed her the address they had.

"The Throstles," she sighed, "there are so many of them. Some of them were knocked down years ago. They're all on the other side of Middleton Park Road, on the old estate, in that direction." She pointed to the way they had come. "There is Throstle Street, Road, Lane, View and so on. Lots of them. Your best bet is to go down there and ask."

After they had finished their tea they set off back towards Middleton Park Circus to make some initial inquiries.

"The pub," said Jack, spotting the Middleton Arms, "someone there'll tell us where to go."

They went into the bar. A group of fairly drunk men said something rude to Jalli but she decided just to ignore it. "We're looking for…" Jack got out the address Marge had written down and showed it to the barmaid.

"Pretty sure that's one they knocked down. Hey George, you know the Throstles."

A middle-aged man with a kind face got up and came across with a smile. "Yeah. Let me look." He took the paper. "No, that's still there. I know this house. Who're you looking for?"

"Shaun Smith."

"Shaun! You are just like him. You have just his whole look. You aren't his son are you?"

Jack nodded. "You walk like him too. (When he's sober that is, and that hasn't been that often.) He's moved though. Only tempor'y like, had to leave. But actually 'e's in Jimmy's now."

"Jimmy's?"

"Yes. St James' Hospital. 'e's been there for about three weeks now. His liver. It's pickled. But perhaps I should not have said it like that, you being 'is son. I'm sure they'll mend him. Trouble was 'e just couldn't stop. The beer had him by the… sorry lady!" acknowledging Jalli whom he judged looked like a person with some sensitivity to bad language. "Now take me. I've been on the wagon for five years. I just come in here for the company and the crisps. That right, Beth?" The barmaid signed her agreement. "When the doc. told me to knock it, I did. But Shaun, 'e just couldn't do it."

"How do we get to St James' Hospital?" asked Jalli.

"Well, it's a bit complicated. You have to go to the city centre and then find a bus… Look, why don't I just take you? You'll be late for visiting time if you go on the bus. I have my van outside – and as I told you I'm on the wagon."

"The wagon?" queried Jalli.

"He doesn't drink alcohol," explained Jack, "so we're safe with him driving."

"Safe as 'ouses. Ain't I Beth? And besides Shaun's my mate. Ought to have popped in meself to see him before now."

"Well. Thanks," said Jack, "we'd be grateful to take you up on your offer."

"Where are you staying?" asked George. Jack told him that they had lodgings in Lovewell View.

"If we go now, we can make the evening visiting. You'll be back by half past eight. I'll just 'phone the missus," George explained that he had to, or she'd worry.

15

J immy's turned out to be a huge hospital. Without George it would have taken ages to find the ward. But George headed in the right direction and soon they were at the nurses' station.

"Shaun Smith? Bay 6, bed 4," directed the nurse, "are you friends?"

"I'm his son."

"First I've heard of him having any relatives. He hasn't told us he had a son."

"I haven't seen him for a bit," explained Jack. "We don't live in Leeds."

Jack and Jalli made their way in the direction the nurse pointed them. They entered Bay 6 just as a weather-beaten man on the left was saying rather loudly, "Take your ruddy religion and get lost!"

"But it is not too late to turn over a new leaf and face up to your past," a rather flustered looking young curate was saying, "God will always accept a sinner who repents!"

"Who says I'm a ruddy sinner? And who says there's any bloody God anyway?"

A gentleman in a bed facing him across the bay, perhaps feeling sorry for the young priest, perked up with, "Nice try vicar! But if you manage to convert him you're doing well!" The curate moved across the ward and began speaking to him.

Jalli was checking the numbers above the beds, but Jack had already decided his father was the weather-beaten man. There was a resemblance that made him shiver inside. "O God, help me to say the right thing," he sighed under his breath.

But it must have been audible because the man in bed 4 came out with, "Oh no! Another blooming member of the God squad!" as he looked directly at Jack and Jalli. "What the hell do you want?" Then he spotted George with them. "George! What the bleeding 'ell you doin' 'ere? What's this? A bloody deputation?"

"Hello, Shaun. These 'ere young people were looking for ya. Dare say you'll get a bit of shock, but I knew as soon as I saw 'im. He's the spittin' image of you."

"Of me. What do you mean?" Shaun studied Jack who stood looking a mixture of embarrassment and confusion. "Stone me! Couldn't be could it? You'd be the right age. What's your name lad?"

"Jack, Jack Smith."

"Well. I never. So you come looking for your old dad, did you?" he said with a smile. Then added in a troubled tone… "What you come for? What's up?"

"I… I just wanted to meet my… my father. I just wanted to see you."

"… and so you've found 'im," Shaun said quietly. "Not quite as you expected, I suppose?" Shaun looked down at his feet beneath the covers, averting his eyes.

"I… I didn't know what to expect," answered Jack.

George, who had fetched some chairs, arranged them around the bed.

"You sound bloody posh," observed Shaun looking Jack up and down. "Your mother brought you up right, then?"

"Yes," answered Jack positively.

"How is she? She's OK ain't she?" A note of alarm in his voice.

"Oh, yes. Very well," assured Jack. "Er... this is my girlfriend, Jalli."

"Pleased to meet you. You're some'ut, ain't you? Got good taste my lad. Eh?"

"Pleased to meet you Mr. Smitt."

"Foreign too, eh? Where'd you find her then Jack? You left school?"

"I've just finished school. I thought I would work with children."

"Good idea."

Jack leaned forward and touched his dad's hand. "Jalli helped me to see that I needed to find you. I missed you without knowing. A boy should know his father... well, I should..."

"Look lad. I wanted to keep in touch," broke in Shaun, "... be a father to you and all that... but Matilda was so wild. Told me to disappear, forever... I don't blame her. I didn't mean to hurt her... Matilda told you about me drinking, no doubt?"

"No, she didn't. She just told me about you and... and... and another woman."

"Well. It was that. But the drink were the worst problem. She couldn't stick it. Daphne took me in – in more than one way. I was proper took in. Then she dumped me. What did Matilda tell you about me?"

"Nothing. She didn't talk about you at all. That was the hardest part. I'm glad I've found you. I'm glad I came."

"How'd you find me?"

"We traced you from Newcastle. Your neighbours had your Middleton address, and then we met George here."

"You done a good thing George. Thanks for bringing 'im. You were too bloody right. You said life would bring some'ut worthwhile in the end. And now something good has turned up. Should 'a taken your advice and did what the doctor said!

"Look lad, yer old dad is sick. I've been here three weeks and they can't do much for me. Liver's totally wrecked. And there's too much else that is wrong for them to give me a new one – even if they could find one." He looked at Jack anxiously and took hold of his hand. "I can tell you there hasn't been a day gone by I haven't thought about you. Often said one for you."

"You pray?" Jack said surprised.

"Well, in me own way. Don't get me wrong I'm not bloody religious! You are, ain't you?"

"No. Well, not really. Mum and me have nothing to do with church or anything. But recently…" he looked at Jalli.

"Oh. I get it now. Should'a known. You look nice." He turned to Jalli. "You look after him. Nothin' too holy mind. You can be too 'eavenly to be any earthly good!"

They spent the next half an hour talking about what Jack had done at school and how things were at home. And now how pleased Jack was to have finally met his father. "Tell your mother you found me," said Shaun, "And tell her I never stopped lovin 'er… I'm not going to make it out of here, lad. You'll come back again before… before I go? You will stop with your old dad…"

"Of course. If you want me to."

"Now he's found you Jack's not going to leave," assured Jalli, "he needs you."

Then, without warning, Shaun began to cough uncontrollably. A nurse came in.

"OK, Shaun. Time to rest," she said taking his pulse. "I won't take them right away, I promise, but I think you've had enough excitement for one day." Shaun nodded and tried to quiet his coughing.

"I'll be back, Dad!" assured Jack, tears in his eyes as the nurse calmed Shaun down and drew the curtains around him. When she emerged she took them to a visitors' room.

"He's very sick," she explained. "To be honest we do not expect him to live much longer. He's being kept going on drugs. He never spoke to us about a son. How old are you?"

"Eighteen. He hasn't seen me since I was two," clarified Jack, "I... Jalli... she helped me see that I must look for him." Jalli put her arm around his shoulder.

"Well, you've found him just in time," said the nurse.

Then Jack began to cry floods of tears, tears that had been there, damned up, for sixteen years. George felt uncomfortable. He wasn't needed for this bit. "I'll wait for you outside," he announced.

"OK," said Jack, "I think we should all be going. We'll come back tomorrow." They inquired when the visiting times were the next day, and asked the nurse to tell Shaun they would be coming.

George took them back to Lovewell View. "Would you tell us

your phone number?" asked Jalli, thinking it would be good to be able to contact George as he had been so helpful.

"Glad to." He wrote it down for them, the young people climbed out of the van and he drove off. Jalli remarked at what a kind man he was.

That evening Jack and Jalli sat and cuddled in silence. Oh, how she loved this boy, thought Jalli. And Jack was so aware of the firm, gentle soft arms around him. He was also conscious of Jalli just talking to her God like she so easily did. He didn't mind.

"He heard you praying when you went into the ward," observed Jalli.

Jack shook his head. "I didn't. I never pray. Not like you."

"But you did. You asked God to help you say the right thing."

"Did I? I can't remember. I must have done it unconsciously."

The next day the ward sister took them aside before they went into the bay. "You see," she explained, "the doctor has just been. We don't think your father is going to live more than twenty-four hours. You can sit with him all night if you like." They found Shaun sleeping. Jack spoke to him but he didn't wake. He seemed peaceful enough and they just sat beside the bed. After half an hour a nurse came to them and said that a social-worker would like to see them. They went back into the little relatives' room.

"I wonder if you could give me a few details about yourselves. We have to check these things through you see."

"But he is my father, isn't he?"

"Well he is Shaun Smith. Now I do need to know your names, how you got here and where you came from, and some sort of ID if you have any."

"Well, of course." Jack gave her his home address and phone number. "But Mum doesn't know I'm here, or that I've found Dad yet. He wanted me to tell her."

"You'd better do that now, then," advised the social-worker.

Jack took out his phone. He had turned it off when he came into the hospital. The woman nodded her consent to his turning it on. The phone flashed up a text message.

"From Mum," he said. "She's worried – as usual." He rang back.

"Yes, Mum. I'm in a hospital. No! Nothing's happened to me! It's Dad. I've found him here, in Leeds."

The call lasted for several minutes with Jack bringing his mother up to date. In the course of it, Matilda said, "Tell him, tell him, I've never really stopped loving him. I just hated the way he went on with the drink and everything. I can't come. Not after all this time. Let him go in peace. You understand?" Jack assured her that he did. Jack then had to put Jalli on to reassure her she was still with him looking after him.

The social-worker checked out Jack's school library card and asked him if he knew his National Insurance number. They needed it for the records. Since he was the next of kin – the only relative if his mother and father were divorced.

Then she turned to Jalli. She wanted to see her passport. The only ID Jalli had was in Wanulkan of course. How had she got into the country? The social-worker became really concerned when she heard that Jalli was only seventeen.

The more they both tried to explain, the harder it became. In the end, the well-meaning social-worker explained, "I have to be frank with you miss. If you cannot answer my questions about how you got here, and you have no papers at all to show me you will be regarded as an illegal resident, and Jack here could be charged with harbouring one. In any case, without proper permission you will be forcibly repatriated and, as someone under age, you could be detained in an immigration hostel until that can be done safely. Under the circumstances I can only suggest you claim asylum."

"But I am not running away," protested Jalli.

"I will see that you get a lawyer, miss. In the meantime I will leave you here, but I must warn you not to go anywhere."

"I shall not leave Jack. Not with his father dying!" Jalli was indignant. But Jack saw the risk they were running.

"Look Jalli. This lady is only doing her job. People are sneaking into Britain all the time. It will not help to argue. We'll pray about it." He squeezed her hand, and stopped her saying more. Jalli calmed down.

"But it's not right."

"No," said Jack, "and so we needn't worry about it. My dad's dying. Can we go back to him now?" The social-worker nodded. As she left she spoke to the ward sister and Jack and Jalli sat quietly with his dad.

Shaun didn't say much more. He just held onto his son's hand and muttered to tell Matilda he still loved her. And that he was sorry. And, "Tell that ruddy vicar I have said sorry to God, and I'll put a good word in for him when I get there!"

Jack rang his mum and heard her cry. Jack passed on his

mum's message. "Bloody good woman," was all that Shaun said. "Yes," agreed Jack, "better than I ever thought."

That night Shaun drifted into a deep sleep. A combination of exhaustion, organ failure and drugs.

Shaun died in his sleep the next day without regaining consciousness. In some ways it was a very special moment for Jack. Later he reflected that it was a privilege to be with someone when they died – but an even more special privilege to be with your own father. It wasn't frightening at all. It was, as he told people later, "More of a 'wow' than a 'yuk' experience!" But after he had gone there was a huge emptiness. The focus of his attention, and even love, was no longer there. The body was empty. Shaun had gone. Jack felt a whole cocktail of emotions. He had both found and lost his father within twenty-four hours!

Jalli said little – she just clung to Jack and Jack to her. They rang Matilda and she said she would travel to Leeds straight away. They also rang George. George came straight round to the hospital.

While they were together in the visitors' suite the social-worker reappeared. She was sensitive and kind and explained she would see that they got somewhere to stay.

"That's alright," interjected George. "They're staying in Middleton."

"I'm not sure if I can allow that."

"Why not?"

"This girl is under eighteen and…"

"I, we, would like to go with George," said Jack decisively. "Mum's on her way. I'll ring her and she will say it's OK."

He did so and, of course, she did. Jack gave her the Lovewell View address.

The social-worker then talked about a funeral. As the next of kin, Jack was responsible she explained. She could arrange for an undertaker. Had he any ideas about where the funeral was to take place?

"Take him back to Middleton," said Jack, "and can we have that vicar who was here yesterday?"

"A church?" mused George.

"Yes. Why not. The local church."

"Never thought 'e were religious."

"Well, he said his prayers. In his own way, he told me. I want him to have the best we can give him."

They went back to George's place and had a cup of tea. George's wife Ann was most attentive. Jack's mum rang to say she was pulling into Leeds City Station. George set off to fetch her and an hour later they were altogether.

"He went peacefully," explained Jack to his mother. "He wanted me to tell you he still loved you."

"So you told me. He was alright when he was sober," she sighed.

"He was rather rough even when he was sober in hospital," volunteered Jack. "But seemed really genuine. I believe he meant what he said. He knew he was dying."

They told Matilda about the social-worker, and the problems with Jalli's non-existent passport. Matilda was alarmed. If they took Jalli into custody things would become incredibly complicated – and her son could end up in serious trouble too.

"Look," she said. "We'll have to get Jalli home before the authorities act."

"But I'm not leaving Jack. Not now!" protested Jalli.

"Jalli," said Jack, "Mum's right. I want you here, too – very much – but we must get you out of Britain in case they put you in a detention centre. They'll never understand about our white gates. I'll be OK. I'll get you back to Persham tomorrow."

"No, I will," intervened Matilda. "Best you stay here and see the vicar and organise things for the funeral. If you're not here that will only complicate things further."

"Well, I don't understand all this completely of course," said Ann, "but if I were you I'd get Jalli here out as quick as you can. They're getting hot on illegals at the moment. It's all over the news. There's a lot of this people smuggling these days, and young women and children are being brought in to be exploited. I saw it on the telly, about the 'Stop the Traffic' thing. It's awful what's happening, and they may think that's how you got here, Jalli."

"But I am just Jack's friend," protested Jalli, "he did not, how do you say it, smuggle me. I haven't done anything wrong!"

"But you have, according to the law," mumbled Jack. "You didn't come into the country with a passport and a proper visa. People coming from outside the EU have to have special permission if they want to come here."

"Outside the EU? What is that?"

"The European Union. Your student card is clearly not European."

"But I want to stay here, Jack. I want to help with the funeral."

"I know," said Jack, "and I want you to stay. But they're right. If you don't get back through the gate they might arrest you. You have to go. I will come to the garden as soon as I get back to Persham. I promise."

After all the "fairytale" wonder of discovering one another, and the excitement of their joint adventures, Jack and Jalli were at this moment experiencing a real dose of reality. In all their exploits, they had not come up against the system of law – government rules that could simply deny them freedom to be together. Like Romeo and Juliet they were not the first in history to suffer this fate. Lovers believe that "Love should conquer all", and that no-one has the right to part them, but the rules to prevent illegal immigration take no account of this. Jack and Jalli now found themselves in the same heart-rending situation that young sweethearts suffer all the time. Ann recollected a Hindu girl in Leeds who fell in love with a Muslim boy. His parents sent him to Pakistan.

George intervened, "Let's give the stories a rest before we make these young people even sadder. The fact is, Jalli must go. And soon. They know where they are of course. I suggest I take Jalli and Matilda down to the station at six o'clock tomorrow morning to catch an early train."

"As soon as that!" exclaimed Jack.

"They'll be round tomorrow for sure. Best get her home lad."

"You're right George," said Ann. And Matilda agreed.

"OK," said George, "We'd better get you back to your B & B. Are you all staying there?"

"I don't know," said Matilda. "I haven't booked anywhere. Will there be room?"

"I doubt it," said Ann, "if not, you can stay here."

There wasn't room for all of them in Lovewell View and after she'd seen they were properly cared for, Matilda was happy to return with George.

That night the young people sat huddled together in the B & B with Jack assuring Jalli he would be alright. "Best you go," he sighed, "it'll only be a week." The cuddles were only matched by the tears.

By day break, everyone was up and ready and exchanging goodbye hugs. Matilda assured them she would be back before the day was out. Jack had to confess he was relieved to see Jalli go. A true lover puts the safety of the beloved before anything else. Jalli took little notice of the journey, she had had little sleep. They went to St Paul's school directly from the station and Matilda saw her through the white gate. When she felt the blessing and the peace of the garden, Jalli realised her tiredness and confusion had prevented her from her normal natural freedom to pray.

"Sorry," she sighed to her Maker, "why was it when I most needed you I forgot you?"

After half an hour Jalli was more herself. She washed and felt better. She set off for home and Grandma.

At nine o'clock the social-worker arrived at Lovewell View and wanted to know where Jalli was. "Gone home," explained Jack. He told her exactly how he had met her and how she came to be in England. Jack assured her she would not see a white gate – unless the Creator intended her to travel between planets herself – but if she needed any proof she could be present when he disappeared through the wall! She wanted to know how she could put all that in her report. It was the truth, Jack assured her.

Later that evening Matilda returned. She had taken a taxi from the station to Lovewell View and was only there for a minute before the police knocked on the door. A policeman and a policewoman asked if they could come in. Jack went through the same story again. They required to know exactly where Jalli was. George thought it best to be as polite and cooperative as possible. The landlady who felt really sorry for the way things had turned out offered to show them round the house. "If you don't mind," said the policewoman, that would be helpful. We have had a spate of cases where young girls have been brought into Leeds for the sex trade and we are obliged to make a full report. We do not think you are part of that, but Jack's story is not believable – well, not without further evidence."

After the police had looked everywhere, including the loft, the garden shed and under the stairs with no sign of Jalli, Matilda said rather crossly, "Look, nothing bad is going on here. Jalli Rarga has gone back home to her own planet. She's disappointed at the lack of welcome the British authorities have for aliens from outer space. She's gone home and she's not coming back!"

"Don't get upset Mum, they do mean well," said Jack, "they have to stop the trafficking."

"Well, I suppose so," agreed Matilda less heatedly, "but Jalli's been an inspiration for you – and for me. Without her you would never have done what you did in finding your father."

"But she's safe now," breathed Jack. Then the policeman bent down to the floor.

"Hello, what's this?" he said as he spied Jalli's student card beside the leg of a chair.

"It's… it's Jalli's card. She must have dropped it. She'll need it to get into the library in Wanulka." He put out his hand to take it, but the policeman held him back. "What's this language?" he asked but without touching the card.

"It's Wanulkan." The card had Jalli's picture and columns of Wanulkan script superimposed on a picture of the beach with the three suns in the sky. "This is the beach there. They have three suns above that planet. Jallaxanya is named after the biggest one."

"We'll take this. It will help us identify where she comes from." The policeman put on a pair of gloves and gingerly picked up the card and dropped it into a small bag.

"She'll need it back," demanded Jack.

"And how do you intend to get it to her?"

"I'll go to Wanulka!"

"Well, make sure you do so legally. You can have this back after it has been properly examined by our experts. They'll tell which country she comes from."

"Unlikely," said Matilda, "if Jack is telling the truth."

The police officers took their leave. "You could try and get a lawyer to help. And your MP," said the landlady.

"No, there would be too much publicity," sighed Jack, "and they would take her apart to find out about aliens! You know what they do on the films." Jack shuddered. They would have to be very careful. It was a pity they had found that card, it might have been better if they hadn't believed him. They would know for sure now that Jalli was not from anywhere on Earth.

The day of Shaun's funeral came. Jack and the vicar had put together a short service, with Matilda's help. The Middleton Arms was there in force, together with a few neighbours. "Dark horse, that Shaun. Never knew 'e were religious!" said one of the men that propped up the bar there most days. Jack told them that his father was, "putting in a good word for the vicar", and they all laughed. "That's just like him," said one. Jack had asked the choir to come and sing the song they had learned in the Newcastle chapel, "Be Not Afraid", and they all joined in with "Amazing Grace" at the end.

As they left the church Jack overheard George saying to Beth the barmaid, "I hope I have as good a send off when the time comes."

Then they all went on to the Middleton Arms where they sang a few other songs that were not in the hymn book!

16

Two weeks later Jack and Jalli were sitting together on the beach in Wanulka. Next to the cottage garden itself, this beach had a special attraction. Sometimes they liked to be together in a public place and "just watch the world go by" as Jack put it. They used the time to talk about their adventures and their lives up to that point.

"You know," reflected Jack, "a month ago I would never have believed it if you had told me I would find, and bury, my father within a week… By the way, I've got your student card back. The police made a big thing of it. It really caused a lot of debate. The card is apparently a type of plastic which, they say, is 'interesting', but which it would be possible to make anywhere in the universe. Of course, nobody could make anything of the script. It was an ingenious 'invention' they said. Oh, and the DNA on it was, apparently, all human. And George and Ann rang my mum and she said they said the police even came back looking for DNA samples at the B & B."

"But I *am* human. Like you. We've already decided that."

"Well, this confirms it. Jallaxanya Rarga is a human being with a sweet heart – and a fantastic body!" He put his arm around her shoulders and pulled her towards him. They laughed. "Anyway, they have dismissed my story of your coming from a different planet, they have your DNA on their database, and mine, and I have received an official warning.

If you come back to Britain you must do so through, 'the proper channels'."

"How can I do that?"

"You can't. So we must just be careful."

"Do you reckon we've had all the unexpected adventures we're going to have?"

"Of course not. Life will always have its surprises right through. My father was surprised by finding me just before he died. Each of us might be equally surprised by some joy at the last minute, too."

"Well, I'm almost alarmed at going back into the garden and finding another white gate. I just like sitting in the shade on a sunny day with my handsome Jack Smitt and having everyone thinking what a lucky girl I am."

"I'm not sure anyone even notices!"

"Oh, they do! You watch them!"

"Well. I'll take your word for it. If they're all looking at us, I certainly don't want to look at them! I don't know about you but I'm hungry. Let's go back to the cottage and get something to eat."

As soon as they got back to the cottage garden there was another small shed and a new white gate.

"What a surprise!" declared Jack.

"We must see it as a compliment, I suppose," suggested Jalli, "we must have done the other tasks with some success or else we wouldn't be moved on to a new one."

"If you put it like that, it does sound rather good: 'Congratulations! You have successfully completed level three. Press "enter" to continue to the next level'! Anyway. Do you think it could wait until we've had our lunch?"

"Most definitely!" Jalli was feeling quite hungry.

Lunch, however, wasn't very relaxed and they were soon finished.

"It's tropical again!" shouted Jack from inside the little shed. "We've both got sun hats made out of coconut palm leaves. Look!" He produced two wide brimmed hats woven out of strips of the palm when green. They were now quite a dull brown so they were by no means new, and, unlike the time when they were at the beach resort with Tod and Kakko and the others, there were no exciting new clothes either, just pairs of tatty trousers, and equally tatty long-sleeve shirts. There were some old plastic sandals but nothing else.

"You look like a scarecrow!" declared Jack as Jalli emerged with her shirt sleeves halfway down her hands.

"Thank you kind sir! You look appropriately dressed for your personality too!"

They stood there and laughed because, in the soft green garden, it all looked rather ridiculous. Jalli rolled up the shirt sleeves. "That better?" she asked.

"A bit," laughed Jack. "I expect that we'll blend in well where we're going though. There's no pack or anything. We must go just as we are I suppose."

"We'll be looked after no doubt. As we always are," volunteered Jalli.

They opened the new white gate and stepped through. They were immediately up to their shins in water – sea-water – sloshing and surging inside a dark cave with a view of the open ocean at an entrance some ten metres in front of them. The salty air smelt strongly of seaweed. They felt its slimy fronds mixed with gritty sand around their toes.

"Wow! We're in a cave!" exclaimed Jack. His voice boomed in the small space above the roar of the sea outside.

"Let's get out!" shouted Jalli and pushed past Jack towards the opening.

"Why the hurry?"

"I spent too long cooped up in a hole last time round," reminded Jalli.

They emerged at the base of a cliff onto a small beach of black sand.

"The tide's out at the moment," observed Jack, "so we'll have to get off this beach before long." He scanned the cliff behind them and plotted a route upwards. "It shouldn't be too difficult."

Jack led the way carefully up smooth wet black rocks at first, then onto grey dry ones which were less smooth and not so kind to feet. Before long they had reached some grass.

Jack looked back to note the way they had taken. "One thing is for certain. We'll have to find our way back down again," he remarked. By the time they had got nearly to the top of the cliff they had dried out, but they were pretty salty. Jalli had even torn an extra hole in the leg of her trousers. They reached the top and stood and stared. They were on an island, and they could see sea in every direction, various shades of blue depending on what lay beneath or the cloud shadows above. In front of them the land dipped more gently leading to a wide open bay curtained by a coral reef. There was a concave strand with sand ranging from deep grey at one end to almost white at the other. The beach was lined with coconut palms.

"Wow!" said Jack.

"Fantastic!" added Jalli, "A real fantasy island! It looks like we have it all to ourselves!"

She put her arms round Jack and gave him a huge hug. "I've only ever seen pictures of these in books. Is this real?"

"Sure is! My left foot is telling me I am standing on a thistle or something!" He sat down and tried to look at the sole of his foot.

"Let me!" said Jalli and found a small thorn sticking in the heel. Her good eyesight and skilful fingers soon had it removed. Jack stood up and readjusted his sandal.

"I could do with a pair of trainers," he grumbled. "Now which way is the Beacon Centre?"

"No point," Jalli returned the tease, "no money!"

"You know, we're not alone here, Jalli. Look. Isn't that a bonfire?" A little to their left on what seemed the highest point of the island was a large pile of brushwood.

They made their way over to it. Beside it was a very large woven coconut leaf mat and three large plastic bottles full of water. "It's a signal beacon. Looks like you light the bonfire and then damp it down and make smoke."

"Down there," pointed Jalli. "I'm sure that's a fence around a garden or something. And, look, among those palms I think I can make out a house – and a whiff of smoke. Let's go down and say hello."

"… And find out what we're supposed to do here. Take it easy on the rough parts. We don't want to cut our feet."

They traced their way down between boulders and scrub until they got to leveller ground covered in tall grasses, shrubs and wild flowers releasing sweet scents into the fresh, salty breeze. The sun beat down and they were glad of their palm hats. When they reached the garden there was a high bamboo fence – too high to see over, but looking through the poles they could see rows of green vegetables and what looked like maize. The fence went round the whole garden. In one corner there was a door hinged and tied with twisted bark.

They almost leaped out of their skins when they heard a loud cry from directly behind them. It was like a child protesting. But turning round they saw, standing gazing at them, a goat. It bleated once more and sauntered off along the fence.

"Now we can see the reason for the fence," declared Jack.

As they left the fence they entered a grove of tall trees and the ground grew soft and lush. They easily discerned a narrow path. It was clearly leading towards the "house".

"No," cautioned Jalli, "not this way. We're not expected. We could frighten whoever lives here just like that goat frightened us."

"Wise words. Let's go down to the beach and call from a distance." They pushed their way through lush undergrowth, stepping over a fallen log and paddling through smelly black boggy puddles. Just before they reached the beach Jalli touched a large green leaf with her arm.

"Ow! That hurts! Don't touch that Jack!"

"What? What've you done?"

"It's that leaf it's stung me!" There was a red splotch over Jalli's lower arm where she had pushed past the leaf. "It hurts! It really hurts!" she complained.

"Look let's get out of here. We've nearly made the beach."

Jack took hold of Jalli and ushered her the last few steps. They sat in the shade of a pandanus palm. Jalli's arm was now quite red. She looked faint. Jack was wondering what to do. "I'll – I'll be alright," said Jalli. "It's just the pain. I expect it'll go off!"

They had been so preoccupied with Jalli's arm that neither of them noticed the man standing on the edge of the surf looking at them for several minutes. Jalli caught sight of movement and looked up. Jack followed her gaze and then they all were looking at each other across the beach.

"Our resident," observed Jack. He stood up and shouted. "Hi. I'm Jack. This is Jalli. We just found ourselves on your island." The man remained where he was, the sea lapping around his feet. He wore a palm hat like theirs and a goat skin across his shoulders. Other than that he wore nothing. Jack wondered whether he should approach but Jalli was still sitting on the sand and he was reluctant to leave her. After what seemed like an age, the man suddenly took off the goat skin and wrapped it around his waist – as if suddenly becoming aware of his nakedness. He stepped toward them and at a distance of about ten metres seemed to try and say something.

"You. H-ho… how? Wh – where?" He struggled trying to get his mouth to go round the words.

"We arrived on the other side of your island," said Jack. "We don't really know why, but we've, kind of, been sent here. Do you need help?"

"H… Help?" stammered the man. He pointed to himself, "J… Johnson," and he held out his hand and a broad smile came across his face. "Ship! You – ship! Sorry, I forget how to speak. Five years!"

"You've been here five years, on your own?" The man nodded with a huge smile across his face and tears beginning

to fall across his cheeks. "Jane," he shouted, "Jane. I...
coming!"

"Jane?" asked Jalli.

"Wife. My... wife." Johnson then spotted Jalli's arm. He
came forward to her and reached, ever so tenderly, to take her
hand. The first human being he had touched in five years! He
held her hand very carefully. "Bad... leaf. Come. I have..."
Jalli stood as he led her by the hand, not once letting go, along
the beach to his "house". It was a single room shelter built
against pandanus palm trunks. He motioned for her to sit
down on a low, shaped, log. His "sofa". From inside the hut,
he found a plastic bottle with a little oily liquid in it and
poured it on the red mark on Jalli's arm. He then took a
bamboo sliver and, holding both ends, scrapped it gently
across the affected area. The treatment certainly helped but
wasn't exactly a cure.

"Bad leaf. Two d-days," Johnson described two arcs with
his right hands, "Two days, better."

"Two days. Like this?"

The man nodded. "Two days. Bad leaf! Don't touch
again!"

"Don't worry! I won't! Thank you." She was reassured
that it was not a permanent affliction, but two days seemed
an awfully long time with that pain.

"You, eat!?" The man went to the base of a coconut palm
and selected a coconut from a small pile. He peeled off the
husk on a sharp stake stuck into the sand and then struck the
shell with a rock, clearly selected for the task. The nut broke
easily. It was obvious he had done this thousands of times
before. Then he went back into the hut and came out with a

medium sized kitchen knife. "Life-saver," he uttered. He cut pieces of coconut from inside the shell and offered one half to Jalli and the other to Jack.

"Delicious," said Jack, "I have not had fresh coconut for ages!" The man smiled.

"Coconut every day. All days. Five years. Fish, yes, fish. I learn catch and cook fish. Then garden. Yams. I'm not the first here. Must be people before with yams, and maize. Not good maize but good… enough!"

Johnson's speech was now improving. His diction was still lacking but he was finding the words easier.

"Ship! Other side? Ship coming here?"

"No," said Jack, "we don't have a ship. It's difficult to explain but we came through a special sort of gate. It's a way of travelling through universes. If you can see the gate you can come back with us. To another universe."

"But he may not be able to see the gate!" emphasised Jalli. "Mr. Johnson, you must not build up your hopes!"

"Jane? My wife?"

"We can't take you back to your wife I'm afraid," sighed Jack, "we are not from your world. But you can come with us – if you can see the gate. If you can see the gate the Owner wants you."

"I understand now. I am dying. You've come to take me to heaven."

"No! No it's not like that, Johnson. We're not angels to take you to heaven. You are not ready for dying yet. Look, we don't know how we can help. But the Owner, God if you like, has sent us. We know there is something for us to do. But we don't know what that is yet. We must wait."

"Wait." Johnson's face fell. But then he began to smile again. "Wait, yes, but now I have friends. Kind friends. Beautiful friends!" Johnson smiled at Jalli. "I have waited five years, two months. Come look!" He motioned to them to look behind his hut where there was a rock with carefully scratched strokes – weeks, months and years. Beneath were six stones – some on a low rock. "Each day when the sun comes up I put one rock here," he explained moving a stone from the ground to the low rock. "On Sunday I put them all back. Today, I think it is Tuesday. I might be... wrong day."

"Wow. Brilliant!" exclaimed Jack. "Do you want to come to the cave and see if you can see our gate?"

"Too late, now. No moon. Tomorrow we will go. Now we will find some... some supper."

Johnson picked up two bamboo spears and beckoned to Jack to come with him to the water's edge. He followed the beach down to where there was a deep pool between high rocks. Here he stood and watched for a couple of minutes and then sent his spear flashing in the water. He went in after it and dragged it up with a large fish. But no matter how many times Jack tried he either could see nothing or missed. "I was hungry for a week, but learned fast," smiled Johnson.

Jalli wandered down the beach after them, feeling a bit better. She was wondering if there was any water to drink. Johnson smiled, "I have tea! But first..." He collected his knife and shinned up a coconut palm like a monkey. He cut three green coconuts that each fell into the sand with a thud. He cut the green flesh off the top of one and then bashed it with a stone – another selected stone from his "tool set".

"You drink that," he ordered Jalli. Jalli put the coconut to her lips and tipped her head. The "milk' was cool, sweet and had a bit of a fizz. She thought she had never tasted anything quite so refreshing. The tea turned out to be a kind of herb that Johnson put into some water he got from a collection of plastic bottles. "Rainwater," he explained.

"Where do you get all these plastic bottles from?"

"Rubbish. They drift up the beach with rubbish!" Johnson pointed to a line of rubbish washed up by the tide. It contained a huge variety of flotsam indicative of the mess of modern society – plastic items of every description, cork, wood, nylon line and netting. He had rigged a series of plastic bags and a tub to catch rain water. Johnson gutted the fish and covered it in a type of clay and laid it on the fire. He turned it several times. Then after only a few minutes he broke open the clay with a stick, scooped it onto a piece of bark and laid it on the sand in front of Jalli. She tasted it and wondered how anyone would want to live anywhere else. The coconut, the fish and the beautiful beach – all were perfect. The only thing missing, she contemplated, was his Jane.

As the sun set he passed around another bottle. For the mosquitoes, he said. The liquid smelt bad, but he assured them the mosquitoes liked it even less than human noses. It seemed to work. Johnson fetched a beautiful soft mattress woven out of some kind of bark and laid it on the sand for Jalli.

"Isn't this your bed?" she inquired.

"No. Your bed tonight," said Johnson, "no rain tonight." He smoothed a piece of sand for Jack and smiled, "Your bed!" and laughed before he himself went down the beach a little and sat quietly under a pandanus palm watching the sun set.

17

The night was calm and the air balmy, but there was little sleep for Jalli. Most of the night she was kept awake by the terrible pain from her arm. In England Jack might have found her some antihistamine or given her some pain-killers. But here there was no such thing.

Jack was concerned but Johnson was not. "It is painful now, but it will pass. Two days," he reminded them as he prepared some coconut and goat's milk for breakfast. Jalli's eyes glazed. "Another night?" she murmured.

"It will hurt again, but less. Tomorrow better. Today we go and look in your cave. I want to see your door. Walking will help the pain."

"So will eating your lovely food."

"Tonight we will have goat and yam."

"But we must not eat all your food," protested Jalli. "If we cannot rescue you, you will need it!"

"I will need to kill a goat. I cannot keep it. There is more than I can eat on a goat. I make sure there are not too many because they break... spoil the island. I have plenty of yams and fish. If you stay we can make bigger garden!"

As they ate breakfast, Jack and Jalli talked about how they met and their adventures, and about the mystery of the white gates.

When they had bathed in the sea and removed the smelly

anti-mosquito liquid they walked along the path to the garden. A much safer way to pass through the wooded area. Johnson explained that he had beaten a way through after he had encountered the same kind of leaf. He had been stung three times in the process! He opened the gate and took them into the garden.

"Hard work!" pronounced Jalli.

"Many stones, then. I dug with this." Johnson showed them a stone plough lashed to the forked end of a wooden shaft. "Then I put grass and leaves and goat... er..."

"Dung?"

"Exactly... and also human!" He laughed. "I mix it up in these piles."

"Composting," declared Jack.

"Yes. Composting! Some people had already started garden, but no fence. I found yams and some maize. I want other things but cannot find the seeds. I would like more fruit."

They trekked on up to the top of the hill and stood by the bonfire. Johnson explained that it was a signal beacon in case he saw a ship – just as Jack had guessed. The mat was to make smoke signals. Johnson demonstrated the method he envisaged. But no ship had been seen in five years.

"How did you get here?" asked Jalli.

"Um – er... place where I lived," Johnson put his head in his hands. "Name's gone. Hard to think. Have not used language for so long. Five years. Place were I lived... fight... coup...ran away and took a boat. Look!" Johnson drew Jalli and Jack to the edge of the cliff and pointed to a small bay at the far end of the island where they could make out some wreckage. "Fuel finished. Made sail and came here. I have not seen a ship since that day. Five years, two months, one w… week! Come, you show me your gate!"

Jack walked along the cliff top until he spotted the way back down to the cave. It was not so easy going back but they slipped and slithered until they came to rocks above the little inlet. The tide was in. "We'll have to wait," called Jack. Johnson pulled a string bag from his back and handed round three plastic bottles of rainwater and some dried sunfish.

"Picnic," he smiled.

"You don't go hungry ever!" rejoiced Jalli.

"Hungry once. Very hungry. Not now!"

The sun was hot, but their big hats and long sleeves, which they had learned to wear rolled down, made it bearable. After an hour the black sand emerged and Jack made his way gingerly down across the slippery rocks. "The cave is not too deep in water," he shouted back. "Come on down. It's slippery!" he warned.

They made their way down to the beach, Johnson offering a hand in the most gentlemanly way to Jalli. It made Jack wonder if he had been a little neglectful. They all stood on the black sand and Jack led the way into the cave. Jalli held back a little as Johnson eagerly, but gingerly, followed. It was clearly visible from the entrance. The gate was there. "Can you see it?" asked Jack. Johnson pushed forward and laid his hand on the top bar. He moved his hand gently over the smooth surface.

"If he can see it," said Jalli, "he's invited in."

"Absolutely." Jack lent forward and opened the latch and drew Johnson in. Jalli followed.

They all stood dripping salt water onto the lawn. Johnson just stood and stared.

"Where am I?"

"It's a kind of reception point between different planets," explained Jack. "Jalli lives behind that gate and my home is through that one." The man looked but all he could see was one gate.

"He can only see his own gate," said Jalli, "he's not supposed to come beyond here."

Johnson's gaze turned to the cottage. He stood in a world entirely different from the one they had just left. He then looked at himself with his goatskin and smiled. He felt completely out of place, not correctly dressed for the occasion.

"Let's take a shower!" exclaimed Jack, "and get you some clothes!"

An hour later they were all sitting in the garden under the tree, clean and dry, although Jalli wondered if her hair would ever look the same again – and her arm still hurt despite some helpful looking cream she found in a bathroom cabinet. The kitchen had been supplied with food. There was no coconut, but heaps of fruit of all kinds. In the fridge they found chicken and cheese, and in the bread bin some of Jack's favourite bread with the poppy seeds on the top. Johnson couldn't believe his eyes.

"You asked for fruit!" suggested Jack. "The Owner must have heard you." They explained how the cottage seemed to work. They were really looked after and given more than they could ever hope for – but white gates kept appearing inviting them to get involved in one corner of creation or another.

"Even places with plants with stinging leaves!" added Jalli.

"Well He did give you long sleeves," suggested Jack. "It was us who decided to roll them up."

"Are you saying I am suffering for my vanity?"

"Exactly!" Jack teased.

Johnson looked troubled. "You did not know. It was an a… accident. You are a *good* girl!"

"He's teasing me," explained Jalli. "He doesn't mean to be cruel. He looks after me very well… most of the time!" It was Jalli's turn to tease Jack.

"Now, the question is," Jack brought the conversation back to Johnson, "where do you go from here? You can come here to eat and clean up, but there is no other white gate for you to use."

"No I cannot leave my world. On my island I am nearer my Jane. There might be a ship." As he said this Johnson began to get agitated. "I have to get back to the island. There might be a ship even now. Thank you for coming. I must go." He quickly returned to the cottage and found his goatskin. "I… can I keep these clothes… and take fruit?"

"Of course," said Jack. Jalli stuffed a large variety of fruit into a bag while Johnson changed. "Thank you I must go. I must go now." And, taking his new clothes and the fruit, he pushed his way through the white gate. He turned and waved as water came up to his ankles. "You will come back and see me!"

"Yes. If we can," shouted Jalli. And he was gone. Jalli and Jack stood hand in hand staring for several minutes. Eventually Jack said:

"I'd better phone Mum."

"And I Grandma. What time is it?"

"Four thirty."

"Perhaps I ought to go home. I didn't say I was going overnight."

"Right. Mum'll be wondering too. She doesn't worry as much as she did because she is sure I'm with you and you'll keep me out of trouble. You'll come back tomorrow?"

"Tomorrow at ten. I'll miss you Jack Smitt!"

"Come here and let me kiss you."

"Be careful. My arm!"

"Is it getting any easier?"

"Well, a bit. But it still hurts a real lot."

"I hope you sleep tonight."

"I'm so tired I think it will take more than a painful arm to keep me awake."

But that night Jalli did wake several times. Although the pain had eased it was still sore when she washed in the morning. She hadn't told Grandma – she didn't want to worry her.

Jack lay awake thinking of Johnson on his island for over five years. He imagined how he would feel if he could not get back into the cottage garden. How he would miss his Jalli if he couldn't see her for just five days! And Johnson had been parted from his wife for five years. She probably thought he was dead. He had no way of communicating.

Jack prayed for him – but he didn't acknowledge to himself that it was prayer. He questioned the Owner of the white gates. Was giving him a bit of a diversion worth it all? It might only have made things worse for him – made him more anxious and less patient. Or given him hope which came to nothing.

But in fact he need not have worried. Johnson was like a new man. He had had contact with human beings once more and they hadn't run away from him in disgust. When he got back to his hut he remembered he had offered them goat and yam. Perhaps another day. They hadn't stayed long enough, he thought.

He resolved to speak to himself and practice talking every day. He regretted not asking for a kettle! He would love to have boiled water and made some tea – but perhaps it might not be good to boil his leaves. The fruit was a real treat. He carefully kept each pip and the pineapple top. He wondered if he would be allowed to go through the white gate again. That night was his second restless one in two days. He was just too excited to sleep.

Ten o'clock came the next day and Jalli and Jack were already in the cottage garden. Jalli's arm was much better. Johnson had been right – two days. They resolved to go back and see him the day after next if the gate was still there.

"We must take him a set of cooking pots, and some matches," volunteered Jalli.

The gate, the shed and the old clothes were indeed still there when Jalli puffed into the cottage garden with a small set of pans and a big box of matches that she had bought in Wanulka. She had carried them further than she had intended because, although the shop was not far from the Municipal Gardens, just as she had emerged from the shop, she had spotted Maik Musula. She had quickly disappeared back inside, had waited for him to pass, and then had gone in the opposite direction – a route that had taken her out of her way.

Having heard the story, Jack sighed playfully, "Well, I suppose you want me to carry them up the cliff then?"

"I expect nothing less from a 'perfect gentleman'."

Jack pretended to look around, "But he doesn't appear to be with us!"

"Well, *you'll* have to do then!" she kissed him on the cheek. Then, in a flurry of flying cooking pans, Jack swept her up and swung her round before setting her down gently on the grass and collapsing beside her.

"I do so love you, Jalli Rarga. It was a brilliant idea these pans. He can cook all sorts of things properly. I reckon if I were a castaway I would like a knife first, and then a cooking pot. Well, after you of course!"

"Then you wouldn't be a real castaway."

"No. You're right. I do hope that Johnson finds his Jane one day."

"Come on. Let's get changed. I reckon I can tie these pans together and sling them on my back." But when they were tied Jack took them and wouldn't hear of Jalli carrying them past the white gate.

"I was only teasing you! I can take them!" But Jack had already settled them on his back.

Twenty minutes later they were half way up the cliff. "Knowing the climb doesn't make it any easier," grunted Jack as they paused for breath. The day was bright, the sea a patchwork of blues and purples under a rich blue sky that grew bluer the more you looked up. There was the sound of gulls, the smashing of the waves on the rocks, and the rattle of pebbles as the sea drew back for another surge. They sat on a small patch of grass beneath a battered bush and became aware of the gentle buzz of bees skipping from flower to flower. Close to the ground, out of the wind, the scent of herbs and pollen lingered and the sound of the sea crashing on the rocks was softened.

"This is lovely," declared Jack. "I do like the seaside."

A waft of some sweet smelling bushes came up from a little hollow to their left. Jack stood up to explore it and his eye caught sight of something on the horizon. It had been unbroken every time they had looked out before. But now he thought he saw something there.

"Look, Jalli, look!"

"What? What am I looking at?"

"There, on the horizon! Isn't that a ship?"

"Where? I can't… yes! Yes! I see it."

"Which way is it going?"

"No idea."

"Quick, let's light the beacon. Johnson can't see this. It's on the wrong side of the island."

"But, shouldn't we go down and tell him?"

"There may not be time."

They clambered up the last few metres at top speed, and ran to the beacon.

"Is it still there?" shouted Jack.

"Yes. But it seems to be moving to the right."

Jack checked the heap. It was really dry. He gave thanks for the matches they had brought. He gathered a few dry pieces of grass and little sticks, set them at the base of the pile and struck a match. But he couldn't get it to catch.

"Let me." Jalli came forward with a heap of dry scrub and dead leaves. "I think these will be better." She pushed them lightly under the windward side and Jack passed her the matches. It lit first time.

"Wow! Great!" danced Jack.

"Thank you kind sir. Useful as well as beautiful you see!"

Jack then carefully poured some water from one of the bottles onto a thick branch and propped it against the heap. It hissed and steam and smoke started to emanate from the fire. They did this with a few more pieces. They were now standing beside quite a blaze, but with only a tiny whiff of smoke.

"Some smoke but not enough," despaired Jack.

"That grass. The sort you couldn't get to burn. Put that on!" commanded Jalli.

She gathered a bundle and threw it against the bonfire. The fire protested and started to issue clouds of pungent smoke.

"More!" shouted Jack. They scooped armfuls of the grass from all around as quickly as they could and soon they had billows of acrid smoke. Jalli ranged around gathering as much as she could and Jack kept piling it on.

"The ship!" skipped Jalli. "I think it's turning. It's bigger and it's stopped going to the right!" Jack emerged spluttering from the smoke.

"I think you're right." Jack grabbed the coconut leaf mat and did his best to make smoke signals. It was easier to say than to do! But he did make a difference in the smoke flow. Jalli came back with even more grass. After five minutes there was sea between the ship and the horizon. Whatever it was it was definitely coming their way. Jack and Jalli hugged one another.

"You go down to Johnson. Tell him!" suggested Jack. "You can be far quicker than me. I'll stay here and keep the fire going."

Jalli leaped down the hillside in the direction of the beach but she didn't get beyond the garden because Johnson had already seen the blaze and was bounding his way up.

"A ship! a ship!" yelled Jalli.

Johnson yelled back. "I knew you had come to rescue me. You are… wonderful!" He shook her hand vigorously and they both ran back up the slope.

At the top of the cliff he stood and stared for moment, then jumped about like a young child. The shape of the ship was now easily discernible and it was heading straight for them!

"Go back to the beach," said Jack. "Jalli and I will stay here and when they spot us Jalli will run down your side so that they know to go round the island. I will stay on the top here and keep them in sight."

Soon Jack was able to make out a white ship that reminded him of a cross-channel ferry advert he had seen at the railway station in Persham. As it approached the island it turned to the right and they waved hard. Then Jalli disappeared over the hill. By the time Jalli had reached the beach the ship was visible coming round the headland. Johnson had made another smoky fire on the beach. The ship anchored outside the reef. After what seemed a long time a small inflatable dinghy was lowered and then they could hear the sound of an outboard motor starting up.

The rescue was somewhat of an anticlimax. Three men dragged the boat up the sand as a fourth stood armed and ready, watching. Johnson indicated to Jalli to put her arms up in the air and walk out onto the beach. Two men approached while the others stood and watched. Jack came running onto the beach too and, seeing the situation, stopped still. He yelled. "We're safe! No-one else here!"

By this time two men had reached Johnson and Jalli, and shouted they were unarmed.

A third approached Jack. Then one of the men spoke and Johnson smiled. He could understand. "Five years," he said, "five years!"

It took some time to explain that Jack and Jalli did not need rescuing, but after some discussion the four men shrugged their shoulders and indicated Johnson to board the dinghy.

"Do you want to take anything with you?" asked Jack.

"No, leave it all here. If anyone else ever gets washed up here it will give them a start!"

"What is the day, the date?" asked Jalli of the crew.

"The third of the eighth. Good luck!" grunted one of the sailors. They really couldn't make out why only one of three people needed rescuing. Johnson took Jalli and Jack into his arms. "Thank you. Thank you. You... certainly been sent – by God. You tell Him... I once doubted Him, I don't now!"

"We will. But you can tell Him yourself," said Jalli.

"I know. I can talk to Him. In my heart!" They pulled the boat out beyond the surf and Johnson got in. As they were rowing out to the ship Jalli shouted, "Give our love to Jane!"

"I will, I will!" waved Johnson.

They saw Johnson climb onto the ship. They stood together, hand-in-hand and watched until it disappeared round the headland. Then Jalli noticed that Jack's face was covered with tears. She bent up and kissed him. "I was just thinking. I couldn't have managed here for five years on my own."

"Yes, you could. But it would be nicer with two."

"That sounds like Pooh."

"Pooh?"

"*Winnie the Pooh* by A. A. Milne. Pooh Bear has friends, like Piglet. He says 'It's nicer with two', and it is."

"You must tell me stories about Pooh."

"They're children's stories."

"I like children's stories. Sometimes they are the best."

"OK."

They went to the little camp and tidied things up. Jalli climbed a short coconut palm, not as dexterously as Johnson but pretty well for a beginner, and cut down two green nuts. Jack fumbled with the knife to cut the top and that took even longer – but the reward was the cool, sweet, tangy liquid that once tasted is never forgotten. It was strange being in this place without Johnson. Jack began telling the stories of Winnie the Pooh and friends – Piglet, Kanga, Roo, Eeyore, Tiger, Owl, Rabbit and Rabbit's "friends and relations". He made different voices for all the characters.

"You are great at telling stories. You should do it all the time. You should have lots of children to tell stories to."

"Thanks. I'll need your help."

"My help?"

"To have children!"

"Well… perhaps… But not yet! I don't think I have stopped being a child myself yet."

"Now how am I to reply to that!? I'll be in trouble if I agree! But, somehow, I think being a mixture of being grown up and still being a child in some ways is something we should always be. I like you as you are, Jalli Rarga. Being here reminds me of Wendy and Peter Pan."

"Who are they?"

"More fictional characters. Peter Pan was a boy who never grew up. He lived in Neverland which was a kind of island and one day went and got Wendy and her brother Michael and taught them to fly. They flew to Neverland populated by lost boys and Red Indians. J. M. Barrie wrote it in the early twentieth century."

"So you must tell me this story too. We have something like that in Wanulka. *Amanu and Zrura*. Amanu never stops being young, but sadly Zrura grows up and is too old to play childhood games. It's a bit sad really."

"Why does Zrura have to grow up?"

"I don't know. But I think the question you are supposed to ask is, why doesn't Amanu grow up?"

"Oh, that's easy. Because he doesn't want to."

"And that's not good. I think you have to grow – as a person I mean – because if you don't it means you have never learnt anything. Learning things means you change."

"Have you changed since we met? We had so many things to learn."

"I have. I think Grandma finds me almost unrecognisable. You have changed too… a lot."

"Oh…"

"But you see you had to. Because now you are part of me, and I of you. We're not the same."

"I know what you mean. I know it isn't saying much, but I'm better than I was."

"And now I want to hear more of your stories – from your land."

"OK. But we can't stay all day. Nice as it might be to spend the night here again, I fear we will be missed."

"Indeed. But we do have a bit of time before we have to go back. I hope Johnson finds Jane. It is important to be missed by someone."

They sat together quietly playing with the hot dry sand, listening to the surf and imagining not hearing another human being for five years.

After ten minutes Jalli shouted, "Jack! You reek."

"I what?"

"Reek. Stink of that awful smoke. We both do." She ran down to the sea pulling off all her clothes and dived into the sea. "What are you waiting for?" she yelled splashing in the surf. "I am not going back clean with a smelly boy."

Stunned by the sight of Jalli skinny dipping, Jack hesitated. She always surprised him this girl. But he quickly recovered, divested himself of the old rags and joined her in the surf. They washed their clothes in the sea too and hung them out on a pandanus palm, and then spread themselves on the sand to dry. Jack told Jalli about Peter, Wendy, Michael and the Lost Boys.

"Hm," sighed Jalli, "so Wendy had to do the housework and cook!"

"Of course. She was the girl!" teased Jack. "But things have mostly changed now in Britain. Young people don't think like that any more. In J.M. Barrie's time the better off people had servants. Few people do these days."

"Jack?"

"Yes."

"I'm hungry!"

"There are some sandwiches in my bag." But he made no effort to move.

"You're lazy!"

"If you say so! Just kidding," he laughed and got his bag. By the time they had finished the chunky cheese sandwiches which he had thrown together in Persham that morning their clothes were dry and crisp.

As soon as they were back in the cottage garden and had deposited their "island clothes" as they had called them in the shed, both it and the gate disappeared.

"That's a shame," sighed Jalli. "I enjoyed that place."

"Job done!"

"Spose so. So what next?"

"I've been thinking!"

"Dangerous! I've been thinking too."

"What?"

"I just thought that I've spent time in England. Perhaps you could come and stay with me and my grandma. She has been really patient letting me go everywhere."

"Actually that is exactly what I was thinking too. I expect she's a bit lonely really. Family *is* important." Jalli reflected on just how much "family" had grown in Jack's priorities since she first met him. She applauded his sensitivity.

"Yes. Come and stay in Wanulka and I'll show you the sights."

"Done!"

"But, one thing I would like to do is stalk the parmanda hives like Mr. Bandi said. And a person has to do that on their own."

"Why? Without even me?"

"I'm afraid so. They are easily spooked and with too many people they retreat inside and don't come out."

"Well OK. But I'll miss you!"

"I won't be gone five years! Just part of a day."

"Five hours is enough!"

"You soppy romantic!" Jalli kissed him. "Look, I've been thinking too. You've met Grandma and I've met your mum but they've not met each other."

"Because they live on different planets."

"Right, but we are making an assumption here. It occurred to me when we took Johnson to the white gate in the cave and he could see it and came through. What if Grandma could see the white gate, or your mum? We've never tried bringing them to our gates."

"No we haven't. It's kind of our place though. I didn't really want to share it with my mum to be honest."

"That's right, and that's fair because we were still finding out just where all this was taking us. But now we are much surer about things and about… about us, we cannot keep from inviting them to meet each other."

"And here is the only place. Would the Owner want us to bring them?"

"Well, that's easy. If they can see the white gates then the answer's yes."

"You know, there's a room upstairs in that house that sort of belongs to my mum. It feels the same as her room at home." Jack remembered the sudden feeling the one and only time he went into the first room down the little corridor.

"I know you told me about it. If we've got rooms then my grandma should have one too because I could not ever leave her. So let's see if they can see the gates."

"OK. We'd better give it a few days because my mum needs time to adjust to new ideas."

"Well let's suggest Saturday – if it's OK for both of them."

"Fine we can decide after we've sounded them out."

Matilda was almost astonished, but because so much was surprising about Jack these days the impact was a gentle one. She had not thought Jack would invite her so readily, but he seemed to want her to be part of all this in a way that he had not wanted her to before. She couldn't get over how much he had changed. She readily agreed, but was quite sceptical about whether it would actually happen.

Momori was pleased, but was prepared to be disappointed. "I have always told myself," she repeated, "that one day I would have to let you go. There will be a time when you are going to have to leave me behind. I'm not so young, and I don't want to leave you before you leave me."

"Oh, Grandma. No-one is going to leave anyone. I would hate it if that happened," said Jalli with a tear in her eye.

"I'll come with you on your agreed day," reassured Momori, "but you must not be too upset if I can't get into your garden."

"I will be upset, Grandma, I could not say I wouldn't be!" Jalli gave her grandmother a strong hug.

"Don't get upset now then," soothed Momori. "Let's both be patient until Saturday. I can wait till then!"

18

Momori looked across the road towards the Municipal Gardens. "I could swear that wasn't here on Monday," she declared.

"So you can see it, Grandma! The white gate, you can see it!"

"Plain as my old eyes will let me! It's bright and new looking. Are you sure no-one else can see it?"

"Well, no-one else has ever come in from anywhere that we have ever met, apart from Johnson – and he came in with us."

"So. This is your very own exclusive white gate into the Municipal Gardens."

"Yours too now Grandma. But beyond it is not the Municipal Gardens but a completely different world."

"OK. So how do we get in without being seen?"

"Oh, just walk in. People don't seem to notice." Jalli walked along the wall, opened the gate and ushered her grandma inside. "So," she said, "I wasn't making it up was I?"

Momori said nothing. She just stood and stared, then breathed the air and turned to her granddaughter with the biggest smile Jalli had ever seen (and she had seen a lot of smiles from her). "Jalli, you are a very privileged young lady. You have been especially chosen. I am honoured to be your grandmother!"

"Oh, Grandma. I am nothing special. It's the place that is special and we are indeed very privileged. Come and sit on our bench."

It was seated like this, with pink blossom in her hair from the tree above them, that Matilda first set eyes on Momori. "Hi, Jalli. It worked!" Jack ran across and caught up Jalli in his arms. "It worked!"

"The Owner wants them to be here!" thrilled Jalli. They danced a little jig on the lawn, while Matilda and Momori smiled at each other.

"Oh, Grandma, this is Jack's mum, Matilda."

"… and this is Jalli's grandmother, Momori."

"Delighted to meet you!" said Momori, doing a Wanulkan curtsy and taking Matilda's hand. Matilda responded less formally, "Honoured, I'm sure!" She felt a bit overawed by everything.

"Sit down, Mum. Sit down," urged Jack and she and Momori sat on the bench together. Momori was quickly aware of Matilda's nervousness and instinctively began putting her at ease.

"You have a very special son," she said. "He has been very caring to my granddaughter. He is such a gentleman."

Watching him with Jalli as they spoke together across the lawn – where they had now drifted out of earshot – Matilda answered, "Yes. Your Jalli taught him that."

"Perhaps in a way. But it had to be there all the time. Meeting each other has brought out some of the best sides of them both I think. Jalli has grown up during these past few weeks. She's always been a happy person but never so happy as this." The conversation developed with each comparing notes about their children, and each increasing in satisfaction at learning about how much the young people had achieved together. Jack had not told his mother half of what he had done in Tolfanland. Momori hadn't realised that the beach resort was chiefly about helping people because Jalli had enjoyed herself so much she had described it as a holiday. Now, it seemed, it wasn't just sand and bikinis but getting young people a good press.

After half an hour the two ladies were really taking to each other – gossiping away as if they had known each other a long time. The young people watched with pleasure. This was easier than they had anticipated. They came across.

"We are so happy you both could come into this garden," said Jalli cheerfully.

"And that you have met each other," added Jack pleased to see his mum happy and smiling.

"How many gates can you see Grandma?" asked Jalli.

"Why two of course, yours and Jack's."

"Can you see two Mum?" inquired Jack.

"Indeed I can," she replied.

"So you are each permitted to visit the other," declared Jalli. "Grandma, can Jack's mum come and stay with us in Wanulka?"

"Certainly, if that's what you both want. Matilda you would be most welcome!" smiled Momori at Matilda.

"Jack!" exclaimed Jalli in a hushed tone, "Can you see a third gate?" One had just appeared between the other two.

"Where?" puzzled Momori, "I can only see two."

"Yes," said Jack. There was indeed a third gate.

"What does that mean?" asked Matilda who could still see only the two gates.

"That," said Jack with a slight tone of apprehension, "is a new adventure!"

"We are not allowed to be lazy," explained Jalli. "There is more work to do."

"I am glad I cannot see another gate!" exclaimed Momori. "I think I am past having the energetic adventures you two seem to get up to."

"I wouldn't be missed," stated Matilda. "It's factory fortnight in Persham. But I must say I don't fancy an adventure really. This place is enough of one for me... but I can only see two gates," Matilda squinted in the direction the others were looking.

"It's over here." Jack led them over to the new gate. He glanced over it and saw hundreds of young people in some kind of field all waving their hands in the air in time.

"Looks like a music festival," he ventured, "isn't that an open-air stage?"

"It's something with many people," agreed Jalli.

"Well, I can only see hedge," said Matilda.

Jalli studied the scene. "I don't think you would like it, Grandma. They're all young people standing in a lot of mud singing pop songs."

"Definitely not my scene then," agreed Grandma. Jack was examining inside the little shed beside the gate. There were two roll-up waterproofs and two pairs of Wellington boots.

"Look, wellies! But only two pairs. Sorry Mum you're definitely not invited it seems."

"That's settled then!" said Matilda in a cross between relief and disappointment at being left behind.

"Matilda?" asked Momori, "If our two young people are

off on another adventure, and if you have a holiday and won't be missed, would you like to come and stay with me in Wanulka till they get back? White gate permitting, of course."

"Well… I haven't been away on holiday for years!"

"That is all the more reason to come," responded Momori to Matilda. "I would value your company."

"You go, Mum. Grandma's food is fantastic…! Not that yours isn't great too… of course…"

"Boys!" sighed Matilda. "All they can think about sometimes is food!"

"… and girls!" joked Jack, squeezing Jalli's hand.

"Girls! How many do you want!?" Jalli made to reprimand him playfully.

"One. One's enough. Couldn't cope with any more!"

"Good job!" laughed Jalli. "But there seems to be a lot of them in this new place," she said, looking over the gate.

"A huge number of young people!" agreed Jack. "I wonder what the Owner wants us to do there?"

"The only way you're going to find out is to go through the gate," said Grandma decisively. "Matilda, I think we should let these people put on these disgusting looking boots and join that festival – or whatever it is. Let's see if Jalli's gate will allow you through into Wanulka." Momori took Matilda's arm and strode off to the Wanulka gate. It seemed to welcome her. "OK, you two if we go off home and leave you to it?"

"But you haven't been here very long," complained Jalli.

"No. Not nearly long enough, but I don't want you two arriving in some strange place too late in the day." Momori took her granddaughter in her arms and kissed her, then grasped Jack's hand and said, "Look after yourselves, both of you!"

"Mum, are you going to Wanulka?"

"Seems so," said his mother with a hint of excitement. "I haven't brought anything to stay overnight, though."

"No matter. We're much the same size. You can borrow some of my clothes," offered Momori. The whole thing was settled and very soon after that the two ladies left through the gate into Wanulka. The garden suddenly seemed awfully quiet. Jack and Jalli stood where they were just inside the gate to Wanulka.

"We've started something there," observed Jack.

"Seems so. Grandma will really enjoy having your mum to stay."

"Good. So let's have a proper look inside this shed." They discovered pairs of scruffy jeans and T-shirts for each of them, and two small bags with some changes of clothes and shoes. Jalli found two long floaty dresses with skirts to the ankles, while Jack unpacked much the same thing in his! He looked at them and wondered if there had been a mistake.

"Robes!" exclaimed Jalli. "Full-length robes. How interesting."

"I'll look stupid in this!" Jack declared holding up a pale yellow one.

"No you won't, because you can be sure that where we are going everyone wears them."

"Not in that festival place."

"No, that's what these other things are for. Got to look quite a mess to fit in there it seems." A girl quite near the gate was sporting a pair of tight blue jeans with a torn pocket and holes in the knees. Girls and boys were wearing all sorts of stuff on the top – in fact some had no top at all (these were mostly boys – but Jalli noticed that was not entirely so!). This venture was going to take some courage.

"It's a bit like diving into the deep-end of a swimming pool," she said.

"The perfect expression," agreed Jack. They got into their scruffy stuff. It was clean, they noted, even if it didn't look it. They re-packed their bags and slung them on their shoulders. Jalli took Jack's hand and led him through the gate.

They were immediately swept up by the crowd. Jack tried to turn and take note of the position of the white gate. It seemed to stand all on its own in the heart of the throng. No-one else taking any notice of course. They pushed their way towards the edge of the crush. The heavy music was compelling – the decibels very high. After three songs from the band on stage there was a short intermission while the next performers got settled.

Jack addressed one of the guys next to him. "Great band!" he declared.

"Yup!" replied the boy.

Jalli tried asking something a bit more ambitious, "Who's next up?" she yelled in the ear of a girl who pressed up against her.

"Cool!" was all she got in reply. The band started up and Jalli and Jack swung with the rest. Communication with the people around them was quite impossible.

An hour later the session ended and people began to disperse. Jack and Jalli tried again to talk to people. All they got were one word answers that could mean anything.

"There's something wrong here," ventured Jalli.

"You're right," agreed Jack. "This mud doesn't feel right either, and the smell is all wrong. All these people in this muddy field should smell quite powerful. I was at a music festival last year for a day. Apart from the music, there's something... artificial about this."

He reflected on the word "artificial" and the more he thought about it the more apt it seemed. Jalli tried talking to some more people. She stopped a screaming girl and her boyfriend.

"Where's it happening now?" she asked. The girl just screamed some more and staggered off.

Just as Jalli was staring after her and Jack was looking round to see what else was happening, a boy and girl both about their age approached them.

"Hi," spoke the girl. "Great concert!"

"Yeah," replied Jack, "we only arrived an hour ago!" The girl and the boy beside her looked amazed.

"You look... are you, real?"

"I hope so," said Jack, "are you?" The girl reached out and stroked Jalli's arm.

"She's real, Matt," she stated. "How did you get here?"

"Well, actually," began Jack aware that they hadn't paid to come in. "We just arrived here from – another planet." He smiled, "Honestly!"

"Obviously," responded the boy called Matt, "which one?"

"Earth, Planet Earth."

"Do you hear that Sass? I've always wanted to meet someone from there. The place where all human beings originate from, they tell us."

"And you?" asked Sass of Jalli, "Are you from Earth too?"

"No, Raika."

"Raika...? I know where that is," said Matt. "It's in the Andromeda galaxy. A rare colony set up over three million years ago. People have been trying to get back there for many years but it requires a special connection. It is far beyond normal space travel. Wow! You are most welcome!"

"Great. Come on, we'll take you to our quarters. Just how did you get into our MIVRE?"

"We just arrived, through a white gate," explained Jalli. "It is a way that seems to connect solar systems and, who knows, even galaxies. There is a cot-tage where the Owner connects up people and places."

"She certainly does! You've been sent. I know you have!" Sass clapped hands in delight. "Come on. Come to our quarters and tell us all about it." Matt took a device from his pocket and held it up in the air. A red light blinked to their left and the throng of people slowed down and stopped. The red light approached them. It seemed to be attached to a platform that settled in front of them. Sass stepped up on the platform and beckoned Jalli and Jack to follow. Matt shepherded them all onto the boards and then held up his device again. Then the platform seemed to sink through the ground like a lift.

After a couple of metres at the most they emerged into a large room, artificially lit with wall lights. The room seemed empty except for a couple of doors, one to the right and the other to the left. Sass took Jalli's arm and guided her off the platform to the left and Matt ushered Jack to the right. He turned determined not to let Jalli out of his sight.

"No, that's the female changing rooms!" squeaked Matt

in amusement. "You don't want to go in there! We'll meet on the other side. Sass'll look after her." Inside the changing rooms Sass went to a bank of lockers and found her day clothes. The mud had mysteriously vanished from their boots and she stuffed both hers and Jalli's back into a drawer of the locker.

"I like that Experience," she said, "we get all the latest music. It's quite cool really. Of course, one day I would like to go to a real festival with real people. But I don't suppose I ever shall. We have another twenty-five years to go until we arrive at our destination and I don't expect they'll have enough people for a music festival there in any case. Anyway the music in the MIVRE is authentic – it's all the up to date stuff."

"So all that is a sort of clever computer program?" asked Jalli.

"You could put it like that. We call it the MIVRE – 'Multi-sensual, Interactive, Virtual Reality Experience.' It's a vast improvement on the virtual reality stuff our parents got when we set out."

"Set out? So where exactly are we? You've a lot of explaining to do here," said Jalli. "I'm confused. Mostly it's us that seem to confuse other people by just turning up from nowhere – but you don't really seem surprised to see us."

"No, we know how people get here. We have had people before – but not for a long time now. We've been asking for ages!" This confused Jalli even more! "We are on our way to a new planet," Sass explained as she got out a long dress very similar to the one Jalli had been given to wear by the Owner.

She began to relax about things – at least this was going the anticipated way.

Meanwhile, Jack had quickly sussed that they were on some sort of spacecraft. Matt was giving Jack some of the technical low-down. The MIVRE had been installed on board before they left but there was a team of geeks on Planet Earth Two (Matt and Sass's home world) responsible for sending technical updates, state of the art programming and new "Experiences". The on-board electronics team had the supplies and components necessary to last until disembarkation to keep rebuilding the whole of the craft's Nerve Circuitry, Computing and Communication Systems or NCCCS that controlled everything. Matt's dad was one of the leading technicians. "On Planet Earth Two he would have been in charge of his own electronics base by now," explained Matt, "but he gave it all up to come on this mission."

"How big is this spaceship?" asked Jack.

"We don't call it a ship. Ships are much smaller and designed to connect places much faster. We call this a 'Mobile Emigration Village' or MEV. All the MEVs are named after villages. Ours is *Great Marton*. It's named after James Cook's village – you know the great explorer and sailor on Planet Earth One in the eighteenth century. It is almost 2500 metres long and 2000 metres wide. There are twelve floors, that makes it over fifty metres high – not counting the expandable dock on the top and the mooring bar on the bottom. There are eight main engines but we have another four smaller backups that sit on swivel platforms on the stabilising wings, fore and aft."

They made contact with the girls again and Matt and Sass turned aside to speak to each other.

"I like what I see!" smiled Jalli as her eyes spied her Jack now dressed in a long flowing robe. "Pity there isn't a camera in the bag!"

"You look fantastic! I love that dress."

"It does feel nice," said Jalli swishing the skirts. "These people are really kind. I think we are in some kind of hotel-type building."

"Actually Jalli we're on a spaceship – a space village. We're not on a planet at all. We're travelling through outer space. I'm not sure where they're going – emigrating somewhere."

"That will explain what Sass meant by talking of arriving in twenty-five years."

Matt and Sass turned to them. "You two OK?"

"Yeah," said Jack, "as newcomers that just walked into your program – your MIVRE – how much can you tell us about where we are – where we really are?"

"It must be awfully confusing," observed Sass, "come to our suite and we'll tell you all about it."

"It must be nearly time for tea," said Matt with enthusiasm. "Are you hungry?"

"Now you mention it, I *could* eat something," reflected Jack. "Do you two live together? I mean, do you share the same suite?"

"No, not yet. We will next year when we're married. Come on!" Matt led them to a bank of lifts, ascended two floors and emerged on a very long corridor the sort Jalli had seen in the big hotel in Wanulka when she had gone inside on a sporting occasion. The doors were numbered and Sass opened the door of number fourteen. The suite consisted of a central lounge with a kitchen on the right and a bathroom with three bedrooms on the left – all on the same level.

"Mum! We've got visitors," yelled Matt. "This is Jack and this is Jalli. They stepped into the MIVRE. We've been praying for someone, and they have been sent. Jack comes from Earth One and – you won't believe this – Jalli here is from Raika in the Andromeda galaxy! The teacher said we hadn't had contact there in four thousand years."

"You are welcome. Raika! It looks as if the colony has evolved beautifully." Matt's mum quickly took stock of the situation. "This is good news. Have you let the commander know?"

"Not yet Mum."

"OK that's fine, we'll communicate straight away. Can't have people thinking we've been boarded by space pirates!" Matt's mum took them by the hand. "Welcome, my name's Yvonne, and this is Will," she said as Matt's dad appeared. Jalli performed her Wanulkan curtsy.

"Charming!" Will declared, too astonished to say anything else. Mum repeated Matt's story. Will walked across to the intercom and left a message on the commander's private number. "She will call round in person, you see. It is not often we get visitors. Only once in a very long while."

Jack and Jalli were ushered to a seat and sat side by side. Will talked about the mission to a new planet. They had left a secondary human colony (Planet Earth Two) almost seventeen years ago when the children were still small. Eighty families had been chosen but not all the children were theirs. Each family had been allocated at least one orphan to look after. They felt they had been sent by God who looked after them and their mission.

They were familiar with the white gates, or their equivalent, because they had kept in touch through very privileged people like Jalli and Jack with the rest of humanity around the universe. "You know, you are very privileged don't you? This only happens once or twice in a decade!" the man emphasised. Jack and Jalli said they knew they were extremely fortunate people but had not thought of themselves as particularly special.

"Oh, you are special alright. But we've been blessed with more than our share of visitors like you. That's why Matt and Sass recognised you. Cut off as we are, we think God knows that we need visitors more often." It quickly became clear that with less than two hundred and fifty people on board, meeting new people was very important. No matter how advanced the MIVRE became, the people in it still lacked the ability to hold much of a conversation as Jack and Jalli had discovered.

Sass explained that the purpose of bringing orphans like her was not just to give them a home – although that was a desirable thing – but to broaden the gene pool for the next generations. Matt was his parent's natural son but Sass had been adopted. Strict rules applied to ensure the best possible success of the new colony, and each of the children had been allotted a future marriage partner from the outset. Matt and Sass had been thus paired, and had grown up with each other knowing that when they got to eighteen they would be married, and then moved into a suite of their own as soon as Sass fell pregnant.

The late afternoon meal consisted of meat and fresh

vegetables and fruit. Jalli wondered how they managed this on their craft.

"Our MEV is very big," explained Sass. "We have a farm – well barns – in which animals are raised. They are very noisy."

"There is also a hydroponics house for vegetables," added Matt.

"But I like the tropical orchard house best," interjected Sass, "it's got real soil in it and trees. There are many species of butterflies and bees for pollination. The bees also give us honey. I'm sure you will be allowed to look round. We aren't allowed in there too often ourselves to preserve the environment, but of course you are our special guests."

Jack asked Matt what it was like growing up with the girl he knew he was to marry. Matt looked at Sass who giggled. "No problem," he smiled, "because I've got a good one! How does it work where you come from?" Jack explained that in most places on Earth they had moved (or were moving) to a system in which young people were left to make their own choices. Those people who were told who to marry were beginning to complain when they learned about the customs in other parts of the world. Jalli said that in Wanulka it was left entirely to the young people themselves – even when their parents thought they didn't like the choices they were making.

"So you can approach someone you haven't grown up with and ask them?" inquired Matt. "That must be very difficult."

"It is," replied Jack. "These days you're supposed to date first, ask them out to do something. Then you're expected to get to know each other very well – then even live together (although that is not universally approved of). But it does mean you don't have to have anyone you don't like. In fact, I never thought I would find a girlfriend because I never met anybody I liked enough."

"Until you met Jalli!" put in Sass.

"Right," agreed Jack, "but Jalli just kind of, well, that was different because we were sort of both given white gates."

"So you were meant for each other. God chose you to be together?"

"Yes," said Jalli, "but we don't feel we have to accept that. I wouldn't be with anyone I didn't want to be with. It always has to be my free choice."

"And that matters," added Jack giving Jalli a little hug, "because that makes me feel really good. It means she wants me for me – not because of any other reason."

"I can see that. But what if you meet somebody you like but they don't like you?" asked Matt.

"Oh. That happens all the time. You thank them for their approach and then politely tell them you're not interested," answered Jalli.

"That must be very difficult… for everyone," stated Matt.

"It is. Especially if people are really keen on someone."

Sass took up the conversation, "It seems a very complicated way of doing things. But I do like the idea of being able to say no if you have been allocated someone who smells and you can't stand them!"

"Sass!" said Will, "You must not talk about people like that."

"But sometimes boys do smell! Anna says her intended stinks. She can't stand him!"

"Well she hasn't grown up yet. She'll think otherwise in a couple of years."

"She'll be eighteen next year. He not only stinks, he's rude to her. And, anyway, he can't stand *her*," continued Sass. "If people were allowed to choose their own partners it would be much better."

"So. Who would you choose?" asked Yvonne.

"Matt, of course!"

"How many people think like you about their intended, and how many people think like Anna?" quizzed Yvonne.

"There's a few like Anna… there's Jo, of course." Jo and Pete were a special case. They hadn't been allocated to each other but had "taken a shine" to each other since they were small. They had become special friends and had lodged an official request to be reallocated to each other. The case was being heard the very next day.

"They are the exception," insisted Will. But it was important to deal with the issue properly now to avoid chaos or even conflict in the future.

"Are they 'in love'?" asked Jack.

"In love?" queried Matt.

"Jo and Pete. Are they 'in love' with each other?"

"Well, they love one another. Most of us do that. They are special friends. What do you mean by 'in' love?"

Jack looked at Jalli. How did one explain it?

Jalli tried, "Well," she smiled and took Jack's hand, "it's like when you meet someone that's really special, really different and you know they… well, when they excite you… they sweep you off your feet, figuratively speaking that is – only in our case Jack actually did it!"

"Did what?"

"Swept me off my feet! He carried me to the bench because of a bruise on my hip… look, it's when your heart beats faster when you are with someone and… you want to kiss them… and be with them all the time. When you're 'in love' you can't concentrate on much else, and your school work goes to pot, and you can't sleep at night, and you can't wait till you see them again and…"

"… you can't stop talking about it!" interrupted Jack laughing.

"… and it is when you forgive them for being cruel and teasing!" Jalli pushed Jack playfully. "It happens when you meet someone that you probably hadn't known about – but is just really different and made for you…"

"So, it's an emotional response to discovering the person you have been allocated to all along," put in Will.

"Well, yes. I suppose so. That is if you believe in Someone who sorts it all out like that."

"So there you are, Matt. Being in love is about finding the person who is right for you," stated Will.

"But is it the same as loving someone?" wondered Yvonne.

"No it isn't," broke in Jack. "You can be in love and have all those feelings, but loving is really about how you treat a person and care for them – not just how you feel about them. I am in love with Jalli, but I am learning to love her not just because she's great but because I want to look after her. My mum keeps reminding me of that. My dad said he never stopped feeling love for my mum, but he didn't love her enough to stop drinking or doing things only for himself."

"Things didn't work out for Jack's parents," explained Jalli.

"But they chose each other?" asked Matt.

"Yes. But my mum wasn't any good at choosing," responded Jack.

"Being able to choose doesn't mean many mistakes aren't made," added Jalli. "I believe young people should listen to the ones that love them, as well as their hearts. I have chosen Jack as my boyfriend, but I do think God has decided Jack and I should be together too. I wouldn't travel around the universe with him if I didn't!"

"And what about your parents?"

"They are both happy," answered Jack. "My mum really likes Jalli. At the moment she's staying with Jalli's grandma. She thinks Jalli's the best person I've ever met."

"You are both much blessed. And very welcome," added Yvonne. "Being in love is wonderful. But giving and receiving true love is forever…"

"I think Jo should be allowed to choose Pete," stated Sass bringing the conversation back home. "Her intended says he doesn't want to marry her if her heart is elsewhere. And I think love is more important than populating a colony! We, our generation, didn't choose to be part of this mission."

"Sass! We have guests. Now is not the time to debate your politics," urged Will.

"OK. But…" Sass was saved from her rebellious fervour because the door buzzer sounded. Will went to answer it.

"Commander Juliet! We were expecting you. Come on in and meet our two guests who arrived this afternoon in the MIVRE through a 'white gate'!" A smart middle aged lady, with the air of someone who knew what she was about, came sweeping into the room. "So, She has sent us some visitors to brighten our MEV. Pleased to meet you both."

"I'm Jalli and this is Jack," Jalli curtsied.

"Jalli's from Raika!" emphasised Will. "Jack is from Earth One."

"So now. Sit down. Tell us your story!" So Jack and Jalli recounted everything. Nothing seemed strange to these people, they all accepted it as quite normal.

"Excellent!" exclaimed Commander Juliet. "You are very welcome indeed. Sass and Matt here have been especially blessed. They are model young people that are most respected on *Great Marton* and thoroughly deserve to be the people to have been chosen to host you."

"We are very honoured to be here," said Jack sincerely. "Whenever we have gone through a white gate before we have been asked to do a special task. Do you know if there is anything we should be doing here?"

"Doing. No. Just being. Being is far more important than doing. You are here to bring a blast of fresh air into our MEV and delight the young people especially. You will not have been sent if you are not excellent examples of human life. And we crave for news, of course, so we will expect you to tell us the latest from your planets. And since we haven't heard from Raika in several thousand years you have a lot to recount," she gave a beaming smile at Jalli. "Sass, Matt, I charge you with writing everything down! You will be welcome tomorrow afternoon on the main deck when we shall all assemble, and I will ask you both to address the whole company. Five minutes about yourselves, and five minutes about your planets. Sadly we have a bit of business to deal with, a representation from two of our young people, but I hope that won't deflect from your visit."

"May we take them round the tropical house in the morning?" asked Sass.

"Of course you may. Just tell the guardian I sent you. Indeed I expect you to conduct them round the whole village." And with that Commander Juliet scooped up her skirts and swept back out of the room.

19

Early the next morning Sass and Matt delighted in showing their guests around the MEV. They were welcomed with great enthusiasm everywhere. Jalli had not been training properly of late and appreciated the exercise as they traversed ten decks hundreds of metres long. The three central corridors were serviced with a moving walkway part of the way. They visited the recycling department that dealt with everything from broken electronics to organic waste, including human. This was on the same floor as the nuclear power plant, a restricted area.

Much of the lower three decks were taken up with hydroponics. Jack was amazed at the density of the production. "We need to have the capacity to feed over four hundred people before we arrive," explained Matt. "This is my department; I have been especially trained for this work. We have tons of fertiliser stored if we need it, but all of our chemicals come from recycling at the moment," he explained. The wheat and barley had been genetically modified to produce a very high yield of grain. The grain to stalk and root ratio was very high. "We've improved it since we started," continued Matt. There was every type of vegetable imaginable. Between them Jack and Jalli recognised most of them, but there were others from planets that had not exported them as far as Earth One and Raika. Some of them needed very extreme conditions – high amounts of ultraviolet light, or a six hour day routine, or very high temperatures and water close to boiling point, or their roots immersed in high amounts of potassium – things that would kill most other things. But these conditions could be reproduced to perfection on board an MEV. The vast hydroponic chambers were sealed behind glass screens to enable these specific environments to be maintained.

Matt took them to the lab where he worked where they met a number of other people their age. They passed offices, a hospital and a school. Sass explained that they had all gone through school together and the same institution had moved from being a nursery to a university. They attended here for the arts and humanities. A history lecture was under way. Sass was training to be a nurse and hoped to do midwifery as soon as the babies started coming along. She showed Jalli the perinatal suite that was presently in moth balls. "Many of us will be turning eighteen soon and then we hope to have some babies," she said. Jalli couldn't resist asking Sass how they managed to maintain such a high degree of discipline. In Wanulka a sizeable number of the students had been engaging in sex long before they were eighteen. It was a national issue. Sass replied that officially it never happened but, and here she bade Jalli not to repeat this, in fact it did happen. "Because it is so easy," she explained, "but it is stupid because if you fall pregnant you are isolated from everybody, have to leave study and lose all honour. There are currently two babies – but they were born secretly in the residential section and they and their mothers are kept incommunicado.

"Commander Juliet will tell you everything is perfect –

but it isn't," continued Sass. "Quite a few of us young ones who cannot remember being anywhere else want to see more honesty and openness, but it's not easy to speak out. We don't have an official say until we're twenty-one. After that there will be some changes. But don't tell anyone what I just told you. Not on *Great Marton*, that is."

"I won't," assured Jalli. "But I do think you have got a lot going for you here. Just being allowed to do what you want is not always the best thing."

"If you lived here for a month you would become very impatient," suggested Sass.

"I'm sure I would!" agreed Jalli.

"We'll take you to the Command Centre next," said Matt indicating a lift. They ascended and emerged into a large, transparent dome.

"Wow!" declared Jack. They could see the whole extent of the upper surface of the MEV shelving away to the stabilising "wings" on the sides and the engine housings aft. Above them was an uninterrupted view of stars and galaxies so clear that Jack and Jalli stood in awe for at least five minutes. Matt pointed to a very faint star off the bow.

"That", he said proudly, "is the Tatania system where we're headed." In front of them was a sort of digital clock that stated, "Estimated arrival at Tatania: 25 years, 215 days, 20 hours, 33 minutes, 25 seconds."

"Planet Earth One is over to starboard," said Matt waving his hand expansively, "The Sun is too faint to be seen except by telescope. Behind us Planet Earth Two, where we came from, is hidden behind the engines."

In the apex of the dome was a large reflecting telescope

with two men perched on movable platforms beneath it. "These are our astronomers," explained Sass. "Mum helps them with a lot of the maths on her computer. She has a direct link to the telescope in our suite."

Towards the forward section of the dome was the helm. There was a remarkably small bank of screens and buttons. There was no-one around.

"Does the MEV drive itself?" asked Jalli.

"Mostly," answered Matt.

"Except in emergencies," said an authoritative voice from behind them, "then we can override the system from here." They looked round and saw Commander Juliet. "Welcome to the Command Centre. You'll take tea?"

Jalli and Jack nodded their assent. She asked her questions presuming the answers. They daren't decline.

"Thanks," squeaked Jack rather overawed.

"This ball in the centre," she indicated a red ball on a plinth behind a security glass, "before you ask as it is so obvious, redirects the MEV in any direction you wish. In an emergency we can break the glass." Jack thought of trains in England but thought it inappropriate to mention the similarity. In fact you just *listened* to this lady, he concluded.

"We can avoid large objects should they not be automatically detected (which they always are of course) by simply rolling it in the direction you need to go. If you lean hard on it then you have five minutes super blast that will move the MEV up to half a light year. One five minute blast, mind you, can't be repeated within seven weeks. The system takes that long to recharge. Persistent use would destabilise the craft anyway – she's not built for it. I'm telling you all this because ever since I was assigned to this vessel people have asked me why that red ball is in an upturned goldfish bowl. It's a very clever device to avoid unwelcome guests, should we encounter any... and before you ask, no we don't carry weapons. All they would do is provoke pre-emptive attack. We are not a battleship and could never compete with any space weapons platform. Our best weapon is surprise speed.

"Now the really interesting thing is this display. It shows our position in the home galaxy. Here we are on the fourth section of the spiral of the galaxy. This is our departure point," – the commander indicated a green arrow – "Planet Earth Two. This is our destination, the third planet in the Tatania system – we'll name it when we arrive..." She threw her arm up to the top of the screen towards a magenta arrow in the fifth section.

"Now if I touch this button... there, it has zoomed out and gives us a picture of the galaxy in relation to it's neighbours and... further out you can see the galaxy in relation to the first section of the universe and finally in relation to the five known sections. Miss Rarga, your Planet Raika is about here. So you can see how completely impossible it is for your people to visit our home galaxy unless it is through an IAS like your white gate..."

"IAS?" asked Jack.

"Immediate Access System – only God can provide those. In point of fact, She facilitates everything but mostly through Her created beings like us. The IAS is under Her direct control and although we can ask Her we have to wait for Her timing... which, of course, is impeccable."

Jalli wondered whether Commander Juliet believed God to be a bit like herself, assured, dignified, assertive and demonstrably "in charge". *She* had thought of God as much closer and more friendly. And sometimes she thought of God as a "she" but mostly, as a "he". "I wonder what Commander Juliet thinks God is like," whispered Jalli to Jack.

"So do I," muttered Jack.

"Questions?" the commander was aware that there was talking going on.

"We were just wondering how far the screen can do close up," said Jack.

"I see, interested in the microcosm as well as the macrosphere! There…" The screen zoomed right back in to the stars in the immediate vicinity. "These are the stars you can see through the dome walls… and we can get it to look in any direction from 'above', 'below' and to… the… 'side'… and from us looking out."

"What's that small bright object on the port bow?" inquired Jack, looking from the screen to the dome wall.

"Passing asteroid, I expect… now this is my office – the hub of operations." Jack and Jalli were ushered into a plush office just as someone was coming with a tray of tea things.

"Thank you, Simon," clipped the commander to the young man with the tray. He left but not without a smile in Jack and Jalli's direction. They took tea as it came, without sugar, as their host asked them about their immediate thoughts of the MEV. They were truly impressed, of course, and Commander Juliet was pleased.

As they passed the screen Jack noticed that the small bright asteroid had got noticeably nearer to the MEV. The digital display now read "Estimated arrival at Tatania: 25 years, 215 days, 19 hours, 22 minutes, 04 seconds."

"Now for my favourite," delighted Sass as they left the lift and entered a door that read, "Orchard Houses". There was a small lobby with a desk in it where the guardian sat behind a computer.

"The Commander has given us permission to visit the Tropical House," explained Sass.

When the man spotted Jack and Jalli he exclaimed, "Visitors!?"

"Yes."

"We are blessed," he said. "Go right in. Take care, it will rain in three quarters of an hour!"

"Perfect, we'll begin here and move round," returned Sass. As they pushed open the doors, she continued, "He knows I like this house better than all the rest of the MEV. If I wasn't destined for midwifery, I would have chosen this place as my favourite place of work." The humidity struck them straight away. "It's usually about 28C to 33C and up to 90% humidity," commented Sass. Through the next door they were among the trees. Bees buzzed all around and large butterflies of different colours and shapes fluttered about. "Here we have paw-paw, over there – those big trees – are mangoes. Along one side was a bed of pineapples and at the far end several rows of banana plants. Sturdy, healthy tomato vines stood against the wall. They walked past squashes and watermelons and several different kinds of plantains, then palm trees including coconuts that reminded them of Johnson's island. These were in a separate room with a bath of salt water that was regularly churned to cause salt spray.

"To make them feel at home?" suggested Jalli.

"Exactly! Coconuts are a real luxury. We don't produce enough for everybody to have some very often." Jack thought of Johnson and how he had lived on them for five years! The tour took them on through a Mediterranean garden with oranges and lemons, passion fruit and grapes of all varieties. Then into a temperate apple orchard which was as near to the cottage garden as they had experienced anywhere. Jalli took special delight in the beehives at the bottom of the orchard. "She loves bees and things," Jack told them. "She has real interest in them and wants to become a specialist one day."

"Does she now," said an orchard keeper emerging from a green wooden tool shed. He walked over to her and they stood engaged in animated conversation for a full ten minutes. Jack studied the different sorts of apples and pears on offer.

"How deep is the soil?" he asked.

"Several metres I expect," answered Matt. "I'm not entirely sure. We don't believe in soil in the hydroponics bays where I work!"

They left the orchards and had a quick lunch before it was time to go to the Main Deck to be formally introduced.

"Ladies and gentlemen," announced the commander, "welcome to our all-member weekly meeting. We are all here I am glad to say. Henry is fully recovered so we have no-one ill at all. Welcome Henry!" There was a general round of applause as Henry stood in acknowledgement. "Now our first business today is to introduce our visitors that have come to us through the latest IAS." There was rapturous applause. Visitors were so rare. "We have been indeed blessed," continued the commander, "because one of them comes to us direct from the Andromeda galaxy and the other from Earth One." (More applause.) "They arrived yesterday. Matt and Sass encountered them in the MIVRE. I will allow them to introduce themselves. Ladies first." The commander motioned to Jalli to begin. Later Jalli remarked that if she ever wanted proof that God helps people then she knew it when she stood in front of two hundred and fifty complete strangers all looking at her and concentrating on every word.

When she said that she brought good news from Wanulka where things continued in their usual safe way there was more applause. The town was growing and she was one of the first recipients of universal education. She told them of her parmanda studies, and how much she appreciated the beehives they had on board the MEV. She sat down with great acclaim.

Then it was Jack's turn who humbly said that he could not boast of coming from a far away galaxy – only Planet Earth One. But this was greeted with no less interest. Humanity's home world, it seemed, always had a special place in the human colonists of the cosmos. When he said he wanted to work with children it had a special impact because the mission was in anticipation of the arrival of a third generation in their midst.

After Jack had sat down, one excited teenager called out. Were Jack and Jalli going to stay? "Now you know the answer to that!" interjected the commander. IAS visits were always of a limited duration. Their task was solely to interest and inform. Although in other places Jack and Jalli had been called to do a specific task, here it would be to encourage people. She hoped their stay would, however, be of a substantial period. "The arrival of these young people," she concluded, "indicates that we have not been forgotten. And they will be equally important because they will be able to report on the good progress and excellent status of the *Great Marton*." There was more clapping as Commander Juliet shook the hands of Jalli and Jack in turn. She bid them remain on the platform. Then addressing the meeting she continued:

"Now we have a short item of business. An application from Jo and Pete for a reallocation of marriage partners. You have all been circulated with the application. I have received fifteen written comments. Ten of them are in favour, one in favour with some reservations and four against. I am going to ask Jo and Pete to give their reasons for wanting a reallocation and then hand over to Judge Joseph."

Jalli and Jack held hands in silent sympathy with Jo and Pete as they put forward their case based on friendship and love. They did their best to make rational arguments but it seemed all the logic was on the side of the status quo. Attraction was not an argument in itself. After a short period allowing both of them to speak it was time for Judge Joseph to make his decision. He was in favour of rejecting their application. He said that the law was the law and if people kept changing things then new precedents would undermine it and chaos would follow. Allowing people to be guided by their hearts rather than their minds was a recipe for disaster. There was nothing wrong with the previous arrangements that would result in a good solid foundation for the health, stability and expansion of the colony.

"Thank you Judge," said the commander at the conclusion of his speech. "Now we have all heard Pete and

Jo's case and the arguments against. You have had your chance to make written representations and these have been circulated for you all to read. We will move straight to a ballot. As the rules state, only those over twenty-one may vote and, as this will result in a constitutional change, it requires 66% in favour to pass."

There was a murmuring around the Main Deck. Young people began whispering into the ears of their parents and guardians. Papers were circulated for the voters to tick in favour of the petition or against the petition. The completed papers were folded and put into a circulating ballot box which was brought up to the table at which the commander was sitting. She called the tellers to come onto the platform. Then, just as the tension arose in anticipation of the counting of the votes, the general alarms sounded! Red lights flashed above the doors.

"Everyone remain where you are!" commanded Juliet. She pressed an intercom to her ear. "Apparently we have more visitors. This time from the Intergalactic Police!" She detailed a deputy to accompany her to the Command Centre while everyone settled to wait in the Main Deck. Jack and Jalli were relieved to be able to leave the platform and moved down to be with Matt and Sass.

"We *are* having a busy time!" declared Will. Jalli noticed Jo and Pete sitting very close with hands held tightly together. What a moment to be interrupted she thought, and found herself saying a prayer for them.

Jack said, "That would be the 'asteroid' then!"

"I would say you are about right," responded Matt. Then, very suddenly, the double doors of the Main Deck burst open and two figures dressed in black uniforms and black helmets covering their whole faces stepped briskly in and each raised above their heads a device, not unlike the one Matt had used on the MIVRE. A high pitched noise filled the room and then ascended beyond earshot. People put their hands to their ears and then began falling to the ground. Jalli saw Jack sway and instinctively grabbed him but his lifeless body slumped over far too heavily for Jalli to hold and she crumpled beneath him.

It only took Jalli a few seconds to work out that the noise from the device had stunned everyone – except her. There was only the noise of the people breathing and the faint sound of the engines that was always there. She could feel Jack's heart thumping in his chest above her. Then she heard what she guessed were the two black figures stomping around the Main Deck. She instinctively decided to keep absolutely still. Her first reaction had been to push Jack off her, but then she considered that, in the interest of self preservation, the best course of action was to pretend to be unconscious like the rest. Out of the corner of her eye she saw the black figures checking the people.

After what seemed like an age, a black leg brushed against her, and then the two figures stomped out of the chamber. She heard them talking outside the doors and could see their legs. They were communicating with their ship. "Confirm. All 'asleep'." one of them reported. "All clear for the boarding party." It sounded like a woman's voice and the accent was almost Wanulkan. "Come on," said the other, "we'll head for the dock. Which way?"

"This way," the female replied. They moved off to the left.

"That is not translated," Jalli suddenly realised, "that *is*

Wanulkan." She struggled from beneath Jack, kissing his sleeping face as she extricated herself. The Wanulkans had left two devices on the table still turned on and obviously left to keep the people under. Jalli wondered what to do. Her first thought was to turn them off, but a quick glance did not tell her how she should do it. To press the wrong button, or turn a knob the wrong way might be fatal. While she pondered this, she recalled the invaders had gone to the dock. If she were to get to the Command Centre first and press the red ball she could… perhaps she could… steer the MEV away from the invaders' ship.

Jalli poked her head around the doors in the direction the invaders had gone, and seeing the way was clear, shot off in the direction of the Command Centre. When she got to the lift door, she found the commander and her deputy slumped on the floor inside the lift. They too had been stunned. There was a device beside them. Should she move it? She kicked it away but it struck a wall and bounced right back into the lift! The commander didn't stir. Jalli couldn't wait. Speed was of the essence. She must get to the Command Centre before the people in black. She stepped over the commander and deputy and pressed the lift button. To her relief it responded immediately and began to ascend.

At the top she lightly stepped away from the door of the lift just in case there were more invaders. There weren't. Or at least she couldn't see any. She could see the invaders' ship bristling with weapons off the port bow. Without a moment's hesitation she ran across to the emergency plinth and gave the glass around the red ball a hefty kick. It shattered – half the weight would have done it. She looked at it for a second. Which way?

That didn't really matter, she told herself, but she must lean down on it to get the sudden speed. She pushed down as hard as she could and rolled it away from her at the same time. The MEV immediately lurched forwards followed by a horrifying crash and a huge shudder that shook everything off the shelves.

Jalli was thrown backwards to the floor. The lights failed and, for a split second, a brilliant flash coming from the port side lit up the whole dome – then there was total darkness. The next thing Jalli was aware of was that the MEV started to hum loudly, and when she looked up she could see stars racing across the sky.

Jalli picked herself up and, using the starlight, felt her way back to the lift. As she arrived a low emergency lighting came on and illuminated the control panels. The black uniformed invaders may not be far away from the Command Centre lift, she feared, and may be sending for it. Jalli did not want to be caught on her own with nowhere to hide.

In fact the invaders had just reached the lift in the dock when the surge had sent them flying across the floor. During the two minute surge, power is diverted from every system except life support and gravity and, like everyone else, they were plunged into the dark. In the Command Centre Jalli worked by a combination of the emergency lighting and starlight.

She tried to drag the commander from the lift but she was too heavy. But, leaving the commander half in and half out of the lift effectively deactivated it when the power was restored precisely two minutes later. The stars stopped moving, the lights came on and the usual hum resumed.

The desperate invaders had taken to the stairs. They were

not sure what was happening, but the answer was bound to lie in the nerve centre of the vessel, and they were making for the Command Centre. Jalli wanted to turn off the stunning device if she could.

She picked it up and stared at it. She wondered what it's range was. She ran to the other side of the Command Centre. Commander Juliet was still asleep. She must turn it off. Which way should she turn the knob? Anticlockwise was the Wanulkan direction for turning everything off, water, gas and electrical devices. She knew in England – and in the beach resort too – it went the opposite way for water and gas. Jack had laughed when she was unable to turn off the water tap above the sink because she was trying to turn it the wrong way. So which way was this going to work?

She pondered. These people had spoken Wanulkan – it wasn't a translation, she was sure of it. So if they came from Raika then perhaps their electrical devices obeyed the Raikan standard. Carefully she turned the knob one notch anticlockwise. The deputy twitched! Was that a good sign or a bad one? She turned it one more notch. This time both people seemed to be waking up. One more notch and they were definitely regaining some consciousness. Jalli turned the knob as far as it would go. To her relief, the commander and her deputy began to sit up.

Stomp, stomp, stomp, stomp – the invaders were coming up the last flights of stairs. Jalli pushed the commander as hard as she could back into the lift from where she had dragged her. The large woman was just trying to get up and fell backwards onto the lift floor. Jalli then stepped smartly into the lift herself and pressed the descend button just as the doors to the stairs swung open and the invaders entered the Command Centre. By the time the lift descended the two floors the commander and the deputy were on their feet.

"Stay there," ordered Jalli in a voice as authoritative as any the commander had heard since the *Great Marton* had left Earth Two space. Rubbing their necks they instinctively obeyed as Jalli bounded back onto the Main Deck, grabbed the devices on the table and turned the knobs anticlockwise. She saw people start to move. Then she sprinted back to the lift.

"All is safe now. The stunning devices are turned off," she panted. "They didn't affect me – probably because I'm Raikan. The invaders are Raikan too, I think. They didn't bargain on another like them being around!"

Commander Juliet uttered a quiet thank you to Jalli followed by a gentle, "Perhaps 'doing' can be as important as 'being' for visitors after all." She pulled at her clothes to straighten them and strode into the Main Deck. "Is everyone alright?" she spoke firmly.

People nodded and grunted their assent. "We have two people claimed to be Intergalactic Police, but who are probably pirates, in the Command Centre. Their ship must be close by and they'll be boarding soon. They have stunning devices that work with sound. Plug your ears at the first hint of contact."

"Excuse me," interjected Jalli. "I think the pirate ship is a long way away. I pushed and rolled the red emergency ball and we surged away."

"Clever girl!" declared the deputy. "But they could still be on our tail. We must apprehend the two men in the Command Centre."

"At least one is a woman," observed Jalli. Why should

people assume they were both men? Interesting. But Jalli did not have time to think about it. The commander detailed half a dozen for the stairs, while she and four more went back up the lift. Jalli felt less important now everyone was awake. For a time she had been in charge of the MEV all by herself. She didn't feel this for more than ten seconds, though, because Jack was beside her cuddling her. Matt and Sass were there too.

"You saved us!" Sass was shouting. "You *did* have a job to do!"

"It seems so," said Jalli. "I am afraid that it is probably because these 'pirates' or whoever they are, are from my home planet. Probably my own city."

"Wanulka?" wondered Jack.

"They spoke Wanulkan without an accent. It was because their stunning devices didn't affect Raikans that I did not flake out like the rest of you."

"But you did all the right things."

"I hope so. There was a huge crash just after I hit the red ball. I hope there isn't any damage."

Half an hour later the commander and the arresting party returned to the Main Deck.

"Ladies and gentlemen," she began, "it seems that we have two more visitors from Wanulka on Planet Raika with us today. Raikan pirates came on board with the express purpose of plundering the *MEV Great Marton* while we were incapacitated by clever devices. However, thanks to our other Raikan guest they did not succeed. Their fellow pirates are now stranded in their spaceship and will probably not make it to a suitable planet for repairs in less than two generations. Our guest Jalli here not only took us half a light year away from them, she also took out half their engines and one stabiliser it seems. Yet, I am pleased to report there is minimal damage to our mooring bar, the operation of which is unimpaired. The whole event was all recorded on the camera array that comes into operation when the emergency ball is operated. Thanks to the initiative and skill of Jalli Rarga, the most dramatic emergency in the life of *MEV Great Marton* to date has been overcome in less than," she checked her watch, "an hour and five minutes. You will also be pleased to know that our estimated time of arrival has diminished by 1 year, 110 days, 16 hours, 33 minutes and 16 seconds."

A loud resounding cheer filled the Main Deck. The teenagers all began chanting, "Ja-lli, Ja-lli…" The commander allowed the chanting half a minute before raising her hand.

"We will all return to our quarters and recover from our ordeal. Reconvene here in precisely twenty-four hours."

That night neither Jalli nor anyone else slept much. Jack crept into her room.

"Jalli, are you awake?"

"Uh -huh…"

Jack knelt beside the bed and kissed her.

"Jalli, you were brilliant!"

"I just followed my instincts. I made lots of mistakes. I was on the verge of panic. I was just going over everything and telling myself how I should have done things differently. Instead of throwing the device away, I kicked it and it bounced right back off the wall into the lift! I keep seeing that. And I was lucky with the red button. Jack, I could have wrecked the whole ship!"

"But you didn't Jalli. You did what you had to. You succeeded. What you did was more than good enough!"

"I guess God was looking after me. God sent us, Jack. He chose us to be here. To do this."

"He chose you, Jalli."

"No, *us*. Without you I never would have dared to come here."

"But you went through your white gate on your own without knowing who you might meet…"

"Yes, but you forget. I was running away from someone!"

"But you didn't run away from what you had to do this time."

"I knew God was with me. As soon as I realised they were Raikan I knew why I was here."

"You did great Jalli. I love you."

"… and I love you! But we'd better try and sleep, Jack. I'm all in."

Jack leaned over her and kissed her again. By the time he had tip-toed back out of the room, Jalli was sound asleep.

At the appointed hour the assembly was reopened. Two unmasked people dressed in black accompanied them. Commander Juliet led them to the platform. She addressed the gathering.

"Welcome everyone. I trust you have all slept well. These two misguided people," she indicated the pirates, "realising the game was up, quickly surrendered. Ladies and gentlemen, whatever their backgrounds they have to remain with us.

They were born on their pirate ship. *They* have no choice and *we* have no choice but to allow them to remain here. They will work – hard. I am putting them under the supervision of Henry in the recycling unit. Everyone knows how gentle and kind Henry is!"

There was a ripple of laughter. Henry was a big man known for his insistence that no-one finished work until his deck was cleared, even if they had to work through tea!

"Now, without more ado, we have interrupted business! Tellers, come forward." At last the votes were counted – Jo and Pete moved close together.

A teller mounted the dais. The hall was hushed. A teller stood forward and tapped the microphone. He cleared his throat and announced nervously, "Ladies and gentlemen, the petition is successful." There was a moment's silence, and then a resounding cheer from the teenagers. The commander raised her hand. The company fell silent. The teller continued. "Out of 128 votes cast, 98 were in favour with 30 against. This is 76%." More cheers. Again the commander waved for silence. She replaced the teller at the microphone.

"I applaud this decision. I think we have done the right thing. My own opinion was swayed by three things. First the readiness of Jo and Pete's intended partners to release them on the ground that it would not work if their partners favoured another. Secondly, the apparent universal support the petition had among the young people themselves, even though they do not have a vote of course. But thirdly, because I overheard, yesterday, a young woman stating strongly that love must take precedence over human plans and human rulings, no matter how well-intentioned. So long as the love is genuine – not about self-gratification to the exclusion of the interests of others – I believe that to be true. There *needs* to be order, as Judge Joseph has quite rightly said, but I believe that if we live within the freedoms and constraints of true self-giving love, then we shall be governed by a higher power than a law of human construction. As Virgil said *Omnia Vincit Amor* – Love Conquers Everything. I congratulate Jo and Pete." There was more cheering until the commander held up her hand to continue.

"Before the celebrations, I must tell you. If there are to be other applications of this kind then they will all have to come before the whole company – and love will have to be proven. True love is not an infatuation or a passing fancy. You are dismissed. All but essential staff may have two days off work!" The commander sat down to more applause. Henry came forward to the platform out of the throng and fixed his eyes on the prisoners. "You two! Recycling is an essential service. You begin straight away. No holiday for you!" and he and his fellow department workers marched them off to the recycling unit.

Matt and Jack watched them go.

"Henry is against any changes," said Matt, "it will take him time to come to forgive Jo and Pete. I hope he doesn't take it out too much on those two."

"I think they have been let off lightly," responded Jack. "I know people who would lock them up and throw away the key."

Meanwhile Jalli was mobbed. Everyone wanted to know about what she had done. Jo and Pete were also surrounded. They looked in a real state of shock. Their parents took them in charge and led them off to rest. An hour later and Yvonne came and rescued Jack and Jalli and took them and Sass and Matt back to their suite. "You know what," said Sass as they entered, "I think Commander Juliet overheard me saying about Jo."

"I am sure she did. I keep telling you walls have ears!" said Will.

"But she agreed with me!"

"This time, maybe. But she won't always agree with your rebellious ways… I think I'd better put in for a re-allocation!" said Matt with mock sarcasm. Sass sent a well-aimed cushion across the room. "Don't you dare!" she yelled.

"Just joking," he laughed. "I just wanted to make sure you still love me."

"Well I did until just then!" Jack and Jalli smiled quietly.

"You two must be exhausted!" breathed Yvonne.

"Jalli might be. I spent a lot of it asleep I'm afraid." He looked down and saw that Jalli was already asleep against him. He gently lifted her from the sofa and carried her through into the bedroom.

Jack and Jalli spent ten days on *MEV Great Marton*. They had sharing sessions and gave talks about the current happenings in their own worlds. The young people were full of questions like all teenagers. When they learned about wars and poverty in what Jack called the "third world" on Planet Earth they were quite upset. Terrorism was something they found extremely difficult to understand, living as they had done in a small, isolated community. Jalli told them about Wanulka, and for the first time told someone else about

Maik Musula. The *Great Marton* young people concluded that, despite the risk to them from the very occasional space pirates (which Jalli had been sent to deal with anyway!) they were in an ideal situation. They were so safe they could not imagine how Jack and Jalli lived with all the threats in their worlds.

"You don't have to go *back*! I'm sure we can persuade the villagers to accept you. They did change the rules yesterday, after all," volunteered Sass. "And we have gained two Raikans already."

"We're very honoured!" responded Jalli. "But we can't stay. My grandma would really miss me... us. And anyway, you've grown up here. I know this MEV is very big and, even with four hundred plus people, would be quite spacious – but we're so used to bigger places, we'd feel restricted."

"They get around at least two galaxies," pointed out Matt. "I can understand that. You don't miss what you can't see."

"We'll miss you," returned Sass, "is there anyway we can stay in touch?"

"Not that we know of at the moment," answered Jack. "But who knows what will happen in the future."

They were exploring the MIVRE Experience in among lakes and snow clad mountains when Jack noticed the gate. He caught Jalli's hand and directed her attention. She saw it too. "It looks as if it is time to go," declared Jalli.

"It looks like it," said Jack. "Are you ready?"

"I hate leaving, but we must have finished what we came here for. It's about time we checked in with your mum and my grandma. I hope they are getting on OK. We've been long enough out of contact."

The others spotted Jack and Jalli looking at something. "What have you found?" asked Sass. She couldn't see anything.

"It's one of your gates, isn't it?" sighed Matt.

"Yes," acknowledged Jack simply.

"So you have to go!?" Sass threw her arms around Jalli. Jalli hugged her in return.

"We have to go!" stated Jalli. "But it's been good, really good!"

"Yes, thank you for everything!" agreed Jack.

"No. It's us that need to thank you!"

"Give our love to your parents," declared Jalli, "and thank them for their hospitality. We won't be able to write I'm afraid. And give our regards to Commander Juliet. We'll keep you in our prayers!"

"What about your things?"

"Keep them as a souvenir. They were meant just for this place. We have our own clothes the other side of the gate. Good luck on your venture. We'll be thinking of you in twenty-four years time!"

"And may your wedding be a good one," added Jalli.

"Thanks. Good luck in Wanulka. I hope you stay safe!"

They all exchanged final hugs. Jack and Jalli found it specially hard to step through the gate but they finally managed it. Suddenly they were back in the familiar cottage garden.

"That was something really special!" stated Jack. "It has been great. I like this robe."

"And I like this dress. We'll keep them and wear them sometimes." Reluctantly they changed into their everyday clothes suitable for Wanulka.

"How dangerous is it? Wanulka."

"I never thought of it as dangerous at all. How those Wanulkans got aboard a pirate ship is something I keep wondering. If you can only 'travel from Andromeda by IAS'," Jalli spoke like the commander, "I can't imagine how they got there."

"Perhaps they have been travelling many generations. It may simply be down to time. They could easily have left thousands of years ago. I guess they have been fleecing vulnerable space travellers for a long time… and now they have met their match in Jalli Rarga!"

"Jack," Jalli looked more troubled than Jack had even seen her. "I know everyone thinks I'm wonderful because I saved them, but it was mostly down to luck. I still shudder when I think about it. I didn't think about steering. I could have run straight into the pirate ship and killed everybody."

"I don't think so. I was talking to Matt and he told me that MEVs are fitted with deflector beams. It wouldn't have hit straight on."

"Now you tell me! I've been worrying about that ever since I touched that red ball!" Jalli was quite upset. Jack took her in his arms.

"You did exactly the right thing!"

"More by luck than judgement," she snuffled.

"Don't knock yourself. Most people would not have done what you did. I think what you did was brilliant! You're quite a girl. We never get everything right, none of us, but what you did *worked*! It's OK." He gave her a special hug. "Now, let's see if we can make a cup of tea in the kitchen."

"Am I allowed sugar?" she smiled through her tear-stained face.

"Look, I'll do you a deal. If I get bossy, you tell me, and if you get bossy, I'll tell you!"

"Done!" said Jalli, "So I can have sugar?"

"Would it make any difference if I said you couldn't?"

"None at all!" she laughed. Jack always made her feel better.

They spent an hour or so relaxing and getting used to just being on their own together again. Finally Jalli declared, "Time to brave Planet Raika!"

"Andromeda here we come! I can't wait to tell Mum just how far away from Earth she is!"

"Earth One, to be precise!" added Jalli. "At least we know we're in the same universe!"

20

"Jalli, you know in my opinion it's not safe." Momori was more anxious than Jalli had seen her for a long time. She and Matilda had got on very well indeed, but as the days their children were on the MEV increased they had both become agitated. Now they were behaving especially protective.

"But Grandma, I know there have been attacks, but there have been thousands and thousands of people in the park over the past three years and nothing has happened in the last two. The chances of anything happening to me are very unlikely."

"There would be no likelihood at all if you didn't go."

"But you know I have taken a special interest in the parmanda hives. This is my chance of seeing them and studying them for myself."

"But sitting there for hours hidden among the trees all by yourself is inviting trouble."

"Lots of people do it, Grandma. You have to be patient, and be alone, or you disturb the insects. You have to become part of the environment. They have to accept you. It takes at least fifteen minutes before they start to behave normally when they are disturbed."

"Well if you must go, you should take Jack."

"I'd like to. But two people in one place is too much for parmandas. They don't act normally." Jalli could be determined when she wanted to be. And she felt they were all making too much of the Parmanda Park predator. The police had been hunting a man who had attacked women in the park for years. He had struck three times but the last attack was over two years ago.

Mr. Bandi was especially keen on her going. He had urged her to follow up her interest. He had often been himself, he had explained, and found the parmanda hives very rewarding. The whole experience was tremendously satisfying, he had declared. If Jalli was serious about her biology, she really ought to stalk the hives. He had pointed out the best place to be from his experience, and described how to get there. Certainly it was a long way off the track, but that made it all the more rewarding because the insects were not as often disturbed. Jalli decided not to share this last piece of information with her grandmother as it would have alarmed her even more.

"… and Mr. Bandi said that if I were seriously wanting to study biology at university, I really ought to go stalking in the park," concluded Jalli.

"And what if Mr. Bandi is the predator?" retaliated Momori.

"Oh Grandma! Poor Mr. Bandi. So wrapped up in his biology and studies, he couldn't possibly be a pervert that attacked young women. You don't know Mr. Bandi!"

"Oh. And how well do you know him?"

Jalli knew she was not going to win this battle of words and fell silent. At the same time, Momori knew that she was not going to change her granddaughter's mind.

A few days later Jack said, "I've been thinking about this

proposed outing to Parmanda Park." They were in the cottage garden behind the house and he had become aware of the gentle buzzing of the bees as they went from flower to flower, "Are you *really sure* it is safe?"

"Perfectly safe," grunted Jalli, "the insects never go for anyone unless you actually physically disturb the hive."

"I wasn't thinking of the insects."

"Oh not you too!" glared Jalli. "No one would ever do anything or go anywhere if you think about every possibility. Look at the adventures we've had!"

"This just feels different."

"That's because I am going without you, and you want to look after me all the time. He is with me even when you're not." She spread her arms to indicate the God who constantly provided for them and loved them so much.

"You're probably right. But, all the same I'll be relieved when you get back safe and sound," smiled Jack.

"It's nice to be loved," said Jalli. "I'm a lucky girl having someone to watch over me and care for me!" and she put a grass stained finger on his nose and kissed him. "But I do want to go!"

"And far be it for the person who absolutely adores you, and loves you, and admires you and thinks the world of you to stop you!" blurted Jack. "But you just look after yourself, that's all I ask."

That same evening they were all together beside a log fire. Grandma was crocheting a bag in the way that Matilda had shown her. She had taken to it very quickly. Matilda was engaged in knitting a chunky cream sweater with some giant-sized knitting needles.

Looking up at Jack she said, "What are you doing, letting Jalli go to this dangerous park all by herself?"

"It is not dangerous!" interjected Jalli. "You all know I really want to go. This is a conspiracy. You've all been talking and plotting to stop me!"

"Not me," protested Matilda. "It is just that even I have heard talk of the Parmanda Park predator. He's infamous!"

"I am not going looking for the Parmanda Park predator. I am going to stalk the hives that's all!"

"I think," sighed Momori, "we will all have to accept that Jalli has made up her mind, and none of us will change it." She was right. Nothing was going to deter Jalli now. It was just a matter of deciding the day she was going to go. "I do think, though, that we all ought to be in Wanulka when you go. And you must take your fancy mobile phone thing to use in an emergency."

"Oh, alright," Jalli conceded, "but I won't have it turned on."

"I didn't expect you would," said Momori.

The very next day Jalli went up to the school. She waited until the students emerged at the end of the day and went to the biology labs. Sure enough Mr. Bandi was there feeding the worms some of the leftovers from lunch. He greeted her with a smile. When the worms had eaten that, he explained, he would have some lovely worm manure to plant his seeds in. He was pleased to see Jalli and asked how things were in her gap year.

"Oh, just here and there," she replied.

"Well, make sure you don't waste your time. A bright girl like you should be having some proper adventures." If only he had known, thought Jalli.

"It's about doing something really special that I've come."

"And what might that be?"

"I've decided to stalk the hives in Parmanda Park."

"Good. You should… but you will be careful?"

"I promise I won't disturb them," she assured him, "I'll go exactly where you said, and I'll not approach too near."

"I'm sure you won't," observed Mr. Bandi as he replaced the lid on the worms, "but it isn't the hives that bother me. I know you will do all the right things."

"What, then?"

"A young woman sitting alone in a secluded part of Parmanda Park needs to take special care these days."

"You're just as bad as my grandma!"

"She's a wise woman. You cannot be too careful. But personally, I would never let anyone stop me enjoying the wonders of nature. Just be aware. That's all."

"OK, Mr. Bandi, I will."

"When are you planning to go?"

"This Saturday."

"The weather should be good. Come back and tell me about it. Take my love to the insects!"

Jalli left the biology teacher straightening the desks in the lab and sighing over the mess his students had made. "It never improves," he mumbled. Jalli smiled. She had always liked Mr. Bandi. He loved his creatures, and his students. One of the best things about being a teacher, he said, is seeing his charges grow to be accomplished young men and women. Not all did, but some like Jalli had been special from the beginning. She took her leave with a smile.

"You look after yourself," he shouted after her. "I haven't

put all that work into marking your essays for you to come to grief!" For a fleeting moment Jalli almost gave up the idea of going to the park. So even Mr. Bandi would be relieved when she got back safe, no matter how devoted he was to watching the parmandas himself. But then her determined nature took over. How dare this man, this predator, whoever he was, stop her and others enjoying God's world! She had made up her mind she was going on Saturday, the weather forecast was perfect and the hives would be at their best.

Saturday soon arrived. Jalli was up at dawn, packing food for the whole day. She would definitely be back before dark she promised. She refused to let them even see her to the bus-stop. They were all disciplined and restrained, doing their best to hide their anxiety, and the sooner they parted the happier she would be. The traffic wasn't too dense and she arrived at the park, some three yukets on the other side of town from her grandmother's house, in good time.

Parmanda Park had been especially preserved because of the parmanda hives the area contained. It was essential to register for permission to stalk the hives, but otherwise people could just walk around so long as they kept to the paths. Dogs were not allowed.

Those who wanted to run or exercise were encouraged to do it elsewhere. (There were many interesting places to ramble in the countryside not far from the park.) Just inside the entrance was a visitor centre with an exhibition about the parmandas, a little about the history of the park, and toilets. On the wall there were maps of the tracks and the park rules. You had to be allowed, of course, to leave the tracks but only to stalk the hives as single people. If you were stalking a hive you had to place a marker, supplied by the visitors' centre, on the spot you left the track. If you caught sight of anyone else you had to leave the vicinity immediately and as quietly as possible. It was known that parmandas were not easily harmed, but if they were disturbed then they would not display. Describing the unique behaviour of a hive in words is difficult. Photographs and movie pictures were no alternative to seeing the display first hand surrounded by the scents and atmosphere of the park. Wanulka was *the* place in the whole country for parmandas. But many people had spent hours in the park and had never witnessed a full display.

A display happens when the vast majority of the insects belonging to a particular hive return from wherever they have been foraging at some kind of signal that isn't wholly understood, and converge on the hive at the same time. At first they do not attempt to enter the hive, but make circles and spirals overhead and around the hive and then, suddenly, when they are ready, cork-screw into the hive's three entrances one after another with a sound that can only be described as a slurp with a pop at the end of it – but that description is very approximate. A person has to hear it for him or herself to really know what it sounds like. The hive is a conical structure made of mud and leaf-litter mixed with secretions from the insects themselves. Each entrance is directed at the spot each of the planet's three suns rise in the morning. There is twenty minutes between the first, Jallaxa and Skhlaia, and ten more before Suuf. But each rises in a slightly different part of the sky, and the parmandas welcome each with a special entrance. It doesn't seem to matter whether the rising sun is actually hidden behind trees, the insects still knew which direction to look. The stalker's trick is to approach from an easterly direction (the Raika's orbit being the opposite of Earth's) from where you could see all three entrances.

Jalli had listened carefully to Mr. Bandi's instructions and stalked the hive he had had most success with. She found it fairly easily. Previous stalkers had installed a log to sit on and so she had no difficulty in knowing how near she could approach. The buzzing quieted as she sat herself down. The insects were going to take some time to get used to her, so she made herself comfortable and sat as quietly as she could.

Jalli was, of course, successful because she was patient. She waited three and a half hours but was rewarded with a superb display. When all the insects had entered the hive, she began to feel stiff and hungry. She also needed the toilet. She quietly withdrew promising the parmandas she would be back in the afternoon. As she neared the path she saw someone quickly get up from a sitting position and run off. This struck her as strange, but if it had been "the predator" he wouldn't have run off, would he? It was probably someone not wishing to approach the same hive.

As Jalli emerged from a wooded part of the path her heart stopped. There on the path in front of her was the bane of her life, Maik Musula. Oh, no! How was she going to get rid of him out here. A shiver went up her spine. He couldn't be the Parmanda Park predator could he? He had been weird and had freaked out, but she never felt he was actually dangerous before. Strange as it sounded, she was quite relieved that when he saw her he approached and started to talk in his usual way.

He explained he had seen her on her way to the park and followed her. He loved her and wanted to make sure she was safe.

"Of course I am safe! Look you're really bugging me. Can't you see that if you felt anything for me you would just leave me alone!"

"No-one loves you like I do," he whined. Well, thought Jalli, as least that bit was true. She went to walk on but he just stood in front of her in the same way he had done before, but he made no attempt to touch her.

"Just go away!" she shouted at him. Shouting seemed to do the trick with Maik. But this time it worked wonders in a way she had not anticipated. Suddenly, running up behind her as fast as his little legs could carry him was Mr. Bandi.

"Mr. Bandi! What are you going here?"

"Is this man bothering you, Jalli?" he breathed heavily as he came up close.

"He's always bothering me. And he knows that he has to leave. Right now!" Jalli glared at Musula. His expression was one of resignation, and deep sadness. He seemed at last to have got the message, and good, kind Jalli began to feel sorry for him. But before he could turn and go back towards the park entrance, Jack and his mother suddenly emerged from a thicket off to the right. Matilda was brandishing her large knitting needles and was yelling terrifying oaths. Jack swooped and sent Mr. Bandi sprawling. Maik was quickly pounced on by Matilda who sat on him and stared into his shocked and terrified face. "How dare you assault my daughter-in-law!" she yelled.

Jalli pleaded: "Jack! Get off Mr. Bandi. He was only here to protect me! You, all of you, you have gone too far!"

Mr. Bandi slowly regained his feet. "I think we have all made mistakes." Mr. Bandi grunted as he rubbed his hip. "In truth I have always under-estimated this young lady. I hadn't the courage to suggest I stood guard. I believed she would have refused." Mr. Bandi rubbed his hip some more, but it seemed to have survived Jack's assault.

"What about this guy?" hissed Jack, ignoring the flustered biology teacher and staring at the terrified Maik Musula.

"He's just a stupid man who can't take no for an answer," stated Jalli. "He's not going to hurt anyone – and, from now on, I think he will give me a huge wide berth."

"The police are on their way," stated Matilda, "I phoned them when I saw that man."

She indicated Mr. Bandi who was now expressing his regret at his lack of courage once again.

"Your grandma lent her a mobile so we could keep her reassured," added Jack by way of explanation.

"Oh, Matilda! What an absolute farce. Now we're all going to look stupid!" sighed Jalli. "Come on, let's all get back to the visitors' centre and clean up."

They dragged Musula back to his feet. He walked quickly ahead of them, but Matilda was making sure he didn't get away. She was going to report him whatever anyone said. As they approached the centre there was clearly something afoot. Half a dozen police officers were manhandling a man into the back of a police vehicle. Sirens on the road indicated more police were arriving. A senior policeman approached them and inquired if they had been the people who sent for them.

"I certainly did!" stated Matilda. "I confess I thought at

first it was this man," pointing out an alarmed and dishevelled Mr. Bandi, "but it turns out that this one is the one you want!"

Maik looked terrified.

"I don't think so, Mrs…?"

"Smith, Matilda Smith"

"Mrs. Smitt. I know this man. His name is Maik and he is stupid. He knows he must take his medication or he will find himself back in hospital where he has been for many months." Turning to Musula, "You are only a fool, you know, if you ignore your doctors! If you promise me you will take your medication, I will let you go home now."

"Oh, I will Inspector, I will!"

"Just make sure you do because if I get any more trouble then I'll have you sectioned again!"

"I promise, I promise," said Maik. And turning to Jalli he said, "I'm sorry. I really am. You have such interesting eyes…"

"Maik!" interjected the inspector, "Home! Take that medicine!"

"Thank you," were the last words Maik Musula spoke as he hurried towards the park gates.

"I don't think you will be bothered by him any more, young lady," continued the inspector. "You see, Mr. Musula has been in hospital for a long time. He could not have been responsible for the attacks in this park. When you called, Mrs. Smitt, we soon discovered a man lurking on the other side of the park. Someone had seen him acting very suspiciously and when he saw us he ran towards the perimeter over there. Apparently he had discovered a gap in the fence. He didn't think we had seen him, but we have caught him and he is now sitting in that vehicle. Thanks to your call we may well have caught the person we have been looking for all the time."

"So, Parmanda Park wasn't safe at all today after all." This was Jack who had his protective arms around his beloved girlfriend.

"It seems not," replied the policeman, "but with you all around with your vigilance and mobile phone it's currently probably the safest place on the planet!"

Later that day the inspector called round to take statements and to thank them once again for their contribution towards solving the case. It was looking increasingly likely that, through the actions of this enterprising family, Parmanda Park was free at last from its notorious predator.

"I've learned a few things today," said Jalli as she stood with Jack against the low veranda fence of the suburban house that had been her home for so long.

"And not just about parmandas," ventured Jack.

"Not just parmandas! To think I actually saw a display on my first visit! You should see one. It was fantastic…"

"So what else have you learned?"

"To listen when people want to keep you safe. You know, Jack, we all made mistakes. I should have suggested you came to the park and patrolled the path. What Mr. Bandi was doing was quite sensible but I hadn't thought about it. And he didn't tell me what he intended because he suspected I would be too stubborn to let him. And, you know, he would have been right."

"Stubborn's the word!"

"Oh. Don't rub it in."

"I was thinking. Suppose that Maik fellow hadn't come along, your Mr. Bandi would have been the chief suspect. After all, you know what your grandma said about how well you knew him. He was the one who knew exactly where you were and he was lurking, even stalking you!"

"That is probably what he meant by saying that he was trying to right his mistake with another mistake," said Jalli.

"Well, all's well that ends well," sighed Jack.

"And I've learned something else," continued Jalli. "Did you hear what your mother called me to Musula as she had him pinned down with her needles?"

"Yes, I did," said Jack, "daughter-in-law." He glanced back through the veranda door where Mrs. Rarga and Mrs. Smith were engaged in animated conversation while they were engaged in their knitting and crocheting. "They have us married off, it seems."

Their eyes met. Jalli's eyes were so beautiful, Jack thought. For him they were far more than "interesting". They were pools of endless delight, a source of a world every bit as wonderful as the cottage garden.

"Do you think we should get married?" whispered Jack.

"What sort of a question is that?" teased Jalli, "You make it sound like a dull duty!"

Jack sunk to his knees. "Jallaxanya Rarga. Will you marry me?"

"Yes! A thousand times yes!" Jalli was dragging him to his feet and kissing him. Kissing his lips, his face, his eyes. Jack held her tight and squeezed her to him. "Jalli you have brought so many blessings you cannot imagine! You have taught me the true meaning of love."

"Not I. We are simply the channels of that astounding love that our creator has bestowed upon us... forever!"

"And I thank God who has brought us together across the universe!" Jack declared.

"But, Jack, I think..."

"You think?"

"I think we should... we should not rush to get married. I do want to marry you. I will never change my mind. But I want to go to university, and to enjoy being... well, not fully 'grown up' for a bit."

"Jalli. I do so love you. You are so sensible. We don't have to be married to be together, or go on adventures. I agree I want to marry you, from the bottom of my heart. But I can wait. And there are things to sort out about my life too."

"But we'll be engaged. Betrothed like they used to say." Jalli danced with joy at the thought and Jack picked her up and swung her round.

The excitement on the veranda had caught the attention of the ladies inside. The chatting, the knitting and the crocheting paused. They turned to one another and smiled.

21

The following day, Momori was looking forward to being able to take her whole new household to her worship centre.

"I haven't been to church for a long time," stated Matilda as she got ready. "They always seem so remote and pompous, and I could never have afforded the collection."

"I expect some churches are," replied Momori.

"What?"

"Remote and pompous. After all they only consist of people, and some people are like that."

"But God isn't."

"No. But not everyone that goes to church, goes for God. They don't all have God in their hearts. We have had our moments in our worship centre, but there have been enough people with a relationship with God to make it worthwhile."

Matilda mused. "I suppose if you are close to God, if He's with you everywhere, you don't really need to go to a church."

"That's true. But we are social beings and we share faith and stories about Him that encourage us when life gets difficult. I nearly always feel better for going. In fact, if I haven't been for a couple of weeks I notice it." Momori turned to the door. "Come on you two, or we'll be late! We really have romance on our hands now, Matilda."

"He's never been a quarter as happy as this in his whole life," observed Matilda, "And, come to that, neither have I."

Jalli emerged with Jack in tow. She was wearing a pale smoky pink dress with white lace trimmings. It was generously flared from below the bust and she looked really feminine. Normally it had been a pair of blue jeans for the church just like any other day – with the exception that they were always her newest pair. But she had taken to wearing the clothes in the wardrobe at the cottage which were a collection of dresses and skirts that she had never thought of as being her style before. Jack liked them, and she had taken to liking the way she looked in them herself – especially as it seemed to please Grandma. This time in Wanulka she had brought this one especially to go to the worship centre. Her grandmother had rarely seen her looking so lovely.

So all were walking on air as they entered the church. Every head was turned and Momori was so proud to introduce Jack (Jalli's young man) and Matilda. Mrs. Rarga was growing a family around her. The pastor was in good form, and his sermon about sharing God's love among them seemed highly appropriate in the circumstances. "No matter what befell us, whether we are sinful or good, whether we are kind or cruel, God never gives up loving us. We are always his children and he is utterly devoted to every one of us. God did not count the cost of love. He hurts with us, weeps with us, rejoices with us and celebrates with us."

Jack and Jalli sat close together in this place where Jalli had sat for many a sermon. Bringing Jack here was bringing him into one of the dearest parts of her life. She smiled as he struggled with the hymns, but admired him for his efforts.

He would have felt like a duck out of water had it not been for Jalli's hand in his pulling him up and down for the hymns, prayers and sermon at the appropriate places. But it turned out to be as friendly as the chapel in Newcastle. None of these people were judgemental – just welcoming and pleased to meet him. It had crossed his mind that some would not approve of Jalli's choice of someone who had not worshipped anywhere before. But instead they were so pleased she had brought him to meet them. "My, how you've suddenly grown up," they marvelled. "Look what finding a young man has done to you! Where did you find him?"

"In a beautiful secret garden," replied Jalli truthfully.

After church, they discussed how to spend the afternoon. It was an absolutely glorious day. "Let's go back to Parmanda Park," declared Jalli. "I want to take you all with me this time so you can see the displays too."

"I think I would rather rest this afternoon," sighed Matilda. "After yesterday's excitement and meeting everyone this morning I think I would prefer just to sit quietly."

"A good idea!" agreed Momori. "Why don't you two go out and enjoy yourselves without us two getting in your way!"

After a quick cold lunch, and having changed into the ubiquitous jeans again, the young people set off for the bus-stop. "If you hurry you should just catch one," shouted Momori. She was never to forget the carefree way the lovers ran to the bus-stop, hand-in-hand, laughing. The next time she would see them, things would be very different.

Jalli and Jack got to the park in good time. They looked at the map and decided to stalk a couple of hives not too far from each other on the other side of the wooded area. On the map,

Jalli traced her finger along the path they should take, and where they should part.

"I'll be lonely without you!" he had replied.

"You won't. Not when you're watching the parmandas. You'll be totally absorbed! And, besides I'll be in easy hearing distance if you need me."

"But not kissing distance!"

"We can kiss on the way! You do want to see a display?"

Jack assured her that he did. In fact, the nearer he got to the hives, the more excited he got. Jalli had taken a little map from the visitors' centre. "This is it, I think," she studied. "Just behind that tree there. We're coming in from the east already. You take that one and I'll be right across there."

"That's at least a hundred metres!"

"Thirteen seconds if I need you, Jack." Jack recalled that was her aim in the sports, and she wasn't far off it!

"You'll be hard pressed to do a personal best across this scrub," laughed Jack.

"Now shhh! Off you go. And be very still remember." Jalli kissed him on the cheek and continued off behind some bushes. Jack carefully made his way forward until he saw the top of a hive. He found a good view and positioned himself on a little stump. The parmandas had spotted him before he spotted them and they were behaving erratically.

He resolved to be very still. How quiet it was, but he knew he was not alone because Jalli was in earshot. After an hour and twenty minutes or so he noticed a change in the insects. They were now behaving more normally. There was a pattern about the way they came and went. Watching parmandas was far from boring. Time passed quicker than you imagined it would. Then slowly the pattern began to change. All the insects hovered and gathered. More and more joined them. They were swirling around the hive and forming a display that Jack could scarcely believe. They were forming up to enter the hive in the dramatic way Jalli had described.

But they never did, because over to the left, the peace was shattered by a loud scream. Jalli was screaming.

"You just shut that mouth of yours," uttered a man with a gruff voice, "or I'll shut it for you and you'll never open it again!"

"What do you want?" Jalli wailed.

"You just do as you're told and no-one's going to get hurt!"

Whatever Jack's personal best had been over the short distance that lay between them, he bettered it that day despite the bushes and uneven ground. Within just a few seconds he burst through a screen of bushes to witness a huge masked man with his hand over Jalli's mouth, tearing at her clothing. Jack was straight into him as he had been to Mr. Bandi only the day before, but this man was of a totally different build and he was hunched over Jalli. Jack simply bounced off him and sprawled onto his back. Before he could recover, the bear of a man lunged at him with what, later, he knew was a baton. The blow caught Jack across the shoulder knocking him back to the ground. The last he saw, he ever saw, was the huge boot of the assailant crashing into his head, over and over again. And the last he heard before he passed out was Jalli shouting at him to stop. Jalli pulled out her mobile. It was turned off!

She pressed the start button and it sang its little start up tune. The monster turned away from Jack and snatched the phone from Jalli's hand, threw it to the grounded and stamped on it twice before kicking it into the bushes.

"Now you do as you're told, unless you want to end up like him!" All Jalli wanted was for this man to be gone as quickly as possible so she could look after Jack. She did not fight. It would have been useless anyway.

"Pathetic! Effing pathetic!" croaked the monster when he had finished with her, "That bloody fellow effed it all up!" He turned, kicked the unconscious Jack in the side and departed angrily beating down at the hive Jalli had been stalking with the baton, and then stomped off, slashing out at shrubs left and right as he went.

Jalli dragged herself up and over to Jack. He was still alive. "Oh! Thank God, he's alive," she whispered. She had feared the worst such was the punishment he had received. But he was completely unconscious. Blood was seeping from both eyes and his nose, which was swollen beyond recognition. His mouth was just a mess of blood. His upper arm was twisted out of shape and Jalli suspected it had been broken.

Then suddenly Jalli was aware of a deep howling sound, as if all the world were wailing. Was it her? Was she weeping so deep she filled the whole world? No. It was the parmandas, gathering around their broken hive, forming a pattern they rarely made and issuing a sound that very few people had ever heard. Later Jalli was to learn that they would rarely do that with anyone around. But this time it was as if they were mourning with Jalli. For that moment she had become one of them.

Jalli dressed herself as best she could with what was left of her clothes. The bright yellow sun on the front of her T-shirt was now stained red with blood, both hers and Jack's.

She tried to shout but could not find the strength. She thought of pulling Jack back to the path but soon thought better of it. He was too broken to move. And then she became aware that she was losing blood herself. She would have to go for help. She got back to the path, but then at the edge of the wood, through a combination of shock and loss of blood, she fainted and collapsed in the grass.

She was fortunate. A little boy saw her fall. He pulled at his mother's arm saying, "Lady, lady! There!" His mother looked but saw nothing. "No lady there," she said, "I see no lady!" But the little fellow was not to be so easily put off and continued to shout and point.

Then the mother spotted Jalli on the ground. She was a nurse from the local hospital and it didn't take her long to work out what had happened. Jalli came to a little and mumbled Jack's name.

"Did Jack do this to you?"

"No! No, he's my boyfriend. He's hurt…"

The woman understood that Jalli was not the only victim of this assault. She quickly led her son over to a group of people passing by and raised the alarm.

Jalli had found the strength to do just enough, or they may both have died that day. That day! It had begun rich with promise and had ended in wretched darkness.

22

"How could God have let it happen?" challenged Matilda. The anger was welling up inside her.

"I don't know how it works," replied Momori. "I've asked that question over and over again in my life. But all I know is that God does not leave us, or stop loving us. I am sure God is hurting too."

"But if he's God why doesn't He put a stop to it?"

"I think He is trying to."

"Trying to! Surely God can do anything he wants!" said Matilda crossly.

"I'm not sure he wants what the world would be like if he just took over everything, stopping and starting things happening, interfering all the time. He seems to come into his world when people ask him, or when they love, or seek goodness. I don't know why there is so much pain, but I do know God is always there to heal."

"I wish I could believe like you. I was just coming out of darkness and beginning to believe, and now my son is in hospital mutilated, and your lovely granddaughter raped..." Matilda never finished her sentence because she was overcome by another wave of anguish; her anger was now giving way to deep sadness. Huge sobs welled up from the depths of her being.

Momori too was shattered. Her faith and spirit were

strong – something learned by hard experience – but her heart was broken. Her beautiful, bright Jalli violated by an evil monster. He might be sick, but that did not lessen the foulness of this. Some girls of her age, she knew, would rather be dead than living so defiled.

But Jalli had been brave at first. Brave because she did not live just for herself. Just as Momori had sunk her whole life into looking after her granddaughter, so Jalli had seen it as her job to make Grandma happy. (She had liked it when she made her smile or clap her hands in joy.)

Jalli's first word when she had come to in the ambulance as it had pulled away from the park was "Jack!". After having been assured that he was on his way to hospital too, she had relaxed. Then she had thought of Grandma. Grandma, who had protected her from evil things for so much of her life, and how she had been stupid and had let her down. She had thought of Grandma's pain.

When she had got to hospital she had asked for her. She was "OK" she had told them. She didn't need any treatment. But she had had no choice. The doctor had been very kind but very insistent. She was bleeding. There had been damage that needed attention. And the police needed a report, and samples had to go to forensics.

"Look," the doctor had insisted, "this man has to be caught. He will almost certainly try this again."

It had not been nice, any of this. The police had wanted to interview her as soon as the doctor had finished. They had wanted a full "blow by blow" account. The last thing Jalli had wanted to do was to recount the details of her ordeal, she had wanted to go home. But the police had needed to know everything. When she thought about Jack she had demanded to see him immediately. The policewoman had said she would inquire when she had finished the questions.

"No!" Jalli had remonstrated. "I want to see him now!" and she had refused to answer any more questions until the policewoman had left the room to ask.

"Like a cup of tea?" asked a cheerful hospital auxiliary pushing a trolley who had put her head round the door.

"The most sensible thing I have heard in hours," Jalli had replied.

"There you go, love. Sugar?"

"Yes please. Lots!"

"Biscuit?"

"No thanks."

"Here, take one of these for later." This lovely woman had been doing her bit of caring. Working at the hospital, she knew more about what happened to people than others might guess, and she ministered through her tea and biscuits, and just bringing an air of everyday normality to the traumatic situations she encountered. "I'm just out here if you need anything." Jalli thanked her.

Then a doctor had come and explained that Jack was undergoing tests. He had arrived at the hospital unconscious with several broken bones – his left cheek, his left upper arm – and a lot of bruising. They had been worried about his eyes too, but the main thing was that they didn't yet know the extent of any internal injuries or what was happening inside his head. They were giving him a scan at this moment. It would be at least a few hours before she could see him.

Then Grandma and Matilda had arrived! The

policewoman had given them a moment while Jalli had briefly explained and had sobbed her apologies for not listening more attentively. Then the policewoman had asked them to leave so she could continue the interview. They had begun to protest, but Jalli had said that it would be best. She hadn't wanted to tell Grandma what happened like this. They had kissed and hugged. It was so good to have such a grandma, Jalli had thought. "I'll be alright," she had said. "I can go after this, can't I?" she had asked the policewoman.

"I'll have to check when we've done, but I don't see why not from our point of view. You'll have to ask the doctor."

The interview had been easier once she had seen her grandmother. Afterwards they had tried to find out more about Jack. He was unconscious, but as he was sedated he was not expected to come round for some time. The doctor had insisted that Jalli had to remain in hospital overnight so he could check that everything was going on OK. After he had been the next morning Momori took her home. Matilda stayed on at the hospital. Jack was still out.

It was three days before Jack regained consciousness. He was making remarkable progress, the doctor said. He was a fighter. Jalli became anxious for him, then weepy, then angry with herself, and then sorry in turns. She begged Matilda's forgiveness countless times because she held herself responsible for his being in the park in the first place. She felt so guilty. She told herself that her relationship with Jack must now be at an end. She felt unclean and unworthy. She was defiled, unfit for a young man so good that he had been willing to sacrifice himself for her. How could she be his now, when some monster had entered her body, her very life, forever, and taken that which should have been Jack's and Jack's alone. No! When Jack was better she would take him back to the garden and his own world, where he could begin again. Then she would devote herself to Grandma as long she needed her. She could never marry Jack now – never marry anyone.

When Jack came to, she was the first person he asked for. He drifted in and out of consciousness. He kept reaching for her hand. He doesn't realise what's happened yet, thought Jalli. They all wondered how much Jack would remember of anything, indeed whether his brain would ever return to normal. One thing the doctors were pretty sure about was that he would never see again, but whilst the bandages remained they could not be completely certain.

Several more days, though, saw Jack much improved.

On the fourth day, they found him sitting up. As soon as Jalli, his mother and Momori came into the room, he asked, "What happened? Why can't I see? Where am I?"

His mother explained that he had had an accident in the park and that the bandages over his eyes would have to remain for some days. He was in hospital in Wanulka. "Of course, Wanulka." He could smell it now. Then it all flooded back.

"The park, parmandas! Jalli! Jalli!"

"I'm here, Jack!"

"Jalli. Are you hurt? What happened? That man!"

"It's alright."

"Did he…? Did he…?"

"You just concentrate on getting better, Jack."

"No. Jalli. Did he hurt you. Did he… you know? I want to know." Jalli burst into uncontrollable sobs. Jack put out his hand towards the sound and pulled her towards him, stroking her hair.

"I'm sorry!" said Jack.

"No! It is all my fault! It's me that should be sorry! It's all my fault. I let you down! I…" Then Jalli was overcome with a sense of her own flawed nature. She pulled away from him and fled from the room, sobbing. Grandma followed her.

"Jalli! Jalli!" Jack was reaching out into the dark.

"She's gone. She's upset. You just rest." It was his mother. Jack had expended all his energy and the doctor came and administered a sedative.

He would need to rest, they said. They planned to remove the bandages the following day and then they would know for certain about his eyes.

Jalli did not return to the hospital the next day, and neither did Momori because she knew she could not leave her. The bandages were removed, and as the doctors had suspected, there was no hope of him ever seeing again. There was too much damage. They had explained it to Jack as carefully as they could. They expected him to make a full recovery otherwise though, and in Wanulka there were all sorts of services he could access as a registered blind person. They would send someone to him to talk about the options.

"Wanulka! I want to go home!" declared Jack. "Where's Jalli?"

"I don't think she wants to see you at the moment," explained his mother.

"Of course not," thought Jack, "who wants a blind person for a husband! I let her down and now I'm blind, useless,

useless. If I couldn't look after her while I could see, how can I look after her now I'm blind? She was always too good for me anyway. I knew that really. She must find someone here in her home town who can love her and look after her!" But all he said out loud to his mum was, "I want to go home!"

The doctors found it odd that they could not refer Jack directly to the doctors in his home town. But at his mother's insistence they gave up trying, and presented her with his records and scans for the doctors there.

Jack and his mother took a taxi to the Municipal Gardens. Matilda had wondered whether she should go back to the Rarga home and explain. But she did not want to leave Jack. She used the phone she had been given to ring them. She explained that they were leaving for Persham. Jack wanted to go home. Momori had asked her to hold on and shouted for Jalli.

"Of course, he wants to go home!" stated Jalli. "Why should he want to stay? It's because of me that he can't see."

"I'm not sure that's true, Jalli."

"I am!"

"Don't you want to see him before he leaves?" Momori was trying desperately.

"Don't you think it hurts enough?" sobbed Jalli angrily.

Momori was sorry the whole business had fallen apart so badly, she lamented to Matilda. She would pray about it.

"Your son made my granddaughter happier than she had ever been in her life!" And these were words that Matilda never forgot.

Back in Persham Jack took to his room. He quickly learned how to get about in the house he had known all his life. But outside it was different. Before, he had taken being able to see for granted. Now he couldn't go out without someone on his arm. He couldn't read, and worst of all he was useless to anyone. He was a liability. The social-workers had come and gone. They had offered him places on courses to learn Braille, presented him with job opportunities "for the blind", and, worst of all, made sympathetic noises. All of which, in his anger, Jack rejected. A Mr. Evans from the church came round. Jack gave him short-shrift. Why should God give them so much just to take it all away? The old man didn't know the answer, but, he suggested, "Don't give up telling God exactly how you feel about it! I shan't!"

One rainy day when his mother was out, Jack felt so fed up he made for the front door, turned the handle and stepped outside onto the pavement. His foot struck something solid and he knew what it was. His kicking tree. He felt the wet leaves now up to his face. It was mocking him! His anger swelled and he lashed into the tree, kicking, pulling, twisting, ripping until he had expended all his pent-up energy, all his frustration, all his anger – and then he sank, sobbing, onto the pavement, soaked to the skin, with his arms about the base of the tortured tree, laying amongst the mess. He remained there for a quarter of an hour before the old man from the church leaned over him and asked, "You alright, lad?"

(It turned out later that Mr. Evans had seen the whole thing, but was wise enough to give plenty of time for Jack's anger to take its course and subside.)

"No!" moaned Jack. "I want Jalli."

"You've certainly let God know how you feel! Not much

left of that tree! Come on let's get you inside." But the door had shut behind Jack and locked itself. The old man and Jack sat on the doorstep to wait for Matilda to come home.

"Tell me about, what's the name you mentioned, Jalli?"

"We were engaged to be married, once."

"What happened?"

For some reason, having expended his energy on the tree and sitting here soaking in the rain, Jack felt like talking.

"Might as well tell you," he said, "it won't make any difference!" The old churchman listened to the whole story.

"Tell me," he asked, "what was the last thing Jalli said to you before she left the room in the hospital?"

"I don't know. She had just told me the man had raped her after I was knocked out. I had let her down. As we were leaving my mum phoned, but she didn't want to talk to me."

"Think about this. Did she actually say you had let her down?"

"No, I said that. It was obvious!"

"It's not so obvious to me. A girl's fiancé tackles an armed monster, despite him being twice his size, and being beaten within an inch of his life! Now if you had run off you might be accused of letting her down, but you didn't."

"I would never have done that! It never crossed my mind."

"Of course not! You loved her. She loved you."

"But we should never have gone to the park in the first place."

"Who's idea was it to go to the park?"

"Well, hers. She wanted me to see the parmandas."

"Which many people have done on thousands of occasions quite safely, I suppose. How could you refuse? How could you know that a monster would be in the park that day? Especially if, as you say, someone had been caught only a day before whom the police had said they were charging.

"Now, I want you to think very hard. Exactly what did Jalli say to you before she left? Do you know how a woman feels after she has been raped? She feels dirty and debased. She might think you wouldn't want her."

"Never! Of course I want her. I love her. It wasn't her fault! Why should it make any difference if she had been assaulted?"

"But she might *think* it does. We men, we can't begin to imagine what a woman feels after something as brutal as this. And it's about what *she* thinks *you* might think."

"I would never leave her because of that. That would be terrible!" But then Jack stopped and stared into the blackness with the rain running down his face. This was the first time he had looked at it from Jalli's point of view like this. His expression told the old man the story...

"In the hospital... she said it was her fault, didn't she?"

Jack nodded. "Mum said she didn't want to see me."

"My guess is, your Jalli was too ashamed of herself to want to see you. Do you still love her?"

"Of course I do! She is the best, most wonderful person I ever met. We had such great adventures together. She made me feel I belonged... but how can she still want me now I am blind!?"

"You haven't given her a chance to answer that. *You* have decided your blindness has meant she wouldn't want you. And I'm guessing *she* has decided *you* don't want *her* for another reason altogether. Has she given you a chance to tell her you still want her, despite what happened to her?"

"We haven't seen each other since the first day I came round and she rushed away…"

"If you ask me, I think you had better get yourself off to Wanulka as quickly as you can and find out the truth! She needs to hear that you still love her whatever has happened."

Later the old man was to reflect that he had never quite felt so much joy before whilst sitting sodden on somebody else's doorstep. Mrs. Smith had been most distressed when she had seen them sitting there so wet, especially as she had been out longer than she had expected. She didn't have to ask what had happened to the tree. She invited the old gentleman in, but he declined in favour of a speedy return home and a hot shower!

After Jack emerged from the bathroom clean and dry, he announced that he thought he wanted to try and visit Wanulka. Perhaps he had been wrong.

"I know you have been wrong!" asserted Matilda. "Momori said you had made that girl happier than she'd ever been and I know that is true. You'll both be miserable until you find each other again."

"But what if the white gate isn't there?"

"We'll have to find that out, won't we?"

That night Jack called upon God, or Whoever, from the bottom of his heart. He prayed and prayed for Jalli. Could it be that it wasn't all finished after all?

23

A week after Jack left, Jalli had thrown herself into her biology text books. But after she had read them she found she had retained very little. She was still in such a state of shock. Her grandmother said that she was sure that that was normal under the circumstances. But Jalli was suffering from a depression that not even the most solicitous care from her grandmother could do anything about. Momori and her friends from the worship centre spent a lot of time praying for Jalli. If it had not been for them, even Grandma would have had difficulty coping. Instead of being a light that lit up the whole room that dispelled people's unhappiness, Jalli had become an ever-deepening black hole that caused those who loved her to be filled with real sadness.

The police didn't leave her alone, and everyone in Wanulka and his dog seemed to know about what had happened. And even if they didn't, Jalli imagined they did. If they ever caught this man, then for sure everyone in the whole land would certainly know about it because of the court case that would follow.

The police came round frequently to report and to make sure Jalli would be sure to press charges when they caught him, especially as Jack, who was central to the case, had gone home before they could question him, and Jalli could not help them find him. They felt she was being obstructive with her descriptions of other galaxies and worlds and they were less sympathetic than they otherwise might have been.

It was clear they were making little progress, and it was obvious they were very fearful he would strike again. The man they had detained had indeed been the man they had been looking for for the previous three years. But this monster was a new predator, and one to be feared. The way he operated was far more violent, and Jalli's descriptions indicated quite a different person from the notorious Parmanda Park predator. There was no saying where or when he would strike again – but the only thing the experts agreed upon was that he would.

The police and the park authorities were losing the public relations battle. The headlines read "Park monster still at large – No clues", and "Exclusive: Predator victim 'flees planet'!"

Then, one day, three of the ladies from Momori's church ladies' group came bounding up the path. "Have you heard on the radio?" they chorused. "A man has been attacked by parmandas. He was not even in the park but on foot near the boundary when a whole hive flew at him and engulfed him.

"They've taken him to hospital but he's in a bad way. Some people are saying it might be the man who attacked you, Jalli." They were still recounting what the radio was saying when the police arrived and asked to speak with Jalli. They suspected the man in the hospital was indeed the assailant. They were doing tests to see if he was a match with the forensic samples they had taken. They needed Jalli to identify him. They produced a picture of a man in rather a bad way. His face was swollen and Jalli could hardly see his eyes behind swollen lids.

"I can't be sure from this, but it could be him. He is definitely the right build." The policeman reluctantly conceded that in the state the man's face was in, it was a "big ask".

And, in truth, although Jalli wanted the man caught, she did not want all that would follow. She had heard tales about what defence lawyers put the victims through in the witness box. And she didn't want to have to stand up in front of the whole world and explain how she had done exactly what the man asked, because she knew there was no way she could have fought him off, and all she wanted to do was be in as fit a state as possible to get to Jack. At first she was convinced she had done the right thing. Her grandma, Matilda and the police had all told her so too. But now, she knew, people were going to doubt her story. The defence was probably going to say she was a consenting partner.

And Jack had gone, apparently forever, to some far away planet. That would not help her story either. In many ways, it seemed it was her word against this monster's. Could he be convicted beyond reasonable doubt? She was even beginning to doubt herself. All her life Jalli had dared to be different. Now she just wished the world would leave her alone. She really wanted to blend into the background and be totally unnoticed. She had given up wearing her bright colours and sought out the drabbest, most shapeless clothes she could find. As the police spoke to her she was wearing a man's shirt two sizes too big for her that she had picked up in a second-hand shop. It was grey and just looked wrong against her, now roughly combed, chestnut hair. In the witness box she would make a poor impression unless she smartened up a lot. By then the defence were going to have the perpetrator in suit and tie, and train him to speak politely to the judge and appeal to the jury.

"Do you think it would help to see him? You could look through a window without him being able to see you," asked a police inspector.

"I suppose I could tell if I could see his thigh. He has a big scar on the outside of his left thigh, high up. People don't think I'm making this up, do they?"

"No, not at all. What he did to you and your boyfriend leaves no-one in any doubt. Look, this man… if it's him, he won't get off. I promise you!"

Jalli consented to go to the hospital. When they arrived they were shown into a small waiting room. Something seemed to be going on. After a few minutes another policeman came in.

"The man's dead," he recounted. "He was too badly stung. There was nothing they could do." Jalli gave an audible sound somewhere between shock and relief.

"Sorry," the officer apologised. "This puts an entirely different perspective on it." And then he mused, "Do you mind viewing and identifying a dead man?"

"OK. Just let's get it over with!" she blurted. Now she was here in the hospital this one more thing was bearable. Besides she needed to be sure herself. If it was the man, that was the end of it. If it wasn't… the policeman left her to see if he could arrange things.

Jalli had no problem identifying him, the minute she saw him, she knew. The scar confirmed it.

"No doubt. It's him," she said flatly. She didn't know what to expect after that.

Back in the waiting room the policeman took another statement in which Jalli said she was completely sure that this was the man who had attacked her and her fiancé.

Fiancé, thought Jalli to herself, the engagement had not even lasted twenty-four hours!

Three days later the papers reported that the police were satisfied the man who had been attacked by the parmandas was the man they were looking for. The forensic samples were conclusive, a police statement said, and the victim had identified him. The case was closed. Momori rejoiced, (although being Momori there was always a thought that it was sad that the man had died, no matter how evil. She would much rather that he had been healed from his illness) but perhaps now Jalli might cheer up.

But the next day things were as bad as ever. In fact, Jalli didn't even attempt to get up. For the first time since Jalli was thirteen, Momori decided to do something for her without telling her. She decided to go to the Municipal Park and check on the white gate.

When she got to the Municipal Gardens, she saw it. It was still there. Then she went round to the school that was just starting a new term and asked to see Mr. Bandi. Momori had proposed, several times, that perhaps Jalli might like to go and see Mr. Bandi, but Jalli had told her that she would not like to see him. She didn't want any more sympathetic noises. Besides, what could he do about it? But Momori was sure this wise teacher could do something. He had written saying that if Jalli wanted to talk he was always there for her, but he would understand if she didn't. In fact, Mr. Bandi was feeling guilty about what had happened as he had been so much part of the parmanda thing, and he had been there and made a fool of himself only the day before.

The next day after Momori went to see him, Mr. Bandi came straight round after school. Jalli was sitting on the sofa just staring out of the window. He was shocked.

"I was wondering how you were. I wanted to come and see you. The school isn't quite the same without you." Momori fussed over him and disappeared to make tea. "You've had a very rough time, but I thought my star pupil was a strong girl and would win through."

Jalli said nothing. He picked up a biology book on the side. "Preparing for uni?" he asked.

"I've decided not to go," said Jalli in a deadpan voice. She had not wanted to see anybody and the immediate emotion was anger that he had come.

"Oh. What are you doing instead?"

Silence.

Mr. Bandi persisted. "I hear they have decided the man stung to death was the man who attacked you. Did he damage the hives do you know?"

"How do you know? No-one reported that!" blurted Jalli.

"I didn't know. That's why I'm asking. So he did?"

"If you must know, he actually bashed a hive to pieces with his stick as he made off. The parmandas made a terrible howling noise, but I didn't give them much thought after that."

"That's why they attacked him."

"What? They smelt him out?"

"Exactly. It is very, very rare for parmandas to attack

anyone. They usually can't be provoked at the time. But they remember."

"So they waited till they smelt him, and then got their revenge."

"No, no. Not revenge. Insects don't harbour such destructive emotions. No. It's self-defence. They attacked him before he could attack them again. The fact that this man had attacked a parmanda hive is the best circumstantial evidence the police could have got. Do you feel you want revenge?"

"No. Wouldn't do any good. Don't feel anything really." Jalli's anger was abating.

The conversation lapsed. Mr. Bandi sat quietly. After a few moments he asked, "What about that young man of yours? Jack isn't it?"

"He's blind. He's gone back to his own planet."

"Blind? How?"

"Haven't you heard?" Jalli sounded cross.

"No. I'm sorry to hear that." Mr. Bandi had heard Jack was no longer in Wanulka but genuinely did not know about the extent of his injuries.

"He tried to protect me and the man beat him and stamped on him."

"I am so sorry. That's dreadful. I knew he was hurt, but I didn't know he is blind... How's he getting on? I mean otherwise."

"No idea. I haven't seen him for ages. He went home. Why all the questions? I don't want to talk about him."

"But... aren't you engaged?"

"Not any more."

"Why? What's wrong?"

Jalli had had enough. "What's this? A cross examination? Am I in the witness box after all?" she shouted. In the kitchen Momori was praying harder than ever. She must come in with the tea at the right time. Too early and she would interfere, too late and Mr. Bandi might already be dismissed.

"No, Jalli. Most certainly not." Mr. Bandi had adopted his "wise teacher" voice, and spoke with a little bit of authority. After all, sullenness, he had long since concluded, was a childish thing. And he had seen sullenness in the way Jalli was behaving. So if she was going to act like a child he would act like an authoritative adult might.

"You and Jack were the most suited teenage couple I have met for a long time. You had a lot going for you. I am surprised that someone with your intelligence, and your devotion, should give up someone like Jack just because he's blind."

"That's not *it*!" She jumped to her feet and screamed. "Don't you see? It's not *him* it's *me*. After what happened in the park how could he want me any more? How could anyone want me any more?"

"But…"

"No, you don't see, do you? You don't know what it's like for a girl that's… that's raped. You're a man!" Jalli sank back into the chair, the tears flowing.

"So is Jack. A man I mean," said Mr. Bandi quietly. "Did he tell you he didn't want you? What was the last thing he said to you?"

Momori came into the room with the tea things as Jalli buried her head in a cushion, sobbing. "I can answer that," she said. "He called her name twice and reached out for her as this young lady here stormed out of the ward."

"He wouldn't want me," mumbled Jalli.

"But surely that's for him to decide." Mr. Bandi leant forward and put his hands on Jalli's shoulders. "You love him. I don't think your biggest problem is what happened in the park, terrible as that is, I think it's being apart from Jack. And I'll venture he wants you, as much you want him. I have the advantage of being a man, and I don't think Jack sounds the kind of boy who would walk away from a girl because she had been attacked. You can't turn love off like that."

The next thing that happened surprised them all. Jalli emerged from the cushion, threw her arms around Mr. Bandi's neck and clung to him.

"Whoa! That's my Jalli," he said. He was glad Momori was in the room. And that Jalli was no longer his student! But before he managed to extricate himself Grandma had her arms around both of them and they stayed like that for a full minute.

"I think," said Mr. Bandi readjusting his glasses that had been dislodged, "I think, ladies, I need that cup of tea."

As he sat with his mug in hand, he declared, "I imagine someone should visit Jack's planet."

"But the white gate. It's probably gone now," sighed Jalli. A note of alarm coming into her voice that sounded like the Jalli of old.

"I don't think so," ventured Grandma. "It'll be there as long as God wants you to use it. That's what you told me."

"How can you be so sure?"

"First, because God is consistent, even if we aren't, and secondly, because I saw it there only this morning!"

"You've been checking up…?"

"I just went to look. No harm in that. If *I* can see it, I'm sure you will be able to."

"Do you *really* think Jack still wants me?" sighed Jalli.

"True love is unconditional," stated Mr. Bandi.

"Which is the same as saying that, if he really loves you, it won't make any difference to him wanting you whatever has happened to you or him," explained Grandma.

24

The very next day two expeditions were embarked upon. In Wanulka, Momori had prevailed upon Jalli to put on a colourful T-shirt. "Jack'll like that."

"But, Grandma, he can't see!" Jalli remonstrated.

"All the same, put it on for him."

In Persham Jack was taking care of his appearance for the first time since he arrived home. His mum was telling him what was clean and tidy. He found it frustrating, but he wanted to look his best. He had no idea what he would say, and he was desperately nervous.

As Matilda had predicted, the white gate was there in the wall as it always had been. She laid Jack's hand on the top of it. He felt the smooth, shiny paint. "What did you used to tell me?" she recalled, "If the gate is there you are supposed to go through it."

Jack hesitated. But his mother opened the latch and pushed him through. Jack's senses came alive at the sound and scent of the garden. He could not see it of course, but the picture of it flooded into his mind. He asked his mother to guide him in the direction of the bench. "Let me sit here and think before we go on to Wanulka."

But just at that moment, across the garden, Jalli had opened her gate. She was describing to her grandma the way to Jack's house in Persham. "I think I remember the way," she was saying, "but I'm not entirely sure. I always went with Jack, of course."

Jack had given hours of thought to what he might say when he met Jalli. As in the past, he had practised several opening gambits. But when he heard her voice, he just shouted, "Jalli! Is that you?"

"Jack! You're here! I was coming to visit you!" She ran across to him.

"I was coming to see you!"

"How are you?"

"I can't see." Jalli took his hand.

"I… I know that."

"Jalli, I just wanted to know if you were alright."

"I've really missed you. Oh Jack, not being able to see must be really dreadful."

"That's not the worst thing… the worst thing is what it has done to *us*. I never thought… I never thought of life without you, but being blind has put paid to that, hasn't it?"

"How does being blind make a difference?"

"I can't look after you can I?" The question was rhetorical.

"But of course you can look after me! You don't have to be able to see in order to look after me!" Jalli led him across to the bench – their bench – and they sat down. "Jack, you being blind makes no difference at all to me loving you…

"… but I let you down. In the park, I failed…" Matilda and Momori quietly withdrew in the direction of the house.

"Jack, you were so brave. You did not think twice about going for that monster. You did all you could. I wouldn't have blamed you for running off to get the police or something when you saw the size of him."

"But he still managed to… to abuse you. I was useless! If anyone let anyone down it was me."

"No Jack. What you did really counted." She continued, hesitantly, searching for the words, "Yes, he raped me when you were unconscious and half dead. But he didn't have all his way with me. You spoiled it for him. He said so. He said that I was no good. And he blamed you for it. He got nothing out of it, he said, thanks to you. So somehow I feel you did succeed, in a strange way… Anyway, he's dead now. The parmandas got him. But the thing is that, now, I am… no longer a virgin. That changes things doesn't it? You are kind, but I know that you deserve someone who is pure and… unused… undamaged…" This speech took a lot of effort and Jalli fell silent, on the point of tears.

"Jalli! Jalli! Nothing that anyone could do to you would change the way I feel about you. I want you, I love you. All I care about is that you are alright. I could never never think that you were anything but pure and good… because, because you're Jalli…! That's not why I stayed away. I didn't think you could want me because I was blind!"

"You silly boy! How would that make any difference? You lost your sight trying to rescue me! How could that stop me loving you? I love you even more for it. It's just that I don't deserve you! You deserve more than I can give."

"Nonsense! All I want is my Jalli"!

She kissed his face, his hands, his eyes. Jack began to weep. The tears flooded from him and she cradled his head against her. She held him tight and felt the wetness of his tears through her clothes.

Matilda and Momori watched in silence. Then the latter

333

said, "Come on Matilda, let's go and put the kettle on!" and they stepped into the cottage as if it belonged to them.

"I think we've both been silly," ventured Jack.

"Downright stupid!" said Jalli. "It was Mr. Bandi who helped me see that perhaps I was not right in thinking you had rejected me. I felt so bad, so horrible, so guilty for all that had happened. It was my idea to go to the park. I took you to those hives and made you leave me. But Mr. Bandi said that if you really loved me that would not stop you wanting me."

"Mr. Bandi was right. Even if you were to blame (and you're not!) how could I do anything but forgive you. But you are *not* to blame. Not ever. Before you screamed I was so happy because the parmandas, my hive, were just forming into a pattern and were ready to dance, to display. I was so grateful that you had thought of going to the park again. Those parmandas were the last happy thing I saw. I know that the universe is a beautiful place. And you make it especially beautiful because of who you are."

"Oh Jack. You say such kind things."

"Well, they're true. I just thought you would be better without a blind person to look after. I want to look after you and I can't. You'll have to take me everywhere, like a pet on a lead."

"But all I ever wanted was to be loved, Jack. That's how you can look after me."

"That's easy. You're so lovable. But I felt so bad about myself. I thought I could never be happy again. Yesterday, I met an old man from the church in Persham."

"I didn't think you went to church."

"No, he came to see me. Twice. The first time I sent him away.

"The second time I… yesterday… I'm ashamed to think about it. Let's just say I was locked out in the rain and… he's a wise man because he asked me what was the last thing you said to me before you left the ward… the last time. And I remembered."

"Don't remind me about it."

"You said it was your fault." Jack paused, and reflected. "He told me to come and see you and tell you it wasn't. And it wasn't, Jalli. None of this is your fault."

"And it's certainly not yours!" They sat for a time in silence.

"I'm so pleased you're wearing a bright T-shirt with a Jallaxa on it. I want you to shine like the sun forever."

"How do you know what I'm wearing? I thought you couldn't see."

"I can't see with my eyes. But I can kind of see with my hands and ears. I felt the appliqué. I felt it straight away."

"Feeling my… front!?"

"Well yes. Sure. With my ear!" They laughed – just like the old times when they teased one another, and the flood gates opened again for both of them. Jack laid his hand on the appliqué. She took hold of him. "Touch me Jack. Love me. All of me!"

"And you have your newest bright blue jeans on. They have a kind of rib pattern." And he moved his fingers from her hip and thigh that was once bruised down over her knee.

"You are very romantic, kind sir."

"Say that again!"

"What?"

"'Kind sir'! That's what my Jalli says. I just want to make you smile and not cry."

"Cup of tea you two?" It was Momori coming across the lawn with a tray with two teacups and a plate of biscuits.

"Thanks Grandma!"

"Matilda and I are having a nice chat. We've missed each other. You two carry on."

"Carry on what, Grandma?"

"Why, making up of course!"

When she had gone Jalli asked, "Do you think Grandma saw you put your hand on my sun?"

"Of course. She and Mum are probably noticing everything from wherever they are."

"I think they're inside the cot-tage."

"They must have gone into the kitchen to get the tea."

They drank the tea and Jalli shared with Jack some of the details of her ordeal. But it would take many months and many more tears before they could talk about everything.

After a while Jack said that he wanted to *do* something. His brain had had enough thinking for one day.

"Come on," he said, "Mum and your grandma are inside. Let's go and join them. And I want you to put on that cotton dress we so admired, the one you haven't dared to before. I think that whatever we may have felt, the older generation have adopted the cottage. They seem so at home."

"Strange that," mused Jalli. "They have taken to it very quickly indeed."

"And found the food," sniffed Jack, who had caught a whiff of something edible. "That's Mum's cooking."

"How can you tell?"

"Mum has her favourites. That's a crumble."

Jalli led Jack by the hand to the door. He stumbled on the

step. "You have to tell me about steps," he explained. "How many, how big."

"OK. The next one's a little one. Then two paces across to the right and we've got the stairs." Jack met the stairs half way through his second pace and sprawled up them. He laughed.

"Should have thought – Jalli-sized paces!" Then Jalli laughed too.

"You shouldn't be so lanky!"

"But without longer legs I could never keep up with you! How's the training?"

"Haven't done any." Jack said it as she did! "How am I not surprised! Get back to your running girl!"

"You're bossy!"

"Well, it seems I need to be!"

"Boss me too much and I won't tell you where to put your big feet."

"OK. Deal. We need each other."

"A real partnership!"

"Jalli, my eyes may not work, but you've helped me to see so many other things. Things that last forever. I love you!"

"And I you! Oh, how stupid we've been! Come on, now let's concentrate. I'll tell you when we get to the top." She put her arms around him and guided him up the stairs. "One more," she said.

"Fourteen," he commented. She guided him round into the front bedroom on the left – her room. She led him across to the bed and he sat on the edge. Then she began pulling off her T-shirt.

"What are you doing?"

"Changing into that dress you said you liked."

"Don't forget, I may not be able to see but I can hear – and I can still see inside my head."

"Then listen to the beating of my heart," she said, as she got out of her trousers and threw them across his lap. She found the dress she thought Jack meant. "Is this it?" she asked, momentarily forgetting Jack couldn't see.

"Bring it here." He hadn't seemed to notice. She held it out for him and he stroked his hand across it and felt the fullness of the skirt. "What colour is it?" he asked.

"It's green, with red and blue splashes."

"That's it." Jalli put it on and stood in front of him as he felt it up and down on her body.

"You're quite enjoying this 'having to feel' bit aren't you?"

"I assure you, madam, I don't 'see' everybody this way."

"I'm glad you don't! I'd be jealous."

"But I want to know what *you* look like. And, yes, you are very delicious to touch." He grabbed her waist and pulled her onto the bed beside him. He found her mouth with his and kissed her with such passion and tenderness that Jalli wondered why she ever thought he wouldn't want her. Then he felt her tighten. Her body, he thought, was as expressive as her face.

"What's wrong? Jalli have I hurt you?"

"No. No. I…" she sighed and began to cry again.

"Listen, I… I think I know what you're thinking. Tell me if I've got this wrong. It's to do with what happened in the park isn't it?"

Jalli sighed an assent.

"That monster may have abused your body, Jalli, but never

reached your heart, your being. That can only happen if you are open, willingly inviting and giving. He knew nothing of the Jalli I love."

Their tears flowed again, wetting the pillow. "I do want you Jack. Touch my heart. Touch my body. It's yours. I give it to you!"

"Now, no more weeping, Jalli Rarga." And he held her tight to him. "I love you! And I assure you, you'll have to put up with me 'seeing you' with my hands every day." And he patted her playfully. They lay there silently in each other's arms and kissing each other for some time. They were roused at last by Matilda shouting up the stairs.

"Do you two want any dinner?"

"Just getting some different clothes for Jack," reacted Jalli.

"Of course! I'm hungry!" replied Jack.

Jalli led him out of "her" bedroom and they went to the bathroom to wash their tear-stained faces. Then Jalli took Jack into "his" room. "Now what have we here? A T-shirt that says in large letters, 'I love Jalli Rarga'. That'll do."

"Perfect."

"Actually, this one's rather nice. It is a deep red with two green stripes down the left side. One paler than the other. And these shorts are perfect – pale beige." Jack felt the clothes, and then began to pull off those he was wearing.

"Just a minute," he said, "you can see me!"

"Saw a lot more of you on the beach," she responded.

"Dare say. That seems so long ago."

"Too long. But let's not dwell on our silliness again or we'll start to cry, and I'll have to wash my face yet again!"

Actually Jack had not worn tailored shorts since he was

little, but Jalli assured him they suited him. She traced on his chest where the green lines went.

"You know all these things are perfect," he said.

"They were made for us," said Jalli. "I should have realised that whatever happened, you were meant for me!"

Downstairs the couple were duly admired, and ushered into the dining room. Jalli hadn't realised how hungry she had been as they tucked into a mixture of Momori's and Matilda's cooking.

"Don't forget to leave room for the crumble," said Jack.

"So you two have decided that you'll do for each other after all," commented Matilda as they ate.

"We've both been rather foolish," acknowledged Jack.

"You certainly have!" exclaimed Momori.

"Grandma?" said Jalli inquisitively.

"Yes dear?"

"Have you been here before? I mean without us – after the 'park thing'. (The 'park thing' soon became the accepted short hand for the horrors they were trying to put behind them.)

"Well, yes. But only once."

"When?"

"Yesterday. Before Mr. Bandi came. It was because… well, I wanted to see if the white gate was still here. I thought I could have persuaded you to go through it. But Mr. Bandi managed to achieve that very well."

"Why did Mr. Bandi come? I didn't ask to see him. And he had written saying he would only come if I wanted to see him."

"Well, if you must know, I asked him to call."

"So you went to see Mr. Bandi?"

"… and then went on to see if I could find the white gate."

Jack interrupted this exchange with, "Mum, what were you doing out so long yesterday? Did you come here too?"

"Well, yes, I did. I was really fed up of seeing you so depressed I thought I had to do something about it. I reckoned that, if I knew anything about Jalli here, she wouldn't reject you for being blind – which was what you kept saying. If she really loved you, she wouldn't do that. Anyway, I felt I had to make sure. So I took the Wanulka phone with me and went to look for the white gate. I thought, if I could just step into the street in Wanulka I could ring Momori and talk to her. But when I got into the street I bumped straight into her! So we came back inside…"

"… and made ourselves comfortable," declared Momori. We quickly learned that what we suspected was true. You were both keeping yourselves from the other because you were too young, too inexperienced – and too impetuous – to know the true power of love."

"But what we hadn't bargained with was that very evening you both would come to the same conclusion," added Matilda.

"Just a minute," Jack was putting all this together, "how come that man from the church came round again when he did? You asked him to call, didn't you Mum?"

"Well, in a way, yes. I met him in the church, on Sunday, and he asked how you were, and I told him how worried I was."

"You went to church?"

"I've been three times now," admitted Matilda. "But you

were too wrapped up in your troubles to notice what day it was, let alone how long I was gone. The last time you were still in bed when I got back."

"And you didn't ask me to go with you?"

"Was there any point?"

"No. I don't suppose there was."

"So," pronounced Jalli. "You've both been plotting?"

"Well, not exactly plotting," said Momori. "We just felt we had to do something. Because we love you. Both of us love both of you. Yesterday, when we met, we just prayed that you would somehow discover that you could still have something together."

"And here we are today!" concluded Matilda. "I have to acknowledge that praying seems to work sometimes!"

25

Everyone appeared to assume that they would spend the night in the cottage. Matilda had found the room that Jack had known was hers from the first day he entered it, and Momori took the one at the end of the corridor. Jalli found the nightdress with the Jallaxa on it that she had discovered in one of the drawers two months previously on her first visit. Although this was their first night in the cottage everyone felt at home as they knew they would.

Jalli had woken at dawn and gone straight into Jack's room. They had talked about Jack's mum going to church.

"Jalli, how do you talk to God about things when the hurt is really, really deep? I mean, it is not easy for me to pray at the best of times." Jalli admitted that she had not said anything to God since the "park thing".

"Why not? You were so good at praying."

"I felt too awful. So empty. The truth is, I just felt cut off from Him."

"Like you felt cut off from me?"

"Yes, but not in the same way. I knew why, I thought I knew why. I believed, like the silly girl I am, that you wouldn't want me. But, I just couldn't face God. I felt... I feel... so ashamed. I was so angry – why did he let that happen – to me... to you... to us!? Then, I blamed myself

343

too. Perhaps it was all my fault. I was so mixed up. I suppose I froze him out."

"But, surely, God would always want you, no matter what had happened – even if you *were* to blame. Didn't you say he loved you right or wrong, good or bad?"

"I know I believed that. But after the 'park thing' it didn't feel like that. I just felt so dreadful. And I couldn't go to church either. I couldn't face anybody asking me questions – or volunteering to pray for me. I felt like… so foul, Jack."

"I'm beginning to understand. I hadn't realised just how this affects a girl – because it all happened to you against your will. You had no part in it. The Jalli I know is as pure and good as the day I met her!"

"Oh, Jack, you do say the nicest things. You might not always feel like that."

"I wish you could 'see' yourself from where I'm sitting! Your whole presence is like the sunshine to me. Jalli, I couldn't live without you! So no more feeling bad. Jalli will you do something for me?"

"Yes. Jack. Anything – if I can."

"Will you pray now. Pray for us?"

"But Jack, I haven't prayed for weeks, I…"

"But you know how. You've done it for years."

"Yes. I know. I just felt OK with it. I felt OK with God. But, what can I say to him. I feel so ashamed now of not praying!"

"Does God love you? We've made it up because we love each other."

"You're right, Jack. But I'm nervous. Not now."

Then something marvellous happened. Jack suddenly

found himself holding Jalli and praying, "Oh God, please help Jalli to talk to you again. Help her to know you still love her, that you've never stopped loving her. Help her to know she's a wonderful, lovely, fantastic and pure girl."

"Yes Jack, yes. You pray for me. Oh, God I have been so stupid. Thank you for sending me Jack. Thank you for sending me this wonderful, fabulous, super boy!"

The next day the sun shone brightly, the birds sang and Jack and Jalli wandered around the garden, exploring nooks and plants they had not had time to really notice before. Jack was more keenly aware of scents and sounds than he had been when he could see.

"If you see something first," he explained, "then the smell is kind of expected, but when you can't see it is the smell that catches you unawares, and if it is a nice one, like in this garden you can just... well, feel like rejoicing!"

They circled the garden until they turned back to the white gates and Jalli stood still. Jack felt Jalli's hand, which he had been holding all the time, tense up.

"What's wrong, Jalli? What's the matter?" And it then occurred to him when he thought about where they were in garden. Before she could say anything, Jack added, "It's another white gate isn't it? I'm registering something. I can sort of 'see' it, but it's not like the usual kind of seeing." Jalli nodded and Jack felt her assent. She stood motionless holding Jack's hand very firmly.

"What are you thinking, Jalli? You're not sure if you're ready for this are you?"

"No, Jack. I'm not. Look, every other time, you've been

there to look out for me. This time… well, you're going to need me to… to guide you. And, I'm still sore, Jack… I mean in my heart."

"I know, Jalli. Look let's sit down on the bench and think."

They walked over to their little bench and sat quietly together.

"Jalli, if a white gate is there, we're meant to go through it aren't we? We've always said that."

"Yes, but Jack, I'm not ready for another adventure."

"Who says?"

"*I* do."

"But what about God. He has always looked after us in the past when we've gone through his white gates."

"But he didn't protect us from that… that man…"

"I agree that's a hard one. But would you say he ever stopped loving you?"

"Well, no. Of course not."

"Somehow, I don't think he always protects us, Jalli. He just promises to be with us and love us… he hasn't left us, has he?"

"No, he hasn't. It's me, I know it's me, Jack. It's just that I don't feel so brave any more."

"So, it may be he wants us to go through that gate so he can heal us."

"Do you mean, wants to make you see again, Jack?"

"Well. I hadn't thought of that. I was thinking about you, and your sore heart."

"But you can help cure that, Jack!"

"Maybe, but…"

Jalli leapt to her feet. God might be offering Jack a cure

for his blindness. She was suddenly full of energy. "Come on Jack. We're going through that gate!"

"Whoa," said Jack. "That's a sudden change of heart. I don't know what's behind it, but I think we *should* go through it. But we have to tell Mum and Grandma what's up first. Are there any special clothes?"

"No. Just a gate." Jalli led Jack over to it and laid his hand on the top bar.

"What can you see?"

"It's like a garden. Not unlike this one. There's a tree with fruit on it."

"OK. Let's go in and tell the ladies. They might not be happy."

But they needn't have worried. The sight of a new lively Jalli, more like the Jalli of old, was such a blessing to Momori. She smiled. When Matilda saw the smile, she felt that she shouldn't raise any objections either. After all, it was good to see her son growing in confidence. She simply said, "You won't be long will you?"

"Mum. You know we don't have any idea how long it will be."

"No I suppose not. But don't be long all the same!"

Jalli smiled, "I'll look after him. I promise. I won't leave him."

Fifteen minutes later they pushed open the new white gate. Four steps took them into a garden with a hedge. The first thing Jack became aware of was birdsong.

"That's a blackbird. Or it is very much like one," he noted.

Another pace and the top of Jack's head struck something round and hard that seemed to be suspended above him. He stopped and reached up and felt a small round fruit hanging from a branch. As he did so another fell on his shoulder.

"Oh, sorry Jack. I didn't think. You're taller than me."

"This is an apple tree I think," whispered Jack.

Jalli bent and picked up the fallen fruit and put it into his hand. Jack smelt it.

"Yes, this is an apple. It's not ripe yet. It's too early. This feels and smells like home... I mean like Britain. Is there anyone there? I thought I heard someone."

"No, I can't see anyone."

"It's over there. There it is again!"

Jalli looked in the direction Jack was indicating. There was a garden shed, and down on the ground round the other side was a foot.

"Hello," Jalli said quietly. There was no movement and she approached nearer so she could see the back of a girl with long, fair hair sitting on the grass and leaning against the shed.

"Hello," said Jalli again. "Are you OK?"

The girl turned sharply. There was panic in her face. "Who are you? How'd you get in here?"

"My name's Jalli. We came through... over there."

"What do you want? You're not from the police are you?" said the girl getting to her feet.

"No. No. We're... we've come to help," Jalli found herself saying. She had stepped through the gate thinking, hoping, that it would lead somewhere where Jack could be cured, but, of course, now they were here it was someone else that needed their help.

"How can *you* help?" And then she spotted Jack and

almost freaked out. "What's he doing here!? Go away!" she shouted.

Jack stood back a pace and got his foot caught on a rose thorn, then he put his other foot into a gooseberry bush and fell backwards with his head among some rhubarb. Jalli couldn't help herself emitting a giggle. He looked so comical.

"That's Jack, my boyfriend. I'm sorry, he's blind. He couldn't see where he was putting his feet." She went over to him to help him but didn't realise that both roses and gooseberry bushes have prickles, and soon found herself in difficulties getting Jack out the way he had fallen in.

The girl came over and suggested they pull him out over the rhubarb, and between them she and Jalli succeeded in getting him back onto the lawn.

"You, OK?" asked the girl.

"Yeah," muttered Jack. "That was rhubarb. What got my feet?"

"Gooseberry bush."

"Are we in England?" asked Jack picking up a southern accent.

"Of course. Tooting."

"London?"

"Of course. Don't you know where you are?"

"Mostly, but sometimes I get lost," said Jack, "Hi. I'm Jack." He held out his hand. The girl took it tentatively. "Sorry, I think I must be a bit muddy."

"I'm Sally," said the girl.

"Pleased to meet you. Sorry if we frightened you."

"You did, a bit. I'm sorry I'm a bit nervous of strange men."

"Oh. Jack's alright," said Jalli, "he's quite safe really," she joked.

"Why do you say that?" the girl looked panicky again. "Look, I don't know you…"

"Come and sit down and I'll explain," said Jalli. They sat under the apple tree. At the other end of the garden was a house, but it wasn't visible from this part of it because of a dividing hedge. "We're not from anyone… from any authority. We're just here to help. We… you won't believe this, but it's the truth. I'll tell you exactly how we came to be here."

Jalli explained about the white gates and how she and Jack had met. Sally sat entranced. It seemed strange but a kind of answer to her prayer.

"I asked God to help me," she said. "I never asked him for anything else before. And you two pop up from another planet!"

"No. I'm from Persham," said Jack. "Jalli's the alien here."

"Oh, don't remind me!" exclaimed Jalli. "I was nearly arrested for coming into Britain, ill… ill…"

"Illegally," Jack explained. "She hadn't bought a proper visa."

"So I can't stay too long!" whispered Jalli, "I don't want to be put in prison. Now you tell us why you were so upset just now?"

"I can't.… I don't want to talk about it."

"But you said that we came when you prayed. We think, we know, we are here to help."

"But… OK. I will tell you – not him!"

"OK. Jack, will you go over there so we can talk in private," said Jalli. Jack was aware that men seemed to be a problem for Sally.

"Lead me to where you want me," he smiled.

Jalli led Jack to the far side of the lawn where there was a stone step. "Sit here, Jack. Don't take this personally. I think she has a problem with boys."

"I guessed that," smiled Jack. "I'll be OK." He sat obediently on the step.

Jalli went back to Sally.

"You won't understand this," explained Sally. "The police don't, my parents don't and the woman from the Victims' Support doesn't. You see, last March I was raped."

"I guessed that it was something like that," said Jalli.

"Why? How could you know?"

"For a number of reasons. The way you panicked when you saw Jack – a strange man – for one. Then I knew there must be a reason why God wanted me to come here, and… and I was attacked too, about the same time. On my planet."

"What, you've been raped too?"

Jalli's eyes filled with tears as she looked at Sally. "Yes. I don't like to think about it, but I can't forget it. I thought I was putting it behind me after… after I got back with Jack, but… it's very hard."

Sally took hold of her and held her. "Tell me about it? No. I shouldn't ask that – that's what I hate about the whole thing for me…"

"No. You can't bottle it up," sighed Jalli. "It'll probably help me to talk about it."

Jalli explained about the events of that tragic day in Parmanda Park. And then the way she had rejected Jack.

"He was blinded at the same time!" declared Sally, "That's awful. It wasn't anything like as bad for me."

"Tell me about what happened to you?"

"I was stupid. I decided to walk home from my evening class instead of taking the bus. It was only nine o'clock in the evening. The buses are only every twenty minutes and I just missed one. This bloke had followed me from the college. I didn't think anything of it. My way took me passed the Bec. Halfway down the road he rushed up from behind and lifted me off my feet and dragged me through some bushes. There was nothing I could do. I screamed but no-one came. He took me quite a way in, and with the traffic and all I don't suppose they could hear me. It was really dark and he had put on a mask. He didn't think I had seen his face, but I had already noticed him outside the college. I recognised it was the same man by his jacket. I was terrified he was going to kill me. But after, after the sex thing, he ran off across the Bec.

"When I got home, I tried to pretend nothing had happened. But it was obvious I had been roughed up. Dad phoned the police and then I was in hospital and they were all asking questions…"

Sally broke down and Jalli held her.

"Go on."

"Anyway after a few days it all died down. I told them all I knew. Then two weeks ago this policeman comes round all smiles and says he thought they'd caught him. He's tried the same trick again, only this girl was aware of being followed and rang 999 on her mobile. They got there just in time. The police car came along and he just ran. He hadn't done anything but the fact that he ran showed he was up to something. She was lucky. But they wanted me to go down to the station and see if I could identify him. Dad took me down. There was a line of them but I picked him out straight away. It was him alright, and I told them so… not thinking what would happen next… Look, tell your boyfriend I'm sorry I sent him away. He looks so lonely."

Jalli got up and went over to Jack. Sally beckoned them both back under the tree and Jalli led him across the grass. As he got near she told him to duck under the branches.

"Jack, Sally's been telling me that she's been through the same thing as me."

"I guessed so," sighed Jack. "I'm so sorry. That's why we're here isn't it?"

"Yes," said Jalli. "Sally needs someone to talk to who understands."

"Jalli's been through a bit herself," explained Jack.

"Yes, I know. And the man… he attacked you too and… and now you're blind."

"But how are *you*?" Jalli took Sally's hand and faced her.

"No. I'm OK. You came off much worse than me. I'm not hurt… nothing that will not get better. I'm sorry about your eyes."

"Can't be helped," smiled Jack. "Jalli's my eyes now. I'm very lucky."

"You are…! I mean you are lucky having her."

Jalli told Jack that they had caught Sally's attacker.

"Yes," continued Sally. "And now they want me to go to court and testify. It'll be all over the papers again. And I know what they'll do to me. His defence lawyer will try to tell the world I'm a bad person. I heard of a girl whose past was all brought up – they actually went round and quizzed her ex and then told the court how she liked to do it!"

"Oh. Sally. I can guess how you feel. I was dreading this happening to *me*. But it didn't come to that. It would have been so hard without anyone to corroborate what you have to say."

"It'll be my word against his. And it has to be proved beyond reasonable doubt. If it isn't, then I'm guilty of being both a slut and a person who accuses people of things they haven't done!"

"But if you don't," said Jack quietly, "he might do it again."

"Yes. That's what they keep saying. The other girl – he never touched her – but he could have done."

"What will they do if you say no?"

"I've got until tomorrow morning. If I refuse to testify they'll have to let him go."

"But you can't…" began Jack, but before he could say anything more, Jalli put a finger over his mouth.

"Shh!" she said. "She knows that. Don't you Sally? But Jack, if I had had to stand up in court and tell the whole world it would have been the bravest thing I did. I don't know if I could have done it. Look, Sally, if you can't do this, then it's alright. You have been bullied and pushed around enough. I guess your family wants justice for you. It's only natural, but…"

"Dad's really keen on me going. He wants to see this man hang, he says. Mum is more reasonable, but still thinks I should do it. My brothers are just angry. I'm afraid that if they see him, they'll kill him… But nobody has said what *you* said, that it's OK if I say no."

"It is. You say no if you want to. Some people will understand. But it might be that if you thought about it you *could* be brave enough. What's the worst thing that a defence lawyer could accuse you of?"

"I don't know. I went to my friend's for a sleepover and we played strip poker with our brothers."

"How old were you?"

"Thirteen."

"And you're sixteen now?"

"Seventeen last month."

"I can't imagine some barrister telling the jury that you played a naughty game at a friend's house four years ago and expect the jury to believe that that makes you the kind of person who would invite a stranger to have sex in a public place. No, to be relevant it would have to be something really shocking. I thought about that. Then I imagined they could make things up, but they can't. They have to be able to prove what they say. I guess the worse thing they can do is ask impertinent questions like, 'Do you enjoy having sex with older men?' in the hope that you will feel guilty or something. The trick is, I'm told, just to keep a level head. But *I* didn't have to go through it. I was spared that. This is *your* choice, Sally. You do not have to do this if you don't want to."

"I…"

"Sal!" It was her mother shouting down the garden. "Where are you? Dinner's ready."

"Quick!" urged Sally, "you've got to hide. They won't believe you are from another planet. There'll be far too much explaining. And Dad'll probably send for the police again. He thinks the garden is safe from intruders."

Jalli led Jack up behind the hedge as Sally shouted, "Coming Mum…! Can you come back tomorrow morning, early. Say eight o'clock? You've given me lots to think about. Then I want to talk some more before I meet the police."

355

"Yes, of course. If we can. If the gate is still here. If not. Good luck. We'll pray. Bye!" Jalli lent over and unlatched the gate and stepped through. Jack followed. All Sally could see from her side was two wonderful, magical people disappearing into a hedge!

"It *was* about healing after all," smiled Jack as they walked across the grass to their bench, "but not ours."

"Speak for yourself," replied Jalli, "Sally has probably done more for me than I for her!"

The following morning they were up early. It was cloudy but dry and the white gate to Tooting was glistening with dew in the morning light. Jalli walked over to it and put Jack's hand on the top rail, or, at least she tried to, but his hand went right through it. Jalli tried again.

"I can't find the gate," declared Jack. He pushed around the hedge but all he could find was hedge. Jalli, though, could touch the gate and clearly make out the garden on the other side. Sally was standing under the tree.

"Jack, I think I'm to go alone this time," whispered Jalli.

"I guess so."

"Girl's talk I expect."

"I'll miss you!" and he took her in his arms and kissed her. He turned and made his way over to the bench and Jalli watched him go. He was magnificent this boy. He just seemed to understand. She turned and crossed over into London. The blackbird was in full song.

"Hi Sally!"

"Oh, you made me jump. I think it's so magical you just appearing through a hedge. You haven't brought Jack?"

"The way wasn't open for him. I think we're meant to talk about things he wouldn't want to hear."

"Like what happened to you?"

"Exactly. And your story too."

"I think I have decided to say yes to the police."

"You don't have to."

"I know, and I would be OK with that now… after what we said yesterday. But this man has to be stopped. Even if he's found not guilty he won't be able to get away with it any more will he?"

"Well, it probably won't stop him trying, Sally. And you would look bad."

"I know but if I don't try, he'll get away with it for sure. Will you tell me what exactly *your* attacker did… I mean, to you?"

"Yes. If you want me to. I've never told anyone all the details, and Jack will never, ever need to know."

"Don't worry, I shan't say anything to anyone. And then I will tell you what happened to *me* on the Bec."

For the next half an hour the two girls shared their nightmares while the other listened. They hugged, but there were few tears. They spoke as mature women rather than the young people they still were. When they had finished Sally said, "I feel tons better, Jalli. I am definitely going to testify. That man is *not* getting away with this. I realised that if I am intimidated by him, or by the system, then it is as if he is still manipulating me, having his way with me. No. I want to see him face up to himself and get taken out of society – not hanged like Dad wants, that's just more of the same, its sick – but just put away somewhere where he can't hurt anyone else."

"Well, go for it, Sally!"

"Yeah. And afterwards, when it's all over, I want you and Jack to come to my eighteenth birthday."

"Next year? Well, we'd love to, but I'm not sure if the gate will work."

"I'll pray it does."

"So will I," smiled Jalli. "I'd like to know how it all goes."

"It'll be fine. I'm strong now. Thank-you. Thank-you so much." Sally took hold of Jalli and hugged her close.

"No, thank *you*. You can't imagine just how much better *I* feel… You be brave."

"I must go. Mum'll wonder what's happened to me. Do come back. Any time."

"Whenever we can."

"Give Jack a hug from me."

"I will," smiled Jalli, as she thought to herself, My man's safe. She *is* stronger.

"Bye! Till next time," called Sally as she trotted up the path to the house.

"How did it go?" asked Jack, as Jalli came across to the bench.

"Wonderful. She's a really brave girl. She's determined to testify."

"I knew she would. That's why we had to go. That's the help she needed."

"Yes, and what I needed too. Jack, I don't think I need you to love me better any more. Just love me because I'm me and not because I need to be healed."

"I'll always love you – just love you. I just want to be with you. And don't think I want you to look after me because I need your eyes to guide me either. Brilliant though you are, you still lead me into apple trees!"

"Love is about giving, not needing, isn't it?"

"Talking of giving, I want to give you this." Jack produced a simple ring with a diamond. "I brought it with me from Persham. I hope you like it."

"An engagement ring! I saw them in a shop window in Newcastle. You put a ring on when you are betrothed. The people we met there had them. That's a lovely British custom."

"Why? Don't you have engagement rings in Wanulka?"

"No. Just bits of signed paper."

"You can have one of those too. I hope you like the ring?"

"I do. Which finger does it go on?"

"This one on the left hand." Jack put the ring on Jalli's finger. It was a perfect fit.

26

"Right," said Momori at breakfast. "We have three choices. Either we stay here, or we go and live in Wanulka or in Persham. You two must stay together permanently because we're having no more misunderstandings through lack of communication."

"Oh, she left me this very morning," said Jack with a mock sigh, "went all the way to London and back without me!"

"I was gone for less than an hour!" laughed Jalli. "It has to be here," she said to her grandma.

"Agreed," said Jack.

"But," troubled Jalli, "will you stay here too, Grandma?"

"Of course," said Momori. "If you both want me to."

"On one condition," said Jack, "that Mum moves in as well."

"Do you think we can put up with each other?" asked Momori looking at Matilda.

"Can't see why not – so long as the young people do some of the housework, cooking and washing up!"

"But the house does its own," said Jack.

"Well it didn't do any washing up last night," complained Matilda.

"Or cooking," said Momori. "And look, the grass needs cutting. Looks as if there is gardening to be done too."

"So we are given the cot-tage to look after," reflected Jalli.

"Looks like it. When we are here, inside it, we are part of it, and we have to play our part it seems," sighed Jack. "I'm very bad at jobs. I can't see to do them!"

"There'll be plenty of things to do. I'll find you some," stated Matilda.

"I'm glad we have to look after the place," said Jalli, "because that means we really belong. But won't you miss your home in Persham, Mum?"

Nice to be called Mum by Jalli, thought Matilda. "No. It was always hard work. And to tell you the truth I was rarely happy there."

"And I have three people instead of one in my family now, and I'm not going to miss Wanulka that much," added Momori.

"What about your friends?" asked Jalli.

"I will miss them, but I belong where my Jalli is."

The following week Jalli and Jack parted to help sort out their moves. "We need take very little," concluded Momori. "We have everything we need there. I shall pack a few personal things." Jalli packed her books. She would need these – eventually, she hoped.

She was determined to pursue her biology. Momori called in to the solicitors' and made over everything to the worship centre. "They can house someone who needs a place to live," she declared, "there is never enough accommodation around here."

Matilda arranged for the furniture in Persham to be collected by a furniture recycling group. "It's nothing special, but it might as well go to someone who hasn't got much. After all, I was helped with some stuff when we first came." She and Jack were packing up stuff to take round to the church for their next sale, when Mr. Evans came round. "That'll take you an age," he declared. "You just put to one side the things you are keeping and we'll come round and help." Matilda and Jack stuffed a few things they felt they wanted to keep in a few cardboard boxes. The next day an enthusiastic party from the church appeared, really grateful for the gifts. They had things and charities they were raising money for, and they were all curious about where Jack and Matilda were going.

Mostly, though, they were so pleased to see them both so happy about it, and kept asking Jack about his "extra-planetary" young lady. Matilda handed the keys of the house to the landlord, and was delighted to be given back her deposit that had been such a challenge for her to find fifteen years before.

A fortnight later, they all gathered in the cottage, exhausted but happy to be together again. The following day it began to rain. A gentle rain that refreshed the garden world. They had never known it rain before but they had concluded the garden must get watered somehow. After the rain they emerged into the garden and Jalli spotted another white gate. No peace for the wicked, thought Jalli.

"Another white gate Jack. No holiday it seems," announced Jalli.

They walked over to it. "I don't think it's for me. I'm getting no vibes like last time," said Jack. Jalli laid his hand on it. He felt it sure enough but it was different. It was not shiny in the same way as the others.

"Jack," declared Jalli, "the hedge is not so thick here." Indeed it wasn't. There was no little alley way through into another world. As they stood there, a couple of people walked by and stopped, looked over the gate and said, "Welcome to Woodglade! So you are the new people who have just moved into 'White Gates Cottage'? My name is Giroonan, Callan Giroonan and this is my Hatta. We live next door in 'Greenlawns Cottage'." He pointed down the lane in the direction they were headed. Hearing voices, Momori and Matilda approached. Quickly sizing up the situation, Momori reached her hand over the gate.

"Momori Rarga and this is my granddaughter, Jalli," said Momori.

"And Matilda Smith and my son Jack."

"Pleased to meet you," said Jack and Jalli together.

"Do come over for tea tomorrow," invited Hatta, "what about four o'clock?"

"We would love too," said Jalli. "Thanks."

"Seem like nice people," said Callen to Hatta as they walked to their garden gate.

"Funny names they have!"

"Foreign I expect," she replied.

Jack, Jalli, Momori and Matilda stepped out of the gate into the lane. The cottage was visible over the whole length of the hedge. On their gate was written in black paint, "White Gates Cottage".

"This is not like the other white gates," observed Jalli, holding Jack's hand. "It's a 'normal' gate. We are not in another world. We are in the same world. This is the cot-tage's world."

"Yes, it smells the same, and the air tastes the same," agreed Jack. They explored up and down the lane, and then returned into the garden. Momori noticed it first, then Jalli. They stopped and stood in silence.

"The other gates! They've gone, haven't they?" said Jack.

"Yes," said Jalli.

"I guessed that might happen. We've done with those places from which we've come. This is a new life in a new place, together. We shall soon have to be working not only to look after the cottage and the garden, but to live with these people in this new world. I feel it."

Jack was right. Communicating with their new neighbours after the first introduction was difficult.

"You must learn our language," said one, as a large group of villagers gathered outside their gate one day and were invited into the garden. They were given lessons by someone with a special gift of teaching. There had been new people in the cottage before, it seemed, that had also come from abroad, and this same teacher had taught them how to speak and read. Jack, however, would need to have finger reading training.

Jalli explained that she had wanted to go to university, and study biology before they moved. That was good, the teacher had said, because their village was the location for an agricultural college where she could pursue her interests and live within walking distance. But perhaps she already knew that, it was probably one of the reasons they had chosen to move into Woodglade, the teacher ventured. Jalli didn't argue with her. If *she* hadn't known, the Owner of "White Gates Cottage" had!

As for Jack, he attended a course for the finger reading in the local town each day. There were a number of people there who had become blind in recent months. He met one young boy of about ten years old who was frightened and upset.

"I'll never be happy again," he moaned.

"Have you got a Mummy?" inquired Jack.

"Yes, of course."

"Does she love you?"

"Yes."

"And have you got a Daddy, too?"

"Yes."

"And does he love you too?"

"Yes. He used to play ball with me when I could see. All the time."

"You are a very lucky boy. So if you have got people to love you, you will be happy again. And it won't take so long."

"How do you know?"

"Because I've got people who love me."

"But you can see!"

"No I can't. Not with my eyes. I'm like you. But I can see with my heart. And I know that wherever you are, even when you don't feel it, there is Someone who loves you, and He or She gives you people to love and people to love you."

"And that makes you happy?"

"Much happier than anything else in the whole world."

Happier than in the whole galaxy?"

"The whole universe!" Jack assured him.

27

Eight years later

Kakko Jallaxanya took a deep breath and blew out all of her five candles in one go.

Everyone clapped.

"Wow!" exclaimed Jack, "Well done! Happy birthday, little lady."

"But I'm not little any more, Daddy," protested Kakko, "I'm five. And I'm big. I'm much bigger than Shaun, he's only three!"

"Can we eat the cake now?" nagged Shaun.

"Yes, let's," urged Jalli, "are you going to cut it yourself, Kakko, or is Mummy going to do it?"

"I will. But you will have to help me. I am going to put the knife right in the middle – I'm going to have the bit with the sun's smile because I am Jallaxanya, the same as Mummy."

Jalli had iced the cake with a smiley sun on it. It was Jack's idea.

"What about my bit?" asked Jack.

"You can have his nose, the bit with the cherry on it!"

"Wow, thanks!"

At that moment Jack's pocket burst into song. It was his mobile that they had all bought him for his twenty-sixth birthday a month before. Someone had written a pop song with the same title as what became known as "the family hymn", "Be not Afraid", sung at Shaun's funeral, and then later at Jack and Jalli's wedding. The song wasn't like the hymn at all, and after the title, the words were completely different, but the kids at Jack's school thought it was really cool.

"Mr. Smith, tell us your phone number," one asked.

"Why? What do you want with my phone number?"

"We want to ring it to play your tune!"

"Be not Afraid" had been a mark of Jack and Jalli's life. The hymn was, indeed, in many ways, their song. Eight years on, the events of those few weeks when Jack and Jalli first discovered their white gates had been dramatic. They had crossed the universe. They had travelled from euphoria to despair – and finally to resolution, where the good things of love had settled richly upon them. They had started that summer as grown-up children, and finished it as mature young people. They had lived a fairytale, and had then been thrown into the icy-cold waters of a horror story. But the true reality – the really real – they learned, was neither in the euphoria nor in the despair, but in the dependable love that the Creator of the universe never stopped giving them. This love both lived in the whole universe outside, but also inside things and people. Inside it was not just in feelings, in the highs and lows of life. It kind of went on underneath, all the time, gently but powerfully making life good.

Another thing that Jack and Jalli noticed, like Momori and Matilda before them, was that He/She mended things. And somehow the things that are mended can be stronger than if they had never been broken.

After the family had left Persham, Mr. Evans had brought along his secateurs to tidy up the "kicking tree". There was one upright shoot that Jack had missed in his final frenzied assault. The old churchman had carefully trimmed off the remains of the others, and the single shoot, at a height of one and a half metres, stood straight in the sunshine. Over the years that followed, it grew proudly, until, at last, the scars of its abuse faded. Below ground the years of struggle had produced bigger, stronger roots than its undamaged neighbours along the street. Regardless of their untarnished beauty, there was an extra robustness about Jack's kicking tree that they didn't share.

The cottage and garden had given up doing things for itself and looking after them as soon as they had moved in and become part of the local community. Jalli's interest in growing things had helped her plant a fruitful garden. Despite his blindness, Jack had no difficulty in finding lots of practical things to do too. He loved simple things like washing clothes and hanging them out to dry. He enjoyed that because, as he came across each garment in turn, he thought about the person to whom it belonged. When they were dry, he folded them neatly into piles, one pile for each person, and was nearly always right – except when Momori and Matilda began to borrow from each other's wardrobes. "They do it just to confuse me!" protested Jack.

Jack, who was now a teacher in a school for blind children, had also begun teaching in the Sunday School, and Matilda delighted in seeing him surrounded by children as he read to them from books in blind script, but more often, told them stories in his own words.

Jalli sank into bed. She was tired. She had had a busy day at the agricultural college where she did research in entomology – bees in particular, and other insects involved in spreading pollen.

Kakko had eventually settled for the night, but not until she had had two stories and several songs. She had not wanted her birthday to end, and they had allowed her to stay up late. Jack put a cup of Jalli's favourite chocolate drink on the table beside the bed and bent over and kissed her.

"Thank you, kind sir!" Jack got in beside her.

"Well, what are we going to call number three?" he asked, patting Jalli's belly. They had known about "number three" for just over a month.

"Well, I was thinking – what do you think about naming him or her after the places we come from? Wanulka Persham!" Jack chuckled. He knew she wasn't serious. He could sense the smile on Jalli's face as she spoke the words.

"Only if it's a girl!" he retaliated. "If it's a boy I want Michael Owen."

"Michael who? Oh, football…! You're teasing me!"

"You started it," laughed Jack. "… Actually, apart from the football and the cricket, I don't miss Persham or England at all."

"I miss Wanulka. It was good to me… I often wonder how Mr. Bandi is."

"Still turning out biologists for the universe, I expect."

"I wonder if I shall ever see him again…" mused Jalli.

You will probably not be surprised to learn that the third child, a little boy, was called Bandi Jack. And they *did* see Mr. Bandi again – as well as many of their other friends from across the universe. But that's a story for another time!

The Other Books of the
White Gates Adventures Tetralogy

Ultimate Justice

Want to be free to expand you horizons – even beyond those you can imagine?

We rejoin Jack and Jalli and their family growing up on Planet Joh as they once again travel the universe to new worlds through the white gates the Creator provides for them.

Each character has his or her own role to play in the exploration – outwards to the stars, but also inwards to what makes us who we are and what we can become…

Winds and Wonders

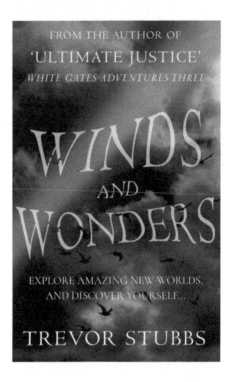

Explore amazing new worlds and discover yourself...

Teenage Abby runs into trouble when she comes up against authoritarian forces in school, as well as the churches she attends. Impatient Kakko still manages to save her millions of people, but goes through the worst pain she can imagine on the way. Shy Shaun makes a great impact on the football field, but how will it turn out in the game of life off the pitch? And parents Jack and Jalli, even Nan Matilda, manage some excitement.

The Spark

The more the darkness squeezes, the brighter shines the Spark.

Shaun has never been as quick or confident as his elder sister, Kakko, or as bright as his younger brother, Bandi. He has been the steady quiet one content to play for his football club, Joh City. But circumstances now threaten to destroy his way of life. How should he cope with the traumas that come his way?

The novel also includes the characters from the earlier books – Wennai, Tam, Dev, Dah, John, the whole Rarga-Smith family and more. There is humour, adventure and romance as, by means of the mysterious white gates, readers dicover new places and revisit old ones.